# FIRE IN THE BLOOD

## POLICE SCOTLAND
### BOOK 4

## ED JAMES

*for Paul*

*Sincerest thanks for the support, advice and friendship over the years,
and for encouraging me to pick up GHOST IN THE MACHINE again -
I had given up.*

# DAY 1

*Tuesday*
*12th June*

# 1

---

Alec Crombie tightened the sporran over his kilt and adjusted the tam o'shanter on his head. He wanted to look the part. He adjusted his bow tie in the mirror and decided he did.

He got his bottle of vocal spray and gave a couple of squirts. He cleared his throat and did a few exercises, passed down through generations of Crombies.

Fraser appeared through the door. 'They're ready for you, Dad.'

Crombie looked him up and down. 'You could have bothered.'

Fraser tugged his Dunpender Distillery polo shirt. 'I'm just the cooper here.'

'Yes well, I suppose you're right.' Crombie made a final tweak to his bow tie, then got going.

Fraser led him through the distillery building, heading to the bar. 'It was a great idea to open this.'

'It was *your* idea.'

Fraser held the door open. 'Doesn't mean it's not great.'

'Very true.' Crombie patted his son on the shoulder. 'It harks back to our family's proud ancestry.'

He entered the large bar area of the distillery, already full of mailing list members. He smiled at a few familiar faces as he made his way to the lectern. A round of applause broke out as he climbed the stage.

He waited for the sound to die down, smiling all the time. 'Thank you, thank you.' He put his notes on the lectern and smoothed the paper.

He held his arm out and made a show of checking his watch. 'It's not even noon yet, but I note a few somewhat ruddy faces in the room already.' He held up the glass of whisky placed on the podium. 'Sláinte.'

Glasses all around the room were raised. 'Sláinte.'

Crombie took a drink, savouring the burn of Dutch courage. 'As you all know, my distillery celebrates its centenary this year. The reason you're all here, of course, is we plan to launch an exclusive bottle to mark the occasion, accompanied by a crystal quaich and an engraved hip flask.'

He looked around the room, noticing more than a few hands putting glasses to mouths. 'Before we let you behind the magician's curtain, as it were, and show you the casks being opened, I wanted to say a few words.'

He turned over the notes. 'We are in the process of producing a book, marking our centenary. This will, of course, be available for purchase through our website and all good retailers, but I think it's important to dwell on the distillery's legacy for a while. Whisky is nothing without tradition, after all.'

He flipped the sheet over, scanning the handwritten bullet points. 'We can't quite pin the exact date the distillery was founded in 1912, so we've decided on the fourth of July in a show of solidarity with our cousins across the pond.'

There were a few cheers from the back of the room.

Crombie held up his glass in acknowledgement. 'Before we started on the whisky, our family used to run public houses in Gullane. We were noted for holding court, but also for our rich voices, passed down several generations from the seventeenth century to my own son, Fraser. People would travel from miles around to hear my grandfather orate — Burns, mostly. I still run the poetry recital group in Gullane.'

He narrowed his eyes, trying to focus on the next point. He reached for his glasses, hands shaking as he put them on. 'What's this got to do with whisky you ask? Beneath his public hostelry, my great-grandfather had an illicit still. He would serve its product at poetry recitals and after hours in the pub. The whisky soon became quite refined and Iain Crombie set this place up as a legal concern.'

He beamed at the crowd. 'I assure you that, apart from the days of the illicit still, this establishment has long since refrained from any lawbreaking.'

A wave of laughter passed through the room.

Crombie took another sip of whisky. 'In July 1912, Iain Crombie purchased a batch of malted barley. He reused the yeast he'd been cultivating for years, which we still use to this day. Of course, we don't know when the process began exactly, but the first batch of whisky was distilled and put in the pub cellar to mature.'

'Fourteen years later, in 1926, the first bottles were sold.' He reached down and retrieved a dusty bottle. 'I tasted this batch when it was worth much less. This is now worth over ten thousand pounds.'

He looked fondly at the bottle as he waited for the applause to die down. 'My grandfather moved the company to these premises not long after. He converted the farm buildings into a medium-sized distillery and we have thrived ever since.'

He held up his glass again, breathing in the aroma. 'Dunpender whisky is softer and lighter than a Highland or Island and it's the product of one of the few remaining independent distilleries in Scotland. *Vehemently* independent.'

He finished the glass and set it down. 'Now, enough from me. I cordially invite you downstairs for some pomp and ceremony in our barrel room.'

Crombie left the stage, leading the forty visitors down the stairwell into the rooms underneath the distillery, his son and a few other employees accompanying them.

He entered the large room and let the space slowly fill up, the low temperature noticeably rising in a short space of time.

Crombie playfully clamped his hand on the shoulder of a man standing by a pair of barrels mounted on racks. 'Doug Strachan here has been with me since we were both wee laddies. We've produced some fine whisky over the years, as I'm sure you'll all agree.'

Strachan held up a hand, bashfully staring at the floor. 'The barrel on the left is made from sherry oak. It gives a nice clear finish to the whisky, almost like a vodka.'

He held up a large mallet and held it against a stout wooden stopper stuck in the side of the barrel. 'This is known as the bung. It keeps the cask whisky-tight, save for the angel's share, of course.'

He smacked the bung with the mallet, before easing it out and placing it in the pocket of his overcoat. He knelt and sniffed at the exposed hole in the barrel, drinking in the aroma of the unblended spirit.

He held up a long copper cylinder on a chain. 'This we call the dog.' He lowered it deep into the barrel and allowed it to fill before pouring the contents into a clear glass bottle. He swirled the bottle and examined the golden liquid. 'See how it looks nice and clean? There are no noticeable impurities. It's taken on the lighter colour of the sherry oak cask it's sat in for the last eighteen years.'

Crombie gestured at the bottle with a flourish. 'This is clearly a worthy candidate for the centenary edition blend.'

Strachan replaced the bung before moving over to the second barrel of the pair. 'This one is a darker bourbon cask, which will complement the softer sherry oak of its sibling when we blend them after dilution.' He gave a cheeky wink to the crowd. 'Of course, we will offer a few bottles of cask strength once they are blended.'

He held his mallet up and hit the bung of the second cask. He hit it again twice, before leaning over to Crombie. 'It's stuck fast.'

Crombie grabbed the mallet and gave it a good few hits, before it finally slackened. He wiped his forehead with a handkerchief then beamed at the crowd. 'I shouldn't be sweating given how cold it is in this room, but I hadn't expected any form of exertion.'

Strachan dipped a second dog into the barrel.

It hit something hard.

He retrieved it and frowned — it was only filled a fraction. It danced about on the chain and spilled its contents onto the cracked flagstones of the floor.

Crombie whispered at him. 'What's the matter?'

'It's hit something.' Strachan picked up a torch and shone it into the barrel. 'There's something in here.'

Crombie's eyes nervously glanced at the crowd before he

snatched the torch from Strachan. He shifted the light about, angling the beam to cut through the liquid. It shone on an object. He struggled to make it out.

He saw a human ear.

## 2

Detective Constable Scott Cullen stepped out of the High Court, blinking in the summer light as he looked down the Lawnmarket and the Royal Mile.

DI Brian Bain rubbed his hands together. 'Good result, Sundance.'

Cullen gave a slight nod. 'I'm astonished it took five months to convict someone with a signed confession.'

Bain patted his shoulder. 'These people change their tunes, you know that.'

'I do.'

DS Alan Irvine was next out, chewing gum. 'Fancy a pint in Deacon Brodie's, gaffer?'

Bain sniffed. 'Aye, maybe.'

Irvine threw another piece of gum in his mouth. 'Our country cousins almost lost us the case.'

Bain led them from the door. 'They're a total disaster, Alan. You know that, I know that, even Sundance here knows that.'

Cullen scowled at the nickname.

'Still, we got the boy.' Irvine clapped Bain on the shoulder. 'He's going away for a long time.'

Bain eyed the front door. 'I've heard whisperings that good old DCI Jim Turnbull had a bit of a bunfight over the bragging rights with his opposite number in Dalkeith.'

Irvine shook his head and laughed. 'E Division. Almost as bad as F troop.'

Turnbull and DS Bill Lamb emerged from the front door, deep in conversation.

Bain grinned at them. 'Good result, sir.'

'Indeed.' Turnbull looked around. 'Thank God the press have already moved on.'

Bain smiled. 'Waiting inside for an hour will help that.'

Turnbull straightened to his full height and looked down at Bain. 'We need to keep the rivers of justice flowing smoothly, Brian.'

Bain thumbed at Lamb. 'Almost froze over back in January.'

Lamb scowled. 'Are you insinuating something here?'

Bain raised his hands in mock surrender. 'I'm just saying what happened out in Garleton.'

Turnbull wagged a finger at both of them. 'Enough. We got the result, that's the important thing.'

Irvine nudged Cullen. 'Here's your bird.'

Cullen turned to see DS Sharon McNeill approach, dressed in off-duty jeans, t-shirt and leather jacket.

She grabbed hold of Cullen and kissed him on the cheek. 'How did it go?'

'He got life.'

She grinned at Turnbull. 'Must feel good, sir?'

'Indeed. Doesn't happen enough for my liking, but it's a good result.'

Bain nodded at her. 'Afternoon, Butch. What you doing here?'

She gestured down the hill towards the Parliament. 'I only live five minutes away. I'm on a stakeout tonight, so I'm meeting Scott for lunch.'

'Good to see you.' Bain nudged Irvine. 'You up for lunch?'

Irvine looked around the rest of the group. 'Anyone else fancy it?'

They all evaded his gaze.

Turnbull rubbed his forehead. 'Please keep your lunch *solid*, gentlemen.'

Bain laughed. 'I never drink on duty unless it's a direct order from you.'

'Very well.'

Bain tugged at Irvine's arm. 'Come on, Sergeant.'

Lamb folded his arms as they crossed the threshold of the pub. 'How many do you reckon they'll have?'

'I'll be keeping an eye on him, don't you worry.' Turnbull went back inside the court, leaving Cullen with Lamb and Sharon.

Lamb offered a hand to her. 'Don't believe we've met. DS Bill Lamb.'

Sharon shook it. 'I've heard a lot about you. Not all of it good, mind.'

Lamb winked at Cullen. 'I know where the bodies are buried.'

'Bill's the most recent addition to Bain's catalogue of enemies.'

Lamb raised his eyebrows. 'I'd keep those opinions to yourself, Constable. Especially if Jim's around.'

'Aye, you're probably right.'

'What were Bain and Irvine saying?'

'They were complaining about your squad.'

Lamb grimaced. 'Typical. I bust my gut and they try to take all the credit.'

'For once, I'd have to side with him. It was us who actually solved the case.'

'Right.'

Cullen tapped his arm. 'I do have sympathies for you, what with having to contend with Bain's antics.'

'Yeah, well, never again.'

Turnbull left the building again, this time deep in conversation with the Procurator Fiscal. He shook hands with Lamb. 'It was a pleasure working with you again, Bill.'

'Likewise, sir.'

Turnbull walked off with the PF.

Sharon nodded after them. 'Nice romantic little lunch.'

Lamb winked. 'They'll be talking shop, you know that.'

Cullen offered his hand to Lamb. 'See you again some time, Bill. Let me know if you fancy a pint in town one day.'

Lamb shook it, covering his own hand over. 'I'll see you around.'

Cullen turned to Sharon. 'Let's go get some lunch.'

They left Lamb and headed down the Royal Mile, weaving through waves of tourists.

'So how was it this morning, Scott?'

Cullen glanced over. 'Don't want to talk about it, if it's all the same. Usual political nonsense from Bain and Irvine.'

'Tell me about it.'

They found a vacant outside table at an Italian cafe. A light summer breeze carried the smell of frying garlic and the occasional fug of cigarette smoke from passing pedestrians.

Sharon picked up a menu. 'Very cosmopolitan.'

'It's rare both of us taking a proper lunch break.'

'This is my breakfast, Scott.'

Cullen laughed and picked up his own menu, immediately finding the spiciest dish.

A waiter appeared, tapping his pad.

Cullen gestured to Sharon.

'Spaghetti Carbonara and a bottle of mineral water.'

'Very well. And for sir?'

'Penne Vesuviana and a lemonade.'

The waiter left them to it.

Sharon raised an eyebrow. 'How's it going with Irvine?'

'He's a wanker. Thankfully Cargill's keeping him in check.'

Her nostrils flared. 'Turnbull's protégé.'

Their drinks arrived.

She looked up, a wry grin on her face. 'Are you ready to talk about it yet?'

Cullen took a deep breath and tried — for once — to think before he spoke. 'I'm just pissed off with him.'

'Bain? What's he done now?'

Cullen took a sip of lemonade. 'It's more that I'm still a DC.'

'And you think you should be an Acting DS?'

'It would help.' Cullen felt the irritation sting again. He watched some Japanese tourists pass near the table, still carrying huge cameras in the age of smartphones. He looked back at Sharon, searching for some sympathy in her eyes. 'It's not like I'm totally stuck with him, but you know as soon as another case gets chucked at him, it'll be all that 'Here, Sundance' shite all over again.'

Sharon winced. 'I can do without his nicknames.'

'Anyway, you've escaped to Wilkinson.'

'It's hardly escape.'

Cullen poured the rest of the can, the drink frothing up. 'Thing is, if I'm doing DS duties, then I should be given the recognition. I'm not after the money necessarily. It would be nice but it's the recognition I want. I'm thirty now. I know DIs younger than me.'

'Here we go again. Scott, you're still a young pup.'

Cullen looked across the street at an obese American emerging from a tourist-trap whisky shop. 'Don't you think I deserve a DS position with the number of times I've saved Bain's arse?'

She wagged a finger at him. 'Leave me out of it.'

'You did ask. I can shut up if you want.'

'It's not that. It's just you keep going on about this. Turnbull's the only one who can sort it out. If you're pissed off, speak to him. He knows full well what you're doing.'

'Thanks for listening.'

She reached over and grabbed his hand. 'Scott, I can't do anything other than listen and you know I have been. You have to speak to Jim about it.' She took a sip of her water. 'There's been a lot of upheaval recently and there's a bigger one coming next year.'

Cullen's phone rang. He fished it out of his jacket pocket — Bain. He let it ring through to voicemail.

He looked at her, frustration biting at him again. He decided to shift the conversation away from his career and avoid another argument.

The waiter arrived with the food, depositing their plates on the table with a flourish.

Cullen tied a napkin on to cover his shirt and tie.

Sharon laughed. 'You look like you're in a Robert De Niro film.'

Cullen tucked into his food, only then realising how hungry he was. 'You're on night shift tonight, aren't you?'

'I am. Me and Wilkinson in a knackered old Vectra outside a house in Lochend. Just what I want.'

Cullen didn't mention the blob of cream sauce that streaked down her cheek. 'I'd almost swap you. Back out to Gorgie to sit with Irvine. Can't believe I'm stuck with him again.'

'Just be thankful Turnbull made Irvine's complaint disappear.'

Cullen finished the lemonade. 'I know. The prospect of days sitting in a backstreet in Gorgie with his jaw pounding away on gum fills me with dread.'

'Wilko's as bad.'

Cullen's phone rang again. Bain. 'Better take this.' He answered it and turned away.

'Here, Sundance, why didn't you pick up when I called?'

'I was driving.'

'I can see you, you silly bugger.'

Cullen turned and got a wave from Bain, standing outside Deacon Brodie's. He pushed his plate to the side and rested his elbow on the table. 'What do you want?'

'Didn't you listen to the voicemail?'

'No, sir. Sorry.'

'I want you to pick up Caldwell from Leith Walk and head out to Dunpender Distillery in East Lothian.'

'Fine.' Cullen rolled his eyes at Sharon. 'Be there in about an hour.'

'Better be quicker than that.'

Cullen ended the call. He looked at Sharon. 'Here we go again.'

## 3

C ullen spotted the distillery in the early afternoon sunshine as they drove down the long straight running parallel to the railway line. 'There it is.'

Dunpender Distillery was a mile or so east of Drem in the East Lothian countryside. It was a set of old farm buildings constructed from purple sandstone, scores of metal pipes emerging from the nearest wall and flowing into towering steel condensers.

Acting DC Angela Caldwell looked up from her mobile. 'You were drinking Dunpender at the Burns Supper in January, weren't you?'

Cullen looked over and smiled. 'Until it ran out.'

'I forgot how much meths you lot got through afterwards.'

Cullen pulled his old VW Golf into the car park. 'How did your appraisal go with Bain this morning?'

'How do you think it went? I'll be lucky to get a one-year tenure at this rate.'

'You'll be all right. You've been in the police for as long as I have.'

'I've not done the Detective Officers' Training, though. You did it, didn't you?'

'I did, aye.'

'What sort of tenure did you get?'

'A decent one.' Cullen didn't know whether Angela would receive anything like the seven years he got.

'How long?'

'That's for me and Bain.'

'Come on. The highest anyone on my courses at Tulliallan has heard of is five.'

'Look, don't worry about it, you'll get a decent tenure.'

'My nerves are shredded. I've got my formal assessment next week. I could just as easily get thrown back to Queen Charlotte Street station as become a full DC.'

'I honestly think you'll be fine.' Cullen pulled his shades off as he got out of the car, pleased to actually need them for once. 'We'd better get in to see the big man.'

They walked across the pebbles to the sign-posted entrance. At least twenty workers were standing outside in the sunshine, most of them smoking.

Cullen stopped outside the door and looked back at the workers. 'I bet they're enjoying the opportunity to skive.'

'Not sure they'd think of it that way.'

'There should be some local detectives from Haddington seconded to an investigation like this.' He winked at her. 'Any local officers here, do you know?

She narrowed her eyes. 'I don't know what you mean. You'd know more than me.'

'Really?'

She ignored him and opened the front door, waiting for a worker in black dungarees to come through first. 'He better not call me Batgirl again. I'm sick fed up of it.'

Cullen grinned. 'You prefer Robin, then?'

'Even less so.' She set off.

Signs pointed to a bar through the back, upstairs to the offices and along the dark stone walls of the corridor to the distillery.

A bored-looking woman in her mid-twenties sat behind the reception desk. Her name badge said 'Amanda'. She was politely listening to a familiar face — PC Johnny Watson, casually leaning against the desk as he flirted.

Angela laughed. 'Look at him go. Five months ago he was a bundle of nerves.'

'He's getting stuck right in there.'

'Good luck to him.'

Cullen called over.

Watson pointed up the stairs. 'Bain's in the owner's office.'

'Cheers.'

They climbed the stairs, finding a large open-plan space swamped with uniformed officers and a few Dunpender employees. The room smelled old, like ancient whisky fumes and cigar smoke had embedded themselves in the fabric of the building.

Bain was at the centre speaking to a red-faced man. He clocked Cullen, his smile without any hint of warmth. 'Sundance, glad you could finally join us.'

Cullen didn't bother rising to the bait. 'Sir.'

Bain nodded at Cullen then at the man next to him. 'This is Alec Crombie, the distillery owner.'

Crombie was a thin man in his mid-sixties wearing full Highland dress — kilt, sporran, jacket, the works. His grey hair was pulled in a tight comb-over with a few loose strands curling off to freedom. He turned his nose up at Cullen before looking away. 'This is an *absolute* disgrace. I'll lose *hours* of productivity and I have twenty people booked on a distillery tour this afternoon. It'll all have to be cancelled and refunded.'

Bain flashed him a polite smile. 'I'm sure you understand we have to go through due process here.'

Crombie flattened his hair down. 'I need access to that whisky. This is costing us thousands of pounds every day.'

'I'm sure you've got insurance.'

Crombie glared at him. 'That's not the point.'

'Once our crime scene officers are finished, we can have a chat about it.'

'I want the name of your superior officer.'

'Do you really need that?'

'Of course, Inspector. This is a matter of grave commercial sensitivity. I've got centenary celebrations to plan and I'd rather this sideshow didn't detract from them.'

'Finding a body in a barrel of whisky isn't exactly a sideshow.'

'Regardless, I'd like to discuss the matter with him.'

Bain gave him a mobile number. 'DCI Jim Turnbull.'

Crombie smiled then headed to his office without a further word.

Bain shook his head at the receding figure. 'Prick.'

Cullen got his notebook out. 'So what's happened then?'

'I wish you'd listen to your voicemails, Sundance.'

Cullen only ignored them if they related to one of many missed calls from Bain — especially if they were followed by another call less than thirty seconds later. He still hadn't bothered listening to the first message.

Bain gestured around the room. 'They're doing some sort of special edition for this centenary he keeps on about, had a load of prizewinners in. They were testing a whisky barrel and one of Crombie's boys found a body in it.'

Angela whistled through her teeth. 'Any idea who it is?'

Bain shook his head. 'That's why we're here, I'm afraid. Anderson's already downstairs. Definitely male. IC1. Not in a good state by the looks of things. The skull is smashed in and all the teeth are gone. No chance of a dental records search.'

Crombie reappeared. 'Your superior officer will be in touch.'

Bain ground his teeth, looking ready to pounce.

Cullen cleared his throat. 'Is the man who found the body still around?'

'He is, aye.' Crombie spoke in the sort of voice normally heard on a regional Scottish radio station, lining up folk music in the wee small hours. 'He's in shock, as I'm sure you can understand.'

Cullen looked at Bain. 'Have you spoken to him?'

'Not yet. Everything we've had so far has come from Mr Crombie here.'

Cullen clicked his pen. 'Can we see if he's ready now?'

Crombie led them over to the corner of the room. 'This is Doug Strachan. He's the chief foreman.'

Strachan sat on a chair just by the open window. He looked about the same age as Crombie and was overweight, his nose bright red and his head entirely bald.

Crombie gripped the shoulder of the man standing next to Strachan, wearing the same uniform. 'This is Fraser, my number two son.'

Fraser offered a large hand. 'I'm the master cooper.'

Cullen shook it, looking blankly at Bain.

Bain rolled his eyes. 'He's in charge of the barrels.'

'Fine.' Cullen smiled at Strachan. 'Can you go through what happened please?'

Strachan rubbed his hand over his red face, slicked with sweat. 'I was just taking a sample of the special edition so I could approve it for blending. Was just away to check it for colour and aroma before we gave a few of our guests a wee taste.'

'How many barrels were you sampling?'

'Just the two.'

'We blend different barrels to get the right texture.' Fraser waved a hand over at the wall. A black-and-white picture showed a man in top hat and tails watching a workman sampling a pair of barrels. His voice was very similar to his father's, deep and rich, with the sort of accent a few grands' worth of education bestowed upon a young gentleman.

Crombie stepped forward. 'It was a special edition. My distillery celebrates its centenary this year and we were launching an exclusive bottle. The event in the bar downstairs was for our most loyal customers to witness the process of sampling the cask-strength whisky.'

'I see.' Cullen glanced at Bain — his sour expression indicating he'd heard a lot of this already. 'DI Bain is a big fan of your product.'

Bain grunted. 'It's *one* of my favourites, put it that way.'

Crombie arched an eyebrow. 'I hope you're not angling for some free whisky.'

'Perish the thought.' Bain glared at Cullen. 'Continue your questioning.'

'Was it the first or second barrel you were sampling when you found the body?'

'Second.' Strachan scratched the side of his head. 'The first looked very good too. It's a crying shame.'

'Where's the barrel now?'

Bain tapped the heel of his shoe into the floor. 'Downstairs in the barrel room. The SOCOs are already going over it.'

'Any idea who's in there?'

Crombie stood up straight and adjusted his kilt. 'We have a possibility. I believe it's the remains of an Irish worker we had here in the early nineties. Paddy Kavanagh.'

Fraser nodded in agreement. 'Paddy went missing around the time those barrels were filled.'

Cullen noted the name. 'I'd suggest we can rule out suicide. Any idea how he got in there?'

'That's what I expect you to find out.' Crombie folded his arms.

Bain's eyes shot over to Cullen. 'You done?'

'For now.'

'I want a word with the pair of you outside.'

# 4

---

Their feet crunched over the pebbles of the car park as they moved away from the buildings.

At the far side was a neatly trimmed hedge, glimpses of a garden across the stream visible through the gaps. Cullen clocked an attractive woman in her thirties reading a book, sending furious glances in their direction.

Angela squinted in the direction he was looking. She looked back at him and shook her head. 'You dirty bastard.'

'Hold on.' Bain pointed over Cullen's shoulder. 'Don't want to spend all afternoon repeating myself to DCs.'

Cullen turned around and spotted DC Stuart Murray sauntering over.

Angela laughed. 'Here's your local CID officer, Scott.'

'Strange how there's no DS coming over from Haddington.'

Angela glared at him. 'Will you quit it with that?'

Bain folded his arms. 'What took you so long, McLean?'

Murray prodded his own chest. 'I'm DC *Murray*. I've just left *McLaren* to head back to base.'

'So where's McLean?'

Murray shrugged. 'There isn't one.'

'Right.'

'We've been looking into an assault in Gullane, some boy got battered on the way home from the pub.'

Bain raised his eyebrows. 'And Lamb's got two DCs looking into that?'

Murray flicked up the front of his hair. 'It's as close as we get to a proper case without you being involved.'

Angela burst out laughing.

Murray grinned at them. 'Nice to see you pair.'

Bain frowned. 'What about me?'

'The pleasure's mine.' Murray offered a hand.

Bain reluctantly shook it.

Murray got his notebook out and clicked his pen. 'How come you're here and not us local boys?'

'Never you mind.' Bain rubbed his hands together. 'Right, this is looking like a bit of a bloody puzzle. First things first, I want to know who the body in that barrel is. They seem to be jumping to conclusions a bit too soon for my liking.'

Murray held up a hand. 'Who's they?'

'The distillery owner and his son.' Bain stroked his moustache. 'Jimmy Deeley is out in Bathgate at a murder, so he won't be here till later to work his usual magic.' He was paying particular attention to a spot buried beneath the stubble. 'The warmer weather tends to bring the bampots out in West Lothian.'

Cullen tapped his pen against his notebook. 'What about Sweeney?

Bain sneered. 'You know as well as I do how often she leaves the lab, Sundance. Besides, Deeley was moaning about her working on the backlog they've managed to build up.'

Angela gestured at the building. 'We can relax. We don't need someone to declare death.'

Bain shook his head slowly, a smile dancing across his lips. 'Less of that, Batgirl. At some point, Deeley will get the body out and we can compare it against MisPer reports. This barrel was filled eighteen years ago. Caldwell, can you get us a list of disappearances from then?'

'Will do.' Angela scribbled in her notebook. 'I'll dig up any case files still open. IC1 males, right? And I'll put a few months around either way.'

'That should be about five minutes, so can you shadow Cullen?'

'Fine.'

Bain looked at Murray. 'Can you look into this Paddy Kavanagh boy Crombie mentioned?'

'I'll need to have a word with him, of course, but aye.'

'We'll chin when we get back upstairs.' Bain eyed Cullen. 'Now, Sundance, I want you to look into this barrel. Who filled it? How did the body get in there?'

Cullen wrote it down. 'I get all the great jobs.'

'Sundance, if you want to wash my car, I've got a bucket and a sponge in the boot. I'm sure they've got water and soap in there.'

'Sorry, sir.' Cullen gave him a fake smile. 'I'll see what I can find out.'

Bain glanced at a sheet of paper in his hand. 'And check the body hasn't been chucked in there recently.'

'Isn't Anderson supposed to be doing that?'

Bain folded the sheet and creased it with his nails. 'Aye, well, I want you to make sure he's doing it properly. As you well know, half our bloody time is spent checking other people's work.'

'Fine. Crombie seems like such a nice man as well.'

Bain put the sheet in his pocket. 'I've got suspicions about him already, put it that way.'

'Would those suspicions be allayed by a bottle of whisky?'

'Watch it, Sundance.'

Cullen was finding it easier and easier to wind Bain up — time was he would have shit himself at the mention of his name, but now it felt like shooting fish in a barrel. 'What about Strachan?'

'What about him?'

'He looks like he's been drinking and not just a cheeky pint with lunch.'

Bain scratched his chin. 'Good point.'

Cullen gestured at each of them in a quick circle. 'There's just four of us. Are we going to get any more help?'

'I've asked. We'll see what happens. As it stands, it's just us and that plonker Watson.' Bain nodded back at the building. 'I've got Irvine as Crime Scene Manager for a few hours.'

Cullen glanced up at the sky, hoping he'd keep away from his DS.

Bain looked at them in turn. 'Right, it's just before two now. I want progress updates from each of you by four.'

# 5

Cullen and Angela sat with Fraser Crombie and Doug Strachan in the stock room just off the main office, small and dusty with no natural light. The shelves on the walls were filled with paperwork in various styles of ring binder.

Fraser sat in front of an old computer, the CRT monitor's grey case long since yellowed, waiting for it to load up.

Cullen tapped the screen. 'Is that Windows 95?'

'It is, aye.'

'Can it even go on the internet?'

Fraser shook his head. 'Doesn't have to. This does everything we need.' The machine beeped and Fraser entered his password. 'What do you want to know?

'I want to know everything about those barrels.'

Fraser frowned. 'Everything?'

'Everything.'

'Right.' Fraser opened a database package and clicked a few boxes. He swore under his breath as it refused to co-operate.

Angela touched the side of the screen. 'Shouldn't you have moved to something that doesn't require a PhD in Computer Science to operate?'

Fraser glared at her. 'Someone looking over your shoulder is seriously off-putting.' He turned back to the machine and seemed to get some joy at last.

Cullen checked his watch. 'Okay, that's ten minutes it's taken just to load up. What can you tell us about this barrel?'

Strachan cut in. 'As young Fraser's father mentioned earlier, the pair downstairs are sherry and oak. We were planning to blend them.'

Cullen almost rolled his eyes. 'Okay, so these barrels, then.'

Fraser tapped the screen. 'According to this, they were filled on twelfth June 1994, exactly eighteen years ago to the day. It was a Saturday.'

Cullen scribbled the date. 'Your father said these were for a special edition.'

'The centenary, aye.'

'How do you know at the time it's actually going to be special?'

Strachan tapped his nose and winked. 'We've learnt to recognise a harvest worthy of such an accolade.'

'Seriously?'

Strachan chuckled. 'No, the product is remarkably consistent. We don't tend to notice much difference year-on-year. All that's made these special is Alec deciding to do an eighteen-year edition.'

Cullen made a note. 'What would normally happen?'

Strachan wiped sweat from his brow. 'Usually, we do a fourteen-year edition, occasionally an eighteen. I would imagine Fraser's father was thinking ahead to the centenary when these were pre-marked.'

Cullen jotted it down. 'Would the barrels have been moved?'

Strachan shook his head. 'Not even an inch since they were filled.'

'Has the distillery always been based here?'

'Since the twenties.' Fraser was smoothing down the hair on his goatee. 'My great-grandfather bought an old farm, sold the land around it to the one next door. Before that, my family had an illicit still in Gullane.' He pronounced it *Gillen*.

Angela smiled. 'Don't worry, I don't think we'll prosecute you on that.'

Fraser didn't respond. 'It took a while before we started using the space here fully, but we're at a comfortable size now.'

Cullen was keen to move on from the potted history of Dunpender Distillery. 'So, these barrels?'

Fraser turned to look at Cullen. 'All we can tell you is just from memory, I'm afraid.'

'You just told me they were filled on the twelfth of June 1994.'

'That's all it has on here.' Fraser scowled at the machine. 'We didn't have any paperwork on them when we computerised in 1997.'

Strachan frowned. 'Fraser, are these the two we found?'

'You *found* them?'

'Aye.'

'I thought you said these were filled eighteen years ago?'

Strachan scratched his ear. 'We *think* so.'

Angela looked up from her notebook. 'What do you mean by 'think so'.'

'What Fraser says. There's not much paperwork on them.'

Fraser drummed on the desk. 'There were a couple of barrels unaccounted for when we computerised. We might have overlooked them at the time.'

Strachan swallowed. 'We just assumed they were part of a private stash for Alec or maybe Fraser's brother, so we added them to the records.'

Fraser looked over from the computer. 'My father takes a private malt most years.'

Cullen frowned. 'Wouldn't they have been recorded?'

Fraser stared back at the screen. 'Sometimes they weren't.'

Cullen put his notebook down. 'Do I need to get some agents from Revenue and Customs in here?'

They both stared at the floor.

Cullen picked up the notebook again and wrote it down. 'Is your brother around?'

Fraser scratched his thick beard. 'My brother's no longer with us. He went missing and was presumed dead ten years ago.'

'Sorry to hear that.' Cullen gestured at the computer. 'Do you know who filled them?'

'No, most fields are blank for these two.'

Strachan's forehead creased. 'There *might* be something in the original ledgers.'

'Where are they?'

Fraser switched off the monitor. 'Dad stored them in his attic when we computerised it all.'

Cullen noted it. 'I need to have a look at them.'

'You'll have to arrange that with Dad.'

Cullen turned to a new page. 'Who was working here at the time?'

'Fraser and I both were. I was master cooper, Fraser was just commencing his training in the art.'

'Would there have been anyone else?'

Strachan stared at the floor for a moment. 'It's just the two of us still around. I can get you a full list of employees, if you want?'

'That would certainly help.' Cullen checked his timeline again. 'These barrels were found in 1997. Was any whisky unaccounted for?'

Fraser switched the monitor back on and tapped the keyboard for a few moments. 'Nothing on here. The originals might be better.'

Cullen got to his feet. 'Can you show us the barrel?'

# 6

Irvine guarded the entrance, chewing gum and messing about on his phone.

Cullen cleared his throat.

Irvine looked up and shoved the phone in the pocket of his white Scene of Crime suit. 'What do you want?'

'Want to look at the barrel.'

'Right.'

'Do you need us to suit up?'

Irvine shook his head. 'You're all right. The body's clearly been in there a while, so we don't need to go through standard protocol.' He handed him the crime scene manifest. 'Sign in.'

Cullen wrote his name before handing it back. 'Is this all you've been doing?'

'It's a key role in the investigation. We'll need to get back out to Gorgie, mind.'

'I'll take it up with Bain.'

Fraser took the clipboard from Irvine. 'We need access to the whisky. My father is going spare.'

Irvine's cheek twitched. 'Not my department, sir.'

Angela handed the manifest back to Irvine. She looked at Fraser. 'I'll see if I can get you an answer soon.'

'I'd appreciate it.'

Cullen nodded at him. 'Can you show us the barrel?'

Fraser led them through the door into the room. Stout pillars were dotted around the cavernous space, roughly thirty metres square and filled with rows of barrels mounted three high. A row of naked light bulbs hung from the ceiling, giving a harsh glow to the place and casting ominous shadows.

Scene of Crime Officers swarmed around. One stood beside the barrel, completely covered except for her eyes, presently obscured by a camera as she clicked at everything.

James Anderson, the lead SOCO, stood examining the barrel.

Cullen called over.

Anderson held up two fingers to indicate two minutes.

Angela whispered in his ear. 'The fingers are usually split apart, aren't they?'

Cullen laughed as he turned to Fraser. 'Tell us about this room.'

Fraser looked at the floor. 'We've got two barrel stores, each occupying half of the cellar.'

Strachan pointed back out the door. 'This is the older of the two. The other half used to be the cooperage, but we built an extension about ten years ago.' He tapped an elaborate winch system on one wall. 'This little baby moves the barrels in and out straight to the cooperage. It's like a dumb waiter in an old hotel, though it's several orders of magnitude stronger.'

'Now, how do we know when they're ready?' Strachan ran his hand along the edge of the nearest barrel. 'We test them, like we did this morning. If they're good, we'll get them winched up and taken to the bottling plant in Alloa.'

Cullen decided the two minutes were up. He looked at Angela. 'I'm going to speak to Anderson. Can you look after these two?'

'Will do.'

Cullen marched over to the barrels.

Anderson pulled down his mask. 'What?'

'Found anything?'

Anderson glanced at Fraser and Strachan before answering. 'Just an annoying DC.'

'Very good.'

Anderson rested his hands on the two barrels, one mounted on a stand and lying on its back, while the other stood upright with the lid off. 'In all seriousness, which I know is something you struggle with, I've found very little.'

'Mind if I have a look inside?'

Anderson handed him a torch. 'Be my guest.'

Cullen shone it into the upright barrel. The body almost filled it. It was pretty much intact, though a cloudy mush sat at the bottom. His buttocks clenched as he saw the head, smashed in and barely recognisable as human. 'Looks like something out of *Lord of the Rings*.'

'Pretty bloody nasty, isn't it?'

Cullen replaced the torch on the floor. 'I thought alcohol would preserve the body.'

'That's right, but you'd need to prep it properly if you wanted it perfect. This was clearly done in a hurry, so it's decomposed.'

'You seem to know a lot about keeping bodies in alcohol.'

Anderson raised an eyebrow. 'Not in front of the public.'

Cullen blushed slightly. 'Any closer to an identification?'

'Not my job. Someone's been at the skull with a hammer or something. Jimmy D will have his work cut out for him when he eventually pitches up.'

Cullen got out his notebook. 'Caldwell's going to look through MisPer reports, so an approximate height and weight would be appreciated.'

Anderson picked up the torch and shone it into the barrel, spending a few seconds looking into the cask and thinking. 'By the looks of things, I'd say most probably Scottish by the colour of that skin.'

'What about Irish?'

Anderson tilted his head from side to side. 'Aye. And maybe Scandinavia, Germany or North America while you're at it.'

Cullen jotted it down. 'Anything else?'

Anderson looked back in the barrel. 'The bits of hair still attached to the skull are very dark. The bit of jaw that hasn't been mangled is clean shaven, for what it's worth. From the way the corpse is positioned, it's hard to tell the height, probably between five ten and six foot. Certainly not overweight.'

'Age?'

Anderson knelt and looked closer inside the barrel. 'No real wrinkling on the skin. I'd expect Deeley to give the official statement but I'd say between twenty and thirty. Anything else is just guesswork and might be misleading.'

'Thanks. Any idea how he got in there?'

Anderson smirked. 'Nothing I'll share with you yet.'

'Is there any way the barrel could have been tampered with since it was filled?'

Anderson scowled as he looked at the ends of the two barrels. 'It doesn't look like it. It'd be a bugger to get a body in there once it was full and surely someone would notice the spilt whisky.'

'Wouldn't be so sure of that.' Cullen looked over his shoulder at the two Dunpender employees. 'Their computer system is somewhat fragmented shall we say, so I don't think there's a high standard at play here.'

'Computers aren't my department.'

'I doubt we'll need Charlie Kidd, put it that way.' Cullen tapped the rim of the barrel. 'So the body was put in before it was filled?'

'They bugger about with the barrels so much it would be next to impossible to say.' Anderson scratched his beard. 'We've got some boys in the Northern Constabulary who know a thing or two about whisky barrels. I was going to give them a call.'

Cullen took a note of it. 'You just about done?'

'Not long now. Tell your boss I'll get him a rough draft report in the next few hours or so.'

'Less of the 'or so'.' Cullen nodded back over. 'I'm going to get those pair over here, so best behaviour, all right?'

Anderson smiled. 'You started it.'

Cullen bit his tongue, before motioning for Angela to bring them over.

Strachan seemed spooked by the barrel, standing a few metres away.

Anderson barely acknowledged them after Cullen's introduction.

Cullen looked at Strachan and Fraser. 'In your expert opinion, does it look like the barrels have been tampered with since they were filled?'

Fraser looked at Angela. 'We were discussing that over there.'

'Sorry.' Cullen smiled. 'Can you repeat for the benefit of Mr Anderson and myself?'

Strachan held up a metal cylinder on a chain, looking like a large shot measure in a pub. 'They were whisky-tight when I popped the dog in. There are no obvious signs anyone has been at them and, believe me, we would know. Other than taking the end off, the only way in would be through the bung.'

He pointed at a wooden stopper protruding from a hole in the side of the barrel. 'We had to give a good dunt to get it off with the... you know.'

'So have they been tampered with?'

Fraser waved a hand into the corner of the room. 'If we rolled the other barrels over from the batch, you'd see they looked the same.'

Cullen gestured at the barrel mounted on its back. 'So it looks like the body has been in there all that time.' He tapped the barrel end with his pen. 'Is this date correct? Was there a batch on the go at the time?'

'Aye, there was. Come here.' Strachan led them towards the back of the room. A row of barrels sat there, all stamped *13/06/94*. 'As we said upstairs, we made a fourteen-year-old batch in 2008 and we kept a fair few barrels behind for an eighteen this year.'

He led them over to Anderson. 'The pair of casks your colleague here is inspecting would have made over a hundred quid a bottle with the quaich and everything. It's all ruined now, of course.'

Angela raised her eyebrows. 'Is that right?'

Fraser folded his arms. 'We can use another of the bourbon casks, nobody will notice.'

Anderson wagged a finger at him. 'Once I let you have this barrel back, mind. Might be a good while.'

'You'll need to discuss that with my father.'

Cullen patted the barrel. 'What happens once you're finished with them?'

'We use the casks three times.' Fraser tapped Strachan on the shoulder. 'Doug and I fix them up in the cooperage. It's a long process. The bits of a barrel could be used for forty-two years, consecutively.'

Cullen made a note to visit the cooperage. 'And how much does each one hold?'

Strachan took a deep breath. 'About six hundred and fifty litres of undiluted spirit. That's when they're filled, mind. They lose some liquid to evaporation over the years. Something like ten to fifteen per cent of the original volume would go in eighteen years.'

Angela whistled. 'Seems like a big loss.'

Strachan winked at her. 'That's the angel's share.'

Cullen checked his watch — Bain would be expecting an update soon. 'Thanks for your time. I'll come find you if we've got any further questions.'

## 7

M urray was hovering outside the stock room, the door now shut. 'Bain's nicked this as a temporary base.'

Cullen looked around — no sign of Bain. 'Thought he'd be looking for a room at Garleton nick?'

'That's bound to happen.' Murray looked past him. 'Where's your shadow?'

'She's just out in the car trying to get an update from Control.'

'Right. I'm going to do something similar. Don't think he'll be too chuffed about a 'no update' update, will he?'

'Never is.'

Murray set off down the corridor.

Crombie shot out of the room, pushing past Cullen with a face like thunder, barely acknowledging him.

Cullen looked inside.

DCI Jim Turnbull stood, arms folded, looking down at Bain sitting in front of the computer.

Cullen knocked on the door. 'Are you busy?'

Turnbull looked over and smiled. 'In you come, Constable.'

Cullen entered, leaning against a filing cabinet. 'Surprised to see you out this way, sir.'

Turnbull inspected his hands. 'I had to come because of a complaint from Alec Crombie.'

Bain looked up. 'We need to keep that whisky held back, sir. If there's another body in there, we're gubbed.'

'That's as maybe.' Turnbull adjusted his tie. 'DI Cargill needs Irvine back.'

Bain pinched his nose. 'I need a strong competent officer.'

'Then I'll send DS McNeill over.'

'Irvine's here, so what's the point in getting someone else over?'

'Let's have a catch-up at Leith Walk this evening, Brian. I expect you to establish an Incident Room on Lothian & Borders premises.'

'This will do just fine.'

'No, it won't. Garleton or Leith Walk. Make a decision.'

'Right.'

'We're done here.' Turnbull buttoned his suit jacket. 'No later than six, okay?'

'Fine.'

Turnbull left the room.

Bain stuck the keyboard on top of the old monitor and pushed it back against the wall. He put his feet up and looked at Cullen. 'You hear much of that?'

'A bit.'

'Christ's sake. Can't be trusted to run my own investigation.'

'He might have a point.'

'Shut your face, Sundance. All right?'

Cullen held his hands up. 'I don't think DS Irvine is actually doing anything down there. You don't want to get your arse kicked because of him, do you?'

'You might have a point for once, Sundance.' Bain cracked his knuckles. 'Right, I'm going to see where that clown Deeley has got to.' He picked up the phone, proceeding to shout at the pathologist. 'I need you out here earlier than Monday, Jimmy.'

Cullen sat at another desk, using the time to consolidate his notes, thinking things through as he wrote.

Angela appeared through the door, clutching her mobile to her ear. She clocked Cullen and ended the call.

Cullen gestured at Bain. 'Deeley.'

'Aha.' She put her phone in her pocket. 'How do you think it's going downstairs?'

'Enthralling. I feel like I know practically everything there is to know about the whisky distillation and maturation process. It's *fascinating.*'

'Tell me about it.'

'Did you get anywhere with Control?'

'Just got passed around from department to department. Finally got hold of someone at the Sighthill document centre who could help rather than make an arse of things.'

'Good.'

'You look like someone's crapped in your cornflakes, Scott.'

Even though Bain was wrapped up in berating Deeley, Cullen leaned away and spoke in a low voice. 'I'm pissed off at doing his skivvy work. Asking some people about the history of a barrel won't be among my career highlights when I retire.'

'You're such a princess.' Angela sat next to him. 'This must beat sitting in Gorgie with Irvine, though.'

Cullen gave a grudging nod. 'That's the thing, though. I'm stuck with flitting between working directly for Bain or Irvine. Neither are doing anything to boost my career prospects and he certainly wouldn't fight my corner.'

'Scott, you've only been a full DC for like a year. It usually takes five to be promoted to DS.'

Cullen was sick of hearing the same things from people. Maybe Sharon was right — he needed to stop waiting and do something about it.

Angela leaned in close. 'Look, Bain's stock's pretty low with the big boys. If what Turnbull told you about his plans for our team are true then Bain will be gone before too long. All he wants from this case is another quick collar to make him look better than Wilko.'

'The few scores Bain has on the board are the results of my efforts. Somehow I've not managed to get any wider recognition.'

Angela laughed. 'Are you serious? You couldn't get any more profile. I'm sick fed up of hearing about you.'

'Really?'

'Aye. Just stop being such a bloody diva. There are worse things happening to people than not getting promoted early, believe me.'

'Like what?'

'Like getting another new nickname.'

Cullen laughed. 'How has he never been formally reprimanded for that?'

'It's actually one of his more endearing traits.'

'Probably the only one.'

Angela laughed. 'Have you ever thought about doing anything about it?'

'I've come close to going to Turnbull. Sharon talked me out of it both times.'

'What did she say?'

'The usual shite about developing a thick skin.' Cullen wondered why it was easy go to Turnbull to complain about Bain but not to further his career.

Bain slammed the phone. 'I seriously can't believe how long it takes him to get over here for a dead body.'

Angela smiled. 'There's no hurry. The body has been dead a while.'

Bain gave her a long hard look. 'There's a hurry if I say there's a hurry.' He jerked round to glare at Cullen. 'What have you found, Sundance?'

Cullen looked at his summary notes. 'Looks like it was filled on the twelfth of June 1994.'

'Looks like?'

'That's just it, they don't know.'

Bain hit the desk. 'What do you mean they don't know?'

'It's not on the computer system. They don't know who filled it or when.'

'So they just found it as if by magic?'

Cullen nodded. 'Aye, sort of. They're consistent with other barrels done at the same time.'

'So you're telling me they don't know for a fact the barrel was filled in June '94?

Cullen held up his notebook, showing them his timeline. 'The barrels were found in '97 when the ledgers were computerised, but they were stamped as being filled in '94. They could have been filled at any point during that time.'

'Any whisky missing?'

'They've suggested looking at the original paper ledgers. Might find whisky volumes in there, too. I'll need to speak to Crombie.'

'Right, get onto it.' Bain looked over at Angela. 'What have you got?'

Angela looked at her notebook. 'Control has six male disappearances in this area in the three months around that approximate date. They've got another seventeen in Edinburgh in that three month period if that doesn't get us anywhere.'

'Good work.'

Cullen showed her his notebook. 'James Anderson gave me some approximate vital statistics of the body. Between twenty and thirty years of age and five ten to six foot.'

Angela scribbled it down. 'Give me a minute.' She started looking through her list and checking them.

Bain looked at Cullen again. 'Was the body put in the cask at the same time as the whisky?'

'That's what Strachan and Fraser Crombie think.' Cullen thumbed towards the door. 'Anderson said he'll confirm. He should be giving you a report this afternoon.'

'I'll chase his skinny arse for it, don't you worry.' Bain drummed on the desk then looked over at Angela. 'How's it going with your search there, princess?'

Angela looked up. 'Good. A lot of short men went missing at that time.'

Bain smirked. 'The sort that would look up to you?'

'Most do.' She crossed her legs. 'I've only got two matches on my list which are now with the Cold Case Unit.'

'Is that Paddy boy on it?'

'He is.' Angela ran her finger along a line. 'Pádraig Seán Kavanagh.'

'Good. I don't like being lied to.' Bain stroked his moustache for a few moments. 'Tell us about Paddy, then.'

Angela scanned the page. 'He was born in Donegal in 1965. He was twenty-nine when this barrel was filled.'

Bain wagged his finger. 'Assuming it was filled in 1994, of course.'

Cullen nodded at Angela. 'See, he does listen.'

Bain stood up and sat on edge of the desk. 'When did he go missing?'

Angela read from her notebook again. 'Eleventh of June.'

Bain clicked his fingers. 'Bang on target. That's when these were barrelled up, got to be him.'

Cullen did the sums in his head. 'Looks likely.'

Angela tucked her hair behind her ear. 'You're not going to like this, sir.'

'Implies I actually like anything...' Bain laughed. 'What is it?'

'The two matches have pretty much the same general description. One is five eleven, the other six foot. Same build, same hair colour. Given the state the body is in, it's going to be tough separating them.'

'Right. And the other match?'

Angela turned the page. 'As I said, I got them to run a fairly wide search to include people who were only reported missing later and who actually might have disappeared earlier.'

'You've got me on tenterhooks here, princess.'

'Reported missing in early July that year was one Iain Malcolm Crombie.'

Bain's eyes bulged. 'You're kidding me. What relation is he?'

'Alec Crombie's number one son.' Cullen thumbed out into the hall. 'Fraser told us his brother was declared dead a few years ago.'

Bain pointed a finger at Angela. 'You knew about this when you came in the room. You should have told me.'

Angela's eyes widened. 'You would have just done your usual.'

'My *usual*?'

'Jumping to conclusions.'

Bain glowered at her, his lips pursed. 'What's the status of the case?'

Angela looked at her notebook again. 'It's still open. Nothing much has happened in the last seventeen years. They got a presumption of death certificate in 2001.'

'Right, good.' Bain looked at Cullen. 'Could it be him in the barrel?'

Cullen thought through what Fraser Crombie told him earlier. 'The time frame is out by a couple of weeks. According to the stamp, it was filled mid-June. Iain was reported missing in early July.'

Angela played with her ponytail. 'He was only *reported* missing in July.'

'I'm not sure this is a coincidence, princess. Are you telling me two people who worked in the same distillery disappeared within a month of each other?'

Angela shrugged. 'Coincidences do happen.'

Bain stared at the ceiling. 'I just know I'm going to have to open every single barrel downstairs.'

Cullen weighed it up in his mind. 'It's a good idea, but I wouldn't do it immediately.'

'Don't worry, I'll give it till this evening before I get the crowbar out. I've told Crombie there's no more whisky being made until this is cleared up. I'll need to get a judge to back that up.'

'Nobody has mentioned Iain as a possibility so far. Everyone is pointing at Paddy.'

'We'll need to speak to Crombie about that, Sundance.'

Cullen turned to a new page and folded his notebook back. 'What do you want us to do?'

'Can you get the original files for both cases, Batgirl?'

'Already requested. All six are being delivered to Leith Walk overnight.'

'*Overnight?*' Bain pinched his nose. 'Can't you go out there?'

Angela shook her head. 'Tried that. I've not got the security clearance to get through the front door. Needs an inspector or above.'

'Well, tomorrow will have to do.'

'Fine.'

Bain turned to Cullen. 'Right, Sundance, can you speak to Alec Crombie about the original paper ledgers and his son?'

'Will do.'

'I've already grilled him. I don't want a complaint.'

'How do you want me to play his son's disappearance?'

'Like I would. Tact and diplomacy.'

'Can I borrow your blunderbuss?'

'Cheeky bastard.' Bain shoved his hands in his pockets. 'Fine, grab Murray if you need any support. Think I saw him having a wank in the car park.'

Cullen frowned. 'Isn't he looking into Paddy's disappearance?'

'Aye, but he's just waiting on some boy in Ireland to call him back. If you could make him useful for once, I'd appreciate it.' Bain shook his head. 'Got to keep an eye on these regional boys, Sundance. This morning should have reminded you of all that shite we had to put up with in January. Abject ineptitude writ large. Murray and his master can get up to some tricks so keep at least one of those beady eyes of yours trained on him.'

'Will do. What about you?'

Bain got to his feet. 'Going to get us an Incident Room at Garleton nick. Need to get a bit of structure around this case. First thing's first, though, we need to get a post mortem done on this body.'

Bain's phone rang. He answered it. 'Jimmy Deeley, you'd better be outside.'

## 8

C ullen held the phone tight to his ear as he looked across the car park. 'Mr Crombie?'

'Yes.'

'It's DC Cullen of Lothian & Borders. We met earlier. Your secretary says you've left for the day?'

'I'm afraid I'm very upset about losing the centenary edition.'

'I see.'

'Are you letting me at my bloody whisky yet? I need to see if I can salvage the edition.'

'I'm afraid not.' Cullen swapped his phone to the other ear. 'I believe you have some ledgers detailing the history of the distillery?'

'I do. A local historian has been going through them over the last few months. He's producing a history of the distillery as part of the centenary celebrations.'

'Do you have them to hand?'

A brief pause. 'They're accessible.'

'Could I come and collect them?'

Crombie sighed. 'Very well.' He gave an address in Gullane.

Cullen wrote it down. 'I'll be there in about fifteen minutes.'

'Then I shall see you shortly.'

Cullen spotted Murray get out of his car, a Golf with 58 plates, a whole different numbering system to the N reg on Cullen's knackered older model. He walked over and patted the roof. 'I've got a Golf myself.'

Murray grinned. 'Yeah, I've seen it. Long after I've heard it usually.'

'Aye, very good.'

'It's not quite a classic, is it?'

'It works.' Cullen shrugged. 'Saving for a mortgage, anyway.'

'I've got a flat in Haddington. It's lovely out this way.'

'I thought North Berwick and Longniddry were expensive?'

'Haddington isn't.'

'It is Haddington, though.'

'Where do you stay, then?'

'Portobello.'

Murray wagged a cheeky finger. 'I grew up in Portobello, you know. It's nicer since they got rid of the syringes off the beach but it's not exactly amazing.'

'It's just a rented room.' Cullen ran a hand through his hair. 'Do you want to chum me over to Crombie's house?'

'Sure.'

Cullen showed him the address in his notebook.

Murray whistled. 'That's a nice place. It'll be expensive.'

'I've been to Gullane once.'

'You mean *Gillen*.'

'What's that all about?'

'I'm only joking.' Murray smiled. 'Gullane is Morningside on sea. The posh types say *Gillen*, the rest say *Gullen*.'

'Got you.'

'It's a funny place. Split between the average Edinburgh commuter and the upper crust.'

'Yours or mine?'

Murray smacked the roof of his car. 'I'll show you what you're missing.'

## 9

M urray pulled into a street at the top of the hill. 'This is the *Gillen* end.'

They got out of the car and started walking down the street, looking south across the East Lothian coastal plain, the sunlight bouncing off rooftops in Drem and Garleton.

Murray opened a gate. 'This is it.'

Crombie lived in part of an old mansion surrounded by high stone walls.

Cullen shut the gate behind him. 'Looks like his grandfather did more than well from the whisky business.'

Murray led up the drive past an old Jaguar. 'Maybe you should drive one of those.'

Cullen knocked on the door. 'I'm hardly Morse.'

The door opened and a Filipino housekeeper answered.

Cullen showed his warrant card. 'We're here to see Mr Crombie. He's expecting us.'

She showed them in, leading them upstairs to a living room on the side of the house. 'I'll just get him for you.'

Out of the north-facing window, Cullen saw a thin sliver of car park at the end of the street which led down to a beach. Across the sands and the Forth, he could see the East Neuk of Fife. He looked at Murray, in the middle of casing the room. 'You can see Anstruther and Pittenweem from here.'

Murray walked over and moved Cullen's hand to the right. 'You were pointing at St Monans.'

'Officers.' Crombie blustered in the room and sat in a green leather armchair. He gestured Cullen and Murray to a leather settee opposite.

Crombie motioned for his housekeeper to leave them. 'Thanks.' He waited until she shut the door. 'The woman has been a godsend since I lost my wife.'

Cullen got out his notebook. 'Thanks for agreeing to see us.'

'It's not that I had a choice.' Crombie retrieved a stack of old ledgers, looking like they told the entire history of the distillery. 'I retrieved these for you.'

Cullen picked up the pile, finding it heavier than anticipated. 'Can I take them away?'

Crombie held up his hands. 'By all means. Feel free to pick up with Fraser or Douglas regarding some of the more arcane annotations.'

'Have you had a chance to look through them?'

Crombie shook his head. 'I'll leave that to you.'

'Thanks for this.' Cullen was already dreading losing days to the infernal things. 'We were wondering if we could ask you a few questions about your son.'

Crombie reached over to a large whisky decanter on a coffee table then filled a crystal glass. 'Fraser?'

'No. Fraser told us his brother passed away a few years ago.'

'It's not Iain.' Crombie shot them a glare, fire in his eyes. 'Those casks were sealed up in the June of '94. Iain disappeared in early July. There is absolutely no chance it is my son in there. None at all. It has *got* to be Paddy Kavanagh.'

Cullen held up the top ledger. 'We need to determine whether the barrels were actually filled at that time.'

'And you've got the ledgers and the assistance of my employees.'

'And that might prove useful.'

'So why all this flimflam about my son, then?'

'We have two possible victims. Paddy and your son both match the description of the body in the barrel.'

Crombie's tongue flicked across his lips. 'Those barrels were filled in mid-June. Iain was away at the time. You should know he wasn't reported missing until July.'

'Which is why we need to go through what happened in the run-up to Iain's disappearance.'

'For what purpose?'

'It might help us exclude him from our inquiries.'

Crombie composed himself, breathing deep. 'Fine.'

'Where was Iain if he wasn't here?'

'He was away at Glastonbury Festival with his brother. Have you heard of it?'

Cullen noted it down. 'I've been once.'

Murray coughed. 'I was more of a T in the Park boy.'

Crombie looked down his nose at him. 'Well, anyway, my boys had talked about going there for years, ever since Iain was eighteen. They decided they would go that year. Some band were playing.'

'Do you know who?' Cullen jotted down *band*.

'Does it matter? They'd been planning their trip a good few months beforehand. They had to clear the time with me before they bought their tickets and I took some persuading, I can tell you.'

Murray frowned. 'For what reason?'

'Well, there was the money, of course.' Crombie took a deep breath. 'It wasn't just travel to the festival, it was their spending money. I wanted to make sure they would focus on finishing the batch and not leave us in the lurch.'

'So when did they leave here?'

Crombie fiddled with his whisky glass. 'It's not my son in the barrel.'

'All the same, when did they leave?'

Crombie took a sip of whisky, draining the glass. 'The morning of the thirteenth.'

Cullen was usually suspicious of such precision in dates. 'That's fairly specific.'

Crombie set the empty glass on the table. 'That morning, we'd just finished distilling. Thanks to my insistence they focus on the task at hand, the boys had worked hard, so I let them go early. Doug Strachan could handle supervising the men.'

Cullen jotted a quick timeline in his notebook. 'That's a bit of a gap between them leaving here and the festival. It's usually the twenty-third or twenty-fourth of June.'

'Aye.' Crombie reached over to the decanter and poured another generous measure. 'The idea was to go down the west coast, through the Lake District and Wales. The boys were big on their hillwalking and their real ale.' He held up his glass. 'And their whisky.'

'Do you know where they went?'

'You'd need to ask Fraser, I'm afraid.'

Cullen noted down an action. 'When did you report Iain missing?'

'It was about a week after Fraser returned from Glastonbury. Iain never came back, so we went to the police.'

Cullen tilted his head to the side. 'Didn't they return together?'

'No. They fell in with some crowd and stayed on at the site for a few days after the festival. Fraser had to come back to start on the next batch of barrels.'

Cullen added another bar to the timeline. 'So Fraser is key to the process here?'

'He is, aye. Wish that weren't the case, but he makes a decent fist of it.'

'Do you not get on well with your son?'

'I don't mean it that way.' Crombie took another drink. 'Anyone who's studied business knows how bad it is to have a key man dependency.'

Murray sat forward. 'You're saying Iain didn't return at the same time as Fraser?'

Crombie looked at him and nodded. 'Iain stayed a few days longer.'

Cullen looked at the timeline again. 'So you reported Iain missing a week after Fraser returned?'

'Correct.' Crombie fixed his eyes on him. 'The body in the barrel is not my son.'

Cullen held his gaze but eventually looked away, thinking they wouldn't get anything more without a positive ID. 'Can I ask you a few questions about the barrels?'

'I doubt I can help, but by all means.'

Cullen flicked back a few pages. 'Doug Strachan said they

found the barrels when they did a stock take in 1997. They thought the whisky might have been for you or Iain.'

'We were trying to expand the business at the time. We simply didn't have the whisky to spare. We were fighting tooth and nail to stay independent.'

Murray tapped his pen on his notebook. 'Did Fraser or Strachan ever take a private malt?'

'Douglas Strachan is *not* a director of the company.' Crombie drained his glass and slammed it down. 'Fraser has had just the one over the years and, even then, half of the bottles are stored here.'

Cullen looked at Crombie for a few seconds before speaking. 'Do you have any idea what happened with these barrels?'

Crombie shook his head. 'Those barrels are nothing to do with me or my son.'

'And the barrels only appeared on the inventory in '97, is that right?'

Crombie pushed the glass around the table. 'There is that, yes.'

Cullen sat forward. 'Why did you earmark these two barrels for a special edition if you didn't know how or when they were made?'

'That's none of your business.'

Cullen stared at him, deciding to show who was in charge. 'It is very much our business. May I remind you this is a murder investigation? I would appreciate if you gave us as much information as possible.'

'Very well.' Crombie lost himself in thought for a few moments. ''94 was a very good malt. We can't just promote any fourteen year old to the exalted position of celebrating the centenary of this company.'

'If it is Paddy in there, do you have any idea who would want to kill him?'

Crombie closed his eyes. 'I have no idea, I'm afraid. I barely knew the man. I only saw him to give him his weekly pay packet.'

'Can I just remind you this is a serious matter we're investigating?' Cullen handed Crombie a business card. 'I want you to think through exactly what could have happened and call me if anything comes up.'

Crombie's eyes narrowed until they were tiny slits. 'Very well.'

Cullen picked up the bundle of ledgers and got to his feet. 'We'll show ourselves out.'

# 10

----

Murray accelerated through the national speed limit sign at the end of the town. 'So you've been to Gullane before?'

'Aye. Came out with my girlfriend a few weeks ago. We went for a walk along the beach. It was quite rare both of us being off.'

Murray looked over. 'Is your missus a copper?'

'That she is. It was absolutely pissing down so we went for coffee and cake in a German bakery.'

'Muirfield is hosting the Open next year.' Murray indicated right. 'Going to be a total nightmare. Doubt I'll get a ticket.'

'Do you play?'

'Aye.' Murray overtook a slow-moving Land Rover, then patted the dashboard. 'See how this baby can shift?'

'Aye, very good.'

'Do you play?'

'No.' Cullen sat up in his seat. 'I really should what with being from Dalhousie.'

'Ever tried?'

'Just some teenage dabbling on a driving range.'

Murray laughed. 'It's all about persistence and practice.'

'I'll side with Oscar Wilde and say it's *a good walk ruined*.'

'That was Mark Twain.' Murray slowed to join a queue of traffic. 'Totally looking forward to the Ryder Cup this year. Europe have a cracking chance of beating the yanks.'

'I can't stand the Ryder Cup.'

Murray was leaning forward, arm over the steering wheel, watching for overtaking opportunities. 'Sunshine and light today, aren't you?'

'Everything that's good about watching golf on the TV with a hangover doesn't apply to the Ryder Cup.'

'Like what?'

Cullen reached for some examples. 'The calm commentating, the fans applauding as they follow the golfers round the course. That sort of thing.'

'You're a right softy, Cullen.'

'Don't you think wedging 'Europe' into football chants is just embarrassing?'

'It's good to have a team to root for. It's one thing golf struggles with.'

'Why should I give a shit about an Italian and a German against two Americans?'

'I see your point.' Murray turned left at Drem, heading towards the distillery. 'I'm playing off four just now. Aim is to get down to two by the end of the year.'

'That's impressive.' Cullen looked over. 'Where do you get the time?'

'You can talk. Heading to Glastonbury.'

'I went once and I had to stand through the White Stripes with my girlfriend pretty much as we were splitting up. And Underworld were playing on the other stage.'

'I quite like Underworld.'

'They're good.' Cullen gripped the grab handle above the door. 'Getting there and back was an absolute bloody nightmare. I borrowed my mum's car and had to spend a whole day cleaning it when we got back. On top of that, it took me weeks of organisation and I had to stay in a phone queue for over an hour to get our tickets.'

Murray pulled into the car park. 'Sorry I asked.'

Cullen spotted Angela leaning against his car, staring into space. 'Good to get it out of my system. Thanks for listening.'

'Right, I'll see you tomorrow, then?'

'Good luck tracking Paddy down.'

'I think I'll need it.'

Cullen got out and retrieved the ledgers from the boot. He carried them over to his car.

Angela scowled at him when he got there. 'Thanks for leaving me with Bain.'

## 11

C ullen stretched back in his chair and let out a deep breath. He glanced at his watch — seven pm already.
He looked at Angela. 'It's been radio silence for the last few hours.'

'Don't tempt fate. How are you getting on?'

'Managed to get through the ledgers in Bain's absence.' Cullen closed the last one. 'You?'

'I got one of the MisPer case files early. Just started going through it now.'

Cullen caught Bain heading their way, hands in his trouser pockets, chewing on gum. 'Incoming.'

Angela glanced up and tore off her glasses.

Bain sat at his desk and put his feet up. He grinned at Angela. 'Hope you don't think I didn't see the glasses, Batgirl. Right little Lois Lane with them on, aren't you?'

Angela rolled her eyes at him. 'I'm hardly a little anything.'

'There is that.' Bain looked over at Cullen. 'Hope you two have been busy here while the rest of us have been doing some proper police work.'

Cullen raised his eyebrows. 'I thought you'd just been irritating the desk sergeant in Garleton until he gave you his whiteboard.'

'Shut it, Sundance.' Bain looked pleased with himself as he

rested his head against his hands. 'He gave me it, though. We'll be based out there for the duration.'

'I take it from the gum you've been speaking to Irvine?'

'He's pissed off I've nicked you from his little skive, but I've had to let him go back to it. Had to remind him who he works for.'

Angela coughed. 'Cargill?'

Bain sniffed. 'Less of that.'

Cullen didn't want them to dwell on the subject too long, in case he got thrown back into Irvine's Astra for another fruitless week. 'How did it go with DCI Turnbull?'

Bain sat forward. 'Need to get a warrant if I want to open the other barrels. The PF knocked me back. I was asking to X-ray them if I couldn't open them. Still a no.'

Cullen frowned. 'Are you serious?'

'Of course I am.' Bain took off his tie. 'It's essential. Could be a treasure trove of bodies down there. She said I need probable cause indicating there's more than one body.'

Angela raised her eyebrows. 'There are *two* disappearances.'

'I brought that up.' Bain inspected his nails. 'She wasn't having it.'

No surprise there...

Bain glanced at a shot of the barrels on the wall. 'They're still impounded. Wee Johnny Watson is looking after them for us.'

'How's Deeley getting on?'

'Don't start me on that work-shy bastard.' Bain picked the gum out of his mouth, before throwing it in the general direction of the nearest bin. It stuck to the outside. 'Earliest he can get out to look at the body is Monday. Had a house fire in Dalkeith, another body in Linlithgow and one in Queensferry.' He screwed up his nose. 'This summer is a nightmare.'

Angela sniffed. 'There's no hurry with ours, though, is there?'

'We're going to solve this, Batgirl, believe you me. How's the detailed forensic analysis of those case files going?'

'Slow, like any detailed forensic analysis.'

Bain smiled. 'Give me a summary.'

She held up a white A4 pad. 'I've been focusing on Paddy Kavanagh as he seems the most likely. I'll give my notes to Murray tomorrow once I've finished.'

'And Iain Crombie?'

'Still waiting on the file. I was going to head home.'

'So you'll have nothing for me at tomorrow's briefing?'

'These things take time.'

Bain peered at the ancient ledgers on Cullen's desk. 'How's it going in the National Library of Scotland there?'

'Only have to focus on the last two, really.'

'Crombie will be glad they're out of his house.'

Cullen laughed. 'Not with the size of it.'

Bain smiled. 'Getting anywhere?'

Cullen slumped back in his chair. 'Not really. They used a pretty weird system. It's taken me about an hour to get my head around it. At some point in the forties, they decided to make the system indecipherable to the common man. I think I've cracked it, though.'

'You think?'

'Well, I spoke to both Fraser Crombie and Doug Strachan about it. They did most of the data entry in the computerisation.'

Bain drummed his fingers on his desk. 'Give me the long and short of it, Sundance.'

'There's no trace of the two barrels. They're not in any records in '94.'

'What about earlier or later?'

'I'd say it's unlikely the barrels were from earlier as there wasn't the whisky to fill them with.'

'And later?'

'Nothing much.' Cullen flicked through the notebook. 'I did find a shortfall of about a hundred litres of whisky in '94. Obviously it hadn't had the time to evaporate.'

'Would that do it?'

Cullen thought it through. 'Strachan told me a barrel contains six hundred and fifty litres. Anderson reckons a body would be about a hundred litres.'

Bain picked at his teeth for a moment. 'That'll cover our two barrels, right?'

'Correct.'

'But we don't know when they were filled?'

'It's highly likely it's 1994, but it's only an assumption at this point.'

'I don't like assumptions, Sundance.'

Cullen looked at his timeline, now in desperate need of redrafting on larger paper. 'It's possible the whisky was stored somewhere else and then poured into the barrel before they discovered them in '97, but it's much less likely.'

Bain started logging into his computer. 'Good effort for once, Sundance. Were there any suspicious splashes of whisky at any point?'

Cullen shook his head. 'Nobody's mentioned any.'

'Have you asked?'

'Not directly.'

'Well, let's ask tomorrow. I'll get our friendly neighbourhood Haddington joker onto it. Either of you two fancy a pint?'

Angela ran a hand through her hair. 'Some megalomaniac has asked me to finish looking through some files by nine tomorrow.'

Bain looked over from his monitor. 'Who said nine? Briefing is at eight in Garleton.'

Angela dropped her pen to the desk. 'Great.'

Bain looked at Cullen. 'Cheeky pint, Sundance?'

Cullen looked at his actions list. 'I wanted to write up my report from today. Keep on top of the paperwork.'

Bain picked up his mouse and dropped it. 'Bottle of Peroni out of Tesco it is, then.'

'All right. I'll come for one.'

'Good man.' Bain stood up and put his jacket on. 'Need a dump, so I'll see you downstairs in ten, right?'

'Right.'

Bain strolled towards the central stairwell, hands in pockets.

Once he was out of sight, Angela looked over. 'Thought you'd already written your notes up?'

'Of course I have, but I was trying to get out of going for a pint with him. Can't believe he guilt-tripped me. I'll only catch the second half at this rate.'

Angela looked into the middle distance. '*He's* been talking all year about spending three weeks watching football.'

Cullen smirked. 'You not heading back out to East Lothian to see lover boy then?'

'That's not even funny.' She got to her feet. 'I'll see you there tomorrow. No need to pick me up here or anything.'

Cullen winked as he got to his feet. 'Very convenient.'

'Scott, I'm serious, stop joking about this. It's not funny.'

Cullen suddenly felt bad. 'Is everything all right?'

She gave a deep breath. 'It's not going well, put it that way.'

'The DC tenure, right?'

She closed her eyes. 'Yes, Scott. Think of it that way.'

## 12

B ain sat, pushing a sparkling pint of lager to Cullen. 'Here you go, Sundance.'

Cullen took a sip. 'Cheers.'

Bain nailed almost half his pint in one go. 'Who's Butch doing this surveillance with?'

'*Sharon* is alternating between DC Jain and DI Wilkinson.'

Bain produced two bags of crisps from his pockets. 'How come I've got this shite little case and Wilko's got the proper one? Christ's sake.'

'You think this is small?'

Bain tore open the crisps. 'Don't you?'

'It's a murder. This is going to keep us going for weeks.'

'Tell me about it.' Bain wolfed down the packet of cheese and onion before opening the salt and vinegar. 'Got a briefing on Police Scotland next week. That'll be a load of bollocks.'

'I've not heard much about it.'

Bain shook his head and took a daintier sip. 'You keep your head buried in the sand, don't you?' He brushed the salt off his fingers. 'All eight police services are rolling into one. Might open doors for people like me. I hear the Strathclyde boy is getting the top job. I played golf with him a couple of times.'

'Didn't take you for a golfer.'

'I've got a lot of hidden talents, Sundance.' Bain started eating the second bag of crisps. 'Cargill coming in means Turnbull's nailing his colours to the mast, Sundance.' He shook his head. 'He'll be Superintendent Turnbull before we know it. Mark my words.'

'He seems to get on okay with the brass.'

Bain finished the bag. 'Don't trust him, though. That fat bastard is only out for himself. Supposed to be bringing some twat in from Grampian soon. We don't need any more bloody sergeants.'

'Sharon and Irvine can get overworked.'

'Piss off, Sundance. Irvine's the laziest bastard I've worked with. Only thing he's good for is handling clipboards.'

'He's not my favourite officer, either.'

Bain took another drink. 'You're lucky he dropped that complaint against you, by the way.'

'He was lying.'

Bain shook his head. 'I don't know who I believe. Never try that shite on with me.'

'Wouldn't dream of it.' Cullen held up his empty glass. 'Another?'

Bain snorted before finishing his own. 'Much as I'd like you to invite me back for coffee, Sundance, I'd better head home.'

'You're very cagey about your private life.'

Bain stroked his moustache. 'Best way to keep it, Sundance.' He tugged his jacket on and led them outside. 'Might head over to Tesco to get that bottle of Peroni. Could do with something in front of the match.'

'Come here, you!'

They spun around. On the opposite side of Leith Walk, a big guy in a suit tore a cyclist from his bike and slammed him to the ground.

Bain groaned. 'Here we go again.'

They ran across the road, weaving through traffic.

The cyclist was on his back in the bus lane, the suit kneeling over him. 'Where is it?'

Bain grabbed the guy's shoulder. 'Where's what, son?'

'This bastard stole my phone!'

'DI Brian Bain.' Bain got his warrant card out. 'Get that boy checked out.'

Cullen helped the cyclist to his feet. 'Do you have his phone?'

The cyclist pulled down his hoodie. 'His phone?'

'This man alleges you stole his phone.'

'I haven't got a phone, man.'

Bain walked up to him. 'You got a name?'

'John.'

'Right, John. Empty your pockets, please.'

John raised his arms. 'I don't have a phone, man. He just assaulted me. I want you to do *him*.'

A couple of uniformed officers walked out of the police station. Bain called them over, then went back to the suit. 'What happened?'

'I was on the phone to my girlfriend and he snatched it out of my hand.'

Bain reached into his pocket and got a packet of mints out, shoving a couple in his mouth. 'It was definitely him?'

The suit shrugged. 'It was a guy on a bike.'

'Was it him?'

The suit looked over at John, then looked away. 'I think so.'

Bain took Cullen to the side, offering a mint then checking his watch. 'We've got two choices here, Sundance. Overtime or pass it to uniform.'

'You mean stay or watch the football?'

Bain chuckled. 'Aye.'

'This isn't a detective case, is it?'

'Agreed.' Bain walked back to the uniforms. 'Right, gents, I'm handing this to you. Make sure you do one of them, okay?'

# 13

———

Cullen was sitting in the hall in his shared flat, watching a string of adverts filling the wall-mounted screen. Rather than a living room, they had a TV in the hall. It wasn't how Cullen would choose to furnish a flat, but he'd got used to it over the years he'd lived there.

He sipped from a can of Staropramen, starting to feel it. 'More comics, is it?'

Tom looked up from his iPad. 'Wish I'd never told you about my dirty little secret. I'd kept it quiet long enough.'

'It's not healthy keeping things from people, comic boy.'

Tom switched his iPad off. 'And here was me thinking it was good to actually be able to spend time with my oldest buddy.'

Cullen smiled and took another drink.

The TV went back to the studio. Tom put the volume back on and they listened to the chat for a few minutes.

'They're two countries away from the match. Bloody joke.' Tom pointed at the Russian player on the screen, Andrey Arshavin. 'The papers were saying he was having a great tournament based on *one game*. He was pish tonight.'

Cullen couldn't remember who Russia played in the first match. 'Who was it they were playing the other night?'

'Very funny. You know full well not to mention that.'

Cullen held up his hands. 'I've no idea what you are talking about.'

'Russia beat the Czech Republic.'

Cullen realised his mistake. 'Please can we avoid your diatribe about how Scotland should have qualified in their place?'

Tom slammed his can down. 'We would have done except for that bloody night in Prague. Tell you, Scotty, if it wasn't for that 4-6-0 formation, we'd have been there.'

'*You* wouldn't.'

'Course I would. I'd have loved seeing the boys at the finals of a major tournament.'

'I don't think you'd have bothered your arse.'

'Whatever.'

'If you'd gone, you'd have seen Scotland getting turned over by Russia.'

The TV switched to a trailer for the Spain vs Ireland match on Thursday.

Tom waved his can at the screen. 'Odds on favourites now. Spain by a country mile.'

Cullen let out a breath. 'I'm so *bored* of them. I hope Germany or Italy tear them apart. This tiki-taka shite is so boring. In their first match they copied Craig Levein's favourite philosophy of no strikers. All they do is pass the ball five yards. I'm so fed up with it.'

'It's beautiful.' Tom shook his head. 'You are such a cynical bastard.'

Cullen finished his can. 'It's a better way to be.'

Tom got up and walked to his room, returning with a bottle of whisky.

Cullen picked up the bottle of Dunpender. 'No thanks, mate.' He got up. 'I'm off to bed. Early start.'

Tom poured himself a healthy measure. 'Suit yourself.'

Cullen went to his room wishing Sharon wasn't working that night. He lay on his bed and called her. 'Hey.'

'Hi, Scott. I'd better be quick, Wilko's out getting chips.'

'How's your day been?'

'Long and boring. You?'

'Frustrating.' He rubbed his eye. 'I miss you.'

'Miss you too. What have you been doing?'

'Sitting watching the football with Tom. Boring myself to tears.'

'Well, you can bore yourself to tears in my flat soon.'

'Definitely.'

'You haven't told Tom yet, have you?'

'Not really. I'm keeping it quiet until it's definitely going to happen.'

'You're the only one stopping it, Scott.'

'Am I?'

'Look, Wilko's on his way back. I'd better go. Give me a call tomorrow, okay?'

'Okay.'

Cullen tossed his phone on the bed and stared at the ceiling, wondering what was stopping him from moving in with her.

# DAY 2

*Wednesday*
*13th June*

# 14

Cullen parked on the high street just outside Garleton police station.

The car in front of him flashed its headlights.

Cullen clocked DC Murray and waved. He turned off the engine and got out, hoping the central locking behaved itself for once, and met Murray at the entrance. 'Morning.'

Murray signed him in. 'Glad I didn't have to drive out here from town.'

'Well, hopefully someday soon the tables will be turned.'

Murray held the door open. 'I hope we nail this today. I can't be arsed with Bain for much longer.'

'I've been with him for fifteen months.'

'Christ.' Murray led them down another corridor, heading for the stairs.

Angela stood at the top, Lamb leaning against the wall next to her.

Cullen cleared his throat as they climbed. 'What's going on here, then?'

They jolted apart.

Angela blushed. 'Nothing.'

'Aye, right.' Cullen offered his hand to Lamb. 'Didn't expect to see you so soon. Tell me Turnbull hasn't paired you up with Bain again?'

'No such luck.' Lamb shook his hand. 'Got a new DC started in the station, supposed to focus on North Berwick, Garleton and Gullane. I'm just doing the rounds and introducing him to the usual faces.'

Cullen held a finger to his lip. 'And you managed to do the rounds when ADC Caldwell was in the station.'

Lamb laughed it off. 'One of those things.' He sniffed. 'I lost Eva Law to St Leonard's.'

Cullen felt a pang of guilt — he hoped he wasn't to blame for her decision and she was in Edinburgh to be nearer him. He tried not to blush. 'My Acting DC tenure was at St Leonard's. I'll put in a good word for her.'

Angela rolled her eyes. 'Oh, I'm sure she'd *really* appreciate that.'

Cullen ignored her. 'Did she make full DC?'

'She did.' Lamb rubbed the triangle of beard below his lips. 'She was too good for us, though, good luck to her.'

Murray stuck out his bottom lip. 'Hey, watch it, Sarge.'

'You know what I mean.' Lamb folded his arms. 'DI Webster's after an update on that assault in Gullane, by the way.'

'I'm a bit caught up with this, Bill. You'll need to get her to speak with Bain.'

'Like that's going to happen.' Lamb looked at Cullen. 'Remember Stuart's got his own caseload.'

'I'd care if I was a DS.' Cullen nodded down the corridor. 'We'd best get on. I don't want you and Bain seeing each other.'

Lamb laughed. 'I've heard his voice already and that's the closest I'm getting.'

Angela raised an eyebrow. 'I'll catch you up.'

Cullen and Murray hurried along the corridor, leaving them to finish their chat.

Murray stopped outside the Incident Room. 'Bill's obsessed with her.'

'Not as obsessed as her husband.'

'Not what Bill says.'

Cullen glanced backwards — she'd moved closer to Lamb. 'Has he been seeing her?'

'He's quite cagey about that sort of thing sometimes.' Murray grinned. 'Are you jealous?'

'Hardly. I'm in a relationship.'

'What did she tell you?'

Cullen tried to think back. 'Lamb tried it on with her in January when we were out here. She's not talked about it since. I think Lamb asked her out and she declined.'

'Interesting.'

The Incident Room door swung open. Bain stood there, glowering at them. 'What are you pair of schoolgirls up to?' He tapped at his watch. 'It's five past.'

Cullen cleared his throat. 'We're just getting our stories straight.'

'I know you, Sundance, and it's never as simple as that.' Bain shook his head. 'Right, I'm just off for a slash.'

They entered the dusty Incident Room with its familiar stench of mould and rotten plaster. Aside from him, Murray and Angela, there was only Watson and two male officers Cullen didn't recognise.

Murray went over the radiator and turned it up. 'Thank God it's June, it was brass monkeys in January.'

Cullen spoke in an undertone. 'See how the mighty have fallen. Turnbull's not even allocated a DS to the case.'

'Does that mean Bain is effectively demoted to sergeant?'

'More likely than either of us stepping up to Acting DS.'

Bain returned. 'Quit whispering the pair of you. Unless you feel happy sharing it with the rest of us?'

Cullen found a seat. 'No, sir.'

Bain stood by the whiteboard, glowering around the room. 'Where's Batgirl?'

Angela waltzed in. 'Right here, sir.'

'Glad someone woke up on the right side of the bed.' Bain clapped his hands together. 'Looks like the gang's all here so let's get started.'

He got out a sheet of notes. 'First, we're in the process of transferring the barrel and the body to sit in Jimmy Deeley's office waiting for him to bother his arse to perform the post mortem. Anderson is taking his time with the Forensic Report as per usual but it's looking like the barrel has been intact since it was filled.'

He cracked open a can of Red Bull and took a deep drink. 'I'd hoped we could get an easy result here, but Batgirl has found both Iain Crombie and Paddy Kavanagh match the description.'

Cullen raised his hand. 'It could be someone from later.'

'Agreed.' Bain looked around the room. 'For your benefit, they don't have records of the barrels being poured in 1994. They first noticed them in '97. It's possible the barrel was filled anything up to three years later than what's stamped on the bottom of it.'

He took another sip. 'Cullen found a hundred litres of whisky were unaccounted for in '94. Someone stole a load of whisky and two barrels.'

Cullen held up a hand. 'There was no record of any missing barrels, but given they reuse them it's possible two went missing without a formal record.'

Bain stroked his moustache and checked the sheet of paper again. 'Alec Crombie doesn't think it's his son in there. Why is that?'

'He's maybe not got over the disappearance.' Angela rolled a shoulder.

'Maybe.'

Murray raised his hand. 'Could he have killed Iain?'

Bain scowled at him. 'We don't have an identified victim yet, so it's going to be a bit tricky catching a murderer, don't you think?'

Murray slumped back in his chair, looking irritated. 'Fair enough.'

Bain stayed focused on him. 'How's the hunt for Paddy going?'

'Not had anything from Aberdeen or Paisley yet. I'll give them a chaser just after this.'

'You do that.'

'Other than the prospects in Strathclyde and Grampian, there are some over in Ireland.'

'Forget about a wee jolly to Ireland.' Bain shook his head. 'Get the road atlas out and head to Paisley.'

'Great.'

Bain crushed the can. 'Can you get a photofit done of Paddy Kavanagh and Iain Crombie with all that fake ageing shite?'

'I'll see.' Murray jotted it down.

Bain looked at Angela. 'What have you got, princess?'

'I've been through the case files for Paddy and Iain that were shipped to Leith Walk.'

'So Iain's file turned up?'

She held up a report. 'Got it this morning. There's a potential break too. Iain was a bit of a lad back in the day. He got done for fighting in Gullane in 1989.'

Bain clenched his fists. 'Did they charge him?'

Angela read from the file. 'Went to the Sheriff Court in Haddington. He got a fine. Breach of the peace.'

Bain grinned. 'You beauty.'

She smiled. 'Never knew you cared.'

Murray glanced at her. 'She only does sergeants.'

Angela hit his arm.

Bain gave her a long, hard look then shifted to Murray. 'Was a DNA sample taken?'

'According to the file.'

Bain clapped his hands together. 'So we should be able to definitively identify whether the body is Iain Crombie?'

'I'd say so.'

'Magic.' Bain looked at the PCs. 'You three, can you get over to the distillery and speak to anyone who was working there between '94 and '97?'

Angela looked at her notebook. 'I've got the name of the officer who looked into both disappearances. A retired DS called Frank Stanhope. Lives in a static caravan by Haddington.'

Bain looked over at Cullen. 'Guess who I want to go speak to him?'

## 15

Cullen turned right onto the A199 heading for Haddington.

Angela looked up from the roadmap. 'How was your pint with Bain last night?'

'Great. He bitched and moaned then pulled apart two boys having a fight on Leith Walk. Palmed it off onto uniform pretty quickly.'

'*Really* glad I didn't go now.' She checked the roadmap again. 'Next right.'

Cullen pulled into a static caravan park set back from the road among evergreen trees. 'Stanhope originally investigated Iain Crombie's disappearance, right?'

'Aye. And Paddy's. He was based in Haddington.'

'So he's, what, some distant ancestor of Bill Lamb in the family tree of Lothian & Borders?'

'Drop it.' She pointed to the right. 'Here.'

Cullen parked and got out, before stepping over a tiny white picket fence barely a foot tall. He tapped it with his foot. 'Why would you bother?'

Angela looked into the distance. 'Why indeed.'

Cullen knocked on the door. It opened. 'Frank Stanhope?'

'Aye.' Stanhope was a gnarled old copper, fat and red-faced. 'Who's asking?'

Cullen held out his warrant card. 'DC Scott Cullen and ADC Angela Caldwell.'

'What's this about, son?'

'Need to ask a few questions about Paddy Kavanagh and Iain Crombie.'

'Both of them?'

'It's complicated.'

'What isn't?' Stanhope gestured to some chairs set around an old whisky barrel now submerged in the earth and covered in the detritus of a fried breakfast. 'Have a seat. I'll get my notebooks.'

Cullen sat, quickly finding he'd picked the most unstable chair.

Stanhope came back out and dumped a stack of notebooks on the barrel. Each had a sticker on the spine indicating active periods and cases.

Cullen grinned. 'I should do something similar with mine.'

Stanhope grunted. 'Kept getting picked up on it in my annual review. Surprised you lot get away with it these days.'

Stanhope's collie ran out and sat at his feet, head bowed between front paws, ears and eyes alert.

Cullen smiled at the dog. 'What's his name?'

'She's called Welshy.'

Cullen grinned at the name. 'That wouldn't be Peter Welsh, would it?'

'One and the same. One of my last cases. Caught him stabbing someone.' Stanhope patted the dog's head. 'Nice to name my dog after a career highlight.' He picked up a half-drunk mug of tea and took a sip. 'What are you after then?'

Cullen tapped the whisky cask. 'A body was found in a barrel at Dunpender Distillery yesterday morning.'

'Good Christ. Who is it?'

'We don't know. It could either be Paddy Kavanagh or Iain Crombie.'

'I did both cases.' Stanhope stroked the dog. 'Which one first?'

'Let's do Iain Crombie first.'

'I remember it well. I can tell you with all honesty I was bitterly disappointed I never solved this in my time in the force. The one that got away.' Stanhope laughed, though his eyes betrayed the darkness of the humour. He held up a notebook. 'Not the only one, of course, but the one that really burned. It always felt so close. You know, I've dreamt of this happening someday. A young copper pitching up to tell me they've solved it.'

'We've spoken to quite a few of the main players in this. You know this much more intimately than we ever will, so could you take us through what happened?'

Stanhope took a pair of reading glasses from his shirt pocket. 'The boys were away at Glastonbury Festival. They'd finished all of the whisky processing and what have you for the year and then went down the west coast through the Lake District and Wales, hillwalking and drinking in small country pubs.'

'Did you retrace the route?'

'Fraser had a few receipts and what have you.' Stanhope flicked over a page then screwed his eyes up, trying to read something. 'According to Fraser, they got to the festival a few days before it started. We've got some of the ticket stubs in evidence somewhere — they were stamped with the dates.

'After the festival, they stayed on partying with some crowd they'd hooked up with. Fraser returned home on the second of July to make a start on the barrels for the next batch. His brother stayed on.'

He blew on his tea and took a sip. 'Iain was reported missing a week later. The ninth. That's when I started investigating.'

Cullen noted it on his timeline. 'What happened?'

Stanhope put his glasses on his head. 'Though the case was initially logged in Haddington, most of my investigation was carried out down south. I worked with cops from Avon & Somerset and was based out of Glastonbury for a few days. That's a weird town, I can tell you. In all honesty, we didn't manage to get much.'

Cullen noted it. 'Any idea why Iain stayed on?'

Stanhope looked into the distance. 'He met a girl.'

Cullen raised his eyebrows. 'This is the first we've heard of it.'

'You calling me a liar, son?'

Cullen shook his head. 'I'm just saying, that's all.'

Angela smoothed her hair. 'Did you ever find the girl?'

'No.' Stanhope tore open a second notebook and put his glasses on again. 'Fraser gave us a description. She sounded like a real pretty sort, the kind you would stay behind for.'

He chuckled. 'We had posters up all through the West Country. At one point, we went nationwide — I saw a poster in King's Cross when I was in London for the weekend. Iain's photo and the artist's impression of this girl.'

Angela crossed her legs. 'Were there any sightings?'

Stanhope went through another notebook. 'If memory serves, a few months after, there was a flurry of sightings in North Yorkshire. The Avon & Somerset boys were leading at that point, though. I spoke to some guys in Harrogate who did most of the shoe leather work but they never found the girl. I guess we'll never know now.'

Cullen clicked his pen. 'What was Fraser's side of this?'

Stanhope put his glasses on the table. 'Fraser last saw Iain at Glastonbury. First of July. Just after the festival. He got an overnight coach from Bristol to Edinburgh.'

Cullen added a couple of bars to the timeline. 'Did you have any clear suspects?'

'Afraid not.' Stanhope poured the tea out on the grass beside him. 'We were split across two jurisdictions with only posters and press releases to help us. It was a missing persons case not a murder. We didn't have a body.' He laughed again. 'In some ways, you're lucky. You've got the body and eighteen years of advances in forensics. I envy you.'

Cullen coughed. 'You wouldn't if you knew my DI.'

Stanhope snorted with laughter.

Cullen dropped his pen on the table. 'At the moment, we don't know who the body is. We're just checking out possibilities and it turns out we've got two.'

Stanhope stroked the dog's head. 'I hope to goodness you find out what happened to Iain.'

Angela picked up the case file from the table. 'Was Fraser Crombie the last person to see him?'

'That we know of.'

'What about before that?'

'Before that...' Stanhope stroked his chin for a few seconds, before picking up the original notebook and flicking through it. 'Before that, it would be their father who saw Iain last.'

He turned to a particular page in the notebook. 'Twelfth of

June it would be. They were in the pub in Gullane after a family meal, the day before they set off.'

Angela scribbled it down. 'Did anything happen that night?'

'We spoke to a few lads who were drinking with them. They seemed fairly cordial.'

Cullen stopped to think for a few seconds. 'Did Alec Crombie directly hear from Iain during their trip?'

'Not *directly*, but Fraser had called home every other night.'

Angela's eyes narrowed. 'Just Fraser?'

'This was before mobiles, remember.'

Angela looked up. 'He was calling his father, right?'

'No, it was mostly their mother.' Stanhope paused. 'She was a severe woman, believe you me, ran that house like an army camp. Never got involved in the whisky, mind.' He picked up the empty mug and held it in his hands. 'She passed away a few years later. It wouldn't be too much of a stretch to suggest the strain of Iain's disappearance did it, if I'm being honest.'

'It's maybe nothing, but did you just take Fraser's word for what happened?'

'Are you saying I did a half-arsed job, missy?'

'No, I'm not. I asked a simple question.'

'Of course I bloody didn't.' Stanhope handed her a notebook. 'Iain's wife got a phone call every night as well. From Iain.'

Angela picked up the notebook and looked through the short-hand notes.

Cullen looked away. 'We didn't know he had a wife.'

Stanhope laughed. 'And they call you detectives.'

'Steady on. It's not mentioned in the file. It isn't us doing the sloppy work.'

Stanhope sat back and folded his arms. 'I'm ten seconds away from asking you to piss off.'

'And I'm ten seconds away from asking you if you want to continue this questioning in the station. You're not a serving officer now.'

Stanhope's eyes scanned the horizon for a few moments. 'There's no need for that either.' He looked at Cullen. 'Her name was Marion Crombie, née McCoull. I think she remarried a couple of years later though I don't know her new name.'

Cullen wrote it on a fresh page. 'Thank you.'

Stanhope rearranged his notebooks.

Angela held up the one with the reference to Marion Crombie. 'I'll bring this back once I've copied it.'

Stanhope handed her another couple. 'I won't exactly need them.'

'Thanks.'

Stanhope's fingers drummed on the whisky barrel. 'Never imagined his body was here all that time.'

'Hold on.' Angela raised her hands. 'We don't know it's Iain.'

Stanhope winked at her. 'Aye, well, I've got a policeman's hunch about this one. It's a useful thing to have.'

'What about Paddy Kavanagh?'

Stanhope exhaled through his nostrils. 'Another of my ghosts. I wasn't directly involved in that one, but it still annoys me. A purer mystery than young Crombie. We had no leads, nothing. Never even came close to solving it. It's a good while since I retired, so who knows what my replacement has managed to do with it. I dig out my cold cases every six months, but that one shut itself again straight away every single time.'

Angela closed her notebook. 'Do you think the body could be Paddy Kavanagh?'

'I don't know.' Stanhope was staring into the distance, focusing on something in the distant past. 'Either way, I sincerely hope you pair can exorcise one of my ghosts.'

## 16

Cullen pulled into the Dunpender Distillery car park and parked alongside Crombie's car.

Angela unbuckled her seatbelt. 'I really think we should speak to Bain about this.'

Cullen turned the engine off. 'We'll go and see him once we've spoken to Fraser Crombie again. I don't like him holding stuff back from us.'

Angela dumped the stack of notebooks in the footwell. 'We're nowhere until we know who's in the barrel.'

'I agree.' Cullen checked his mobile for messages — nothing. 'Something doesn't feel right to me.'

'Policeman's hunch?'

'Aye, very good.' Cullen thumbed behind them. 'You did well back there. I was thinking the same thing.'

'He was looking down your top as well?'

Cullen laughed. 'No, I meant about him doing a shoddy job.'

'Like he said, it was just a missing person case.'

Cullen wondered if that was all there was to it. He looked over at the building. 'Come on.'

They got out of the car and walked across the gravel. It was quieter outside than the previous day, but there was loud machinery noise coming from inside the buildings. A few workers were taking cigarette breaks — one of them using the end of one to light another.

Cullen held the door open. 'Can barely hear myself think.'

'You thinking is always a danger.' Angela stopped and folded her arms. 'Seems like everyone's forgotten what happened yesterday, though.'

Cullen gestured for her to enter first.

The receptionist was behind her desk, leafing through a magazine. She wore a short skirt and crossed her legs as they approached. Cullen tried to look elsewhere but he could see why she'd been getting so much interest from Watson.

She looked up, her mouth chewing gum like a certain DS. She looked Cullen up and down. 'Can I help?'

Cullen held up his warrant card. 'We need to speak to Fraser Crombie.'

'Think he's in the cooperage.'

Cullen placed his hands on top of the reception desk. 'Would you be able to show us where it is?'

She tapped a greyscale CCTV monitor to the side. 'I'm covering the security guard's break so I can't just leave my desk.' She pointed to a door to the left, the opposite direction from the staircase they'd climbed the previous day. 'Just head through there. Pass the bar, head to the end of the corridor. You can't miss it.'

'Fine.' Cullen smiled at her. 'How long have you been working here?'

'Five years. Why?'

'We need to speak to anyone working here in '94.'

She folded her arms. 'The policeman who was chatting me up yesterday was back asking about that earlier.'

'What did you tell him?'

'I was two in 1994.'

'What about your predecessor?'

'That would be Elspeth. Elspeth McLeish. She left when I started.'

Cullen wrote it down. 'Did she retire?'

She shook her head. 'Don't think so. She just got fed up. She shacked up with some bloke who was loaded.'

'Do you have an address for her?'

'I'd have to dig it out.'

He handed her a business card. 'Call me when you find it.'

'Will do.'

Cullen walked over, pushed the door and headed on down the corridor.

Angela caught up with him. 'Bloody hell, Shagger, you've fair lost your mojo since your thirtieth birthday.'

Cullen stopped and stared at her. 'Shagger? I seriously don't need any more nicknames.'

Angela held her hands up. 'Sorry.'

'Leave those to Bain.'

Cullen set off again, passing the busy bar. At the end of the corridor was a mesh glass fire door, which he managed to open after a couple of pushes.

There were two other doors leading off a small corridor — the one to the right read COOPERAGE. He knocked on the door — no response. He put his ear against the wood, finding the source of the loud noise.

Cullen pushed the door and it swung open. He entered the vast room, at least forty workbenches dotted around, scattered with half-finished barrels. A team of four men were at work halfway down, Doug Strachan among them.

Cullen walked up the middle, noticing Fraser Crombie sitting further back on an old wooden chair, his face stretching with exertion as he tore away at a barrel, pulling the rim off. He then set about the body, ripping the spars apart.

Cullen leaned against the nearest workbench. 'Looks like tough work.'

Fraser looked up at Cullen, before setting the barrel on the floor and hanging up the hammer. He grabbed a towel smeared with oil and rubbed his hands.

Strachan nodded recognition but kept his distance.

Fraser wiped his forehead. 'How can I help?'

'Quite some place this.'

'This is the extension we told you about yesterday.' Strachan smoothed a hand over the rough walls.

'Must have cost a small fortune to build.'

'It'll be worth it.' Fraser pointed at a row of completed casks from a variety of different woods. 'We doubled our capacity.'

Cullen motioned at the far wall, covered by some complicated-looking machinery — conveyor belts, winches and large funnels. 'What's all that?'

Strachan thumbed up through the ceiling. 'That's the other end of the dumb waiter you asked about yesterday. We're just away to fill another batch.'

Cullen tilted his head to the side. 'Thought you were told to stop production?'

'We're not touching anything in that room. Doesn't stop us filling new ones, does it?' Fraser got to his feet. 'You've not come here to ask about my barrels now, have you?'

'We wouldn't mind asking you a few questions.' Cullen looked around the room again. 'Is there somewhere private we could go?'

## 17

T he distillery's small canteen was a tiny, windowless room just by the reception. Fraser closed the door behind them. 'Am I under suspicion here?'

Cullen got out his notebook and clicked his pen. 'This is just for information. If anything particularly useful comes up, we may take you up to Garleton for a formal interview.'

Fraser folded his arms. 'Fire away, then.'

'Tell me about Paddy Kavanagh.'

Fraser scratched his beard. 'Nothing much to tell. I've worked here full-time since I left school. Paddy was here all that time until he disappeared. He kept himself to himself but I got the impression he was a bit of a drifter.'

'In what way?'

Fraser shifted on his seat. 'I mean, I was just a laddie at the time, only twenty-one, but I could tell a drunk from a mile off.'

Cullen jotted it down. 'Go on.'

'He liked a drink, did Paddy, like all the other casual labourers we've had in here. They tend to be Polish or Czech nowadays rather than Irish. They drink themselves stupid at the weekend and usually on lager rather than whisky.'

Cullen tapped the desk. 'Do you think it could be Paddy in the barrel?'

Fraser shrugged. 'I've no idea who's in that barrel.'

'Do you know anyone who could have cause to harm Mr Kavanagh?'

'You mean anyone who might want to kill him and put him in a whisky barrel?' Fraser smirked. 'As I say, Paddy was a drinker. He stayed up in Garleton and used to cycle down the back roads here every morning. He was usually still pissed from the night before.'

Cullen turned to a new page. 'Tell me about the trip with your brother.'

Fraser screwed his eyes up. 'Thought you just wanted to know about Paddy?'

'It might help if we know about Iain.'

Fraser stared at the desk then up at Cullen. 'I suspect you've heard it five or six times over already. What more's to tell?'

'We haven't spoken to you since we found out it could be your brother in there.' Cullen leaned forward. 'We've heard the story from a few people now, but not you.' He prodded his notebook. 'What's interesting is we've only just heard about a girl Iain met at Glastonbury. Your father didn't mention it either.'

'We agreed not to talk about it.' Fraser looked away. 'Iain was going to handle it when he got back. He was married.'

'To Marion Crombie, right?'

'She's remarried since. Marion Parrott now. Lives in Gullane. Don't have her address.'

'We can get it.' Cullen started another timeline. 'So, Iain was married and yet he got involved with this girl at the festival?'

'He did, aye.' Fraser didn't seem intent on providing any more information but Cullen let him sit there. Eventually, he looked up at Cullen. 'We went there to see Spiritualized. They were Iain's favourite band. He'd been big into Spacemen 3. You ever heard them?'

Cullen shook his head. 'I'm more of a techno guy.'

'I remember it like it was yesterday. They met right at the front in the middle of their set. Their eyes just locked onto each other and that was it.'

Cullen noted it down. 'How was your relationship with your brother?'

'Fine. We were pretty close.'

'No big arguments or anything?'

Fraser shook his head. 'Not that I can think of.'

Cullen gestured for Angela to take the lead.

She cleared her throat. 'And you left them at the festival?'

'Aye. They spent every minute of every day with each other. The bands stopped on the Sunday night. The twenty-sixth, I think. We stayed partying for a few days. There were loads of hippies and crusties sitting around campfires. It's not like nowadays, they were pretty cool about you doing that. I mean, half of our group had just jumped the fence.'

'Why did you come home separately?'

Fraser fiddled with a piercing in his left ear. 'I left on the first of July. Dad told me to get back home. Needed to get on with the barrels for the next batch.'

Angela scribbled something down. 'And why did your brother stay on?'

'He was really into this girl. I mean *really* into her. Besides, he had nothing much to come home for — his work was mostly finished till September. Iain was treating it like he was on a long holiday. He knew he'd get a bollocking off the old man, but he didn't seem to care too much about it.'

He licked his lips. 'We were short on barrels that year so I helped Doug fix up the ones we'd just got shipped over from America. We use second-hand barrels from the big bourbon companies.'

'How did Iain seem when you were leaving?'

'He was pretty blissful, to be honest with you. He was in love with this girl, I think.'

'So why do you think nobody heard from him, then?'

'What do you mean?'

Angela leaned across the desk. 'I mean why do you think he disappeared?'

'It was probably the prospect of coming back here. He seemed really happy at Glastonbury. Maybe he did escape with her and they're living in Ibiza or Pontefract. I'd put money on her working in a solicitors in Wakefield or a supermarket in Watford and being as boring as the rest of them. It was an illusion, that's all it was.'

'What makes you say that?'

Fraser focused on the table. 'The prospect of coming home to see Marion again was what did it to him. He wanted to escape that and to escape working here. He had a degree, which I don't. He was a smart guy.'

'Was he having difficulty with his wife?'

Fraser looked away. 'You'd really need to ask her that. It could get really heated, that's all I'm prepared to say.' He sat forward on the seat. 'My brother was an angry man. It was never far below the surface and usually came out when he'd been drinking.' He closed his eyes. 'He might have killed himself.'

'Why do you think that?'

Fraser's eyes locked onto Cullen. 'You're thinking from the perspective of it being him in the barrel. I think he isn't in that barrel but I think he is dead. Iain was a man of passion. He was fed up working here. The same thing, day in, day out, year in, year out. I don't mind, but Iain felt restricted by it.'

'Why didn't he leave?'

'Loyalty to the old man.'

'Wasn't Iain in love with this girl at the festival? I wouldn't have thought someone in a new relationship would kill himself?'

Fraser shifted his seat forward, the leg scraping on the ground. 'Iain was maybe placing a bit too much hope in her. He said he felt insanely happy. I spoke to her a bit and I kind of got the impression she was hiding something, maybe a boyfriend back home. Festivals are fake cities that just exist for a few days of the year. It's not real, there's a day job and a real world back home.'

It made logical sense to Cullen, but he wasn't going to mention it to Bain any time soon. He went back a few steps in his notebook. 'You said your brother was an angry man.'

'Angry and impulsive. His marriage was a classic example. One morning, he had a big raging argument with Dad. That afternoon him and Marion went into Edinburgh and got married at the registry office.'

'Was your father against Iain seeing her?'

Fraser smoothed down his beard again. 'You'd need to ask him the exact details but he didn't like Marion and hasn't had much to do with her in the last eighteen years.'

Cullen exchanged a brief look with Angela. 'Assuming it is your brother in the barrel, would there be any likely suspects in your mind?'

Fraser sat back in his seat for a few seconds. 'It feels like I'm betraying a trust here, but I'd say the only likely person would be Doug Strachan.'

'Why?'

'You've met him, right? His face is red from the drink. We all drink more than we should in this place, it's part of the job, but Doug used to take liberties.'

'What kind of liberties?'

Fraser glanced at the door then leaned forward. 'Iain caught Doug stealing a couple of times. He reckoned he'd taken a litre in a fortnight. We're talking the undiluted cask strength stuff here, which he could dilute at home. That's the best part of three bottles. Iain didn't know how much more he'd taken over the years.'

'Is there any way of corroborating this?'

'You'd need to ask Doug. I don't think Iain went to Dad about it.'

'Why not?'

'Doug knows the whisky process inside out and, if you pardon the expression, he knows where the bodies are buried.'

'I see.' Cullen tapped his pen on his notebook for a moment. 'If he was so impulsive wouldn't he just have sacked Mr Strachan there and then?'

'He'd threatened him.' Fraser was playing with his piercing. 'He was going to confirm his decision when he got back. We spoke about it a few times when we were away. I tried to talk to him about it but Iain was going to get shot of him.'

Angela frowned. 'Did Iain have the power to sack him?'

'He was going to take it to Dad.' Fraser shook his head. 'Dad was hard on that sort of thing. Iain would have persuaded him pretty easily.'

'Did Mr Strachan think your brother was going to make him lose his job?'

'He's not had a drop since, as far as I'm aware.'

Cullen thought it through for a few moments. Killing someone over the threat of being sacked seemed extreme, but Doug Strachan had kept his job, livelihood and reputation. It was the germ of a motive — means and opportunity could come later. Strachan had certainly benefited from it, if what Fraser said was true.

Cullen noted it down. 'And you think this is enough for Mr Strachan to want to kill your brother?'

'I'd say so.'

'Could Mr Strachan have carried it out?'

'Don't let his current appearance fool you. Doug was a fit man back then, he was certainly capable of doing it. If my brother is in there, then Doug is the only person who had a good reason to do it.'

Cullen got to his feet, intent on finding Doug Strachan.

# 18

Fraser gestured around the empty cooperage. 'I don't know where they've gone.'

Cullen looked at Angela. 'Come with me.' He led her back into the corridor. 'What are you thinking about Strachan?'

She leaned against the wall. 'Assuming it's Iain in the barrel, then could he have done it?'

'Aye.'

She took a deep breath. 'He's grossly overweight now. His belly stretches below the bottom of his polo shirt. It's rank. Take eighteen years of boozing off and he might be stronger and fitter. Probably capable of doing it.'

'Agreed. Let's get him down the station.'

'Near Bain?'

Cullen laughed. 'Near Bain. Wait here and see if he turns up. I'll call you.' He walked back to the reception desk, noticing the bar was busier, and peeked in the room. No sign of Strachan. He continued on.

The receptionist looked up at him, pushing her magazine to one side. She fluttered her eyelids at Cullen. 'How can I help?'

'I'm looking for Doug Strachan now. He seems to have disappeared.'

The receptionist stared over at the door. 'I think he went out.'

'When?'

'An hour ago, maybe?'

'Any idea where?'

'He didn't say. I don't keep a log of what everyone's up to.'

'Is his car still in the car park?'

She looked over at the security monitor on her desk. 'Looks like it's gone.'

'Shite.' Cullen took a deep breath. 'Does he do this sort of thing often?'

'He can do, aye. Sometimes he'll be gone for a few hours at a time.'

Cullen felt his guts contract. 'What car does he drive?'

'It's an old Audi, I think. It's purple. P reg.'

'Almost as old as mine. Thanks.'

Cullen went outside into the car park and stood thinking for a few seconds. He noticed a gap between a Peugeot and a SUV.

He clenched his fists, struggling to think what to do. Strachan was becoming a suspect and he'd let him go.

He got his mobile out ready to phone Angela when he heard a grinding noise from the main road. He half suspected it to be a tractor for the farm. An Audi 80 flew across the car park and pulled into the space, just missing him.

Strachan struggled out of the driver's door. 'What do you want now?'

'I need to speak to you about your relationship with Iain Crombie.'

# 19

Cullen started the tape machine. 'Interview commenced at twelve twenty-six pm on Wednesday the thirteenth of June 2012. Present are DC Scott Cullen, ADC Angela Caldwell and Douglas Strachan.'

He looked over the desk. 'Mr Strachan, would you confirm for the tape that you have foregone the offer of a solicitor?'

Strachan cleared his throat. 'Aye.'

'Mr Strachan, as you know, we're investigating the discovery of a body at Dunpender Distillery.'

'Aye, I know. I found it.'

'We don't have a positive ID at this point. Who do you think is in the barrel?'

'Alec thinks it's Paddy Kavanagh.'

'Who do *you* think it could be?'

Strachan took a few seconds to stare up at the ceiling then threw his hands up in the air. 'I've no idea.'

'Were you acquainted with Mr Kavanagh?'

'I was.'

'What can you tell us about him?'

Strachan looked at the table for a few seconds. 'Paddy was into his hillwalking. He used to head off somewhere every weekend, up to Aviemore, down to Northumberland, off to the islands off the west coast. There were a couple of times when we didn't see him at the start of the week, but he'd pitch up on a Tuesday lunchtime and just get on with it. He'd usually be caught up by the end of day on a Thursday.'

'What happened when he was reported missing?'

Strachan scratched his neck. 'The landlady at the B&B he was staying at in Garleton reported it. He hadn't turned up by the Wednesday morning, so I gave her a phone to see if he was ill or something. He hadn't come back from his weekend adventuring. She went into the police station in Garleton that afternoon to see if he'd been in an accident or what have you.'

Cullen flicked through his notes — Stanhope hadn't mentioned who had reported it. 'Do you have her name?'

'I could try and look it out.'

'So, in your opinion, it could be Paddy in that barrel?'

'It could be, aye.'

'Any idea why? Or who did it?'

'Paddy was a bit of a lad, you know?' Strachan rasped a hand across the stubble on his chin. 'He was a regular in the Tanner's Arms up in Garleton, drank there most nights. It was a pretty rough place.'

Cullen jotted it down. 'Did you ever drink there?'

'I did, aye.'

'And did anything happen?'

Strachan leaned forward. 'He got into arguments at the bar a couple of times. You know how it is with these places. There's always a wee bit of bother but it was usually forgotten about by the next evening.'

'Was he ever barred?'

'They'd threaten it but he'd be back in there again the next night.'

'Did he get anyone else barred?'

'Not that I can think of. He was a sociable drinker was Paddy.'

'Are there any likely suspects from the crowd he drank with? Anyone he might have upset or maybe owed money to?'

'I was just there for the drink. You'd have to track down some people from back then.'

'Was anyone from the distillery a regular?'

'Other than me, no. Fraser and Iain were up there for a few pints with us every so often.'

Cullen noted it, wondering if there was anything there. 'How was it with them?'

'It was usually a lot tamer. Paddy would be on his best behaviour if they were around.'

Cullen nodded. 'What about his past in Ireland? Any angry spouses or children?'

Strachan stared into space and smiled. 'Paddy always told funny stories about Ireland. Drinking and working in distilleries.'

'Did he have any family?'

'His parents were both dead.'

'Was he married?'

'If he was, he certainly didn't tell us. He was one for the ladies, that's for sure, but never anything serious.'

'Was he involved with anyone here?'

'Just Elspeth McLeish.' Strachan hesitated for a few moments. 'Well, Paddy had a thing with her. Lasted a good few months. They both liked a drink, so I don't think it was a particularly healthy relationship. Elspeth always had a few guys on the go and she never made a secret of it. Whether any of them would have wanted to kill Paddy, well you'd need to ask them that. I just know there were some, that's all.'

Cullen didn't want to have to track them all down, looking for a spurious motive. 'Tell me about your relationship with Iain Crombie.'

Strachan took a few seconds to compose himself. 'Iain was a good lad.' He held his hand out just above the tabletop. 'I knew him since he was yay high and taught him everything he knew about whisky.'

'So you don't think it's him in the barrel?'

Strachan shook his head. 'I don't. I think he's still out there.'

'Any reason why?'

'I just do. Iain left in strange circumstances, I'll give you that, but it doesn't mean he's been murdered.' He leaned forward on the seat. 'Mind that barrel downstairs was filled three weeks before young Iain went missing.'

Cullen tapped the table. 'We don't actually know that.'

Strachan shrugged. 'That's for your CSI girls and boys, I suppose.'

'How did you get on with Iain?'

'Fine. He was a good lad. He was passionate about the product here. He was a fine heir to his father's legacy.'

'If it's Iain in there, who would want to kill him?'

'It's not Iain.'

'If it was.'

Strachan exhaled slowly. 'I honestly can't think of anyone who would want to kill him.'

'Nobody at all?'

'Honestly, no.'

Cullen jotted it down. He swallowed hard. 'Did Iain ever catch you stealing whisky?'

Strachan's yellowy eyes squinted at Cullen. 'I beg your bloody pardon?'

Cullen leaned forward. 'Mr Strachan, I need to know if Iain Crombie ever caught you stealing whisky.'

Strachan glanced nervously at the tape recorder. 'Is this why you've brought me here?'

'Just answer the question, please.'

'Are you accusing me of murder?'

'Mr Strachan, you're not under caution. We're just gathering information.'

'Aye, right.' Strachan's eyes swept between Cullen and Angela. 'If you think I don't know you'll use some comment against me, you must think I'm a bloody fool.'

Cullen rested his hands on the table. 'We just want to confirm whether you stole whisky or not.'

Strachan leaned back and folded his arms. 'Fine.' He stared at the floor then up at Cullen. 'He caught me taking some whisky one night. I'd got about eight hundred mils.'

'What were you going to do with it?'

Strachan rested his chin on his hands. 'I was diluting it at home so I had a personal supply of the good stuff.'

'Why?'

Strachan took a few moments before he answered. 'Because I'm an alcoholic.'

'I see.'

'It's an illness I can't escape. I've tried AA, but I just can't give it up.'

Cullen had seen functioning alcoholics in the force — guys

who could tuck a fair few pints and whiskies away and then be fresh as a daisy the following morning. There were fewer of them these days, though. 'Do you still steal?'

Strachan shook his head. 'No.'

'Did Iain threaten to relieve you of your duties here when he caught you?'

'I'm sorry?' Strachan laughed. 'It would have been a bloody blessing. This place needs me far more than I need it. I've had offers from all over Scotland, sonny, I could have worked at any distillery I bloody wanted. They didn't rate Iain Crombie or his father, they knew who was really doing all the magic.' He stabbed the finger on his chest. 'Me.'

'I see.'

Strachan was breathing heavily, his face almost purple. 'Who told you about this?'

'I'm not at liberty to divulge information, I'm afraid.'

'Figures.'

Cullen looked over at Angela. 'Anything else from you?'

'No, I'm good.'

'Interview terminated at twelve forty-one pm.'

Cullen got up and left the man looking destroyed.

## 20

C ullen chewed on a meatballs and cheese sub as he crossed Garleton High Street.

Angela caught up with him. 'Shouldn't eat as you walk.'

'I'm starving.' He took a drink of water as they waited for the oncoming traffic to clear. 'What did you go for?'

Angela held up her bag. 'Chicken pesto and a Diet Coke.'

They crossed the road and Angela opened the front door. 'Thought you were a wanker about Subway?'

'Sharon likes it. We've gone a few times at the weekend.' Cullen started up the stairs and led along the corridor. The Incident Room was empty.

Angela hung her coat on the back of a chair. 'Where's Bain?'

'No idea. I expected them to be here.' Cullen looked at the whiteboard. 'He's been busy.'

'He's not even punched it yet.'

Cullen laughed as he sat at a desk. He got his drink and crisps out, doubting he'd get tucked into them until mid-afternoon.

Angela unwrapped her sandwich. 'It's about time he pulled his finger out on this case. As far as I can tell, he's done *nothing*.'

'Don't let him hear you say that.'

Bain stormed into the room, eyes blazing, Murray and Watson

following. On the board, he scored the third of the Paddy leads out. 'So that's Grampian out as well.'

'Sorry.'

'Despite your best efforts, DC Murray, we've got nowhere with this Paddy boy. You'd better hope against hope it turns out to be Iain Crombie in there, cos we're bollocksed otherwise.' Bain stabbed his finger in the air. 'And it's your fault.'

'Understood, sir.'

Taking the last mouthful of sub, Cullen read over the rest of the board, now covered in lots of scribbles. There were four large boxes — *Paddy*, *Iain*, a question mark and *94-97*.

There was very little detail around the *Paddy* box, just what Murray was chasing — *Paisley* and *Ireland* were already scored through, with *Aberdeen* having just been struck out.

Bain looked over at Cullen's lunch. 'Afternoon, Sundance. I see you've thought to get yourselves sandwiches.'

Cullen raised his eyebrows. 'There are three shops a two minute walk from here.'

'Still could have got me one.' Bain rustled about in a carrier bag on the desk, producing a can of energy drink. 'Anderson popped in. They've finished finding the square root of bugger all at the distillery, but his laptop ran out of battery so he hasn't completed the report.'

Cullen grinned. 'That's a decent excuse to get close to you.'

'Don't even go there, Sundance.' Bain downed the can in one and tossed it in the bin. 'So what have Batman and Robin been up to?'

Cullen dropped his notebook on the desk. 'We've spoken to Stanhope, Fraser Crombie and Doug Strachan.'

'I thought I told you to focus on Stanhope, Sundance?'

Cullen took a long drink of the Coke, before pointing at the board. 'We did, but we had some pretty good leads to follow up there. Got a few more bits on Iain and some on Paddy.'

Bain walked over to the board. 'Paddy first.'

Cullen looked through his notes. 'Used to drink in a pub called the Tanner's Arms in Garleton. He was a barfly, in there most nights. Fraser Crombie and Doug Strachan both witnessed him getting into fights. So there's a possible avenue.'

Bain uncapped his pen, his face looking like someone'd booby-trapped the lid. 'How did some boy from the boozer get him in a barrel in the bloody distillery?'

Cullen stretched back in his seat. 'I meant it's an explanation for his disappearance, not for ending up in the barrel. We have got two cases here.'

'With you now.' Bain wrote *Tanner's Arms*, connecting to *Regulars 1994*. He looked over at Murray.

Murray deflated. 'Are you serious?'

'Aye. Get a list.'

'How?'

Bain grinned. 'Mine is not to worry about the how, just the what I want.' He held Murray's look for a few seconds. 'Right, Sundance, have you got any more on him?'

Cullen turned the page. 'He was having a fling with the receptionist at the time. Woman called Elspeth McLeish. She subsequently married according to the current receptionist.'

'Elspeth?' Bain put the cap back on the pen. 'So she could be Elizabeth, Elspeth, Liz, Beth or Betty or pretty much anything?'

'The receptionist was going to look through the files for me.'

Bain stroked his moustache. 'I don't fancy our chances. This is a company who found two extra barrels of whisky.'

Angela balled her sandwich wrapper and put it in the bag. 'She had a few men on the go. Could have been one of them.'

'For the love of goodness.' Bain uncapped the pen and scribbled it on the board. 'So we're going to have to hunt down ex-flames of an ex-receptionist?'

'Maybe.' Angela took a drink. 'Strachan could win *Mastermind* with 'the life and times of Paddy Kavanagh' as his specialist subject.'

Bain laughed. 'If Paddy's in the barrel then finding who killed him is going to be next to impossible.'

Murray nodded. 'We're not exactly drowning in leads and suspects for Iain but at least we've something to go on. We're nowhere with Paddy.'

Bain tossed the pen in the air and caught it. 'Anything else, Batgirl?'

'Strachan also told us it was Paddy's landlady who reported him missing.'

'Didn't this Stanhope boy tell you?'

Angela shook her head. 'Afraid not.'

Cullen burped from his lunch. 'Strachan is going to try and find a name and address for her.'

Bain wrote it on the board. 'Great, so a lush is pretty much our only lead in this case?'

Angela held up the case file. 'Might be in here. I haven't checked.'

'Get onto it.' Bain grinned. 'You need a proper nickname by the way.'

'You seem to call me McLaren a lot.'

Bain scowled at him. 'Less cheek.'

'Sorry.'

Bain looked back at Angela. 'Any more?'

'Not on Paddy, other than he used to travel far and wide at the weekends to go hillwalking. Highlands, Northumbria, west coast.'

'Great.' Bain drew a few more boxes around Paddy. 'Right, what have you pair found out about Iain Crombie? It better be more than 'he was called Iain and he disappeared'.'

Cullen flipped through his notes, trying to calm down. 'We spoke to Stanhope, the DS who investigated both cases at the time. The reason Iain stayed on at Glastonbury was he'd met a girl.'

'Right.'

'You don't seem particularly pleased.'

'Do you want a round of applause, Sundance? One of them ones where someone starts clapping and then the whole audience joins in like in some film.'

Murray's phone rang. He held it up to Bain as he left the room. 'Better take this. It's the gaffer.'

'I'm the only gaffer that matters just now.' Bain took a deep breath. 'Go on, Sundance.'

'It was in the official report, but nobody else mentioned it.' Cullen flipped the page. 'However, Fraser Crombie knew about it. He told Stanhope but not his father.'

'Why not?'

Cullen sat back in the chair. 'Turns out Iain was married.'

Bain thumped his hand on the whiteboard, eyes dancing at each of the officers. 'How did we not know?'

Cullen shrugged. 'Sorry, sir.'

Bain pinched his nose. 'Right. What do you know about her?'

'She's remarried and is now called Marion Parrott. Like the bird but with an extra T.'

'This sounds like shite to me.'

Cullen looked up. 'I worked with a Sergeant Jim Parrott in West Lothian.'

'Bet he got fed up of your antics, Sundance.'

'He took no end of stick, but reckoned its French.'

'Think they're related?'

'Doubt it. She still lives in Gullane. Can we speak to her?'

Bain scribbled *Marion* up on the board. 'Fine.'

Angela put her drink down. 'Sounds like they had a fiery marriage.'

Bain made a clicking sound with his tongue. 'Good. Anything else?'

Cullen scanned the notes, searching for anything. 'Fraser Crombie thinks suicide is a distinct possibility for his brother.'

'Like the boy in the Manic Street Preachers?' Bain snorted at Cullen's blank expression. 'The boy who played guitar ran away. They never found him and they put it down to suicide. I liked their first couple of albums.'

Cullen smiled. 'You've got a fairly catholic taste.'

'Lower case C, Sundance.'

Cullen went back to his notes. 'Iain fell out with Doug Strachan before he disappeared.'

'Looks like he drinks like a fish.' Bain sniffed. 'You think he could be a suspect?'

'Could be.'

'What did they fall out over?'

'Iain caught him stealing unblended whisky.'

Bain shoved his hands in his pockets. 'Isn't that like drinking meths?'

'Wouldn't put it past him.' Angela smirked. 'He was going to dilute it at home.'

Cullen sat forward. 'These are guys who do this for a living, year in, year out. He knows exactly what he's doing.'

Bain scowled. 'Why wasn't he sacked?'

Cullen turned forward a few pages. 'Strachan reckons he was too heavily embedded in the process. The whisky would be crap without him.'

'Jesus wept.' Bain turned back to the whiteboard, drawing lines from *Iain* to *Strachan* and scrawling *Argument* on the line.

Cullen got up and joined him. The *Iain* box had four times as many leads than *Paddy* — *Fraser, Alec Crombie, Doug Strachan, Glastonbury, Glastonbury Girl, Marion Parrott* and *Frank Stanhope*. He tapped the board. 'Our biggest problem is we don't know who our body is.'

'You're telling me.'

Cullen tapped on the *Paddy* box. 'How's the hunt for him going?'

'That Murray boy's just back from Paisley, tail between his legs. He could show a tortoise a thing or two about slowing down, I tell you.'

'Remember the tortoise beat the hare.' Murray sat at the desk, tossing his phone in front of him.

Bain glared at him, before tapping a finger on *Alec Crombie*. 'What about the old man?'

Cullen twisted the top of his bottle. 'He's a bit of knob, but we don't have anything pointing to him killing Iain. He seems upset by it more than anything. He's heavily in denial that it's Iain in there.'

'Seems like a dodgy bastard.' Bain grunted. 'He's still a suspect.'

Cullen didn't have the energy to press the point. 'What do you want us to do then?'

'You pair go and see this Marion woman.'

'Will do.'

Bain looked at Murray. 'You'd better find someone who knows about the Tanner's Arms while I try and work out a nickname for you. And a steak sandwich from Subway wouldn't go amiss.'

## 21

They waited outside Marion Parrott's house, a brick semi at the opposite side of Gullane from Alec Crombie's. The street was quiet, the only noise coming from cats fighting on a stone wall.

Cullen looked up at the clouds sweeping in overhead threatening the morning's bright blue sky, rare for a Scottish summer. 'No doubt it'll be pissing down by the time we finish tonight.'

Angela swept her hair over. 'Aren't you watching the football?'

'Maybe.'

Cullen rang the doorbell again. 'She better be in.'

A sullen looking teenager answered the door. Skinny jeans, shirt, jumper, messy hair. 'What?'

Cullen showed his warrant card. 'We're looking for Marion Parrott.'

'That's my mum.'

'Well, is your mother in?'

'Are you the police?'

Cullen held up his warrant card. 'That's what this means, aye.'

'Is this about my dad?'

'I need to speak to Mrs Parrott.' Cullen nodded into the house. 'Is she in?'

The boy looked at him for a few seconds. 'I'll just get her.' He headed off inside.

A woman in her early forties came to the door, red hair tied back in a ponytail, eyes surrounded by dark rings. 'Can I help?'

Cullen introduced them. 'Do you know why we're here?'

Marion frowned. 'Has there been some news?'

'We're here to speak about your ex-husband.'

'*Iain?*'

'Is there more than one?'

'No.' Marion swallowed. 'Come on in.' She led them through the kitchen, a kids' breakfast bomb site waiting to be cleared, and into the garden, nothing more than a patch of grass, some neglected flowerbeds and a tiny patio. She pulled over an ashtray as she sat at the patio table and picked up a cigarette. 'Do you mind?'

Cullen gave an open-palmed gesture. 'Go ahead.'

Marion sparked the cigarette alight then took a deep drag, looking at him with cold eyes. 'Has Iain turned up?'

'Not exactly.' Cullen reached into his pocket for his notebook and pen. 'A body was found at Dunpender Distillery yesterday morning. It was in a barrel we believe was processed in 1994.'

She closed her eyes. 'So it could be Iain?'

'It could be. There's at least one other avenue we're actively investigating.'

'Have you spoken to Frank Stanhope?'

Cullen nodded. 'We'd like to hear it from your perspective, if that's okay?'

'Fine. Where do you want me to start?'

'He was away from home for a few weeks, is that right?'

'It is.' Marion sat staring into space for a few seconds. 'He loved his music. Him and his brother wanted to see Spiritualized at Glastonbury. They were away for a couple of weeks before. Fraser said Iain stayed on partying after the festival. He could really get lost in a good piss-up.'

'Did he come home after it?'

Marion shook her head. 'Fraser told me Iain met someone there. It broke my heart.' She took another drag, eyes trained on Angela. 'I was two months pregnant. When he didn't come back, I almost had an abortion.'

Angela raised her eyebrows. 'Is that Iain's son who answered the door?'

'It is, aye.' Marion's expression softened. 'He's on exam leave just now.'

Cullen wrote it down. 'Did Iain know about the baby?'

Marion rubbed her eyes. 'We'd been trying for a few months. We'd already lost one so Iain wrapped me up in cotton wool as soon as we knew I was pregnant.'

Cullen struggled to reconcile the caring would-be father with the whisky-fuelled young man, away sowing his wild oats at a music festival. 'We believe while they were away on the trip to Glastonbury, Iain was phoning you every night. Is that correct?'

Marion wiped her eye. 'Every night. Kept asking how the baby was. Iain wasn't even a bump then but that's what we called him. The bump.' She sniffed. 'I've had two kids since with Craig, but it wasn't the same as with Iain junior.' She smiled. 'He's off to university next year. He's like his father in so many ways. I'm not much of an academic.'

'Does Iain know about his father?'

Marion fiddled with the lighter. 'He does.'

'Go on.'

'He's become obsessed with his dad's disappearance. It's only natural, I suppose. I told him about his real father on his seventeenth birthday, three months ago.'

'What did he do?'

'I was cleaning his room recently and I found a journal he'd been keeping. He's spent a lot of time speaking to people and putting together a story of his dad's life.'

Cullen noted it down. 'Who has he been speaking to?'

'His grandfather, his uncle. A few others who knew Iain. Some guys who worked with him.'

Cullen leaned over the table. 'We believe Iain's presumption of death was declared in 2001. Did you benefit from it?'

Marion sat back and folded her arms. 'What are you suggesting?'

'We have to consider every possibility in a case like this. We have to consider you a suspect if you gained financially from his disappearance.'

Marion waved the hand with the cigarette at him. 'The only good thing was it meant I could remarry.'

Cullen focused on the rings on her left hand. 'So you weren't able to cash in on any life insurance or anything like that?'

Marion stabbed her finger in the air again. 'That family ripped me off. They just cut me off, excluded me from anything and everything they could.'

'So you got nothing from Iain's estate?'

Marion laughed as she exhaled smoke. 'There wasn't one to speak of. They totally controlled Iain and Fraser, right down to the last penny. He got hardly anything in his salary, it covered our rent but that was it. They used to give him cash to see him through.'

'Why?'

Marion took another puff. 'They kept absolute control over him. Alec and his wife. Iain never had any life insurance or savings. He didn't have any shares in the company, either.'

'Wasn't he good with money?'

Marion took a final drag before crumpling the butt in the ashtray. 'He wasn't financially astute, not like his brother. They both had trust funds. Fraser still had his by the time Iain died. Iain had spent his on God knows what.'

'It would be useful if we could see any of Iain's documentation.'

Marion pushed the stub around the ashtray. 'I've got a box full of stuff in the attic — bank statements, photos, that sort of thing.'

'That would be good.' Angela grimaced. 'Do you get any money from the family for your son?'

'They offered to pay me a couple of grand to have an abortion. I didn't and that was the end of the matter. I could have progressed it through the courts, I suppose. I got money every Christmas but that's it.'

Angela tapped the edge of the table. 'You were married, weren't you?'

'Aye, well, our marriage wasn't exactly blessed by them, put it that way.' Marion picked up the ashtray and gently tilted it, rolling the ash around. 'We were only nineteen when we got married. We were young and Iain was a real romantic. It was a registry office affair, though his dad has enough money to hire Edinburgh Castle.'

She looked at the sun. 'Going to Glastonbury was a good

chance for the two of them to get away. They'd worked hard all year.'

'Do you still see Fraser?'

'Aye.' Marion lit another cigarette and took a deep drag, holding the smoke in her lungs for a few seconds. 'We meet up every year. We go for a drink on the anniversary of Iain's disappearance in July. We're supposed to meet up in a few weeks.'

'How does he seem about Iain?'

Marion took another long puff and spoke through the exhalation. 'He misses him. Fraser's not the warmest of people, you know, but losing his brother really changed him.'

'What about Doug Strachan?'

'What about him?' Marion took a deep drag. 'He could make a solid barrel if you ever caught him sober.'

'Was he an alcoholic?'

'Still is. I bumped into him in the Tesco in North Berwick last year. He had a trolley full of cheap whisky. I'm surprised he's able to work.'

Cullen jotted it down. 'How did Iain get on with Doug?'

'Fine. They had a bit of a run-in once. Iain caught the old idiot stealing whisky.'

Cullen flicked back a few pages. 'Do you know why he didn't sack him?'

'Iain wasn't like that. He could be a bit of a hippie at times. He believed in forgiveness.'

'Assuming it's him we've found, do you have any idea who would want to kill him?'

She shook her head. 'None at all.'

Cullen turned to a new page. 'Did you know a Paddy Kavanagh?'

She furrowed her brow for a few seconds. 'Vaguely rings a bell. Who was he?'

'He worked at the distillery. He's the other potential victim.'

Marion closed her eyes. 'I keep forgetting it might not be Iain in there.'

Cullen smiled. 'I understand. I'm sure this has come as a big shock.'

'I think Iain went out drinking with this Paddy guy once or

twice up in Garleton, but that's it. If I remember correctly, he used to come home even more pissed than usual.'

Cullen closed his notebook and handed her his card as he got to his feet. 'If you think of anything please feel free to give me a call at any time.'

Marion finished the cigarette and ground it into the ashtray. 'Do you want that box of Iain's?'

Angela smiled. 'That would be good.'

Marion got up. 'I'll be back in a few minutes.'

Once she'd gone, Angela shut her eyes. 'That's my afternoon gubbed.'

## 22

C ullen held the Incident Room door open. 'You first.'

Angela raised her eyebrows. 'Remember, you're updating him not me.'

'Fine.'

She stormed off to the corner of the room.

Cullen headed over to the whiteboard, where Murray was facing Bain's full wrath.

Murray put his hands on his hips. 'So what do you want me to do?'

'For the love of goodness.' Bain stroked his moustache. 'Right, this Paddy investigation is going nowhere. You've done the square root of hee-haw on it, other than waste a tank of petrol as you barrelled through to Paisley.'

'It was under your orders, sir.'

Bain prodded the whiteboard. 'We've got bugger all, Constable.'

Murray sniffed. 'Another couple of leads have just come through from Ireland.

'There's a million bloody Paddy Kavanaghs over there.'

'What do you want me to do?'

'Go and have a think on what you should be doing.'

Murray grabbed his coat before storming off and slamming the door behind him.

Bain watched him go with a smug grin. His eyes swivelled round to focus on Cullen. 'What have you made a mess of now, Sundance?'

'What's that supposed to mean?'

Bain smirked. 'You're only here when you've cocked something up. I'd be the last person you were speaking to if you were onto something.'

Cullen leaned against the desk. 'We spoke to Marion Parrott.'

'And?'

'There's nothing new really. She backed up the statements we had from Fraser Crombie, Alec Crombie and Doug Strachan. Strachan stole whisky, Iain caught him. Iain was phoning her every night when they were away.'

'Nothing new?'

'Iain's got a son.'

'Christ's sake, Sundance, that's new.'

'Doesn't get us anywhere, though.' Cullen looked around the room. 'What have you been up to here?'

Bain shrugged. 'Strategising.'

'*Strategising*? What for?'

Bain glared at him. 'This bloody case.'

'Excluding you, there are only six officers on this case. Who are you strategising for?'

Bain tapped his nose. 'You wouldn't recognise it if you saw it.'

'So, I'm doing everything on this case, as per usual, right?'

'Is that what you think?' Bain laughed. 'That's a classic, by the way.'

Cullen looked up. 'Tell us your strategy then.'

'It's not finished yet.' Bain's nostrils flared. 'If we don't get a collar on this your arse is getting introduced to my left boot's steel toecap.'

Cullen's calm disappeared. 'What more do you expect us to do?' He flapped his arms around. 'Make shit up like you did?'

Bain took a deep breath and stabbed a finger at him. 'Don't start on that shite again. It worked.'

'It didn't. You were trying to frame the wrong man. *Again*.'

'Just as bloody well there's no skeletons in your closet, Sundance.'

Cullen tried to slow his breathing and deflect Bain. 'She didn't know Paddy Kavanagh, so we're no further forward with it.'

'Do you think it's Paddy in the barrel?'

'Probably.'

Bain clenched his fists. 'So it's the one we're getting nowhere with.'

'I don't think the likelihood is related to the number of leads we've got.'

Bain glared at him. 'But you think it's him?'

'Aye. Almost certainly.'

'Cullen, I shouldn't be the one telling you to stop focusing on only one victim. Especially after all that shite you put me through last summer.'

Cullen folded his arms. 'Excuse me?'

'Jesus Christ. You and your bird put me through the ringer over that Schoolbook killer.' Bain made a puppet out of his left hand. '*Don't focus on him, sir.*' He switched to the right. '*Are you sure it's not this guy we've not even told you about?*'

Cullen felt a prickle of sweat in his armpits. 'What do you want me to do?'

'Write it up.'

'Is that it? Caldwell's started.'

Bain peered over.

Angela didn't look up from her laptop. 'Leave me out of this.'

Bain looked back at Cullen and grinned. 'Help that clown Murray find something about this Paddy boy. I'm sure you'll be able to keep an open mind on it.'

Cullen clapped his hands together. 'Nice to have some direction at last.'

'If this is a disaster, Sundance, it's your fault. End of.'

23

---

Cullen found Murray hiding in his car outside the station. He opened the passenger door and got in. 'If it's any consolation, I just got a kicking off Bain.'

Murray looked over briefly before looking away again. 'Wouldn't say I came off on the winning side either.'

'Yeah, I saw. I'd describe mine as more of a score draw.'

'Just as well away goals don't count double.'

Cullen laughed as he ran his hand through his hair. 'He's been *strategising*. Can you believe it?'

'Seems more like he's been doing jack shit to me.' Murray gave a slight chuckle. The coolness he usually exuded seemed to have just been shot to bits. 'What do you want, Cullen?'

'Bain asked me to help with the Paddy Kavanagh investigation.'

'What, because I'm messing it up?'

'Whether you are or not isn't something I can comment on. The Iain stuff is grinding to a halt. There are a couple of people I could chase up but it might be better if we team up for now.'

'I'm not a charity case.'

Cullen held up his hands. 'Not saying you are. We need to find out as much as possible about Paddy before Bain arses this up and we're kicked off back to our other cases.'

Murray nodded slowly. 'So what do you want to do?'

'Who have you asked?'

'I've been through Watson's notes. Spoke to Fraser Crombie and that Strachan guy.'

Cullen frowned. 'Not Alec Crombie?'

'Chance would be a fine thing.'

'Let's head back to the distillery.'

## 24

T he receptionist folded her arms. 'I can't let you up.'
Murray leaned across the partition to her. 'Come on,
Amanda.'

'Stuart, I just can't.'

'Why not?'

Amanda looked away. 'Because Mr Crombie is busy and asked
not to be disturbed.'

Cullen felt his blood boiling. He smiled at her. 'Did you
manage to get an address for Elspeth McLeish?'

'Eh?'

'You were going to get me her address.'

'Oh, right, aye.' She scribbled something on a notepad at the
side of her keyboard. 'I'll see what I can find.'

'Thanks.' Cullen headed off to the stairwell leading up to
Crombie's office.

Amanda lifted the partition and ran after them, tugging
Cullen's sleeve. 'I've told you. Mr Crombie is busy.'

Murray got between them. 'Come on, Amanda. We'll make
sure he doesn't blame you.'

She looked at the floor. 'Fine.'

Murray patted Cullen's arm. 'Come on.'

They marched on down the corridor, climbing the stairs to the
office.

Cullen gave him a wink. 'First name terms with her, eh?'

'What can I say? Must be the car.'

Cullen opened Crombie's door and knocked.

Crombie sat at a large oak desk, entirely covered in papers. He looked up and scowled. 'Yes?'

Cullen stepped through the door, opening his notebook as he walked. 'Just need to ask you a few more questions.'

Crombie leaned back in his chair. He gestured to the two leather seats in front of his desk. 'As long as you're quick.'

Cullen clicked his pen as he sat. 'We're investigating whether it's Paddy Kavanagh in the barrel.'

Crombie crunched back in the seat and fiddled with his fountain pen. 'I'm very pleased you've dropped the fantasy of it being my son in there.'

'We haven't dropped anything. Until the body is formally identified, we're investigating both prospects as equally likely.'

'Very well.'

Cullen smoothed down a fresh page in his notebook. 'How would you describe your relationship with Mr Kavanagh?'

Crombie carefully set his pen on his desk and put his hands together as if in prayer. 'As I explained, there wasn't one. He was an employee. All dealings with him went through Iain or Doug.'

'Besides Mr Strachan and your son, would any of the current workforce have worked with Mr Kavanagh?'

Crombie sat forward and ran a hand over his forehead. 'Let me think. I still run all the personnel files myself. Could never see the bloody point in paying someone.' He sat in silence for a few moments. 'There were a lot of people who worked here at the time. We were very busy, but I'm struggling to think of anyone who is still alive I'm afraid.'

Cullen gestured to the other end of the room. 'Perhaps if you looked on your computer?'

Crombie patted the side of his head. 'It's all up here. As I said, I don't see the need in all the expense of getting someone else to do it for me.'

'So there's nobody?'

Crombie tapped his fountain pen on the desk a few times. 'The only person I can think of is Eric Knox. He would have worked with Doug Strachan for a good twenty-five or thirty years. He retired two years ago, lives up in Garleton.'

Cullen wrote the name, not particularly hopeful he would get anywhere with it. 'Can we have a contact address or phone number for Mr Knox?'

Crombie reached down and unlocked a drawer in the desk. He pulled out a large ledger, its dark green cover faded and tattered. 'This is all the information I don't keep in my head.' He flicked through the thick book, his hand eventually stopping at a page. 'Here we go. Eric Charles Knox. Lives in Garleton, as I said. Queen Street. Here.' He swung the ledger around.

Cullen glanced at the page. It looked like the ledger stored personal details of every employee over a long period of time, perhaps as many as fifty years. He took a note of the address before returning the ledger. 'Thanks. We understand Elspeth McLeish was involved with Mr Kavanagh.'

'I try to keep myself distant from staff relations.' Crombie licked his finger and leafed through the ledger, finally stopping halfway. 'Here we are.' He traced a line on the page. 'Ah.'

'What is it?'

'I'm afraid we had returned mail from the address we have on file for Elspeth.' Crombie slammed it shut. 'I can't help you there.'

Cullen tapped the desk. 'Can I ask you some questions about your daughter-in-law?'

'You can ask.'

'We spoke with her earlier this afternoon. She told us you tried to pay her to have an abortion.'

Crombie's shoulders seemed to deflate. He twisted to look out of the window.

Cullen waited almost a minute. 'Is it true?'

Crombie looked down. 'It was my wife's suggestion. She didn't take the money.'

'And you've had little to do with her and your grandson since?'

Crombie turned back round. 'I kept a distance from Marion because I don't trust her. She'd take me for all of my money if she could.'

'How would she be able to do that?'

'She has means.'

'Can you expand on that?'

Crombie exhaled. 'All I'm saying is you shouldn't take everything you hear from her at face value.'

'We're trained not to do that, sir.'

'Yes, I'm sure you are.' Crombie smiled, but with no warmth in his eyes. 'I've made sure I have a continual dialogue with my grandson, young Iain. He's so much like his father.'

'Do you pay any money to Mrs Parrott or to your grandson?'

'I do. I make sure the boy has everything his mother can't provide for him.'

'And how often do you see him?'

'Every fortnight or so. We have lunch up at the house every six months or so.'

Cullen added to the list, doubting it was salient. 'Were you aware your son met a girl at Glastonbury?'

Crombie scowled at him, eyes ablaze. 'I beg your pardon?'

'We have it from a number of sources Iain met a woman at Glastonbury.' Cullen sniffed. 'It's the reason he didn't return home.'

Crombie threw his pen down, almost knocking it on the floor. 'Absolute balderdash. I've never heard such rot in my life. Even though she didn't deserve it, Iain was a faithful husband to Marion. Any notion my son was up to no good at this infernal music festival is slanderous to his legacy.'

Cullen decided not to ask what sort of legacy a twenty-four-year old would have left. 'Can I ask what Mrs Parrott did to leave such a negative opinion?'

'She was a gold-digger and she took my son for everything he had.'

'Do you have anything to back that up?' Cullen set his notebook on his lap. 'She seems to have gone out of her way to avoid any charity from you.'

'She didn't deserve any money.'

'Mr Crombie, the information regarding your son's infidelity came from three sources.'

Crombie pushed the personnel ledger to the side. 'I'm asking you to leave. I agreed to discuss Mr Kavanagh's disappearance. It is not my son in the barrel. I don't know where he is but I do know he is not in that barrel.'

Cullen sat there, eyes trained on Crombie. 'Why are you so certain it's Paddy and not Iain?'

Crombie leaned forward. 'Are you trying to imply something?'

'I'm just a bit perturbed by it.' Cullen scratched the stubble on his chin. 'At the moment, we have two potential victims. It's a bit unnerving you are putting up the shutters on us investigating one of them.'

Crombie narrowed his eyes. 'I've spoken to you twice now and that gorilla of an inspector once. I hardly think that's putting up the shutters.'

'Both times I've spoken to you, you've told me it's not Iain in there and encouraged me to discount it as a theory. If you have evidence or any information as to his whereabouts then you really should share them with us. Even though you have received a presumption of death certificate, your son's disappearance is still currently an open investigation.'

Crombie made a steeple with his fingers. 'I *know* my son is still alive.'

'Is that from a postcard or a letter, maybe?'

Crombie smiled. 'I just know.'

'Unless you have actual evidence that would stand up in court, then I'm afraid we have to consider it a valid possibility your son is the body in the barrel.'

Crombie shook his head in despair. 'Very well, but you are wasting your time and incurring taxpayer expense for no good reason.'

Cullen's blood was pumping — the vein in his forehead usually reserved for particularly heavy hangovers was throbbing. He decided to drop it for now, but this wasn't the end of the matter.

'I had your DCI over here yesterday. He asked me to give him a call if anything goes amiss. I'm still no further forward with getting my barrels released. I'm losing money hand over fist here.'

Cullen got to his feet. 'I'll speak to him directly about it.'

# 25

M urray pointed out of the car window. 'This is Queen Street.'

Cullen pulled in. 'Thanks.'

'You certainly got a rise out of Crombie.'

'Why does he keep saying it's not his son in the barrel?'

'It's beyond me.' Murray leaned forward against the dashboard. 'What's with all this mystical 'I just know' bollocks?'

'I'm fed up of that.' Cullen's blood was still boiling, almost bubbling over — he took a deep breath as he undid his seatbelt. 'Let's go see this Knox character, then.'

They got out of the car and headed across the street.

Murray pressed the buzzer. 'Do you think there's anything in what Crombie's saying?'

Cullen mulled it over as they waited. He'd been thinking of nothing else as they'd driven from the distillery. 'There are a few things spring to mind. He could have been involved in his son's disappearance. Similarly, he could have been involved in Paddy's disappearance and is trying to throw us off the scent.'

Cullen squeezed his eyes shut — he'd been wondering why Iain and Paddy disappeared at approximately the same time. 'Are you saying Iain Crombie could have killed Paddy?'

'That would explain the disappearance.' Murray nodded. 'That's good, Sundance.'

Cullen wagged a finger at him. 'Don't. Scott's more than fine. Cullen is better.'

'Sorry.' Murray grinned. 'Reckon Crombie's involved?'

Cullen hit the buzzer again. 'I don't know. If Crombie's right and it is Paddy in the barrel, why tell us it couldn't be his son?'

'I'm liking the theory Paddy killed Iain and scarpered.' Murray's eyebrows flicked up. 'We'd better add that to Bain's strategising board when we get back.'

Cullen laughed then hit the button again. 'Is this guy in?'

The speaker crackled. 'Okay, okay. Who is it?'

'It's the police.'

'Up you come.'

The buzzer sounded and Cullen opened the door. 'You lead.'

Murray started up the stairs. 'We're the same rank, you know.'

'It's your turn, that's all.'

Eric Knox stood in his doorway, a big barrel of a man set on spindly little legs, rheumy eyes struggling to focus.

Murray held up his warrant card. 'DC Stuart Murray and this is DC Scott Cullen.'

'What do you want, lads?'

The closer Cullen got to him, the stronger he could smell the second-hand booze. Cullen hoped he was sober enough to give them anything useful.

Murray put his card away. 'We want to ask you a few questions about a Padraig Kavanagh.'

Knox tilted his head slowly. 'Paddy?'

'Can we come in?'

Knox's bottom lip protruded. 'Certainly, boys, in you come.'

He led them through to the sparsely-decorated living room, before collapsing into an armchair. He offered them both a seat but Cullen preferred to stand.

Murray sat on a wicker chair near the door.

Knox's eyes were on the mostly empty bottle of Likely Laddie on the coffee table alongside a glass that hadn't been cleaned in days if not weeks. 'So, boys, what do you want to know about Paddy, then?'

Murray got his notebook out, pen poised. 'We believe you worked with him at Dunpender Distillery.'

'He was a good lad was Paddy. I knew him well.'

'How close?'

Knox mulled it over. 'As close as you'd get being workmates. We'd go out drinking most nights after we got back up to Garleton. We both used to cycle to the distillery. It was a right bugger in winter.'

'Where would you go drinking?'

Knox picked up the dirty glass and inspected it. 'The Tanner's Arms. We both had a tab there. Not sure how much was on Paddy's when he ... you know.'

Murray licked his lips. 'Know what?'

Knox set the glass down. 'He disappeared.'

'Do you know what happened to him?'

Knox shook his head in an exaggerated motion. 'No idea, son. It was a right bloody mystery. Disappeared round the time Iain Crombie did.'

Murray looked at his notebook. 'Eleventh of June, 1994.'

'That sounds about right, son. I went for a few scoops with him in the Tanner's the night before. He was worried about something.'

Murray jerked forward in the chair. 'Any idea what?'

'None at all.' Knox laughed. 'Paddy always had a wee trick up his sleeve, though, always had something on.'

'And you don't know what?'

Knox shook his head.

Cullen cut in. 'Did you know Iain Crombie?'

'Never gave me the time of day, that one. Head up his own arse.'

'You never socialised with him or anything?'

'Didn't like to fraternise with the likes of me. He did go out for a pint with Doug Strachan and Paddy on a few occasions, mind.'

'Did you ever go?'

Knox sniffed. 'I wasn't invited into their inner circle. I was in there by coincidence more than anything.'

'Did anything ever get out of hand?'

Knox stared at the bottle again. 'Paddy occasionally had a bit too much to drink and got chucked out. Water off a duck's back to the barman in there. He was back in the next night as if nothing had happened.'

Murray wrote something down then looked up. 'We under-stand Mr Kavanagh was a bit of a traveller?'

'He was always on his travels. Up to the Highlands and Islands, Aberdeenshire, down to Northumberland. Always put in a good shift with us. I kept telling him to slow down. He was showing the rest of us up.'

Murray smiled. 'Did he ever speak of the time before he came to Dunpender?'

Knox's head lolled from side to side. 'Not really, no. Got the occasional wee snippet. He was based all over the place.'

'Was his background in whisky?'

'Whisky with an 'e'.' Knox gave a wide smile, showing a row of black stumps. 'Irish whiskey. He was mainly a carpenter. Used to help out with the barrels and that but he soon got stuck in else-where. A good learner was Paddy.'

Murray leaned forward. 'Mr Knox, we believe Mr Kavanagh may have been murdered.'

Knox scowled. 'Murdered?'

'Yesterday morning, a body was found in a barrel of whisky at the distillery. We have reason to believe it could be Mr Kavanagh.'

Knox took a deep breath. 'That would explain his disappear-ance all right.'

'Would anyone wish to cause him harm?'

Knox drummed his fingers on the armchair for a few seconds. 'Nothing springs to mind, son. Paddy was well liked. Got into a few scrapes in the Tanner's, but didn't we all?'

'So nobody springs to mind?'

Knox shook his head slowly. 'Not that I can think of.'

Murray tapped his pen against his notebook. 'No enemies, either at work or otherwise?'

'Can't think of anybody, really.'

'How was his relationship with Iain Crombie?'

Knox stared at the glass. 'As I say, I don't really know. They were drinking buddies on a few occasions but that's it.'

'You mentioned he lived here in Garleton?'

'Aye. Used to have a bedsit on John Knox Road.' Knox chuck-led. 'No relation, by the way.'

'Do you have an address?'

'Excuse me.' Knox reached a trembling hand over for the

whisky bottle, pouring a good few fingers into the glass. He took a deep drink of the spirit before blinking his eyes a few times. 'That's better.'

Murray waited a few seconds. 'So this bedsit?'

'It fell into disrepair about ten years ago. Got sold off and it's now flats. You know, proper ones.'

'Do you know anyone else who lived there?'

'Even better, son.' Knox stumbled to his feet, staggering across the room towards a large sideboard near Cullen. He reached into a drawer and retrieved a notebook, handing it to Murray.

'What's this?'

Knox grinned. 'Paddy's landlady's address. Catherine Wilsenham.'

## 26

Cullen trundled over the level crossing before accelerating hard. 'You sure the other way isn't quicker?'

Murray looked up from the map. 'This is shorter.'

'But is it quicker?'

Murray thumbed behind them. 'You're just frightened of the level crossing.'

Cullen tried to laugh it off, not even convincing himself. He had to switch down to second to make it up the hill. At the top, he indicated right for East Linton. 'I don't think we got much out of Knox there.'

Murray looked round as they descended the hill. 'He was a fair few sheets to the wind.' He put the roadmap in the footwell. 'Reckon this Wilsenham woman will be any use?'

Cullen pulled in again to let more cars pass. 'I think the only use will be in covering our arses.'

Murray looked over. 'How?'

'You should have spoken to her by now.'

'You're starting to sound like Bain.'

Cullen shook his head in disbelief. 'You've had the file for over a day. She made the initial report of his disappearance. Don't you think you should have tried to track her down?'

'I thought she'd be dead.'

'Well, good luck when you try that defence with Bain.'

Cullen turned left off the high street into a large car park. A grand old building sat to one side, surrounded by a sprawling sheltered-housing complex.

Murray let his seatbelt rattle up. 'Don't say anything to Bain, all right?'

Cullen nodded. 'Wasn't planning to.'

'Fine.' Murray slammed the door.

Cullen sighed before getting out.

Murray was leaning across the roof, staring at him. 'Do you want to show me how it's done then?'

Cullen raised his hands. 'I was just saying. I know how Bain thinks — he'll be chipping away at you.'

Murray tapped the car roof. 'I'll lead.'

He walked over to the building and introduced himself to the warden at the front desk. 'We're looking for a Catherine Wilsenham.'

The warden smiled. 'I'll just show you through.' She led them down a long corridor then opened a door. 'Do you want to wait in the TV lounge?'

'Okay.' Cullen entered the room. The volume on the TV was ridiculously loud, especially as the room was empty. He found the remote and muted it.

Murray sat, crossing one leg over the other. 'Depressing place this.' He frowned at Cullen. 'You okay, big man?'

Cullen rubbed his eye. 'It's nothing.'

'Really?'

'My contact lens is dry.'

Murray licked his lips. 'Don't believe you.'

Cullen slumped on an armchair. 'My gran lives in a home. This reminds me of it, that's all.'

'You big softy.'

'Yeah. Guess I am.'

'You hide it well.'

The door opened again. The warden led a frail old woman, hanging off her Zimmer frame as she juddered through. She looked at least eighty.

The warden stayed by the door. 'Will you be okay, Catherine?'

Wilsenham waved her away with wide flicks of her wrist as she ambled forward. 'My body might be failing but I've still got my wits about me.'

The warden smiled and left them to it, Wilsenham carefully sitting in the chair nearest the window.

Murray creased his notebook, pen poised over the page, and introduced them. 'We need to ask you about Paddy Kavanagh.'

Wilsenham was heavily out of breath from the walk. 'Oh God, that's taking me back. What do you want to know?'

Murray looked at his notebook. 'We may have found his body.'

Wilsenham held her hand over her mouth. 'Oh my heavens.'

'We're just looking for general information at the moment.'

Wilsenham nibbled her lip for a few seconds. 'I was only his landlady, you know. Paddy used to disappear for long weekends every so often and then magically reappear, ready and raring for a week's work.' She sniffed. 'One week, he hadn't turned up by the Wednesday.'

'What happened?'

'I spoke to his work. I can't remember the name of the chap. They hadn't seen him either. I did my Christian duty and went to the police station in Garleton to report him missing. I spoke to a very nice man there, I think his name was Stanhope.'

Murray scribbled something down. 'What else can you tell us?'

'Paddy used to like a drink. I'm teetotal, myself. I would have a sherry with Christmas dinner when my Gerald was still around.'

'Paddy was another matter entirely, though. He was always up the high street at the Tanner's. That was a bad place. It was full of rough sorts, you know, the sort who would sell anything for the price of the next drink.'

'Was Paddy ever thrown out?'

'I believe he was asked to leave on occasion. Why?'

'Just corroborating information.' Murray looked at his notebook. 'Could we go back to his travels?'

'I'm not sure I can add much information to what you may already know.' She laughed. 'We weren't exactly travelling companions.'

Murray grinned. 'I was wondering if Mr Kavanagh was visiting anyone. Did he have any family up north, for instance?'

She tapped the arm of her chair for a few seconds. 'He did

have some family. I can't remember where, but he did occasionally go and meet relatives.'

Murray sat forward on the sofa and held his hands out, palms facing upwards. 'Mr Kavanagh is either a potential murder victim or he's a missing person. If you could try and remember where his family were, it could aid our investigation immeasurably.'

Wilsenham turned to the side and looked out of the window, across the car park. She looked back at Murray, her swift movements in stark contrast to the drunken motion of Eric Knox. 'I can't recall, I'm afraid.'

Cullen cut in. 'Was this mentioned to the original investigation?'

'You know, I don't think it was.'

Cullen jotted it down — something, at last. 'We know Mr Kavanagh used to travel. Up to Aberdeen, Aviemore, the western islands, down to Northumberland. Could his relations have been in any of these locations?'

A light suddenly went on in her eyes. 'You know, I think he had family just outside Newcastle. For some reason, Morpeth springs to mind.'

---

## 27

Cullen locked his laptop and looked over at Murray. 'How are you getting on?'

Murray's eyes stayed focused on his screen. 'Just about finished typing up the statement from Wilsenham. Watson can get it signed tomorrow.' He finished typing and looked over. 'What about you?'

Cullen held up some reports. 'Just been looking through the statements Watson got from the distillery.'

'Sounds like you're putting off setting finger to keyboard for your own report.'

'I'll get on to it when Bain's back. That'll hopefully help me avoid him.'

'Any idea where he is?'

Cullen shrugged. 'Not seen or heard from him since we got back.'

Angela looked up from the far end of the room. 'Any chance you love birds could give it a rest?' She held up the box of Iain Crombie's personal effects. 'I'm still not even halfway through this and our glorious leader will go mental if I haven't finished by the time he gets back.'

'Have you seen him?'

She shook her head. 'He's not been here for the last hour or so. Before that, he was pissing about at the whiteboard.'

Cullen's phone rang. He looked at the display — Bain. He answered it.

'Sundance, could you get back to the Incident Room?'

Cullen could hear his voice from the corridor. 'We're already here.'

Bain marched into the room, PC Watson following him, and headed straight to the whiteboard. 'Right, you lot, gather round.' He wrote some notes in the bottom right corner.

Cullen and Murray wandered over, Murray stopping halfway to crack his spine. They pulled seats up and sat in a small semi-circle.

Bain uncapped the black marker pen.

'That looks like a flip chart pen.' Angela was squinting at it. 'You don't want to write on a whiteboard with one of them.'

Bain checked the marker for a few seconds before glaring at her. 'It's a whiteboard pen.'

They all laughed.

'Aye, when you've had your fun.' Bain looked at his watch. 'Right. It's half six now. I've got to head back to Leith Walk to update Turnbull and Cargill.' He sneered, clearly resenting having to report progress to DI Cargill, the same level as him. 'I need quick updates.' He looked at Murray. 'Stuart, can you start?'

Murray cleared his throat and flicked through his notebook. 'DC Cullen and I spoke to two acquaintances of Paddy Kavanagh. Eric Knox was a co-worker and drinking buddy. He had clearly been drinking this afternoon and wasn't holding himself together. That said, we managed to get the name and address of Mr Kavanagh's landlady, Catherine Wilsenham.'

He turned the page. 'We spoke to her in East Linton. She's backed up a lot of the information we have. She did mention he had family in Morpeth, just north of Newcastle.'

'Sounds like you've bothered your arse for once.' Bain wrote it on the whiteboard. 'That's Northumbria Constabulary, right?' He tossed the pen in the air. 'Got anything more on these Morpeth people?'

Murray held up a couple of sheets of A4. 'I've run a search. There are two Kavanaghs in Morpeth. Also need to think about the possibility of it being a married female relative.'

'Next steps?'

'I was going to get in touch with the local police and see if they have anything further before I approach the relatives directly.'

'Why?'

Murray folded his arms. 'If Paddy is still alive then we need to speak to him. We don't want him running.'

'What the hell are you talking about?'

Cullen cleared his throat. 'We think Iain and Paddy disappearing within three weeks of each other is suspicious. We suspect whoever's not in the barrel to be involved in the other's murder.'

Bain shook his head. 'Christ's sake, Sundance, I have absolutely no idea where you get half this shite from.' He took a deep breath. 'Try and keep it simple for once. Baby steps. We don't want to arse this one up.'

Cullen smiled. 'Wasn't going to.'

'You never do. Doesn't stop you.' Bain's eyes focused on Cullen, the ice blue almost freezing him. 'If it's not Paddy in the barrel, it's Iain. Right?'

'We still need to positively identify the body. If it's Iain Crombie, then it follows that Paddy could still be alive.'

Murray rapped on the table. 'And we don't want to alert him to us being on to him.'

Bain narrowed his eyes. 'Feels a bit too much to me.'

Cullen bit his bottom lip, chewing some skin off and tasting blood. 'We'd like to speak to the Morpeth police and see where it takes us.'

'Fine, but you're not going.' Bain looked at Murray. 'Turnbull has secured your partner in crime, DC McLean.'

Murray grinned. 'You mean McLaren?'

Bain jabbed a finger at Murray. 'Stop correcting me.'

'For the sake of clarity, I'd appreciate it if you could try and get our names right. Sir.'

Bain put his hands in his trouser pockets. 'Pick up your buddy first thing tomorrow then head down the A1. Better hope you don't get stuck behind a bread lorry doing forty on the single carriageway bits.'

'Thanks.'

Bain tapped the *Ireland* box on the whiteboard. 'Heard anything back from our pals across the Irish sea?'

Murray looked at his notebook and scratched the back of his neck. 'No. Still nothing.'

'Which is what I've been doing.' Bain grinned. 'I phoned your buddies in Ireland. None of those Paddy Kavanaghs you found is our boy. We're back to square one. Better hope our Geordie cousins come up with something.' He looked at Angela. 'Right, Batgirl, hopefully you've got something more than this pair of clowns.'

'Wish I had.' She looked at her notebook. 'I've been through the box of Iain Crombie's documentation but I've not found anything even vaguely relating to a life insurance policy. There are still new letters coming in every year but nothing related to life insurance.' She flicked the page. 'Of course, that's only half the battle. I need to get a search done with insurers to check he didn't have one. That might be slightly tricky.'

Bain grinned. 'Well, I'm glad one of my officers has been doing some proper work.'

Cullen rolled his eyes. 'And what great police work have you been doing while we've wasted our time on activities allocated by you?'

Bain laughed at him. 'I've been busy.' He counted off on his fingers. 'One, I've been on the phone to the Garda in Ireland. Seem to remember having to do that before cos one of you lot couldn't be bothered doing it properly.'

He added another finger. 'Second, young Watson and I have been speaking to local officers who may have picked up Paddy back in the day. Got nowhere, other than North Berwick, Haddington and Dunbar police stations.'

He counted a third finger. 'Three, Watson spoke to a few workers at the distillery, including Strachan and both Crombies. No telltale splashes of whisky were ever found between '94 and '97. Doesn't look like our body was put in the barrel after '94.'

He took a deep breath and tapped his ring finger. 'Finally, we went to see your pal Stanhope at his caravan. Senile old bastard told us nothing. Waste of time.'

Cullen licked the blood on his lips. 'What do you want us to do, then?'

'Sundance, I want you to look into this bird Iain was supposed to be off with. Anything you can find. If it's a dead end, it's a dead end.'

'Fine.'

'Murray, you and McLean head to Morpeth first thing.'

'McLaren.'

Bain stabbed the air with his finger. 'I'm *warning* you.'

Murray held up his hands. 'I just want to make sure we're being precise and there's not some other officer I'm supposed to take.'

Bain held his eyes for a few seconds then looked over at Angela. 'Batgirl, if you continue your search into Iain Crombie's policies and anything else. Actually, you might as well look for Paddy at the same time.'

'Great.' Angela scribbled in her notebook. 'Add another week on.'

'If you can all rendezvous here at two pm tomorrow I'll be a happy man. I'll be here all morning.' Bain sniffed. 'Right, you can piss off home.'

Cullen got up, heading straight for the door.

Murray followed him. 'He's on fire today.'

'Tell me about it.' Cullen held open the door at the bottom of the stairs. 'I'll be in Leith Walk tomorrow.'

Murray laughed. 'At least I'll be bombing down the A1 and not stuck here.'

Cullen's phone rang, the volume at full blast.

Murray covered his ears. 'Jesus, turn it down.'

He held the phone to his ear. 'Cullen.'

'Sundance, get your arse back up here. Fraser Crombie's been assaulted.'

## 28

M urray pulled in behind Bain's Mondeo on Gullane's Main Street.

Bain was already out, talking into the intercom for the flats next to the post office. He looked back and shook his head as they got out of the car. 'Hurry up the pair of you.'

They followed Bain up the stairs, avoiding any running commentary as they climbed. Bain rapped on the door, warrant card out.

It was opened by a uniformed officer, who thumbed inside the flat. 'Through here, sir.'

They entered the hall.

The uniform stood in front of a shut door. 'We're taking his statement just now. The doctor was called out from North Berwick, she's just checking him over.'

Bain nodded. 'And you've got uniform scouring the area?'

'Yes, sir.' He held up his Airwave. 'PC Watson's just got there now.'

'Come on, then.'

In the living room, Fraser sat on a sofa clutching an ice pack to his head. The doctor knelt at his side.

Bain walked over to the uniform sitting next to Fraser and stood aggressively close. 'You got the statement yet?'

'Yes, sir.'

'Care to read it back for our benefit?'

The uniform checked his notebook. 'I think we're finished anyway.' He looked over at Fraser. 'I'll read back a summary just now. We'll need to read back an unabridged version later, which you'll sign. Are you okay with that?'

Fraser winced as the doctor took the ice pack off, revealing a red graze on his temple. 'Go for it.'

The uniform cleared his throat. 'You were taking your usual walk from Gullane to North Berwick along the cliff tops by the golf courses. You didn't see it but someone attacked you with a brick. You managed to get onto the course where two golfers spotted you and provided assistance before calling the police. PC Hughes and myself were in attendance.'

'Correct.'

'You were brought back here where you recalled seeing a man dressed in black while you were out walking.'

'Correct.'

The uniform nodded at Bain. 'That's the summarised version. Do you want the detail?'

Bain folded his arms. 'That'll do.' He tapped the doctor on the shoulder.

She jumped, before scowling at him. 'What?'

'Are you finished there?'

'For now.'

'Can we go into the hall?'

She got to her feet.

Bain shut the door behind them once they were in the hall, leaving the two uniforms in the living room. 'What's going on?'

The doctor took a deep breath. 'He was definitely assaulted. Quite a nasty wound as well. He's going to be off work for a week or so.'

'We've had a couple of assaults in the town recently.' Murray gave a shrug. 'Might be connected.'

Cullen sniffed. 'This wasn't in the town, though.'

'That's just semantics.'

Bain nodded at the doctor again. 'He said he was attacked with a brick.'

The doctor got an evidence bag out, small fragments of debris rattling around. 'I got these out of the wound. I'm no expert but it looks like quite an old brick.'

Bain took the bag and held it up to the light. 'Thanks, you can go back through.' He looked at Murray as she left them to it. 'Tell me about these assaults.'

'Nothing much to tell, sir. Couple of guys were assaulted on separate occasions walking back from the pub.'

'No leads?'

Murray exhaled. 'Nothing.'

The uniform came through the door, holding up his Airwave handset. 'They've spotted someone who fits the description by the rocks at Yellowcraig.'

## 29

C ullen twisted round in the car. 'Fraser, are you sure you should be here?'

'I insisted at my flat, didn't I? The doctor didn't have any complaints either.'

'She said you'll be off work for a week or so.'

'No chance of that.'

Murray braked suddenly before turning left through ancient stone walls and following Bain through an open expanse. 'I don't think you should be with us, Fraser.'

'I want to help you identify who attacked me.'

'Okay, but you're staying in the car.' Cullen pointed at a grand old house on the right. 'What is this place?'

Murray slowed. 'Archerfield estate. It's full of golf courses and a new housing estate. It's twenty-five grand a year in one of the clubs. Got a few ex-Premiership footballers for members.'

Fraser thumbed at a right turn. 'My old man owns a few invest-ment properties in there.'

Murray whistled. 'Must be worth millions, right?'

Fraser looked away. 'Something like that.'

Murray sped on down a road twisting between greens on the golf courses, the sea becoming visible through the thick pine trees. They came to the end, pulling up outside a hut.

Bain was already out of his car, shouting into an Airwave. They got out and started off ahead.

Fraser pointed at the hut. 'I was attacked in those trees just there.'

Murray put a hand on his chest. 'Fraser, I told you to stay in the car.'

'Right, sorry.' Fraser took a deep breath, before slowly getting back in.

Bain shook his head. 'You pair shouldn't have brought him out here.'

'You didn't object back at the house.' Cullen nodded at the Airwave. 'Any update?'

'Nothing, Sundance.' Bain took a good look around. 'Played here once with Turnbull and Whitehead. Decent course.'

Murray grinned. 'I shot an eighty here last year.'

'Decent. Maybe you should give up on policing.'

The Airwave crackled. 'Control to DI Bain. Over.'

'Bain here. Over.'

'We think the target is heading to the Archerfield estate.'

Bain rolled his eyes. 'Golf course or houses? Over.'

It was a few seconds before the Airwave sounded again. 'Houses. Over.'

Bain pointed at Cullen and Murray then the car. 'On our way. Over.'

Cullen didn't have his seatbelt on by the time Murray was reversing, swinging the car round in a tight arc. He rolled the steering wheel with his palm, before putting his foot down and jolting forward.

Bain's car bombed ahead of them, increasing the distance by the second.

Murray's hands gripped the steering wheel tighter. 'Shouldn't be outstripped by a bloody Mondeo.'

Cullen clutched the grab handle. 'That thing can shift.'

'Tell me about it.'

Bain's car indicated left after some partially built chalets before dodging past two oncoming BMWs.

Murray drove into an estate filled with large houses. 'Place is filled with McMansions. It's like *Desperate Housewives*.'

Cullen laughed. 'Single men shouldn't watch that programme.'

Murray blushed as he raced past the gated houses.

Cullen looked to the left, seeing a second street in varying stages of completion.

They screeched to a halt at the end. Panda cars with flashing blue lights were abandoned in front of a grand mansion, at least the fourth they'd seen in that exact design.

Cullen got out, clocking Bain talking to a pair of uniforms. He felt a tap on his shoulder and spun round. Lamb. 'Surprised you're here, Bill.'

'Whole unit's short staffed. Trying to keep away from your guv'nor.'

'Don't blame you.'

Bain called over to Cullen, his eyes narrowing as he spotted Lamb.

'We're heading into the woods towards Dirleton.' Lamb marched off, speaking into his Airwave.

Cullen trotted over to Bain. 'What do you want us to do?'

'They reckon there's a path behind those trees leading down to the beach where this boy was spotted. We'll go that way.' Bain pointed at Lamb. 'That arsehole is heading back to Dirleton. Can you and Mc— *Murray* check along the backs of the houses?'

'Will do.'

Bain extended his baton and nodded at two uniforms. 'Come on, boys.'

Cullen looked at Murray, eyebrows raised. 'Let's go.'

They jogged down a path, following Bain until it branched at the end where they went right.

Cullen dodged between the trees, looking right at the empty back gardens of the houses and left across the fields. 'Can't see anyone.'

'Me neither.'

'I mean no-one. There's nobody in the gardens.'

Murray laughed. 'Half these houses are empty.'

'Really?'

'I'm not joking.'

They jogged on until they came to a fork in the path. One branch continued, while the other led along the edge of the field.

Cullen made a snap decision. 'You go into the field, I'll keep on this path.'

'Right.'

Cullen got his own baton out as he ran, the trees becoming tighter knit as he progressed. He spotted a figure in a garden and slowed to a halt. He squinted through the mesh fence, deciding the thirty-something woman hanging out washing wasn't their quarry.

Something hit him on the head from behind. He stumbled to his knees, clutching his skull. He doubled over in agony, eyes locked shut. His fingers traced over his crown, immediately recoiling. He looked at his left hand. It was covered in blood.

He stumbled to his knees and looked back the way.

Nobody.

He took a deep breath and felt his vision blur. He struggled to keep his eyes open.

'Are you all right?'

He looked up, focusing on the figure standing over him.

'It's Murray, Scott.'

Cullen took his hand and got to his feet. 'Somebody attacked me.'

Murray inspected the wound. 'Doesn't look too bad.'

'Feels it.'

'They caught you good and proper.'

'Did you find him?'

Murray shook his head. 'I saw one of Bill's lads coming back the way. Then I heard your cry.'

Cullen tried to slow his breathing. 'How did they get away?'

'Maybe you were knocked out?'

Cullen dabbed at his crown. 'This bloody hurts.'

'There's no way out, by the way.' Murray looked up and down the length of the path. 'That end is covered by Bill's team and we came the other way.'

Cullen waved at the fence, the gates already rickety and mostly unlocked. 'Must be through one of the houses.'

'It wasn't me.'

Cullen laughed, sending another wave of pain across his skull. 'Didn't think it was.'

Murray's Airwave crackled. 'All units. PC Watson has found the target entering a deserted property on the Village Road.'

Cullen hauled his door open. 'Right. Come on.'

Murray raised his eyebrows. 'You sure you're okay?'

'I'll live.'

Cullen trudged down the path, his head thrumming with pain, ending up back on the road. A crowd of uniformed officers congregated around a house halfway along.

Lamb was leaning against the high wall around the perimeter, looking up at the house. He nodded at them as they approached. 'Wee Johnny Watson's caught him.'

Murray laughed. 'Wonders will never cease.'

Cullen pointed down the road. 'Better go get Fraser to identify him.'

'I'll do it.' Murray jogged off.

Lamb stood on tiptoes, looking at Cullen's head. 'That's not too bad.'

'Murray said it was nasty.'

'He's a drama queen.' Lamb inspected the wound. 'What happened?'

'Someone jumped me.'

'Did you see them?'

Cullen shook his head. 'No. I must have blacked out.' He glanced at the house. 'What's the story here?'

'Just been on to Control.' Lamb held his Airwave up. 'It's vacant. One of the banks owns it. Can't rent it for love nor money.'

Cullen whistled. 'And nobody lives there?'

'That boy that managed Hearts last season lived there until he got the boot.'

Cullen looked around at the soulless estate. 'How can people afford to live here?'

'The Chief Constable lives round the corner.' Lamb waved at a hulking McMansion, at least two wings too many. 'Unless you plan on ascending to that rank, I'd forget it.'

'With my record? I'll be lucky to be chief paperclip procurer at this rate.'

The front door opened and Watson led out a man clad all in black, holding up the handcuffs.

'Bless him.' Lamb chuckled. 'That boy's been hanging around Gullane and Dirleton for months. He fits the profile of a few unsolved crimes we've got on the books.'

Murray's car pulled in at the kerb, Bain's following closely behind. Fraser got out and Murray led him over to Watson and his captive. Fraser looked at him for a few seconds before nodding.

Murray smiled and led Fraser over as Watson took his prize to the waiting meat wagon. 'That's him all right.'

Lamb flicked his eyebrows up. 'Nice to see an arrest within a hundred yards of Bain.'

Cullen clutched his head. 'Any danger you can get that doctor over here?'

## 30

Cullen pulled up behind an orange Ford Focus. He killed the engine and got out of his car, carrying a box. He patted the bandage on his head before walking over to the passenger side of the Focus and tapping on the window.

The door opened and DC Chantal Jain got out. 'How's your bollocks, Cullen?'

Cullen shook his head. 'You never change do you?'

Jain's eyes bulged. 'What happened to you?'

Sharon got out of the driver side. 'Would you pair get in? We're supposed to be subtle here.'

Jain saluted. 'I'll just go for a walk, then. Let you and lover boy have a nice cosy chat, Sharon.' She winked at Cullen as she marched off, pulling her mobile out of her pocket.

Cullen got in the passenger seat and dumped the box on the dashboard.

Sharon leaned over and kissed him. 'Nice to see you.'

'And you.'

She winced at his bandage. 'Scott, what have you done?'

'Someone hit me with a brick.'

'Christ. You need to be careful. You haven't learnt not to plough in, have you?'

Cullen sighed. 'No.'

'Did you get them?'

'I think so. It was at those new houses by Dirleton. One of them backed onto this lane I was checking out. Must have jumped me when I was investigating a garden.'

'Nasty.'

'I'll be okay.' He opened the pizza box. 'Here you go. I stopped off in Musselburgh on the way through. Half spicy chicken, half margarita.'

'I'm starving. I'll even forget my diet.' She tore off a slice. 'Hope none of the spicy stuff has got on my side.'

He got the bottle of diet cola from his jacket pocket. 'They didn't have any cups. You okay sharing with me?'

'Sharing body fluids with you hasn't been a problem so far.'

He took a glug. 'Chantal okay with me sitting in her chair for a bit?'

She spoke through a mouthful. Gone were the days when she'd cover her mouth while eating. 'It's good to have a break. Can't believe she was standing there chatting to you. Don't want our cover blown.'

'Still the football hooligans?'

She nodded. 'I hate the sport at the best of times. I really can't understand people knocking lumps out of each other because of it.'

'I don't get it either and I'm a fan.' Cullen folded the crust in half and dunked it in the dip. 'Well, I hope your day's been less eventful than mine.'

'I couldn't conceive of a less eventful day. Watching cars and people going up and down the street. We're getting nowhere with this, but Wilko's criminal intelligence is renowned.'

'I thought it was his lack of intelligence that's renowned?'

She laughed. 'There is that, of course.' She took another bite of the pizza and chewed. 'Rumour is he's getting that detachment to HQ. This case is part of it. Can't believe Turnbull's letting him get away with it.'

'In his interests to get shot of him, though, isn't it?'

'True. We're supposed to be busy, though.'

Cullen stared down the street. 'Bain isn't balancing many cases just now. He's barely balancing one, in fact.'

'How do you mean?'

Cullen finished chewing, already tearing off the next slice.

'He's not actually done anything today. He's been in the Incident Room in Garleton, *strategising* at his whiteboard. It's ridiculous.' He swallowed a chunk with some more cola. 'I've put in over a hundred miles today, traipsing around half of East Lothian, and he's just arsing about in that office.'

Sharon closed her eyes. 'I can just see you telling him exactly what you thought of him.'

He chewed another slice. 'I might have done. I picked him up on his strategising, told him I thought I was doing everything on the investigation.'

'You better watch, you'll get as bad as him one day.'

'Hardly.' Cullen stuck half the slice in the sour cream dip. He put it in his mouth and chewed. He took out his notebook and flicked through as he ate. 'I've filled out twenty pages of my notebook today. He'll be lucky to have filled half of one.'

'Keep your powder dry, Scott. It's not going to do you any favours fighting with him. He'll be moaning about you to Turnbull, asking to get someone else, and I'll end up losing Chantal or something.'

'I'll bear that in mind. I've half a mind to go to Turnbull myself. Could do with a DI that's actually bothering his arse. Even Wilko would be an improvement.'

'In a way, I've got sympathy for Bain.'

Cullen almost spat cola over the interior of her new car. 'Are you kidding me?'

'Think about it. Bain was the big boy in the team under Whitehead. Then he moves upstairs and Turnbull comes in as DCI. Pretty quickly, he brings Cargill in and he's been vocal about moving Bain and Wilko on.'

'I think he's getting what he deserves. He's had this coming for a while.'

'He's got a good track record, though. He could go to HR with this. He's solved two high profile murders.'

Cullen poked a finger at his chest. '*I've* solved two high profile cases. Me, not him.'

'Were you Senior Investigating Officer on either?'

He looked away. 'No.'

'Well, then. You're his resource and any collars are his collars.'

'I suppose so.' He looked at the pizza box, just two half-empty tubs of dip on his side. 'I went for a pint with him last night.'

'My God. Why?'

'Nothing else doing. It was that or sit with Tom.'

'So what happened?'

'He moaned about Turnbull and Cargill then about you then me and Irvine.'

'That complaint's still gone away, right?'

'Right.' He looked out of the window — the sun was hiding behind the taller buildings towards Seafield Road, but the sky was still bright blue. 'He broke up a fight on Leith Walk.'

She put her head in her hands. 'I can just picture it.'

Cullen cleared his throat. 'You going to be here all night?'

She looked over. 'I'm afraid there's no nookie for Scotty boy tonight.'

'Fine. There's football on. Back to world war three with Tom and Rich, then.'

'They're like an old married couple. Tell them if they shared a room it'd mean Tom could get more money in.'

He laughed. 'I just might do that.'

'You don't have to credit me, either.'

'It'll be different when we move in together.'

'I know. The sooner you tell Tom, the better.'

A text message blinked onto Cullen's phone. It was from Derek Miller, brother of a former colleague who had died. *'U want 2 meet on 25th? Deek'*. They had an arrangement to meet up on that date every month to remember Keith.

Cullen texted a response. *'Aye — sure. Windsor Buffet? SC'*

'Who was that?'

'Derek. I'm meeting him a week on Monday.'

'You're doing a good thing there.'

'Certainly hope so.'

He looked down the road and saw Jain walking toward them, a blue carrier bag in her hand. He checked the pizza box.

'You going to eat that last bit?'

She pushed the box over. 'You're such a pig.'

Cullen sat at the table in the hall, wincing at his head. 'What's the score?'

Tom tipped his can at the screen. 'Two one to Germany with ten minutes to go.'

Rich took a sip of wine, his lips dyed red. 'It tells you at the top of the screen, Skinky.'

'Very good.'

'Germany must be favourites now.'

Tom shook his head. 'I'm telling you, it's Spain.'

'It's Germany's, man.' Rich laughed. 'They're absolutely tonking Holland here. That's got to make them favourites.'

'Spain have a much easier route to the final. Germany will probably have Italy and England.'

'And they'll beat them. And then they'll beat Spain. They are much better. I'm so fed up of that 'no striker' shite Spain do.'

'Not you as well, Rich. Scotty was moaning about that the other night.'

'Good man, Skinky.'

'Can't you see Spain play beautiful football?' Tom tilted his can towards the screen.

'It's the Harlem Globetrotters.' Rich topped his wine glass up. 'It's technically impressive but it's about as exciting as listening to you having a wank.'

Tom's eyes were like thunder. 'I'm warning you, Richard, this is my flat. I can kick you out.'

Rich smirked. 'You won't, though, will you?'

Cullen finished his cup of tea. 'You pair are like an old married couple.'

Rich burst out laughing, smacking his hand against the table.

Tom's expression worsened. 'Scott, I'm warning you as well. Any more of that shite and you're getting kicked out as well.'

Cullen refrained from telling him he wanted to move in with Sharon. 'It feels like I live with two gay men sometimes rather than just one. You know, if you moved into one room, you could rent out Rich's and make more money.'

Tom wagged his finger at him. 'If I had a red card, I would be waving it right now.'

Rich swirled the wine in his glass. 'Sure it's not a pink card?'

Tom got up. 'You're both out of order.' He headed to his room, slamming the door.

'I've seen that sort of behaviour so many times from you, Rich.'

'So what? I can be a cheeky bastard.' Rich sniffed the wine then sipped, grimacing as he swallowed. 'At least part of the shit from Tom is because I'm gay.'

Cullen coughed. 'Yeah, maybe I should have told him before you moved in.'

'See, you're as bad as me.' Rich licked his lips. 'Sod it, it's good for him. Character forming.'

Cullen stared at the screen, watching Germany play keep ball. 'How's work?'

Rich yawned. 'The news desk is pretty slow just now. Talk of more cuts.'

'I never understood why you left Fleet Street for the *Edinburgh Argus*.'

'I'm a bit of a vulture. The opportunities can be decent when an industry is in free fall. I saw that in London. You just need to know where to look.'

'You can always surprise me.'

Rich snorted. 'You better watch out, Skinky. They'll be getting rid of coppers next.'

Cullen sighed. 'Don't say that. I'm struggling to become a sergeant as it is.'

'Just saying, mate.'

Cullen got up. 'I'm going to bed.' He took his mug through to the kitchen, leaving Rich in front of the dying embers of the match.

He collapsed on his bed, wincing as his wounded head hit the pillow. He got his phone out and texted Sharon.

*Fed up with the pair of them. Can't wait to move in with you. x*

# DAY 3

*Thursday*
*14th June*

## 32

C ullen cradled the phone between his neck and shoulder, upsetting his wound. He washed down more co-codamol with a large filter coffee he'd been working through for the last half hour.

His belly rumbled. He looked over at Angela. 'You fancy heading up to the canteen for an early sitting once I'm off this call?'

'Sounds good.' She nodded at the file on his desk. 'You getting anywhere with that?'

Cullen glanced at it, just received from the Lothian & Borders archive. 'Not really. It was very careful not to name any officers in other jurisdictions active on the Iain Crombie investigation.'

'Funny that. Anyone would think they were lazy.'

'I tried old Stanhope but I couldn't get a hold of him.'

'Who are you on the phone to?'

'Avon & Somerset. There was a reference to a case number on their books. I think it's my needle.'

'Just hope you've got the right haystack.'

Cullen chuckled. 'I've spent all morning with them. I've finally got hold of an Inspector Harvey down there.' He held up the original case file. 'He's listed as DC Harvey in here. Done well for himself.'

'Heard from Bain this morning?'

'Just the three phone calls.' He glanced at his watch. 'And it's only just gone eleven. I bounced two of them but he caught me out at half nine. There wasn't any point, other than checking I'd bothered turning up for work.'

'What's he doing out there?'

'Strategising again.'

Angela snorted with laughter.

'Hello?'

Cullen sat up. 'Hi, is that Inspector Harvey?'

'It is. Is that DC Scott Cullen?'

'Aye.'

Harvey laughed. 'Someone gave me a note to call you back. Bit surprised you're still on the line.'

'Aye, well, I'm known for my persistence.'

'Is that Glasgow you're based?'

Cullen was continually astonished at the ignorance of Scottish geography among those south of Manchester. 'Edinburgh.'

'Oh, I've been there. Lovely city.'

Cullen sniffed. 'There's another side to it.'

Harvey laughed. 'I can well imagine. Reminds me of Bath. The stories I could tell you about that place.'

'I've heard it's nice. Only seen it on the TV, mind. Looked quite like Edinburgh. I don't imagine it's got a Niddrie or a Wester Hailes.'

'They're all in Bristol.' Harvey laughed. 'How can I help?'

'I gather you were involved in the investigation into the disappearance of an Iain Crombie at Glastonbury Festival in 1994.'

'That's correct. One of the strangest cases I've ever worked. You know, we get five disappearances every time that festival runs. Kids from all over the country. Not all of them turn up.'

'What can you tell me about Mr Crombie's disappearance?'

'It was long and drawn out. I'll give you a summary off the top of my head. Apologies if I miss anything.' Harvey cleared his throat. 'We got a call from a DS Stanhope up your way. This lad was last seen by his brother. DS Stanhope came south for a bit. We had a couple of good nights in Glastonbury and Bristol. The investigation ran for a period of months, I think, but it was down to a few hours a week after the second month.'

Irvine sat down opposite Cullen, dumping a polystyrene container on his desk, the smell of vinegar and chips wafting his way.

Cullen turned away. 'We understand Mr Crombie met a girl.'

'That's right. The trail ended with Miss Wiley.'

Cullen grabbed the handset with his left hand. 'Say that again?'

'We believe Mr Crombie had disappeared with a Mary-Anne Wiley. She lived in Harrogate.'

'Where's that?'

'North Yorkshire.'

Cullen wrote it in large text. 'Did anyone speak to her?'

'The difficulty with a case involving two active constabularies increases exponentially when you add a third. My DI was under pressure to pass it on. This was a Scottish disappearance, not a local one. So we handed it to North Yorks.'

Cullen was flicking through the Lothian & Borders file as he listened, but there was no reference to a Mary-Anne Wiley. There was a Post-It with *North Yorkshire police* on. Stanhope hadn't mentioned them and no detail was recorded. He drummed his fingers on the desk. 'Who was your source?'

'We had a nationwide missing persons campaign running. There was a photofit of the girl your colleagues got from the MisPer's brother, which went out with the photo of Mr Crombie. Someone in Harrogate came forward.'

'And you just passed it on?'

'We did, I'm afraid.' Harvey sighed. 'I wasn't too keen and I've spent the last eighteen years eradicating that sort of small-mindedness from our force. This 'you touched it last' nonsense is a blight on cases like this. We had a similar one a few years later where someone from Bristol disappeared in London and the Met were playing games with us.' There was a pause on the line. 'I can send the case file up if you want.'

'That would be a great help.' Cullen gave him the address. 'Do you have any North Yorkshire reference numbers or contacts in the file?'

'There's a number here. I'm not sure how reliable it'll be, mind.'

Cullen got a mobile number. 'Thanks. I might phone back.' He ended the call.

He sat there, pleased he'd managed to get a lead in the case. He had a decision to make — call Bain, call Yorkshire or get something to eat.

## 33

C ullen chucked the food container in the nearest bin, just missing.

Angela tutted. 'You better pick that up.'

'I will.'

'I'm not doing it for you. I'm still not speaking to you.'

'What?'

'Scott, you asked if I wanted to go for lunch with you. You were on the phone all the time and we just came straight back.'

The hold music stopped. 'Is that DC Cullen?'

'It is.'

'PC Seth Neely, Harrogate station. How can I help?'

'I'm looking into the disappearance of an Iain Crombie.' Cullen gave the case reference number. 'I want to speak to anyone who worked on the case eighteen years ago.'

Neely laughed. 'Good luck with that. I'm in the document centre just now, so I'll dig the file out if you want to stay on the line.'

The line went back to hold. Cullen started typing up notes.

After a few minutes, his phone showed a call waiting == Bain. He ignored it.

Neely came back after about ten minutes. 'You still there?'

'Still on, aye.'

'Just got the file. Had a look through and I've got a list of offi-cers involved at the time.'

'How many are still active?'

'I'll need to check.'

'How long will that take?'

There was a pause then Neely exhaled down the line. 'Might be about an hour or two.'

Cullen leaned back in his chair, reckoning it should be twenty minutes tops and most of that would be remembering passwords. 'Could you send the file up?'

'No can do.'

'I'm getting files sent up from Bristol.'

'I can get you the number of our Chief Constable's office if you want to take it up with him?'

'What about a copy?'

'I'm afraid not. They took all the machines out of here to stop illicit copies being made. It became a big problem a couple of years ago.'

'So the only way I'm seeing this is if I come down to Yorkshire?'

'Afraid so.'

'What about meeting in Newcastle?'

'No can do.'

'Where are you based?' Cullen got an address for an industrial estate on the outskirts of Harrogate. 'I'll get back to you.'

'Okay, well, I'll look forward to it.'

Cullen tossed his phone on the desk and tried to think through his next steps. Whichever way he looked at it, he needed to speak to Bain.

After he'd finished typing up the notes.

## 34

Cullen rapped on the door to the caravan again.

Angela folded her arms. 'For the third time, I don't think he's in.'

'He's got to be in. I need to speak to him.'

'Because Bain will kick your arse? He's already spoken to him.'

Cullen knocked on the door again.

Angela laughed. 'That's it, isn't it? You want to show him up.'

Cullen swallowed. 'I just need to speak to him about this Yorkshire case.'

'I know. I remember the monologue from the car on the way over. My ears are still burning.'

A collie bounded up, expecting to be patted. Cullen knelt down and complied. He checked the dog's tag. 'This is Welshy.'

Angela used her hand to screen her eyes against the sun. 'I can see Stanhope now.'

Cullen turned and watched the old man stagger over, carrying a plastic bag. He whistled and the dog shot off towards him.

Cullen met him halfway. 'Do you have a minute?'

'Feel like I'm back in active service with the number of questions you lot are asking me.'

Cullen smiled. 'I've been on the phone to Avon & Somerset police. Wonder if you could add anything.'

'Sure.' Stanhope dumped his bag on the barrel and sat down. 'Who've you been dealing with?'

Cullen avoided the same seat as before. 'DI Harvey.'

Stanhope grinned. 'Good old Bob managed to make Inspector. Well, I never. He's a good copper. Kept in touch after that case. Went for dinner when he was up at the Festival about ten years ago. Lost touch since I moved out here.'

'I'll pass on your regards if I speak to him again.'

'Was he playing games, son?'

Cullen shook his head. 'No, he seems keen to avoid games, to be honest. It's North Yorks we're having difficulty with.'

'Some things never change.'

'Were they obstructive before?'

'Not really, but they didn't go out of their way to help. Mind, I'd handed off the case to Avon & Somerset and they did the same to North Yorks. Pass the parcel.'

Cullen nodded. 'Did you investigate any of the sightings?'

'It wasn't my case any more, son. I knew they had some responses to the press release with the photofits of the woman Iain went away with.'

'What about when you dusted the case off every six months?'

'No need to be smart, son.' Stanhope stroked the dog's fur. 'I didn't get involved in any of the interviews. Wasn't allowed to.'

Cullen looked across the caravan park, a few other old men basking in the summer sunshine. His little gamble had failed to pay off. 'Thanks for your time.'

'I'd rather you visited than that DI Bain.'

Cullen smiled. 'I gather he visited yesterday.'

'Aye, son. I've got a bit more sympathy for the pair of you. That boy is a dinosaur. Lucky to still have a job.'

Cullen got to his feet. 'That's what I keep saying.'

Stanhope narrowed his eyes before clicking his fingers. 'It did jog my memory, though.'

'Oh?'

'Aye, Fraser and Iain had a big row before they went to Glastonbury.'

Cullen sat down again and got out his notebook. 'Go on.'

'If I remember correctly, they had a big bust-up. Alec took them out for a meal to try and resolve it.'

Cullen looked up. 'What was it about?'

'Something to do with the company.'

'What sort of thing?'

'A takeover.' Stanhope frowned. 'Sounded like the boys were going to cancel their trip. Iain had an advert in the *Courier* trying to flog the tickets. Nobody took them up — imagine if they had...' He broke off, lost to some strand of what if.

Cullen flicked back a few pages, finding a reference to the family meal. 'You told us about this before, right?'

'Did I?'

Cullen held up his notebook. 'You said they went to the pub in Gullane the night before they left but it seemed fairly amicable.'

'Aye, that's right.'

'What happened at this dinner?'

Stanhope leaned against the barrel, resting his head on his fist. 'They were supposed to come to an agreement about the company. Given Dunpender is still independent eighteen years later, they must have done. The boys made up and put their differences behind them.'

'Who told you this?'

'Doug Strachan, I think.'

## 35

'There he is.' Cullen marched off down the length of the cooperage, Angela following in his wake.

Strachan and Fraser sat on wooden chairs, mangling barrels with claw hammers. There were another ten workers dotted around.

Strachan looked up at their approach. 'Officers.'

Cullen leaned against a workbench and got out his notebook. 'Need to ask you a few questions, Mr Strachan. Just following up on our interview the other day.'

Strachan scowled as he checked his watch. 'Supposed to be going on my break just now.'

'We probably won't be long.'

Strachan huffed to his feet. 'Right, come on then.' He led them down the far end of the room. 'I assume we don't need to go back to the station this time?'

'You assume correctly.'

Strachan gestured at some seats looking like a makeshift tea break area. 'What about here?'

'Suits me.' Cullen pulled the chairs close together and sat, looking back down the room, aware of Fraser's gaze diverted their way.

Strachan's chair groaned like an old man as he sat. 'What do you want to know?'

'We've heard about an argument Fraser had with his brother.'

Strachan rubbed his head. 'That was nothing.'

'Really?'

'Aye. They were always teasing each other. It's what boys do. One said sugar, the other said shite.' Strachan dug at his left eyebrow. 'This one was about the continuing independence of the distillery.'

'Who was for it?'

'Iain.' Strachan took a deep breath. 'Could so easily have been Fraser siding with independence, mind, and Iain pushing for a sale.'

'How so?'

'Like I say, one says sugar, the other says shite.'

'Did it ever get violent?'

Strachan screwed up his face. 'It's not really for me to say. I've already told you all I know.'

Angela folded her arms. 'Mr Strachan, we need to know if the relationship ever got violent.'

Strachan took a deep breath. 'Boys will be boys.'

'What's that supposed to mean?'

Strachan looked up at her. 'There were a couple of times when they got into heated arguments which turned into, I don't know, fights? Usually when they'd been drinking.'

'How bad are we talking here?'

'Nothing too bad. Slaps and a bit of grappling. That's all.'

'So, toy fights?'

'Aye.' Strachan held up his hands. 'Look, that's all I know.'

Cullen thought it through. It was something they needed to investigate further, just maybe not with Strachan. 'Right. Thanks for your help.'

Strachan got to his feet. 'That it?'

'Aye.'

Cullen followed him back to the other end of the room.

Fraser dropped his hammer to the floor. 'My turn, is it?'

Cullen set off back again, sitting down beside Angela, who looked bored. 'We understand you were arguing with your brother about the future of the company.'

Fraser eased himself into the seat and took a deep breath. 'Is this what you were asking Doug about?'

'Partly.'

'Well, I was right. We should have sold out.'

'Who to?'

'Scottish Distillers.' Fraser slouched back in his seat, pointing round the room. 'This place was dying on its arse at the time and it's just got worse since. My old man makes a decent living but everyone else earns bugger all. We should have taken the money when we had the chance. We'd never get the same now.'

'Is there talk of another takeover?'

'I shouldn't be telling you this but aye, Diageo is trying to buy us out.' Fraser sniffed. 'We'll get about half what Scottish Distillers offered in '94, you know. Bear in mind inflation and it's something like a quarter or a fifth of the amount. We should have sold out back then.'

'And that's what you were arguing about?' Angela's eyebrows hovered halfway up her forehead.

'It was. Iain wanted to stick with what we had. All right for him, educated man and all that. I've got nothing.'

'Which side was your father on?'

'Do I need to even answer that? We're still independent.'

'And you were for selling out?'

'Aye.'

'Why?'

'What we should have done was focus on the things those big guys don't understand and sell the skills into their company. That way, we could have gained a bigger piece of the pie. I could have got a decent salary out of it instead of the pittance I receive now.'

'And yet you're still here.'

'Aye.' Fraser laughed. 'You know, I've learnt the craft of being a cooper. It's been hard but it's something that has been in our family for one hundred years, almost eighty of them in this building. I could take that elsewhere.'

'Why don't you?'

'I'm a loyal man. I feel I owe it to my ancestors.'

'You didn't think to tell us this before?'

'I didn't deem it pertinent.'

Cullen couldn't tell whether it was or not. 'I gather it turned violent.'

'Violent?' Fraser laughed. 'Have you got a brother?'

'An older sister.'

'Right. You'll have had fights with her then, aye?'

'I suppose.'

'That's what I'm talking about. Shouting matches, bit of push-ing. That's it.'

'Anyone who can corroborate this?'

Fraser thumbed back up the room. 'What about Doug?'

'Other than Doug?'

'You can ask my old man. You could ask Marion. You could ask anyone.'

'We might just have to.'

## 36

Cullen tried to sneak into the Garleton Incident Room for Bain's two pm briefing without too much hue and cry.

'Here they are.' Bain stood at the whiteboard, hands on hips. 'Batman and Robin. Been up to something important, have you? Didn't fancy coming in to the actual Incident Room of the case you're on.'

Cullen collapsed into a chair. The wonky leg clunked. 'We've been following a couple of leads.'

'Phono leads for your stereo, no doubt.' Bain looked over Cullen's shoulder. 'Oh, we're lucky today. Feels like a royal visit.'

Cullen turned around. Murray and McLaren ambled in.

Cullen's mobile rang. He didn't recognise the number. Bain scowled at him as he got up, heading for the corridor.

'Cullen.'

'Hi, lad, it's Seth Neely.'

Cullen'd have to start chasing Neely later. 'Thanks for calling me back.'

'Not good news, like.'

'Hit me.'

'Both officers on that investigation have since retired. Both died in the last five years — one from cancer, the other a heart attack.'

Cullen jotted it down. 'Thanks. I'll be in touch if I need to come and see that file.'

'Be looking forward to it, lad.'

Cullen pocketed his phone and took a breath before returning to the Incident Room.

Bain stared at him as he sat. 'Murray and McLean here are proving yet again how useless local plod are.'

Murray coughed. 'McLaren.'

'What?'

'You've done it again. It's McLaren, not McLean.'

Bain smacked the whiteboard. 'I don't care! You pair of useless idiots have wasted a tank of petrol getting nowhere!'

Murray snorted. 'We got to Morpeth.'

Bain paced up to him and stared into his eyes. 'You shut your mouth, all right? You've come back here with your tails between your legs so don't give me any of your lip, son.'

'I don't think it was a—'

'Of course it was!'

Murray sat back and folded his arms. 'If you'll let me finish?'

Bain held up his hands and took a step back. 'Of course, I'll let you say your piece before I tear you another arsehole. That must be about six you've got now.'

Murray spoke through gritted teeth. 'As I was saying, I don't think it was a waste of time. We've managed to confirm Kavanagh's relatives haven't seen him in eighteen years. That's not nowhere.'

'We're still nowhere near somewhere, though.'

'Still, that's not nowhere.'

Bain shook his head. 'What about that boy last night who chucked a brick at Fraser Crombie?'

'Still being questioned as far as we know. DS Lamb is leading it.'

'That's all we need.'

'The boy's got alibis for the other assaults.'

Bain stroked his moustache. 'Not for the one last night, though, right?'

'No.'

'Right.' Bain looked at Cullen. 'The big prize chopper, Captain Sundance. Tell me some good news.'

'Well, I managed to track Iain's girl to Harrogate in Yorkshire. Mary-Anne Wiley.' Cullen picked up a copy of the poster. 'There was a publicity campaign based on a photofit of her from Fraser Crombie's description.'

'Aye, your pal Stanhope told me last night.'

'We went to see him this afternoon.'

Bain shook his head. 'What were you doing there?'

'Checking up on stuff from the old case files. There was a sighting of Mary-Anne Wiley in Harrogate. The bad news is they won't release the file. If we want to see it, we'll have to go down there.'

'Right.' Bain stayed quiet for a few seconds, arms folded, looking at the whiteboard.

'So can I?'

'Can you what, Sundance?'

'Go down there.'

'No.'

'No?'

'No.'

Cullen hit the table. 'But this is a lead. We might get something from it.'

'Aye, well.' Bain avoided eye contact. 'Instructions from DCI Turnbull. Until this is confirmed as Iain or Paddy then we're not to incur excessive expenses.'

Cullen waved at Murray and McLaren. 'But they've just visited Morpeth.'

Bain leaned over the desk at him. 'Hence the policy, Sundance. Anything else from you?'

Cullen looked away. 'Stanhope told us Fraser and Iain had a fight before they went to Glastonbury.'

'Hallelujah. Some bloody progress at last. Go on.'

'According to Fraser and Strachan, they made up before their trip. They had talked of cancelling it.'

'What were they arguing about?'

'A takeover offer from Scottish Distillers.' Cullen flipped through his notebook. 'Iain and Alec were against it, they wanted to stay independent. Fraser wanted to sell out and incorporate themselves in the bigger company.'

'And they argued about it?'

'Aye. They had a family meal and made up.'

Bain noted it on the whiteboard, connecting *Iain* and *Fraser* with a line marked *Argument 2*. 'Right, so this Fraser boy looks like a suspect?'

'Potentially. Well, it's not a motive to kill him, is it? He's clearly not benefited from his brother's death.'

'Fair point.' Bain looked at Angela. 'What about you, Batgirl? Uncle Brian won't bite.'

Angela raised her eyebrows. 'From the din that's coming from you, I'd say you just might.'

Bain laughed. 'I feel like shite, but you can make me laugh.'

She crossed her legs. 'What do you want to know?'

'Nothing much, princess, just the small matter of a progress update.'

'Fine. First, there's no DNA sample from Iain Crombie's arrest.'

Bain's eyes almost popped out on stalks. 'You are kidding me.'

'No. Central records told me it wasn't policy until the early nineties and this was 1988.'

'For Christ's sake.' Bain pinched the bridge of his nose. 'What else?'

'The insurance policy search for Iain Crombie came back negative.'

'So no policies?'

Angela shrugged. 'That's generally what's meant by a negative result.'

Bain folded his arms. 'You wouldn't think you were looking for a positive reference from me, would you?'

She smiled. 'I doubt it would be worth anything anyway.'

Bain laughed. 'Brilliant. So we're buggered?'

'I wouldn't use those words, but aye.'

Cullen clicked his pen a couple of times. 'What about Deeley or Anderson?'

'Don't start me on that pair. They're still backed up, no chance we're getting anything for an age of man.' Bain rubbed at his forehead. 'Pair of them are just a pair of walking excuses.'

Angela sniffed. 'So, four excuses?'

Bain pointed his finger at her. 'Less—'

There was a knock on the door. Turnbull stood there, arms folded. 'The desk sergeant said you'd be up here.'

Bain leaned against the wall. 'Welcome, sir.'

'I've had further complaints from Alec Crombie.'

'It's nothing, sir.'

'Have you made any progress?'

'I'm afraid not.'

'Right. Given you still haven't got an identified victim, this investigation is being shut down.'

'Really?'

Turnbull nodded. 'I want you to write everything up and lock this room. I'll see you in the Starbucks next door in five minutes, Brian.' He turned and left.

Bain exhaled and stared out of the window. The rest of them started packing up.

Cullen went over to join him. 'So that's it?'

'Watson, Murray and whatever his bloody name is, get them to send their reports to Leith Walk by the end of the day. Can you get back to your previous duties?'

Cullen let out a groan. Back to working with Irvine.

# DAY 4

*Tuesday*
*19th June*

*Five days later*

## 37

G orgie Road was heavy with foot traffic, cars and belching
buses, as commuters headed home at the end of another
day, just as Cullen's was beginning. Gorgie was an area
he didn't know particularly well, but he was beginning to get
acquainted with it.

Cullen ambled down the street, carrying a plastic bag in one
hand with his mobile clasped to his ear in the other. 'That's us just
settling in for the night.' He yawned. 'Clocked on at four pm and
I'm dreading the next fourteen hours.'

Sharon laughed down the phone. 'You'll get through it.'

Cullen shook his head. 'That's four days straight now. I'm
beyond fed up sitting with Irvine.'

'How's it going?'

'He keeps threatening to reopen the complaint. I'd say our
working relationship has gone from strained to almost nuclear
war.'

'Just don't choke him again.'

'I'll try not to.' Cullen grinned. 'I almost got to the point of
feeling nostalgic for one of Bain's investigations.'

'Don't speak too soon. He's been running around here all
afternoon.'

Cullen sighed. 'Cargill's stakeout must take precedence,
surely?'

'Gorgie isn't strictly on our patch, though. Turnbull had a DI over from Torphichen Street earlier. No idea what happened.'

Cullen stopped in the street and leaned against a wall, hordes of people milling past. 'I'm getting a bad feeling about this.'

'Sorry to be the bearer of bad news, but I haven't seen you for days, Scott.'

'Yeah, sorry.' Cullen sniffed. 'You on earlies, me on nights. Not good.'

'Hasn't stopped you popping into mine at six in the morning, getting your way then falling asleep.'

'Need to keep the physical side of the relationship going.' Cullen chuckled. 'Any other juice?'

'Cargill's supposed to be bringing in more detective sergeants.'

Cullen smiled for the first time that day. 'I might be able to get that promotion after all.'

'Don't count your chickens, Scott.'

'I'm close to putting my feelers out and seeing what's available in St Leonard's, even back out in West Lothian.'

'Now you're just getting desperate.'

Cullen laughed as he turned the corner into a quieter side street. Tynecastle, the Heart of Midlothian football stadium, loomed over him as he stopped at a black Vauxhall Astra. 'Look, I'd better go. I'll give you a call later now you're back on office duties.'

'Love you.'

He pocketed his phone, opened the passenger side and got in. TalkSport was on the radio, building up to some more Euro football commentary.

Cullen screwed up his eyes, looking out of the window. They were conveniently parked for a view across the road of the block of flats. He looked over at Irvine. 'Anything?'

Irvine rattled a chewing gum drum and threw a couple of pieces in his mouth. 'Nothing.'

'Nothing at all?'

Irvine snorted. 'What do you think? We're wasting our time here.' He rubbed his hands together. 'I'm just thinking of the overtime, though. Got a boys golfing weekend in the Algarve coming up in October. Might treat myself to a new driver.'

Cullen dreaded another soliloquy on the relative merits and

demerits of Titleist versus Nike versus some other brand he'd never heard of. He handed Irvine three newspapers and took his own pair out.

Irvine picked up Cullen's *Guardian* and *Independent*. 'You gone for your poof's papers again?'

'Do we have to keep going over this?'

'I'm just saying, that's all.'

Cullen chucked his papers on the dashboard. 'What do you mean you're just saying?' He stabbed his finger in the air. 'Since I let slip that I've got a degree in English, I've had no end of abuse from you about it.'

Irvine folded his arms. 'Do you really want to go there again?'

Cullen sat back and shook his head. 'I've not seen that sort of behaviour since high school.'

'You saying those papers aren't for poofs?'

'Given more people read your papers, there are probably statistically more homosexuals reading yours than mine.'

Irvine laughed. 'Like buggery there is, Sundance.'

Cullen leaned over, resting on the handbrake. 'I've told you not to say that again.'

Irvine backed off. 'I'm just making a point, that's all.'

'I'm not asking you to read them. Besides, I've not seen any direct evidence you can read. It's just the pictures you look at, isn't it?'

Irvine scowled. 'Does your dyke bird read them?'

Cullen's hand was reaching for Irvine's throat when his phone trilled. Bain. He almost muttered something like *Here we go*, but he knew it would get back to Bain within an hour. 'Saved by the bell.' He got out of the car and answered.

'Sundance. You and Irvine still in Gorgie?'

'Afraid so. The only good thing is it's June and I'm not freezing my nuts off.'

'Reckon Irvine can manage on his own?'

'Why?'

'Deeley's just done the post mortem on the body in the barrel.'

## 38

C ullen walked into the Incident Room in Leith Walk. Murray, McLaren and Angela sat around looking bored as they waited for Bain.

'The gang's back together.' Cullen gestured around. 'No Watson?'

Murray grinned. 'No uniform yet.'

Cullen checked the whiteboard, already decorated with Bain's scribbles. 'Where's our lord and master?'

Angela pointed at the floor. 'Down with Deeley.'

Murray got to his feet. 'You fancy a coffee?'

Cullen smiled. 'Americano, two extra shots.'

Murray and McLaren left them to it.

Cullen found a seat next to Angela. 'What's Bain been working on?'

'No idea. This, probably.'

Cullen laughed. 'I'm just glad I've avoided the double-whammy of working with both Irvine and Bain again.'

'How's that been?'

'Lucky I haven't received another complaint, put it that way.'

Angela closed her eyes. 'Oh, Scott.'

'What about you?'

'Tulliallan. Passed the final module. I'm now an accredited detective.'

'Well done. That'll be a weight off your shoulders.'

'One weight anyway.'

'What's that supposed to mean?'

She tugged her fringe across her forehead. 'Nothing.'

'Is the old college any closer to looking like Police Scotland headquarters?'

'Didn't notice any difference.' A smirk danced across her face. 'Guess who was on my course?'

'I've no idea.'

'Go on, guess.'

'You know I hate guessing.'

'All right. Eva Law.'

'Great. How's she doing?'

'All right.' Angela nodded. 'We had a drink at the bar one night. She was asking about you.'

Cullen swallowed. 'And what did you say?'

'Nothing much. She's got a boyfriend in Edinburgh now.'

'I'm very pleased for her.'

'You love treating them mean, don't you?'

Cullen looked at her. 'I have absolutely no interest in keeping her keen. On that topic, how's Bill doing?'

'Making an arse of things is what.' Bain slapped a hand on Cullen's shoulder. 'Welcome back to a proper investigation, Sundance.'

Angela was about to retort but Murray and McLaren appeared.

Bain's eyes shot to their coffee tray. 'Where's mine?'

Murray treated it with a bemused look.

McLaren avoided eye contact with anyone.

'Right, now you're all here, let's get started.' Bain sat at the head of the table and picked up a sheaf of papers, looking less stressed than a week ago. 'Jimmy Deeley has completed the post mortem report on the body in the barrel. I've got extra copies being produced for you to digest at your leisure, but I'll just run through it in summary to make sure we're all singing from the same hymn sheet here.'

Cullen noted it for buzzword bingo.

'Most of it confirms what we already knew, so I'll just run through some salient points and you can read it afterwards.' Bain put on his glasses. 'The skull was caved in, most likely with a hammer or a wooden mallet.

'There's still a lot of ambiguity about when the body was put in the barrel, but the volume of whisky in the lungs means it's likely the victim was still breathing when placed in the liquid, even though there was substantial brain injury inflicted.'

Murray cleared his throat. 'So when was the body put in there?'

Bain took off the glasses. 'Nothing we can confirm either way. Looks like it could be anything from '94 through to '97.'

Cullen rolled his eyes. 'We've been over this. What about the volume of whisky that went missing?'

Bain grinned. 'Sundance, that's where we come in. There's no forensic or medical evidence confirming when the body was put in the barrel, but it's likely the barrel was filled in the summer of '94, even on the twelfth of June as it said on the barrel. So you're perfectly correct — we need to investigate that further.'

Angela looked up from her notebook. 'Has Deeley given a positive ID yet?'

Bain grimaced. 'Afraid not. As far as he is concerned it could still be either Paddy Kavanagh or Iain Crombie.'

Murray folded his arms. 'So we're no further forward?'

'I wouldn't say that.' Bain sniffed. 'We're still in the situation where we have two victims of a similar height, build and hair colour.'

Cullen frowned. 'What aren't you telling us?'

Bain grinned as he passed round a set of photos, clearly taken at the post mortem. The stills showed a male arm, the skin dyed a yellow colour. He ran his finger across the left arm. 'See this scar?'

Cullen looked closely at his copy. There was a deep ridge in the flesh. 'What about it?'

'This is in neither MisPer report.' Bain tapped his stack of files. 'This could be someone else. Given we've got two disappearances from the same distillery within weeks of each other, I think it's highly unlikely there's a third body.'

Murray got up and walked over to the whiteboard. 'Don't think we should be discounting it just yet. One or both of Iain Crombie or Kavanagh could have killed this third body and run away.'

'And I'm not discounting. I just want us to focus on eliminating

Paddy and Iain first, or confirm it's either one of them.' Bain took out an A4 notepad and flipped to a page halfway through. 'Right, Deeley reckons this scar was still in the process of healing at the time of death. Definitely not *perimortem*. While it's a distinguishing mark, it would appear the people who reported them missing didn't include this little factlet.'

Cullen tried to peer over at Bain's notepad, but it looked like Swahili to him. 'What do you want us to do, sir?'

Bain gave each of them a hard look, settling on Murray last. 'First, Murray, go through Paddy's medical records, find out if he'd had an accident.' He looked at Cullen and Angela. 'You pair, I want you doing the same for Iain Crombie.'

McLaren waved at him. 'What about me, sir?'

'You work with McLaren.'

'You mean Murray?'

Bain smacked his hand off the desk. 'Just get on with it.'

---

## 39

Cullen dialled the number then cradled the phone between his neck and shoulder, slouching back in his chair. Angela and Bain sat across from him, both on calls. Crombie answered the phone. 'It's been a while.'

Cullen took a deep breath. 'Unfortunately we've had a number of serious accidents and that's caused a backlog in processing the post mortem.'

'So you are confirming it's Paddy Kavanagh in the barrel?'

Cullen gritted his teeth. 'I'm afraid not. It's still ambiguous as to who it is.'

Crombie chuckled. 'I keep telling you this, it's not Iain.'

'I understand, sir, but as we have discussed several times, I'm afraid we have to investigate it as a possibility.'

'Is that what this call is about? Are you still clinging to the possibility it's Iain?'

'If that's how you wish to portray it, then yes.'

'I really could do without this just now. We don't need this getting all over the press again like it did last week. We are in the midst of takeover talks and this isn't putting me in a good position.'

Cullen flicked back through his notebook, finding a mention from Fraser. It seemed like the talks had advanced beyond the point of being an aside.

'And I've still not got access to my barrels yet.'

'I've told you before that's not my department.'

'You said you'd have a word with DCI Turnbull. Have you?'

'No, sir.'

'I'm sure you have leverage with the Procurator Fiscal.'

'Not personally. Listen, I'll see what I can do.' Cullen made a note to chase it. 'I would've thought you'd defer the takeover talks with all this going on?'

'I wish we could. They're very persistent.'

'I see.' Cullen switched the phone to his left hand. 'Mr Crombie, I'm investigating the medical history of your son. The body in the barrel has a scar on his arm and we need to identify whether Iain or Paddy had one.'

Crombie paused. Cullen didn't fill it. 'Well, there you go. Iain didn't have a scar on his arm.'

'Mr Crombie, the scar was still fresh.'

'Let me get this straight. You're looking to analyse my son's medical records to ascertain whether he had a scar he didn't have?' Crombie laughed. 'I hope you realise how ridiculous that sounds.'

'I still need to do the check, Mr Crombie.'

'I won't approve it. I'm his next of kin. If you wish to progress this, then some sort of warrant will be required.'

Cullen stayed silent for a few moments, mulling it over. He threw his pen on the desk. 'Mr Crombie, if I was to get a warrant, it would imply there is some level of guilt or suspected guilt regarding Iain's disappearance. Would you be happy with that insinuation?'

'I *know* it's not my son in the barrel. You will *not* be getting my permission to review any of my son's medical records. It's eight o'clock, I'd appreciate if you didn't follow this call up today. Good evening.'

The line clicked dead.

Cullen slammed the receiver. 'For Christ's sake.'

Bain looked over. 'That's not the sort of language I want to hear so early in the investigation.'

'This is coming from you?'

Bain chuckled. 'You're not mucking anything up are you, Sundance?'

Cullen folded his arms. 'Pot, kettle.'

'Don't start.' Bain waved a finger at him. 'I'll beat you at any game you want to play.'

'Crombie won't approve access to his son's medical records.'

'This is really getting on my tits now, Sundance. What reason could he have for blocking the request?'

'Surely if he's sufficiently convinced it's not Iain in the barrel, then allowing us access will prove him right and show how idiotic we are.'

'Unless there's something more to it.' Bain cracked his knuckles. 'Iain disappeared under a cloud. The argument between him and his brother drove a wedge through the family. What if something happened and there was a cover-up?'

'My brain's already sore with the number of possibilities I'm coming up with.'

'You're welcome to go back to reading papers with Irvine.'

Cullen grasped the edge of the desk, breathing slowly. 'I'll pass on that kind offer, if it's all the same.'

Bain stroked his moustache. 'Crombie can go to hell. We'll get a judge on the case.'

'Could you get on it?'

Bain scowled. 'You want me to get you a clean pair of pants after I've finished wiping your arse?'

## 40

Half an hour later, Cullen managed to negotiate the complex net of police and NHS interrelations and got through to a call centre in Inverness.

'How can I help?'

Cullen sat forward, leg jigging from the second coffee of the evening. 'I need to track down records for an Iain Crombie. He was declared dead in 2001.'

'I see.' There was a long pause with only a small amount of background chatter. 'I'll need to pass this to my manager.'

'Fine.'

The line went dead. Cullen got out a packet of gum, worrying he was on the road to becoming like Irvine.

'Constable?'

'I'm here.'

'I'm afraid we're unable to give you detailed information relating to Mr Crombie. We need a court order to give you the detailed case history of a specific patient.'

'Can I ask why?'

There was a pause. 'The data agreement between the NHS and the police services govern where there is 'an overriding public interest' and where the data is pseudomised.'

Cullen could just imagine Bain going on about data being sodomised. 'What does that mean?'

'Each unique identifier in the data is replaced with another one, without any link to the original patient's record.'

Cullen was relieved she used the word patient and not customer or client. 'So you're telling me it's a no?'

'Of course it's a no. Unless you have a court order or there's express approval in the considered opinion of the GP or other doctor who treated the patient then it's got to be a no.'

Cullen twirled his pen between his fingers for a few moments. 'So if I spoke to the GP or consultant or whoever then they could approve my request?'

'That is the case, yes.'

'Can you give me the name of the GP, then?'

'Very well.' Loud tapping at a keyboard. 'Dr Adrian Berry was the family doctor. He was based in Gullane Medical Practice at the time, but he's moved to North Berwick. There's a mobile number on the file.'

'Can I have it?'

She gave it somewhat reluctantly. 'Is there anything else?'

'No, thanks for your help.'

He ended the call then dialled the number for Dr Berry — it bounced straight through to voicemail. He left a message and then immediately tried again.

He tried the number for the health centre's reception.

A grumpy-sounding woman answered the call. 'This is out of hours.'

'This is a murder investigation.' Cullen gave her his warrant number.

'I see. How can I help?'

'I'm looking for Dr Berry.'

'I can pass him a message. I'm not promising he'll call back'

'Thanks for your help.'

Cullen put his phone on the desk and tried to think through his next steps, coming up blank. He looked over at Angela. 'How are you getting on?'

'Getting nowhere.'

'I might be onto something but nothing's happening until tomorrow. I didn't clock on till four what with the overnight stake-out with Irvine. Do you reckon Bain will mind me pissing off now?'

Angela frowned. 'You're asking me?'

'A problem shared is a problem halved.'

'Hung, drawn and quartered, more like.'

Cullen laughed. 'Have you seen him?'

'He left after a meeting with Cargill and Turnbull about twenty minutes ago. He was moaning about reporting to a DI.'

'Right. You heading soon?'

'Yeah, think I will.'

'Fancy a pint?'

'Not tonight. How's Sharon?'

'Her stakeout finished on Saturday night. They caught two Hibs casuals red-handed. The silly twats were carrying the knives they used in a stabbing.' He sniffed. 'Perfect timing. My stakeout started that night. Haven't properly seen her for days.'

'I bet you've seen to her, though.'

Cullen laughed. 'That's below the belt even for you.'

Angela tugged at her hair. 'Say hi from me.'

'Will do.' Cullen put his suit jacket on, grabbed his phone and dialled Sharon's number, wondering if she fancied going for a drink.

# 41

Cullen squinted into the evening light as the sun crept over the rooftops of the taller buildings on Broughton Street. He'd met Sharon and they were in The Outhouse bar's beer garden, still warm from their table's patio heater.

He took a sip of St Mungo, a German lager brewed in Glasgow, quickly becoming his favourite. 'This definitely isn't a gay bar?'

Sharon laughed. 'No.'

'So why is it called Outhouse, then?'

'Because of the beer garden. Which we're sitting in.'

'And it's nothing to do with *Planet Out*?'

'God, stop being so homophobic.'

'I'm not homophobic. Rich is gay.'

'Rich is hardly a raving queen, though.'

Cullen leaned forward. 'I'm not homophobic. I just didn't know if this was a gay bar or not.'

'Worried about the skinhead that's checking you out at the urinals?'

'Very funny.'

She laughed. 'I'm just winding you up.' She took another big drink of rosé. 'Nice to be able to have a drink with you. I'm so glad the surveillance is over.'

'As long as Bain doesn't catch me. I've only done four hours today.'

'Yeah, but you're in at seven tomorrow, right?'

'Right.'

'And you've put in the hours this week.'

'Don't I know it.' He shielded his eyes from the sun then shifted his seat to the side. 'Really wish I had my shades.'

'Angela's right, you are a princess.'

Cullen smirked. 'How's your day been?'

'Slow. Problem is Wilko's got a carrot dangled in front of him. He's driving us hard for the first time ever, making sure the paperwork is done to a high standard. Me and Chantal have been chained to our laptops all day.'

'When's it going to court?'

'Monday morning.'

'Wow.'

'Aye. They're fast-tracking it. There's a big initiative on. I'm keeping a million miles away from it.' Sharon took another drink. 'Must be a relief to be away from Irvine, though?'

Cullen took a long drink of the sharp lager. 'Tell me about it. He was nipping my head today. Called me a poof again.'

'See why I don't want you sounding homophobic? You need to be whiter than white if you want to get him done.'

'I know, I know. I just can't believe Cargill has paired us up again, given Irvine's complaint against me. Buxton told me Irvine was moaning about Turnbull getting him to drop it.'

'Better just to forget about it. He's a wanker, you're not stuck with him now.'

'No, I'm stuck with Bain again.' He finished his pint and checked his watch — twenty to ten. 'We've got time for another.'

She held up her glass. 'Same again. *Small*, this time.'

He grinned, eyebrow raised. 'We'll see.'

'No, really. I'm half-cut as it is. I need to be focused on the report tomorrow morning. Turnbull wants a run-through in the afternoon.'

'Giving him a helicopter view?'

'I think the exact phrase he used was thirty-thousand feet.'

Cullen snapped his finger out like a pistol. 'Bain wants us singing from the same hymn sheet.'

'Oh, classic.'

Cullen grinned and picked up his glass. He headed inside,

finding it busy for a Tuesday. He had to queue behind a group throwing shots down their throats. Cullen started to question Sharon's assertion of it not being a gay bar.

The barman took his order. Cullen's phone rang — an 01620 number. He couldn't place it. He went back outside to take the call, spotting Sharon playing with her phone.

'Mr Cullen, this is Dr Adrian Berry returning your call.'

Cullen's heart rate increased. He got out his notebook, cradling the phone between his ear and shoulder. 'Thanks for calling me back. I'm working on a murder investigation and I need to trace the medical history of an Iain Crombie.'

'The son of the distillery owner?'

'Aye. He disappeared in 1994. He was presumed dead in 2001.'

'Yes, I remember. I was involved in the presumption of death. Have you found his body?'

'We're investigating that possibility.' Cullen clicked his pen. 'I was wondering if I could speak to you tomorrow.'

'Well, this is most unusual.'

'It's unusual for me too. I just need some information from his medical history.'

'Very well. I can meet you at eight am at the surgery in North Berwick. Otherwise, we're talking seven pm.'

'Eight would be perfect.'

Cullen ended the call and headed back inside for a celebratory beer.

## 42

C ullen lay on his back, staring at the ceiling.
Sharon was stroking his flaccid cock. 'I'm going to
have to declare death.'

'Give him five minutes.' He looked at her hand. 'He's just run a
marathon.'

'He is very small, after all.'

Cullen laughed. 'Don't hear you complaining.'

She let go, his penis slapping back against his sore balls, and
snuggled into him. 'Clock's ticking.'

He kissed her head. 'I love you.'

'You're only saying that because you're pissed and you've just
come.'

'Should have maybe stopped with that pint.'

'You definitely shouldn't have ordered a bottle of wine.'

'I felt in a good mood. Away from Irvine. Prospect of a DS position. Things are looking up.'

She squeezed him tight. 'I want you here.'

'I am here and you've just had me.'

She giggled. 'I mean I want you to move in.'

'Right.'

'You need to talk to Tom about it.'

'I will.'

She tweaked his nipple. 'When you called me last week, you were so bored with them.'

'I know.' Cullen sighed. 'The flip side of sitting with Irvine is I haven't been back to the flat since Friday. That's three matches I've missed. Maybe four. I've stopped caring.'

She got up on all fours, biting his nipple. 'I mean it, Scott. I want you to move in.'

Cullen nodded towards the pair of eyes staring across at him. 'Will Fluffy welcome me?'

She glanced over then grinned. 'If you feed him and change his litter every couple of days, he'll love you.'

'He's that easy is he?'

She looked at the alarm clock then got on his stomach, pushing her breasts in his face. 'Ready?'

Cullen looked down. 'He's awake again.'

'Don't need the defibrillator?'

He pulled his arms around her and kissed her.

# DAY 5

*Wednesday*
*20th June*

## 43

C ullen sat down in the Incident Room in Leith Walk station, sweat already dribbling from his armpits.
Murray sniffed the air. 'What's that smell?'

Cullen cleared his throat. 'I had a couple of pints last night. Didn't have time for a shower this morning.' He glanced at his watch. 'It's gone seven. Where's Bain?'

Angela tugged her hair. 'I saw him arriving this morning. Not seen him since.'

'You okay to head out to North Berwick after this? I'm meeting Iain Crombie's doctor.'

'Fine.'

Bain barrelled into the room, before standing by the flip chart and rubbing his hands together. 'Thanks for bothering to turn up.'

Murray held up his hand. 'Bit of a mare getting out here this morning, sir.'

'Just think of what I have to go through getting from Bathgate to Garleton.' Bain squinted around the room. 'Where's your wee pal?'

Murray thumbed upstairs. 'He's getting you a coffee.'

'Good man.' Bain uncapped a marker pen. 'I want an update on where we are with the actions I gave you last night.' He looked at Cullen. 'Sundance, you first.'

'I'm making slow progress.'

'As ever.'

Cullen raised his eyebrows. 'I need to get permission from Alec Crombie to get access to Iain's medical records.'

'And have you asked?'

'Aye. He refused.'

'Have you got a plan B?'

Cullen looked at his notebook. 'I've got hold of the family doctor who saw Iain back in the day. I'm heading out to North Berwick to meet him at eight.'

'Keep a lid on it, Sundance. I don't want Crombie putting in a complaint about this.'

'We need to find out who's in that barrel.'

'I know, I know, but just don't piss him off, all right?'

Cullen swallowed hard. 'Fine.'

'Batgirl, you next.'

Cullen didn't listen to her update, instead focusing on calming himself down. Bain wasn't the sort to give anyone free rein, especially someone known to stray down unapproved paths.

Just as she finished, McLaren walked in and distributed coffees to Murray and Bain. He looked at Cullen. 'Sorry, I didn't know if you wanted one.'

'Always assume I do.'

'Never bothers to get anyone else one.' Bain grabbed his and took a drink. 'Murray, how's it going with Paddy?'

'Like Scott, I've managed to get hold of Paddy's doctor. His records turned up here overnight.'

'Good work. Find anything yet?'

Murray turned to McLaren. 'Ewan?'

'Turns out Mr Kavanagh had a scar on his arm.'

Bain's fists pumped the air. 'You dancer.'

McLaren nodded. 'Pretty pleased with it, gaffer.'

'Right, so it's Paddy in there.' Bain let out a deep breath. 'Sundance, you can stop pissing off Alec Crombie.'

Cullen pinched his nose. 'I'm not giving up.'

'Yes, you are. It's Paddy. Case closed.'

'Sorry but you've asked me to look into it and I'm looking into it. I'm not dropping it.'

'Cullen, I'm not going to tolerate any more of this from you.

The Chuckle Brothers have just told us Paddy had a scar on his arm. Case closed.'

'Until we've matched it with the scar on the body, then we should keep checking. Right?'

Bain stroked his moustache. 'Look, Sundance, it's Sod's Law you picked the wrong one. Our country cousins have come up with the goods for once. You can't be a superhero every time.'

'I'm not trying to be a superhero. We still need to investigate the possibility it's Iain.'

'All you've done is find the family doctor. Big deal, Sundance.'

Cullen clenched his fists under the table. 'So I'm getting shut down?'

'Aye.' Bain folded his arms. 'I don't want to hear any more of it.'

'But—'

'But nothing, Sundance.' Bain looked over at McLaren. 'How did Paddy get this scar?'

McLaren glanced at the file. 'Says in here he was knocked off his bike two months before he disappeared. He was rushed to hospital in Edinburgh and they stitched him up.'

'I thought Deeley reckoned the wound was healing?' Cullen looked around the room for some support. Didn't get any. 'Two months is a long time to still be healing.'

Bain rolled his eyes. 'I've warned you.'

'Why wasn't the scar on the MisPer report as a distinguishing feature?'

'Your guess is as good as mine, Sundance.' Bain leaned back against the whiteboard. 'Murray, can you check with the landlady?'

Murray noted it down. 'Will do, sir.'

Cullen rubbed his hands over his face. 'If I'm not allowed to speak to the doctor, what do you want us to do?'

'Write your shite up this morning, Sundance. Let me think about what I'll get you to do after.'

'Fine.' Cullen marched off, feeling anything but.

## 44

C ullen got his change and waited for Barbara to pour his
coffee. He snatched it.
     She didn't let go. 'Say thank you.'
Cullen exhaled. 'Thank you.'
'Doesn't cost anything, does it?'
He laughed before walking to where Angela sat. He looked
over at her. 'What were Murray and McLaren up to back there?'
'Eh?'
'All that 'sir' and 'gaffer' shite. It's weirded me out.'
'Just toeing the line, I suppose.'
Cullen tore open the lid of the coffee, the burnt smell infil-
trating his nostrils.
'What are you doing, Scott?'
Cullen looked over. 'Watching this cooling helps put my anger
in context.'
'I meant about Bain telling you to stop.'
'I'm ignoring him.'
'Bain was right when he said you're acting like a superhero.'
Cullen blew on the coffee. 'I'm just trying to do the right thing.'
'Part of you wants to prove Alec Crombie wrong, doesn't it?'
'While it's still not definite, I'm just trying to keep our minds
open to any possibility.' He took a drink, savouring the acrid burn.
'This is typical Bain. Get a sniff of a lead and close everything else

down.' He prodded his chest. 'Close *me* down. Write everything up, put it in a box.'

'You think this is personal?'

'If I hadn't stuck my hand up last summer or in January, the wrong convictions would have been made.'

Angela smiled. 'Superhero.'

He took a sip of the coffee, just about at drinking temperature. He spotted DI Cargill heading over, carrying a tray and looking for a spare table. Turnbull followed close behind.

Cullen closed his eyes — just what he didn't need.

Cargill stood by the table, a bacon roll and coffee on her tray. Her hair had just been cut short — even shorter than before — with the hair-clip as a token gesture at femininity falling well short of the mark. She had a trouser suit on, the jacket just about covering the worst of her saddlebags. 'I didn't expect to see you here, Scott. I thought you were supposed to be on overnight surveillance with DS Irvine.'

'I was.' Cullen returned Turnbull's nod and wrapped both hands around the coffee cup. 'DI Bain took me off it.'

'He what?'

Cullen paused. 'Didn't you know?'

'No, I didn't.' Cargill licked her lips, eyes full of fury. She turned to Turnbull. 'Did you know?'

Turnbull tilted his head to the side. 'Brian may have mentioned something along those lines, but it was neither explicitly stated nor agreed to.'

Cargill turned back to Cullen. 'I need to have a word with DI Bain.'

'Let me know the outcome, ma'am.'

'You're not to do anything under DI Bain's instruction without consulting me first. Am I clear?'

'Absolutely.'

Cargill gave a polite nod and gestured towards a table by the window. 'Shall we?'

Turnbull grinned at Cullen. 'DC Cullen is one of our rising stars, you know.'

Angela raised an eyebrow and looked as if she was stifling a laugh.

Cargill narrowed her eyes as she focused on Cullen. 'I'll bear that in mind.' She lifted her left wrist to check the time, almost tipping the tray up. 'I've got a seven thirty with Deeley, so can we get on?'

'Give me a second.' Turnbull watched her walk over to the window.

Cullen's heart started fluttering. Turnbull speaking to him directly couldn't be good.

'Everything okay, Cullen?'

Cullen smiled. 'Yes, sir. Juggling seven cases, none of which are going anywhere, but I'm okay.' Lying bastard, he told himself.

Turnbull breathed out hard. 'How's Brian faring on this case?'

Cullen raised his eyebrows. 'DI Bain is okay, sir.'

Angela kicked him under the table.

Cullen tried to avoid glaring at her. 'It's difficult at the moment but we'll get a result.'

'Nothing funny in his behaviour?'

'Define 'funny'? This is DI Bain we're talking about.'

Turnbull chuckled, before looking at Angela. 'And you?'

'No, sir.'

'Okay, well if either of you see anything outside the particularly wide set of parameters DI Bain usually operates in, you let me know straight away.' Turnbull stomped off.

'Rising star.'

Cullen looked across at Angela. 'Stop it.'

'Rising star.'

Cullen snorted. 'Rising stars usually get promoted and not stuck with the worst DI in the force. Rising stars aren't used as pawns in some shitty game of chess between DIs.'

Angela laughed. 'Why did you defend Bain? That was a chance to get him down the pecking order.'

'Like it would work.'

'You never know.'

Cullen took a long drink of coffee and did some calculations in his head. Cargill would be in with Deeley for a good hour at least. Then she'd spend about another finding Bain, followed by Bain giving her the verbal runaround — call it another hour.

He looked over at Angela. 'I reckon we've got a window of three hours where we're not directly under Bain's command.'

Angela pushed her empty cup into the middle. 'You're up to some cowboy shite, aren't you?'

'I wish people would quit with that.'

'Most wish you'd quit with the cowboy shite.'

'Very good.'

Angela leaned in close. 'Whatever it is, you're on your own, Scott.'

Cullen took a deep breath. 'No, you're coming with me.'

Angela sat back and scowled. 'You can't order me about. We're the same grade.'

'It's my fault, okay?' Cullen tapped a rhythm on the table. 'If it goes well, you'll look good out of it. Deal?'

Angela looked at the scarred tabletop for a few seconds. 'Fine.'

Cullen finished the coffee and grabbed his suit jacket from the back of the chair.

**45**

---

'H*is* family moved here when we were at uni.' Angela waved out of the window as Cullen slowed to forty.

They drove past Victorian mansions on a long tree-lined road heading into North Berwick. Seemed a pretty place, a small fishing town a few miles east of Gullane, kind of like a slightly smaller version of St Andrews.

Cullen glanced over. 'I didn't know that.'

'Aye.' She folded her arms. 'Spent a few Christmases here, I can tell you.'

'What's it like?'

'It's okay. It's got the train to Edinburgh so it's full of lawyers and actuaries. All their kids go to school in Edinburgh though. The trains in the morning are stuffed with them.'

'You still not planning on having kids?'

Angela just looked out of the window.

Cullen cut up past the railway station, avoiding the town centre, but soon hitting traffic lights. He pointed to the post-war houses just down the road. 'They could be in Corstorphine.'

'I see what you mean. It's just in there on the right, by the way.'

The health centre was next to the Edington Hospital and, fortunately, had a reasonably sized car park. Cullen pulled into an empty space. He undid his seatbelt and looked across at Angela. 'Is this about the cowboy stuff?'

She sighed heavily. 'No, it's not, Scott.'

'Is it about me coercing you into coming out here with me?'

'Just drop it.'

'Fine.'

They crossed the car park and found Berry's office, at the end of a corridor that seemed to double back on itself.

Cullen rapped on the door and looked in. 'Dr Berry?'

'Yes.' Berry leaned back. 'I thought we said eight o'clock?'

'Sorry about that, sir. There were some guerrilla roadworks on the A1.'

The large man's face seemed to disapprove of everything Cullen said. 'Very well. In you come.' He beckoned them in.

They sat opposite his desk. Cullen got his notebook out, turning to a fresh page. He clicked his pen then introduced Angela.

Berry leaned across his desk, his tie sprawling over some files. 'Can I just remind you I'm doing you a favour? Without the necessary paperwork, it's entirely at my discretion how much or how little help I give.'

'I understand.' Cullen smiled, trying to disarm him. 'I appreciate your help. We're in the difficult situation of not having a confirmed identification, so we're unable to get a warrant. However, it could help us in that identification.'

'So be it.' Berry licked a finger and turned through the pages in the file. 'I had a look while I was waiting for your somewhat delayed arrival. There was a mark you were looking for, wasn't there?'

'There was. An injury to the left arm, probably less than a month before death.'

'I see.' Berry flicked quicker. 'Well, we might have something for you. Mr Crombie was treated at the Edington Hospital A&E six weeks prior to his disappearance.'

Cullen's heart raced. He leaned across the desk. 'Can I have a look?'

Berry pulled the file away. 'I wish you could. Sadly, I've not got the full report here, just a note.'

'Where would the report be?'

'Edington next door might have a copy.' Berry closed his eyes briefly and shook his head. 'No, I'm forgetting. The records across the Lothians were all centralised when they built the new ERI at Little France.' Berry paused for a few seconds before scanning through the stub record. 'There's the name of a doctor here, an Amardeep Singh.' He turned to his computer and typed in a reference number. 'Here we go. You're in luck. He's still active — now based at the ERI, as it happens.'

Cullen craned his neck around, trying to see the extension number. He managed to catch a few digits. 'Would you be able to phone him for me?'

'I most certainly will not.' Berry tilted the monitor away. 'I need you to submit a formal request, ideally signed by a superior officer.'

Cullen swallowed, knowing that was unlikely. 'This is a murder inquiry, Dr Berry. I really need that information.'

'And unless you provide a signed request, you're getting no further assistance.' Berry smiled. 'I'm sure it should be easy to obtain if it's a murder inquiry?'

## 46

B ack outside, Cullen slumped on a wooden bench outside
the small hospital next to the health centre.

Angela grimaced at the steady stream of traffic passing
on the main road in the early morning sunshine. 'See all the SUVs
on the school run?'

'I'm not in the mood.'

Angela chuckled. 'You're such a blagger, Scott. It's got to fail
sometimes.'

'Does it?'

'I think it's only likely.'

Cullen stared at his notebook, the name of the doctor and the
four digits screaming out at him. 'Sod it.' He got out his mobile,
finding the number for Edinburgh Royal Infirmary's switchboard.

'How can I help?'

Cullen gave his credentials. 'I'm looking for a Dr Amardeep
Singh.'

'Which one? We've got three.'

Cullen hoped Berry had given him the correct one. 'I've got the
last four digits of his extension.' He read them out.

'Putting you through now.'

'Cheers.'

'This is Mr Singh. How can I help?' Singh's accent was upper
crust Edinburgh with only slight traces of Indian ancestry.

'This is DC Scott Cullen of Lothian & Borders. I'm looking into the possible murder of one Iain Crombie. I believe you operated on him in 1994.'

Angela shook her head at him before getting to her feet and walking back to the car.

'Give me a second.' Singh tapped at his keyboard. 'Ah, yes. I did.'

'I need to speak to you about the operation.'

Singh sighed down the line. 'Then I insist you provide some formal documentation, Constable.'

'This is a murder inquiry.'

'But *I* insist.'

'This would really help me out.'

'Constable, the General Medical Council guidance explicitly states it is my duty to protect patient confidentiality. Only in cases where there are proven and direct links to a crime should I hand any information over to the police.'

'So what do I need to show you?'

'I'm sorry?'

'What do I need to give you if I want more information?'

Singh took a few seconds. 'I need written permission from the next of kin. No particular form, just something signed and witnessed.' He paused. 'And that's witnessed by someone other than yourself.'

'Thanks. Can I arrange an appointment for ten, please?'

'I suggest you get the permission first.'

'Are you free at ten?'

The pitch of Singh's voice went up a few tones. 'Very well. I can rearrange my schedule, but if you can't make it I would appreciate some prior warning. And I will escalate the matter to your superior officers in the event of non-attendance.'

'Of course.'

Cullen got the location of Singh's office in the hospital and ended the call. He took a moment to calm down before looking across the car park at Angela, hands gesticulating wildly as she spoke into her phone. She ended the call as she spotted him heading over.

Cullen smiled. 'Thanks for reminding me how good I am at blagging.'

'Don't tell me you've got something.'
'Got to get Alec Crombie's approval first.'
'You're such a cheeky bastard, Scott.'

## 47

'I really do not have any time for you and your wild goose chase.' Crombie slammed his fist on the desk. 'You've somehow managed to engineer your way into my office once again. I've got a board meeting on Friday and I need to focus on it.'

Cullen took a step forward from the door. 'As I've explained, this is a serious matter. You'll know we're still actively investigating both your son and Paddy Kavanagh as potential victims. I could very easily call up my DI and get a court order in place. It wouldn't reflect well on your business.'

He exchanged a look with Angela, realising just how far he was pushing it.

'You can't come in here with your constant innuendo and expect me to comply with your outrageous behaviour. Perhaps I should be having a word with your superior?'

Cullen tried to stare him out, but had to look away finding a formidable adversary in Crombie. He decided to try another tack. 'This is your opportunity to prove us wrong.'

Crombie narrowed his eyes. 'How?'

'You're convinced it isn't your son in the barrel. This is a chance to show how much of an idiot I am.'

Crombie turned and looked out of the window for almost a minute.

Cullen's heart raced as he wondered if his gambit had paid off or whether Bain would get a call from the distillery owner.

Crombie turned around. 'I know it's not Iain in there.'

Bain was going to give him such a doing. And Cargill and Turnbull wouldn't be too enamoured with his behaviour either.

Cullen opened his mouth to start pleading. 'But—'

'I will approve your access to my son's medical records. I would stress a vital condition that this represents the very end of the matter. We will not discuss any further suggestions about my son. You do not go to Fraser or Doug with it. You do not go to anyone else. Do I have your agreement?'

'You do.'

'Have a seat.'

Cullen took the seat on the left, Angela sitting on the right.

Crombie took out his fountain pen from an open drawer and produced a printed letterhead from another, before fixing his stare on Cullen again. 'So you only require a letter expressing my permission to look at Iain's medical records?'

'I believe that would be sufficient. I'll pass it in for evidence in the case file when I get back to the station.'

Angela coughed. 'It needs to be witnessed by a third party.'

'Very well.' Crombie reached across his desk and pressed an intercom button on the phone. 'Amanda, can you come up, please?'

'On my way.'

Crombie started scribbling — the way the ink appeared, it looked like high quality paper. He wrote his name at the bottom.

Crombie leaned back in his chair, crossing his legs and adjusting the kilt between his thighs. 'You're taking your time with this case. That's almost a week since I last heard from you. I'm surprised you haven't got it all wrapped up by now. Edinburgh's finest and all that.'

Cullen got out his notebook, struggling to find his pen. 'We've had our challenges.' He found it in his trouser pocket. 'There have been some higher profile incidents hit us. There were two separate RTAs on the bypass and the M8, and a murder in Bathgate.'

Crombie frowned. 'What's an RTA?'

'A Road Traffic Accident. There's talk of upgrades to both roads all over the news again.'

Crombie laughed. 'That the main trunk road between Glasgow and Edinburgh is a dual carriageway is a national disgrace.'

'Agreed.' Cullen was surprised to find common ground with the man.

The receptionist entered the room. 'Sir?'

Crombie signed and dated beside his name and wrote 'Witness' below. 'Amanda, I need you to witness this.'

She went round to the other side of the desk and signed the letter. Cullen clocked Crombie letching at her as she bent over the desk.

Crombie licked his lips and smiled at her. 'Thank you. That'll be all.'

Amanda left the room, closing the door behind her.

Crombie held the note out for Cullen. He reached for it but Crombie pulled it back. 'Not so fast. You will desist when this proves fruitless?'

Cullen's mouth was dry. 'Absolutely.'

'Very well.' Crombie handed him the paper.

## 48

Cullen marched across the new Royal Infirmary's car park. As he approached the main entrance to the huge white building, he looked over at Angela. 'Is this the right way in?'

Angela looked around then threw up her hands. 'No idea.'

Cullen's phone rang — Bain. His earlier calculations were on the optimistic side. He cleared his throat as he answered. 'Sir?'

'Cullen, where are you?'

'I've got an errand to run.'

'Do you. I've checked with Wilko and that witch Cargill and you're working for neither of them. What are you up to?'

Cullen turned away from Angela. 'I'm just away to speak to a doctor who operated on Iain Crombie before he disappeared.'

'Are you kidding me?'

'I'm serious. I don't know exactly what—'

'Why are you off doing that, rather than what I told you to do?'

'I wanted to rule Iain Crombie out entirely.'

'And I wanted you to do the paperwork on this, Cullen. Murray's been in with Paddy's doctor. The boy definitely had a scar on his arm.'

'Does it match?'

'He's not back yet.'

'Well, I'll call you back in half an hour and let you know if Iain

Crombie's one matches. In the meantime, I'd suggest you get Murray to check Paddy's actually fits the description.'

Cullen ended the call and turned off his phone, before taking a deep breath.

Angela folded her arms. 'I only heard about one and a half sides of that conversation, but it didn't sound like it went well for you.'

Cullen looked away. 'Could have gone better.'

'Your calculation was short?'

'Aye.'

She raised her eyebrows. 'You're going to get your arse kicked for this, aren't you?'

'I'm past caring, to be honest.' Cullen looked over at the building. 'Shall we?'

Angela gestured for him to lead. 'On you go.'

Cullen entered the hospital, determining *Orthopaedics (Trauma)* was at the far end of the building. 'This is going to take us hours to get there. Been here a few times. The architects didn't exactly prioritise ease of navigation.'

Cullen set off through the main mall area, before turning right down a long corridor. 'Like a bloody shopping centre this.'

'I'm sure there's an M&S going in.'

'Really?'

Angela laughed. 'Of course not.'

Cullen grunted then started up the stairs to ward 108. He asked at the reception area and was shown down another corridor towards Singh's office.

As they entered, Singh glanced up at the clock. 'Right on time.'

Cullen smiled. 'We're lucky.'

Singh gestured to the two chairs in front of his desk, which was covered in papers and x-rays. 'Have a seat.'

Cullen tried to catch his breath as he retrieved his notebook and pen. 'Thanks for seeing us, Dr Singh.'

'I am now a consultant, so please only refer to me as *Mr* Singh.' He adjusted his turban. 'Do you have the letter?'

Cullen handed it over. 'Hopefully this is what you need.'

Singh examined Crombie's permission letter then tossed it on the desk. 'This is not something I am particularly happy with.'

'Mr Singh, this is a very serious matter. We found a body in the distillery owned by Mr Crombie's father. Both Iain Crombie and another man disappeared around the same time. We're unable to identify the body as the face is unrecognisable. The teeth have been removed so we can't check dental records. We could run a family trace on the DNA but that will take weeks and meanwhile we're burning taxpayers' money.'

Singh nodded, the sob story having some effect. 'Very well.' He reached over and picked up a paper file, the red cover bleached pink around the edges. 'I went to the trouble of retrieving the file from our document retention facility.'

'Thanks for doing that.'

Singh flicked through the file. 'As you know, I was working at the Edington Hospital in North Berwick at the time in question. Mr Crombie was admitted in May 1994. He had a cut which required a number of stitches.'

'How would you describe it?

'It was a deep laceration. It wasn't a clean separation of the flesh and there were signs of trauma and tearing.'

Cullen wrote in his notebook, trying to hide the excitement. 'Where was the cut?'

'It was on the left arm.' Singh held up a black and white photograph. 'Here.' His finger traced the line across the arm, perpendicular to the vein.

Cullen took the page and focused on it, mentally trying to match it up with the body in the barrel. 'Do you know what caused it?'

'It was some sort of sharp object, though not a knife. The cut wasn't particularly clean.'

'Do you mean hygiene clean?'

'I mean both. The wound did take a lot of scrubbing, but it wasn't a neat cut. I would suggest a serrated blade was used. These wounds make it very difficult to get the sides to knit together. We were close to taking Mr Crombie to the old Royal Infirmary.'

'But you did manage, right?'

'I sewed the injury up, prescribed painkillers, antibiotics and rest.'

'Do you know who brought Mr Crombie in?'

Singh paused for a moment, before leafing through the file. 'It doesn't seem to have been recorded, I'm afraid. I only patched Mr Crombie up. Admissions was another department entirely.'

Cullen noted it down. 'Okay. What sort of action would have caused it?'

Singh fiddled with the band on his wrist. 'All I can say is it was caused by a trauma. Whether it was a blow, a collision or a fall, I can't say, I'm afraid.'

Cullen held up the photo. 'Would I be able to have a copy?'

Singh took a deep breath. 'I can arrange for one to be made. The quality of the copies is incredible these days.'

Cullen smiled. 'That would be useful, thanks.'

Singh left the room.

Angela crossed her legs and folded her arms. 'You spawny bastard.'

'I prefer to think of it as skill.'

## 49

S lightly out of breath and clutching a copy of the picture, Cullen made a beeline for Bain, Angela lagging behind.

Bain stood with his arms folded, staring at Cullen. Murray and McLaren were keeping a safe distance. 'Here he is, John Wayne coming in from the sunset. I've told you so many times I've lost count, but don't you *ever* hang up on me again. If I've told you once, I've told you a hundred times.'

Cullen ignored him. 'It's Iain Crombie in the barrel.'

'Sundance, it's Paddy Kavanagh. Murray's already ascertained that fact.'

Cullen paused for a moment, a smile on his lips. 'Can I at least say my piece?'

'You're pissing about here on your wee trips. I wonder what you're up to half the time, Cullen. I've not seen you for *four hours*, but I've had DI Cargill on my back. You're playing us off against each other, aren't you?'

'If anyone's playing, it's you.'

'Less of that, Cullen. Now, where have you been?'

Cullen looked up at the ceiling, desperately trying to remain calm. 'As I explained earlier, I've been speaking to Alec Crombie and the doctor who sewed up Iain Crombie's arm.'

'What for?'

Cullen held up the photo. 'Iain was admitted to the hospital in

North Berwick a month before he went to Glastonbury. He had a deep cut to his left arm.'

Bain gestured for Murray to come over. 'Did you speak to Wilsenham?'

'Paddy's landlady? She didn't know about Paddy's injury which is why it wasn't in the MisPer documentation. Nobody at the distillery knew either.'

Bain stepped in. 'We've already spoken to Paddy Kavanagh's doctor. Tell him, Murray.'

'He had a cut to the arm. We're just away to confirm it with Deeley.'

Cullen showed them the photograph. 'This matches the injury on the body.'

Bain snatched it from him. He looked at it for a long time. 'Christ, Sundance.' He handed the photograph to Murray, then undid his tie. 'Why do you have to be right all the bloody time?'

'I'd rather be right and trusted.'

Bain stroked his moustache. 'These games you keep playing don't help, you know that?'

'I'll keep playing them as long as you do.'

'We need to get this confirmed.' Bain turned to face the others. 'Has anyone seen Anderson?'

McLaren put his hand up. 'I chased him up for you, sir. He's still not finished his report.'

'I saw him downstairs when we parked.' Angela glanced at the window.

'Deeley's lair.' Bain pinched his nose. 'Where they've been taking the body out of the barrel. Very slowly.'

Angela smiled. 'Must be like *Time Team* down there.'

Bain bellowed with laughter. 'Aye, well, there's no yokel in denim shorts in my police station, that's for sure.'

Cullen narrowed his eyes at Bain. 'So you're in agreement it's Iain Crombie?'

Bain fixed a stare on him. 'I'm saying I'm open to the possibility again. Need to get an expert to confirm it.'

---

## 50

Bain ploughed into Deeley's office, leading Cullen, Murray and Angela behind him.

Jimmy Deeley sat in his office chair, speaking into a Dictaphone. 'The body has proved difficult to identify for a number of reasons. The skull was smashed in by a hammer and no teeth were found.'

Murray whispered at Cullen. 'Who's he?'

'The Edinburgh Chief Pathologist.'

'That's him? Thought he was a janitor.'

'Thought you guys would be using him now, too?'

'Supposed to be but I've not dealt with a body in a while.'

Deeley continued talking into the machine. 'Now, I don't know under which assumptions our killer was operating as to what the liquid would do to the body, but the corpse is reasonably well preserved. Not perfect, but good enough.'

He finally stopped the machine. 'How can I help, Brian?'

Bain beamed. 'Think we've cracked it.'

'Chance would be a fine thing. Go on, then, Edinburgh's finest, who's in the barrel?'

'It's Iain Crombie.' Bain flashed the photograph. 'He was admitted to hospital with an arm injury six weeks before he was reported missing.'

Deeley took the photo and compared it with another. 'Certainly bears a striking resemblance. I'll need to speak to the doctor and check the medical records for veracity, of course. Wouldn't be the first time you've tried to pull a trick, Brian.'

Bain screwed up his face. 'You'll get yours.' He sniffed. 'Where's your pal Anderson?'

'He's in next door.' Deeley chuckled. 'One of our main rooms has been repurposed for the time being to house that barrel. Katherine is going spare. Mr Anderson has been collaborating with me today.'

Bain nodded at Angela. 'Be a good girl and get Anderson through here for Uncle Brian.'

She headed off, face like thunder.

Bain rubbed his hands together. 'Hopefully get some answers out of that prick.'

Deeley winked at him. 'No love lost between you two, is there?'

Bain snorted. 'He's a liability.'

'I'm sure the feeling's mutual.'

Anderson appeared holding a wad of paper. 'What is it?'

'Could have sworn somebody promised me a forensic report on this barrel a week ago.' Bain eyes suddenly widened and he started prancing around like a children's TV presenter. 'I wonder who it could have been?' He looked around them, one by one, then finally at Anderson. 'Ah, yes, it was James Anderson.' He glared at him. 'Update. Now.'

'The report's in your inbox, Brian.'

'I'm not at my desk. Summarise it.'

'Fine.' Anderson dumped his papers on Deeley's desk. 'I'll give you a summary, then, seeing as you're asking so very nicely.'

'That would be smashing.'

Anderson read from his notes. 'Couldn't get anything off the barrel. It's been contaminated so many times. Christ knows how often they move those things. We got two clear sets of prints matching Doug Strachan and Fraser Crombie.'

Bain took a deep breath. 'That narrows it down by exactly bugger all.'

Anderson flipped through a few more pages. 'The barrel has definitely not been opened since it was filled. We opened another one from the same batch and they were virtually identical, give or take very slightly different wear patterns.'

'Crombie let you do that?'

Anderson smiled. 'Just a case of asking nicely. One day you might get taught that on one of your jollies up to Tulliallan.'

'You didn't have to put up with an earful about how much he was losing every day?'

Anderson looked away. 'Well, there is that.'

'So it's definitely from 1994?'

'I'm not saying that.' Anderson smirked. 'That barrel hasn't been tampered with since it was filled and it's consistent with the barrels filled in 1994. I'll let you detectives draw the conclusions and conjure it into your case. Happy to present my findings in court.'

Bain's eyes homed in on Cullen. 'Right, so given they had enough missing whisky that year to fill the two barrels, we can deduce it was filled in 1994.'

Deeley cleared his throat. 'Impressive as it is seeing the cogs turn, I presume there's a point in you coming down here other than to pester James?'

Bain shoved the photo in Deeley's face. 'This looks like it matches the body.'

'Come on through.' Deeley took them into another room and pulled out a rack from a unit at the side. A body lay on it, covered in a plastic sheet. He lifted it up, revealing a pale arm.

Bain motioned at the body. 'This him?'

Deeley focused on comparing the photo to the arm.

They waited a few more seconds, before Bain coughed. 'Well?'

Deeley looked up. 'It's a match.'

'Happy to sign your life on that?'

'Afraid so.'

Bain pointed at the body again. 'Is it in a fit state to show to people?'

'Like who?'

'The family.'

'Why?'

'Alec Crombie's son has been missing for eighteen years, Jimmy. I think he's allowed to see the body, don't you?'

Deeley nodded slowly. 'Give me an hour to get it shipshape.'

'It'll take that long to get the bugger brought over here.'

'I'll be off, then.' Deeley turned and marched out of the room.

Anderson moved to follow.

Bain grabbed his arm. 'Where do you think you're going?'

Anderson glared at his hand. 'I need to prep with Jimmy. I'll leave all the Sherlock Holmes magic to you boys, I'm merely a Doctor Watson.' He shrugged past Bain and left.

Bain looked like he was going to kick an inanimate object. 'Right. Let's get back upstairs. This place gives me the creeps.'

## 51

Cullen hung around, feeling like a spare part as Deeley finished setting up the room.

Cullen lifted the sheet off the body, lying on a slab in the middle of the room. It was well preserved — there looked to be blood underneath the skin and signs of bruising. His stomach lurched as he looked at the face, all smashed in. Whoever had done this had gone to town. The skull was collapsed, the teeth removed.

He looked at Deeley. 'I'm surprised these bits of flesh are still attached and haven't floated off in the whisky.'

'It's a messy business, young Skywalker.'

Cullen's finger hovered over the scar on the left arm, careful not to touch. 'Why didn't they cut that off?'

'How do you mean?'

'The killer went to all the effort of smashing the head in, but he left a distinguishing mark.'

Deeley shrugged. 'A hammer would be so much easier to come by in a distillery than a knife sharp enough to cut flesh.'

'True.'

There were voices from the corridor. Deeley quickly covered the body. Cullen moved away and stood in the corner.

Bain was first through the door, followed by Crombie and

Fraser. Doug Strachan entered some seconds later, his fat face red from the walk from the car park.

Bain gestured for them to stand by the table.

Crombie scowled as he paced over. 'This is a pointless charade. There is no *way* it can be Iain.'

Fraser Crombie and Doug Strachan shuffled to the opposite side of the body.

Bain moved to the foot of the table. 'You'll be wondering why you're here. We've managed to identify the body by matching it against missing persons reports from the time.'

Crombie cut in. 'It's not my son.'

'If you'll let me finish?'

Crombie held up his hands. 'Go on.'

'We'll have to confirm the identification by means of some secondary checks, though our options are somewhat limited in this case.' Bain paused and stroked his moustache. 'The bad news, I'm afraid, is it looks like the body is that of your son, Iain.'

Crombie closed his eyes for a few seconds. When they opened, it was as if fire burnt there. 'We've been over this before. *Many times.* The body in that barrel *cannot* be my son.'

Cullen noticed self-doubt creeping into Crombie's deep voice for the first time.

Bain looked at Deeley. 'Dr Deeley here is the City of Edinburgh Chief Pathologist. Now we've identified the victim, he'll be leading a detailed autopsy following the preliminary post mortem he carried out yesterday. We wanted to give you the opportunity to confirm the identification before proceeding.'

Deeley started before Crombie could chip in. 'I'm afraid the identification was difficult due to significant physical damage to the skull. The actual cause of death, however, appears to be drowning.'

'Good Christ.' Strachan's face had slipped from dark red to pale cream.

'The post mortem revealed the victim was still breathing when he was put in the barrel.' Deeley folded his arms. 'Drowning is the cause of death I will formally record, along with the additional injuries.'

Crombie glowered at him. 'That's all very well but what makes you think this is my son?'

Deeley held up a finger before lifting the sheet, revealing the left arm and part of the torso, but keeping the face covered. 'Somebody took great care to smash the skull, but they neglected to remove a key distinguishing mark.'

Crombie's eyes locked on Bain. 'Inspector, this isn't evidence.'

Deeley held up Singh's photo. 'This photo is from your son's records. You gave permission to DC Cullen earlier and we now have a copy of his full medical file. I spent some of the ninety minutes it took for you to arrive perusing the file. I can confirm that the body does indeed match Iain's photograph.'

'Nonsense.'

Deeley pointed to the arm. 'Did Iain have a scar like that?'

Crombie shook his head. 'Not that I know of.' He looked over at his son. 'Did you know anything about this, Fraser?'

'Afraid not. Maybe Marion would know?'

Cullen closed his eyes — he should have thought of that earlier. It would have saved hours of pissing about with doctors, permission forms and playing DIs against each other.

Bain took a deep breath. 'Mr Crombie, this is your son. We have confirmation from a medical practitioner that this injury related to your son and it's been independently matched against the body by Dr Deeley here.'

The only sound in the room was the drone of the electricity.

Crombie licked his lips and hissed. 'Let me see him.'

Deeley's eyes darted between Bain and Crombie. 'I would advise against it. As I said, the body is heavily damaged.'

'*Please.*'

Deeley raised his eyebrows, before pulling the sheet away from the face.

Cullen watched the three men for their reactions.

Alec Crombie started crying openly. He began moaning, muttering 'Oh, Iain' over and over.

Fraser closed his eyes and gave a slight nod, as if acknowledging his brother's death.

Strachan looked away from the body. 'Cover him up, for goodness sake.'

Deeley pulled the sheet back.

Bain patted Crombie's shoulder. 'I'm sorry to have to do it this way.'

'I understand.' Crombie slumped back against the wall, his muscles seeming to lose their tension. He looked at Cullen, tears streaming down his face. 'I owe you an apology, Constable. You were right.'

Cullen stared at the floor. 'Believe me, being right gives me no pleasure.'

Bain cleared his throat. 'We'll have to formally interview all of you at some point later today.'

'I understand.' Crombie wiped tears from his cheeks. 'I want you to find out whoever did this to my boy.'

Bain nodded. 'We will.'

Crombie looked at Fraser and Strachan. 'Someone's going to have to tell Marion.'

Cullen locked eyes with Bain. 'I'll do it.'

## 52

Bain rested his head on Cullen's shoulder from behind, tapping the sandwich wrapper in front of him. 'Mm, appetising.'

Cullen wriggled away from him, the coffee breath almost voiding his stomach. 'Hummus and falafel. No meat.' His brain had struggled with conflicting information from his stomach, eventually deciding hunger outweighed revulsion.

'Man up, Sundance.'

Cullen pushed the wrapper away. 'How did it go with Turnbull?'

Bain sat beside him, putting his feet up. 'Good.' He picked at his teeth. 'We've just been agreeing the next steps. He's pleased we've identified the victim.'

'I hope some of the credit is heading my way.'

'Don't worry, Sundance.'

'Well, is it?'

'Would I steal your thunder?' Bain got up and walked to the whiteboard. He underlined *Iain* three times, scoring out *Paddy* and the mystery box. He turned and looked around the Incident Room. 'Come on. Look lively.'

The others sauntered over.

Angela sat next to Cullen. 'Am I getting any credit?'

'Need to see if I'm getting any first.'

Bain clapped his hands together. 'Right. I think we've made some solid progress today. We've finally confirmed who the body is. Cullen has been his usual sneaky bastard self and come up with a result out of nowhere, so top marks, Sundance. Zero out of ten for team play, mind.'

Murray grabbed Cullen's shoulder and shook it playfully. 'Good work.'

Cullen brushed him off.

Bain looked back at the whiteboard. 'I want us to focus on our activities. We need to find Iain Crombie's killer. We have a list of suspects and we need to close it down. DCI Turnbull wants us to use the momentum we've now got and get a result as quickly as possible.'

He tapped on *Iain*. 'Fraser told us he was at Glastonbury with Iain, his brother, who pulled some bird and stayed down there, never to be seen again. Right?'

Cullen nodded. 'Until he showed up in a barrel eighteen years later.'

Bain tapped the box marked *Barrel*. 'How did he get himself into a barrel filled ten days before this festival started?'

Cullen thought it through for a few seconds. 'Anderson said they're consistent with being batched up in 1994. A couple of weeks wouldn't be easily identifiable.'

'So basically, we know bugger all.'

Cullen folded his arms. 'That's a bit harsh.'

Bain stared at the board. 'Iain could have got back from Glastonbury and gone straight to the distillery where he met someone. Nobody knew he was back and got his pan done in. Whoever did it stamped the barrels with three weeks earlier.'

Angela smirked. 'Seems like science fiction.'

Bain scowled. 'Eh?'

'He's not likely to just turn up there, is he? He's been at a festival. I don't know what the weather was like that year, but he'd been sleeping in tents for over three weeks. Wouldn't he have gone home and got a bath or a shower first?'

Bain nodded his head slowly. 'Aye, good point.'

Cullen bit his lip. 'Don't think we should exclude it, though.'

'Agreed.' Bain pointed to the whiteboard. 'What about suspects?'

Cullen flicked through his notebook. 'Fraser implicated Strachan. Iain caught him stealing whisky and Strachan himself confirmed the story. His motive was saving his job. If he's the culprit, he's clearly benefited as he's still employed there.'

'Right.' Bain underlined *Strachan*. 'Go on?'

'It just fits. He's got a motive and he benefits from Iain Crombie disappearing.'

'What about Fraser?'

'Well, he had an argument with Iain and their father about the future of the company.'

Bain tossed the pen in the air. 'Is that it?'

'That's all we've got on him.'

'Do you think he's a suspect?'

'I'm not ruling him out.'

'Okay, so who else?' Bain set the pen down. 'His old man?'

Angela leaned forward in her chair. 'What about all that stuff with him refusing to acknowledge it could be Iain in the barrel?'

'He was going mental at me earlier.'

'You've maybe got something.' Bain tapped at Crombie's name on the board. 'He kept on telling us it was Paddy. He was being a right fanjo about it.'

Angela frowned. 'What's a fanjo?'

Bain rolled his eyes. 'What you've got and I don't.'

'A functioning brain?'

Bain scowled. 'No, a fanny.'

Bain picked the pen up again and underlined *Alec Crombie*. 'I'm putting him up as a suspect.'

Murray got a call on his mobile. 'You okay if I take this, sir?'

'Seeing as how you asked so nicely.' Bain turned back around as Murray headed out of the room. 'Any other suspects?'

'Paddy Kavanagh disappeared just before Iain Crombie did.' Angela waved a hand at the whiteboard. 'It's suspicious.'

'Good point.' Bain circled *Paddy*. 'Anything else pointing to him?'

Cullen flicked through his notebook. 'He used to drink with Iain Crombie up in Garleton. The Tanner's Arms on the high street, a pretty rough bar.'

'Place was notorious.' McLaren was nodding. 'Shut just after I started in uniform.'

Bain glared at him. 'So you *can* speak, McLean.'

'*McLaren.*'

Bain's eyes bored into him.

Murray appeared in the doorway, looking at McLaren. 'Got a minute, Ewan?'

McLaren shuffled off out of the room.

'Liability, those pair.' Bain stared back at the whiteboard. 'Anything else about Paddy? Cullen?'

'Not that I can think of.'

'Batgirl?'

'Nope.'

'Right.' Bain twirled the pen between his fingers. 'Anyone else? Sundance?'

'Marion Parrott?'

'The ex-wife?'

'Aye.'

'Why?'

Cullen found the first interview with her in his notebook. 'Her son stands to inherit the distillery.'

Bain screwed his eyes up. 'He was a foetus when this happened, Sundance.'

Cullen snorted. 'Iain was sleeping around at Glastonbury. She might have killed him when he got back because of that.'

'Wouldn't she need help?'

Angela rolled her eyes. 'What, because she's a feeble woman?'

'That's not what I meant, princess.'

'No, it is what you meant.' Angela narrowed her eyes. 'You think she couldn't do it cos she's a woman.'

'I'm saying it needs a strong person to do this. The others suspects are all big men. How tall is she?'

Angela looked through her own notebook. 'Five six, five seven.'

'How heavy?'

'Not very. Ten stone, maybe?'

Bain tapped the whiteboard. 'Iain Crombie was a big lad. I can't see her getting him in the barrel. And I don't think she knows how to use the machinery, either.'

Angela smiled. 'Okay, so for once you're not being a sexist pig.'

'Hey, I'm an equal opportunities bastard, Batgirl.'

Cullen waved a hand at the whiteboard. 'Are we done with Marion, then?'

'Think so.' Bain drew a line to a new box, *Accomplice*.

Cullen got up and joined Bain at the whiteboard. He tapped on *Iain*. 'Now we know it's him, can I go down to Harrogate?'

'Fine. Just you. Cheapest train down and up. No overnight stay and no taking the piss.'

'I want ADC Caldwell to come with me.'

'Why?' Bain glared at her. 'Are you two at it?'

Angela burst out laughing. 'Hardly.'

Bain rubbed his forehead for a few seconds. 'Fine, you can both go. Get Holdsworth to sort your tickets out. I'll need to speak to Jim about approving it.'

'Fine. We'll go first thing tomorrow.

'I haven't forgotten about you speaking to Marion, either.'

'I will do that.'

'First though, you need to head back to that surveillance obbo with Irvine.'

Cullen's eyes shot up to the ceiling. 'You're joking, right?'

'Wish I was. That witch Cargill was busting my balls. A load of shite about me grabbing you to do 'non-core activities'. I'll show her some non-core activities.'

Cullen took a deep breath. 'So that's it? I'm back with DS Irvine?'

'Afraid so.'

'Fine.' Cullen tapped the board. 'I'll do it when I'm finished typing my notes up.'

'Fine with me.'

Angela brushed her hair over. 'What about me?'

Bain looked around the board. 'Can you get everything logged onto HOLMES and all that shite? Be a good development opportunity for you, princess.'

'When was the last time you did any of that?'

Bain grinned. 'The privilege of rank.'

'I could think of a word that rhymes.'

Murray and McLaren reappeared and sat.

Bain nodded at them. 'The wanderers return.'

'Problem brewing back at the ranch.' Murray clamped a hand

to his neck. 'That was DS Lamb. Our DI got wind of us both being seconded to this investigation.'

'Wonder how she got wind of it. I'll sort her out, don't you worry.'

Murray smiled. 'Assuming we're still on this case, what do you want us to do?'

Bain tapped the board. 'We came up with a couple more suspects while you were grassing me up. Can you go back to looking into Paddy Kavanagh, this time as a possible suspect?'

Murray wrote it down. 'Will do, sir.'

Bain put the pen on the table. 'He disappeared when this Iain boy went missing. Now we know who's in the barrel, this Paddy boy's a suspect.'

Angela stood up. 'Is that us?'

Bain grinned. 'The rest of you can go. Caldwell, get me a sandwich, I'm starving.'

## 53

C ullen sent the report to the printer. Faced with the alternative of surveillance with Irvine, he'd taken his time typing it up.

He checked his watch, realising he only had two hours left.

He looked at the whiteboard, his eyes dancing through the actions Bain captured at the briefing. He decided he should speak to Marion Parrott before heading out to see Irvine.

Corroboration would be handy — if she slipped up when they broke the news, Cullen didn't want to find himself out on a limb.

The Incident Room was mostly empty. Murray was on a call and Angela was on HOLMES duty.

Cullen sat next to her. 'How's it going?'

'Keep away from me, cowboy.'

'Woah. What's up?'

'Bain gave me a leathering about going with you earlier.'

'Sorry.'

'Yeah. Thanks for covering my arse.' She folded her arms. 'You'll get all the credit for it.'

'I'll sort it out.' Cullen smiled. 'Look, I need to speak to Marion Parrott. I could do with some back-up.'

'This is to avoid Irvine, right?'

'Maybe. I'm just away to let her know her husband's genuinely dead.'

'Forget it. I'm finishing this then heading to my sister's.' She nodded at Murray. 'Try him.'

Cullen smiled. 'Look, I'm sorry I got you in the shit with Bain.'

She took a deep breath. 'Don't worry about it. Just get out of my hair.'

Murray was on a call, slumped back in the office chair, his feet up on the desk. He sat up as he slammed the phone on the desk and started slapping his fingers against the laptop keys.

Cullen wheeled himself over. 'How's it going?'

'Shite. No chance we're finding Paddy. Meanwhile, my caseload is building up back in Haddington and Bill will be down on me like a ton of bricks.'

'Where's McLaren?'

'He headed back to Haddington to keep our DI sweet. Bain's managed to piss her off so much she's called Turnbull to complain.'

'Fancy heading back out east? Need to speak to Crombie's widow.'

'Is this to avoid that Irvine wanker?'

Murray's Airwave crackled to life. 'Control to DC Murray. Come in.'

Murray reached for the device and plugged in the headset. 'Receiving.'

He sat listening for a few seconds. 'Whereabouts?'

A pause. 'How long ago?'

Another wait, longer. 'Aye, I know where that is.'

He ended the call and looked over to Cullen.

'Got a sighting of Paddy Kavanagh in Haddington.'

## 54

Siren blaring, Murray's Golf flew along the A1 in a way Cullen's just couldn't. 'Times like this make me glad I spent the extra five grand on the GTI. Can't touch it in a pursuit.'

'We're not technically in pursuit.'

The speedo was clearing ninety just as they spotted the sign for Haddington. Murray pulled off the dual carriageway. He skidded to a halt at the oval roundabout and punched the steering wheel.

Cullen could see he had been planning on going for it, but an articulated lorry and two white vans persuaded him otherwise. 'Steady on.'

'You're just jealous.'

'I'm just wanting to get there in one piece.'

Murray turned right, heading into the town. Through the trees, Cullen could make out the blue lights of squad cars surrounding the place.

Murray turned into a concealed entrance and parked alongside the row of panda cars. He reached for the Airwave. 'DC Murray to DS Lamb. That's us here. Over.' He chucked the Airwave over.

Cullen put it back on the dashboard. 'So where was the sighting?'

Murray pointed at a grey concrete building. 'The only thing left standing.'

'What is this place?'

'Used to be a service station when the dual carriageway ended here. Been derelict a good few years since they dualled all the way to Dunbar. We get the odd call out, usually for a break-in. Supposed to be turned into a Sainsbury's soon. Can't come quick enough.'

'And they reckon it's Paddy Kavanagh in there?'

'A man matching his description, certainly.' Murray let his seat-belt go. 'Come on.'

They got out of the car before jogging to the throng of officers standing a couple of hundred metres from the single storey petrol station.

Cullen recognised a few of the faces from the case in January.

Lamb stood at the front, speaking to a heavy woman unseasonably dressed in a long overcoat.

Cullen nodded at them. 'Who's Bill speaking to?'

'That's our DI. Sandra Webster. Total nightmare.'

'Got you. Surely not Bain bad, though?'

'Who could be?'

'Quite.' Cullen looked around. 'Surprised he's not here.'

'He was up speaking to Turnbull, wasn't he?'

'That'll be it.'

Lamb walked over, before clapping his hands and clearing his throat. He stood, hands on hips, taking in the group of officers. 'Okay. We're here in response to a sighting of one Padraig Kavanagh.

'We have the place surrounded, all exits blocked and squad cars ready to jump.' He stroked his moustache. 'Our objective is to enter the building while maintaining full operational control of the site and to apprehend the suspect for further questioning.'

One of the older officers held up a hand. Cullen could just about place his face.

Lamb nodded. 'Go ahead.'

'Who is this Paddy Kavanagh?'

Lamb smiled. 'I was just coming to that. Kavanagh has been missing for eighteen years and is the lead suspect in a murder investigation dating back to 1994. We believe he is moderately dangerous and should be treated as such. He may be armed. I don't want any heroes here. If he escapes, we've got officers in cars and on mountain bikes. We will catch him.'

Cullen turned to Murray and whispered. 'Didn't think you lot could rustle up a cup of tea in less than two days. This is impressive.'

'Careful, you're sounding like Bain there. Besides, Bill's had a rocket up his arse from Webster. Doesn't want to look bad in front of the big city police.'

Lamb narrowed his eyes as he scanned the crowd. 'Any more questions?'

Nobody had any.

'Okay, I want four squads.' Lamb split the twenty or so officers into groups. 'One, three and four cover the east, north and south of the building.'

He looked directly at Cullen and Murray. 'Group two, I want your DCs to enter the building. Groups one and four need to leave a flanking officer to provide cover when the DCs go in. Once inside, I want you to apprehend the suspect or at the very least flush him out.' He looked around the group. 'Are we clear?'

A ragged chorus of 'Yes, sir' broke out.

Lamb punched his fist into his open hand. 'Let's get to it.'

Cullen retrieved his baton from his jacket and extended it. He put the can of pepper spray in his trouser pocket.

They got into formation. Group three headed off first, covering the rear of the building. There was already a wide perimeter of officers providing an inner cordon to support Cullen and Murray's entry.

Cullen felt a surge of excitement in the pit of his stomach. He glanced at Murray. 'It's been a good few months since I've done anything like this.'

'What about Archerfield last week?'

Cullen touched the scab on the back of his head. 'That's nothing.'

Lamb approached them, shaking hands with Murray.

Cullen grabbed his hand. 'Thanks for nominating us.'

'No problem.' Lamb looked around. 'Most of these lads are only useful for getting in the way.'

Cullen smiled. 'Better keep that away from Bain.'

Lamb grinned before snapping his baton to full extension. 'I'm coming in with you.' He took a deep breath. 'Come on, then.'

Lamb led them and two uniformed officers into position, waiting for the flanking officers from the other groups. 'On my mark. One. Two. Three. Go!'

Cullen followed in Lamb's footsteps, hugging the ground, before stopping outside the door.

One of the uniforms snapped the lock with bolt cutters.

Lamb yanked it open, motioning for Cullen to lead.

He ran inside, heart pounding as he switched on his torch. The light danced around. They were in the vestibule of a restaurant. A stack of tourist leaflets sat on a stand just by a door marked *Welcome.*

Cullen eased the door open with his baton. The room was pitch black, the windows boarded up. A single crack let a shaft of light in.

His nostrils twitched. There was a pervasive smell — a mixture of mould, mildew and rotting meat.

Lamb whispered from behind. 'Try the lights.'

Cullen fumbled on the wall, finding a set of stubby switches. He turned them all on, surprised when the overhead lights flickered into life.

The large room must have been a diner. The nearest section appeared to be a shop. The till was still there, mounted in a wooden frame with a seat. Next to it was a pile of dismantled metal shelving. Cullen prodded it with his baton, but it wasn't budging.

In the restaurant area, old laminated tables were pushed against the walls. Red plastic and metal chairs were scattered through one half of the room — in the other, they were stacked neatly. A serving hatch ran down one side of the room, half-closed.

Cullen went into the furthest half of the room, with Murray taking the other. He crept on, checking between seats and tables.

Halfway down, Cullen knelt to look under the tables.

Nothing.

He got up and continued, eventually meeting Murray at the far end.

Murray turned and gave Lamb an okay sign.

Cullen stopped in front of a large double door in the wall with the serving hatch. 'What do you think?'

Murray looked back at Lamb and got a nod.

Murray snapped his baton out. 'You first.'

Cullen prodded the door. It shuddered open. He entered cautiously, his baton brandished in. He found another light switch and flicked it.

Slowly, a strip light came to life. They were in a kitchen, empty of all appliances.

Murray looked round at the cabinet carcasses. 'No hiding places here.'

Cullen pointed at another door at the far end. 'Your turn.'

Murray carefully opened it with his baton. He entered with Cullen following closely.

It was colder in there.

Murray fumbled at the lights. Nothing happened. He clicked on his torch, flashing the beam around the room. There were coat racks, lockers, some seats, a kitchen area and a kettle. 'Looks like a staff room.'

Murray's torch caught a dark shape on a cursory scan.

Cullen grabbed his wrist, pushing the light back. 'There, middle of the floor.'

There was a sleeping bag.

Murray looked round. 'Someone's been here.'

Cullen went over to the windows and ran his fingers down the side of the boards. The second one wasn't well attached, coming free easily.

Light blasted into the room, making them blink. The window glass had been removed.

Cullen propped the board up. 'Given the front door was locked, this would make the most logical entrance.'

'Agreed.'

Cullen clocked the ring of police officers around the building. He called over to the nearest, who cupped his hand to his ear. 'Have you seen anyone come out of here?'

The officer shook his head. 'I would have called if I had.'

Cullen turned to look back into the room.

Murray was crouched, prodding at the sleeping bag with his baton. He slipped on a pair of rubber gloves and touched it. 'It's cold.'

Cullen joined him. 'So it's not like we've just missed him?'

'Can't say either way but he's not been in it in the last half an hour, I reckon.'

Cullen had another good look around the room. He went over to the lockers, the doors all open. He looked through every one — empty. There were no other entrances. 'Were there any other doors back there?'

'There should be, aye. I'd expect a stock room at the very least.'

'Come on. We can get forensics in here later.'

Returning to the main room, Lamb still stood guard at the far end. He gestured over. 'You found him yet?'

Cullen held up his hand, open-palmed and signifying another five minutes.

Lamb gave a slight nod.

Murray was trying to shift a stack of dining tables, the tops cracked and scarred. 'There's a door behind this lot.'

Cullen looked around. 'Come on.' He jogged over to a table. 'Here, grab this end.'

'Got it.'

'Slowly. *Slowly.*'

'Christ's sake, Cullen.'

'I'm taking the bulk of this.'

'Right, drop it now.'

Cullen let it go. The space in front of the door was now clear.

Cullen got out his pepper spray and looked at Murray. 'Ready?'

'Ready when you are.'

Cullen tugged the door open. Bile rose in his throat. The room stank, the off-meat stench he'd picked up earlier.

Cullen pocketed the spray and covered his mouth with a hanky. 'Get your torch out again.'

Murray shone it into the room. 'See? It's the stock room.'

'Well done.' Cullen coughed, desperately trying to not vomit. 'Looks like they didn't bother to clear it when this place shut.'

He stepped into the room. His feet stuck to the floor.

Murray shone the torch at his feet. The surface was covered in a thick goo. 'Jesus Christ, Cullen. This is rank.'

Cullen got out his own torch. Two large chest freezers hugged the far wall, lights off and silent. 'The power on the freezers must have been cut when the building was shut.'

'Different circuit to the lights?'

Cullen nodded. 'And I bet the freezers weren't empty when they were turned off.'

Murray took a deep breath. 'If there's someone in there, that's desperate, man. Let's have a look.'

'You first.'

Murray shook his head. 'No way. You first.'

Cullen took the room in for a few seconds. 'I'm not walking through that stuff.'

'Give me a hand.'

Murray led them back into the restaurant, standing at the other end of the table they'd pushed aside. 'After three. One, two, three.'

Cullen lifted his end. 'Slowly this time.'

'I am going slowly.'

Cullen dropped his end. 'You bugger.'

'What's the matter with you?'

'You're going too fast. I'm going to end up walking in all that shit.'

'Okay. Bloody hell. Help me push it, then.'

Cullen joined him at the far side. They slotted it through the door, making it halfway across the floor. He checked it was steady. 'Should just about reach both freezers with my baton.'

'I might film this.'

Cullen laughed, almost losing control of his nerves. He got up on the table and inched his way along, worried about falling in the goop as he progressed.

He stopped and reached out with the baton, struggling to grip the handle. Eventually, he managed to budge the lid, prising it open.

Large black flies swarmed him. The stench increased dramatically — the freezer was full of something. He let the lid drop down again.

He opened the second freezer — empty. He let the lid fall again, returning to where Murray stood.

'Well?'

Cullen rubbed his eyes. 'The one on the left has something in it. I don't even want to think what but it doesn't look like Paddy Kavanagh. I'll be buggered if I'm touching it.'

'You've got to.'

Cullen shook his head. 'You're welcome to. I'm leaving it for the SOCOs.'

Murray took a step back. 'Good plan.'

Cullen leaned against another table, thinking things through. 'There are no windows or doors in that room and we've got the place covered. If there's someone hiding in that freezer they're not getting out of the building without getting caught. It's a job for a SOCO, not us.'

'Good point.'

Cullen waved at Lamb. 'Let's go and brief the big man.'

## 55

Cullen got out of the car and spotted Lamb. He headed over. Murray stayed back and made a phone call.

Lamb grinned. 'Good work back there, Constable.'

Cullen pulled his shirt away from his skin. 'Doubt I'll ever get that stink out of these clothes.'

'I thought we had him.' Lamb gestured at Murray. 'Who's he speaking to?'

'Trying to get a trace on the call reporting the sighting of Paddy.'

'Good luck with that.'

'Come on, then.' Cullen led them upstairs, Murray following.

Angela was sitting in the corner of the Incident Room, tapping on a laptop. Her eyes bulged as she saw Lamb.

Bain stood by the whiteboard, his hands a blur as he redrew the mind map. He turned round as they sat. 'Evening, gentlemen. Nice disaster out there.'

Lamb rubbed his stubble. 'Paddy wasn't there.'

Bain rapped the whiteboard. 'This is seriously stretching my patience.'

Cullen tried to remain calm. 'We received an anonymous call stating that someone matching Paddy Kavanagh's description was staying at this old service station.'

'We issued a photofit last week.' Murray held up the standard notice, the ancient photo glaring at the camera.

'Why didn't you run this by me?'

'You were going ballistic at me for not finding Paddy. I worked on the assumption he was still alive and got a press release issued. The *Courier* and *News* both ran with it. And we got a result.'

Bain exhaled deeply. 'Not finding him isn't a result.'

Lamb got up and joined Bain at the whiteboard. 'Brian, we believe he's alive and is staying in Haddington. Assuming he killed Iain Crombie, Paddy Kavanagh is your number one suspect now, right?'

'Right.'

Lamb took a pause. 'If you're smart — and I know you can be — then you can use this to your advantage. Your objective is to solve this case, but if there's a dangerous killer who has returned then it represents a very real threat to the public. You can go to Jim Turnbull and get a bigger squad on this.'

'You've got a good point there. I'm due to meet Jim in twenty minutes. Had a right good mauling from him earlier. Looks like I've finally got something positive to talk about.'

Lamb patted his shoulder. 'Damn right you do. This is a chance to get back on top.'

'Who says I'm not?'

Lamb held up his hands. 'All I know is what I hear.'

'And what have you heard?'

'Just that Cargill has become the golden girl through here, right? She's got her hands full. This is a chance for Jim to have a golden *boy* — you.'

Bain stroked his moustache. 'I like your thinking.'

Cullen watched their old pals act. He leaned across to Murray. 'What's Lamb playing at?'

'No idea.'

Bain wheeled round to face Cullen. 'So Sundance, you were supposed to be back out with Irvine on Cargill's obbo. How come you were in Haddington?'

Cullen cleared his throat, trying to keep his cool. 'I accompanied DC Murray after he received the call about the sighting of Paddy Kavanagh.'

Bain shook his head. 'Always got an answer for everything,

haven't you?' He switched his glare to Lamb. 'Does this have anything to do with Fraser Crombie and Sundance getting hit with a brick?'

'What, you mean did Paddy do it?' Lamb thought it through for a few seconds, a clenched fist covering his lips. 'Well, it's certainly possible. Now we've got a sighting, it's an avenue we can investigate.'

'What about that boy Watson arrested?'

'We've interviewed him.'

'And?'

'We didn't charge him.'

'How come?'

Lamb's eyes darted around the room. 'Well, he obviously didn't assault Cullen given he was inside the housing estate when the attack occurred.'

'What about Fraser?'

Lamb folded his arms. 'Fraser didn't see his assailant. He merely spotted the suspect in the vicinity prior to the attack.'

'For crying out loud.'

Cullen raised a hand.

Bain scowled at him. 'Do you want to go to the bog or something, Sundance?'

'I'm just wondering if you want me to head out to see DS Irvine?'

'No. I'll sort Cargill out.' Bain shook his head. 'Did you get your train tickets sorted?'

Angela didn't look up. 'Holdsworth's just printing them for me.'

Lamb's forehead creased. 'Who's Holdsworth?'

'Turnbull's office manager.'

'Bit of a luxury, isn't it?'

'We've actually got proper crimes through here, Sergeant.' Bain let it settle for a few seconds. 'Right, I'm off upstairs. Can you lot try to stop anything else falling apart while I'm gone?' He strode off out of the room, slamming the door behind him.

Lamb sat on a chair, straddling it back-to-front. 'He doesn't exactly improve with age, does he?'

Cullen smiled. 'He's more like a mouldy tub of Philadelphia than a blue French cheese.'

'Think he'll get anywhere with Jim upstairs?'

'Who knows? He's been getting a pasting off Turnbull and Cargill for the last week or so. Maybe this is a chance for him to get one back.'

Angela joined them, leaning against the table near to Lamb. 'It's a chance to get Bain to take his swearing elsewhere.'

Lamb smiled at her. 'Good to see you again.' He looked her up and down. 'Did you hear any of that?'

'Hard to hear anything apart from you rams butting heads.'

Cullen nodded at the door, looking like it was still bruised from Bain's exit. 'You're acting a bit out of character'

'I reckon Bain might be a useful ally to have at the moment.' Lamb smiled. 'The force is changing. Who knows what we'll all be doing in a year's time. Us country cops need as many city allies as we can get.'

Cullen winked. 'Nothing to do with DI Cargill?'

Lamb looked away. 'There is that, I suppose.'

# 56

Cullen reached forward and poured another cup of decaf tea from the pot on the coffee table. He leaned back on the leather sofa. 'I'm just fed up with being saddled with him. He's an arsehole.'

Sharon took a sip. 'He's your arsehole, though. Get used to it.'

'All right for you, you get paired with someone competent.'

'Caldwell's okay.'

'Aye, well, she's junior. It won't stop me getting paired up with Irvine when he needs someone to do his work for him.' Cullen blew on his tea. 'I can just see Bain acquiring him now Turnbull has made his investigation current.'

'Be thankful Jim got the complaint to disappear.'

'You're right. At least I won't see him until I get back from Harrogate.' He glanced at the TV, some tedious celebrity show playing on mute. 'Thank God I'm not at the flat.'

'You really need to speak to Tom, you know?'

'I know. He'll no doubt be suffering withdrawal symptoms. It's a break in the Euro schedule today.'

Sharon lifted her left leg and placed it over his. She leaned over and kissed him.

He adjusted himself and pulled her close. He kissed her on the cheek and nibbled her earlobe, just how she liked it.

He whispered into her ear. 'I've got to get up early tomorrow.'

'Better take my time, then.'

She got up and led him through to the bedroom. 'Come on, you.' She pushed him back on the bed and started undoing the buttons on his shirt, her fingers clawing at the fabric.

Cullen reached over for her blouse. She slapped his hand. 'Wait.' She pushed him on his back and tugged his trousers off, chucking them on the bedroom floor. She yanked his trunks off. 'He's standing to attention.'

Cullen looked down. 'He's certainly ready.' He reached over to the bedside table and retrieved a condom. By the time he'd torn open the packet, she was naked.

She crawled up the bed, dangling her breasts over his cock. He reached down and put the condom on.

She slid on. Her hands gripped the bed frame above as she started gyrating on top of him, getting faster and faster, her breasts dancing in front of his face. Cullen felt her close up around him, clenching him tight.

She ground him hard, eyes closed. Cullen reached up and grabbed her breasts, massaging the nipples with his thumbs.

She buckled on top of him. 'God, God, God.'

Cullen started thrusting, his hands clawing her breasts. He spasmed as he filled the condom, endorphins striking his brain.

She rolled off and cuddled into him, heavily out of breath.

Cullen took the condom off, tying it off but keeping a hold of it. 'Wow.'

'Wow.' Her face was flushed and she looked blissful.

Cullen held the condom up, the sperm sliding to the bottom. He tipped it up again and watched it flow back. He looked over. 'Thought you were going to take your time?'

'Don't know what came over me.'

'I know what came over me.'

She slapped his chest.

Cullen laughed before rolling onto his side. 'I'm worried about how quickly you were on me there.'

'How do you mean? I thought you liked it rough?'

'I barely had time to get the condom on. I don't want to become a dad, you know?'

'Believe me, I don't want to become a mum.' Sharon grabbed his nipple. 'Besides, you're growing a lovely pair of boobs there.'

'That's why I let you go on top. They look better that way.'

She lay back in the bed and pulled the duvet over her. 'Good night.'

Cullen reached over and kissed her. He turned away from her, worrying about her aggression and lack of care.

# DAY 6

*Thursday*
*21st June*

## 57

Cullen stretched out his legs in the standard class carriage of the East Coast train, catching something fleshy. He glanced over at Angela. 'Sorry.'

She looked up from her book. 'Don't worry about it. We're both tall.'

'Right.'

Cullen took in the Northumberland countryside, the beautiful sandy beaches and the sprawling fields.

He checked his watch — just after half six. They'd managed to get a table to themselves and Cullen had covered it with the case file and was currently going through the old disappearance Frank Stanhope had worked on.

They pulled into a town Cullen didn't recognise. 'Where's this?'

Angela looked over. 'Berwick-upon-Tweed. It's okay.'

As the train pulled off from the station and started trundling across the Victorian railway bridge, he could see the town sprawl across the bay at the mouth of the river, anchored to an old seafront.

Cullen added it to the list of places to visit on a day trip. 'Are we in England, then?'

'Two miles in or something.' Angela laughed. 'Did you know Berwick was at war with Russia for a hundred and fifty years?'

'No?'

She leaned forward. '*He* told me. Something to do with how it historically switched between Scotland and England so many times that it was listed independently on the declaration of war for the Crimean. They left it out of the declaration of peace. They signed a peace treaty a couple of years ago.'

'That's pretty funny.' Cullen went back to scribbling in a notepad.

Angela looked up from her book. 'You're such a noisy writer.'

Cullen sat back and tossed his pen down. 'How can anyone be a noisy writer?'

'I've no idea, but you manage it.'

'What can I say, I'm an active thinker. I always need to jot things down and connect them.'

She arched an eyebrow. 'You do realise that's a characteristic you share with a certain individual we work with?'

'Right. Hopefully the only one...' Cullen took a deep breath and looked out of the window, the sun already rising in the sky. 'Can I go through some stuff with you?'

'Don't you ever take any time off?'

'Not really.'

She dropped her book to the table. 'Fine, go for it.'

He showed her his notepad. 'Here's my list of suspects.'

'Looks just like Bain's whiteboard.'

'Very funny.' He looked at the pad, starting at the top right of his mind map. 'This is in no particular order.'

'Fine, just get on with it.'

Cullen looked around the carriage. It was largely empty. The nearest passenger was a fat man in a suit battering a laptop with his headphones on.

Cullen spoke in an undertone. 'Okay. Paddy Kavanagh is now our prime suspect. He disappeared really close to Iain's death. I don't like coincidences.'

'Why would Paddy kill Iain?'

Cullen traced his arrows. 'He was a heavy drinker. I know from bitter experience that rational behaviour for the average piss artist is simply out of the question.' His finger moved down. 'The information we've got about the Tanner's Arms shows a violent man, one who is prone to getting barred but never for long.'

'It's not a lot for a prime suspect.'

'That's what I'm struggling with. The sighting of him at the old service station in Haddington has changed everything. The case has suddenly switched from an intriguing cold case into a live manhunt. Bain is using it to gain influence and officers and Turnbull's letting him.'

'Other than Paddy disappearing at the same time as Iain, what have you got indicating he has something to do with his death?'

'He could have killed him and run away?'

'You're clutching at straws, Scott. If so, why is he back?'

'You've got me there.' He looked at a different box. 'Doug Strachan was the previous favourite. Iain caught him stealing whisky.'

'Right.' Angela tapped the pad. 'When we spoke to him, he just laughed it off, right?'

'Right. Could there be something behind it?'

'Is there anything pointing to him doing it?'

'Maybe.' Cullen looked at the other boxes. 'That's pretty much it for him.'

'Right. Next.'

'Marion Parrott has been ostracised by the Crombie family.'

'You better not bring that shite up about her being a weak woman.' Angela folded her arms. 'I bet I can bench press more than you and Murray.'

Cullen held up his hands. 'I don't doubt it.'

'What's her motive?'

'There's a blood relation. Iain junior. She might think he was due to inherit the company.' Cullen still had an action to check the ownership.

'Is that enough?'

Cullen shrugged. 'It's plausible.'

'Really?' Angela rolled her eyes. 'You need some more evidence.'

'Agreed.'

'What about Fraser?'

Cullen looked around the boxes on the page. 'With Fraser and his old man, I just can't see clear motives.'

'What about the family power struggle?'

'That's just hearsay, right?'

Cullen thought about it. 'Yes and no. We've had it from Crombie and a few others. I don't see there being much in it.'

'Think about it then.'

'Right.' Cullen looked out of the window, trying to grasp hold of the strands of the case.

Angela took the pad. 'Let's take a step back, okay?'

Cullen stared at the file open on the table. 'I need to—'

She shut the file. 'Scott, why have you got me man marking you in bloody Harrogate?'

'Because Bain is an arse?'

Angela laughed. 'Very cute. No, because you've got a lead.' She tapped the file. 'Go through it again.'

Cullen took the pad back and looked through it. 'Iain met Mary-Anne Wiley at the front of a Spiritualized set at Glastonbury, no doubt off their heads on booze and pills. They clung to each other after, stayed on partying and delayed their return to the real world.'

'Go on.'

'The trail ran cold when Fraser returned on the second of July.'

'And he didn't report Iain missing until the ninth?'

'Right. The gap's probably explained by the fact this is before anyone had a mobile phone.'

'Possibly.'

'This time gap is really annoying me, though. Three weeks lost.'

'It's all from Fraser, though, isn't it? Has anyone backed up his statement?'

'He gave us the itinerary of their travel. Had ticket stubs for the festival. Iain had phoned his mother and Marion.'

'Okay.' She tapped the pad. 'Anything else on the girl?'

'There were a couple of sightings of Mary-Anne Wiley in Harrogate, in response to the national campaign.'

'What else?'

Cullen tapped his pen on the table. 'That's it. I've got nothing else on the sightings.'

'What about Stanhope's file?'

Cullen shook his head. 'Been through it.' He held it up. 'Nothing.' He checked through his notebook. 'Bollocks.'

'What?'

'Harvey was supposed to send the Avon and Somerset case file up. I haven't received it yet.'

'You should chase it.'

'Later in the day, maybe.'

'Yee-hah, Sundance.'

'Stop it.' Cullen tried to laugh it off. 'That was useful. You can tell you've been on detective training.'

'Gee, thanks.' She picked up her book again.

## 58

C ullen got off the train onto the busy platform, Angela lagging behind as she fiddled with her phone.

People milled about as he tried to find the exit.

Angela pointed at the signs. 'It's that way.'

He followed her out. 'It's just after nine and I'm already shattered.'

She tucked her book in her handbag. 'And we've got a long day ahead of us as well.'

Cullen gestured around the modern station. 'When we were on the train I read Harrogate was supposed to be nice. I expected an old country-style station.'

'You're a bit of a weirdo for your architecture.'

'It's not all boozing and shagging with me.'

'I really don't want to hear about your sex life, Scott.'

Out front a middle-aged police officer leaned against a squad car. 'DC Cullen?'

Cullen offered his hand 'Aye. This is ADC Caldwell.'

'PC Seth Neely.' His eyes crawled all over Angela before shooting back to Cullen. 'Can I see your warrant cards?'

'Really?' Cullen got his out. 'Here you go.'

Neely checked them both. 'Thanks. The brass have been on at me to make sure this is above board.'

Cullen pocketed it. 'Let me see yours.'

Neely peered at him for a few seconds before slowly shaking his head. 'If you want to be like that.' He got his out. 'Happy?'

'That'll do.'

Neely tapped the car. 'Let's get going.'

Cullen got in the back. Angela raised her eyebrows as she buckled up next to him.

Neely drove them through the streets of Harrogate, then through a wide and green park.

Cullen looked at Angela and murmured. 'It does look nice.'

Angela looked out of the window. 'This is like the Meadows.'

Neely looked back. 'What's that?'

'Just saying this is like a park in Edinburgh.'

'Right you are.'

Cullen texted Sharon — *Harrogate lovely. Fancy a dirty weekend here?*

They left the greenery, driving past a supermarket and a retail park before heading through a rough area of the town.

Neely pulled into an industrial estate, parking outside an unmarked building.

Cullen got a text back from Sharon. *You book it in then. Looking forward to it. xx*

Neely unfastened his seatbelt. 'Here we go.' He led them inside through a heavy security door, before signing them in at the front desk.

Cullen's mobile rang. He gave them an apologetic look and took the call, leaning against a wall.

'Is that Detective Constable Scott Cullen?' A male voice, young but deep.

'Yes, it is.'

'I need to speak to you.'

Cullen was struggling to place the voice. 'Can you tell me who you are?'

'I'll meet you in the Old Clubhouse in Gullane at eight tonight. You'll see me then.'

'Unless you stop all this cloak and dagger stuff, we're not meeting up.'

There was a pause. 'Fine, it's Iain Parrott.'

It clicked — the boy's voice was similar to his uncle and grandfather, though the accent was less refined. 'Marion Parrott's son?'

'I prefer to think of myself as Iain Crombie's son and heir. Can you meet me?'

Eight pm in Gullane felt a *long* time away. 'Fine, I'll see you there.'

Cullen turned back to face them.

Angela looked bored. 'Who was that?'

'Iain Parrott.'

'What does he want?'

'No idea. I've not told his mother about his father's body yet. Bain will no doubt give me a doing for it.'

'His mum said he'd become obsessed about his dad, right?'

'Right.' Cullen stabbed the appointment into his phone, setting a reminder.

Neely coughed. 'You pair done?'

Cullen pocketed his phone. 'Sorry, but you know how it is.'

'Don't I just.' Neely led them down a long corridor, deep into the bowels of the building. He nudged a door open with his foot. 'In here.'

Inside the room were six study desks, each with a pair of chairs and a lamp. There were no windows, just a flickering strip light. One of the desks at the back had a paper file on it.

'I've left it over there.' Neely handed them a key. 'Remember, you can make some copies on the photocopier next door, but the file stays here.'

Cullen scowled. 'You told me on the phone they'd taken all the photocopiers out of the building.'

Neely looked away. 'All but one, lad.'

'You've just wasted two train tickets.'

Neely shrugged. 'Not my job to photocopy.'

Cullen marched over to the desk and sat, readying himself for a tedious morning.

## 59

C ullen's pen bounced off the desk, before skidding across the floor. 'Buggery.'

Angela didn't look up. 'Wondered when that was going to happen. You've been huffing and puffing for the last hour.'

Cullen reached down to pick up the pen, then flicked through the few photocopies he'd shoved in the lever arch binder. 'This has been a complete waste of time.'

'You're only just realising that now?'

'Mary-Anne Wiley is as elusive as Paddy Kavanagh.' He pushed the folder to one side. 'I've gone through the file four times now. All I've done is made sure the expenses weren't totally wasted.'

Angela took off her glasses. 'We should probably compare notes, just to make sure we've not overlooked anything.'

'Right.' Cullen looked at his pad. 'I've got three recorded sightings of Wiley. Two in supermarkets and one in the train station. All were dead ends. You?'

'The same. I've been through the statements. They were pretty lengthy but, when I got into it, the detail around the actual sightings of Wiley were vague as hell.'

'This is a disaster.' Cullen drummed his fingers on the table, before checking the train time app he'd bought on the way down. 'Assuming we can get to York in the next hour, we can catch the next train to Edinburgh.' He glanced at his watch. 'Sod it, let's get back home.'

'Agreed.'

Cullen wedged the ring binder in his rucksack and left the file on the table. He locked the door behind them, before marching back down the long corridor, stopping at the front desk.

The guard looked up. 'Something wrong?'

'Looking for PC Neely.'

'I'll give him a call for you, then, lad.' The guard gave a wheezing cough then picked up a handset. 'That Scottish boy's looking for you. Aye. Okay, Seth.' He pointed out of the door. 'He's out having a smoke.'

Cullen thanked him, before heading out of the door.

Angela shook her head let out a sigh. 'Neely's clearly enjoying this.'

'He's a wanker.'

Neely was round the corner, smoking and chatting up a woman with blonde hair who didn't look like she worked for the police. He spotted their approach and tossed his cigarette in the gutter. 'Catch you later, Jackie.' He slowly walked over to meet them. 'That you done, then?'

'Aye.'

Neely nodded at the building. 'Best go lock the file away.'

Cullen held up the key. 'We need to catch the train back to Edinburgh, so I'd appreciate it if you could give us a run to the station first.'

Neely sniffed. 'I do have some of my own activities to do here.'

Cullen folded his arms. 'What have you been doing all morning then?'

'Get a taxi.'

'Look, we don't have time to get a taxi and then make our connection.'

Neely smirked. 'Right, lad. I'll drive you.'

# 60

The train lurched across the Tyne, stopping every hundred or so metres. Cullen looked down at the river, his phone clasped to his ear. 'That's not what I said.'

'You've found bugger all, Sundance.'

'We've managed to conf—'

Bain started shouting, so Cullen held the phone away from his ear.

The elderly couple sharing their table scowled at Cullen as Bain's swearing bled from the speaker. He got up and moved to the passageway. 'As I said, we've eliminated a potential line of inquiry.'

'I'll eliminate you, Sundance. So this Wiley bird wasn't found then?'

'Correct.'

'For crying out loud... Waste of a hundred and fifty quid.'

'You're not the one who had to sit on a train for three hours and then in a little room in Harrogate.'

'This was your idea, Sundance. Don't go looking for sympathy, okay?'

'Wouldn't dream of it.'

Bain paused for a few seconds — it sounded like he was drinking something. 'Murray was digging into Paddy again. Did you speak to the woman he was slipping a length to?'

'Elspeth McLeish?'

'If that's her name. Have. You. Spoken. To. Her. Yet?'

Cullen moved out of the way of the queue of passengers looking to disembark at Newcastle. 'No.'

'What do you mean, no?'

'When do you expect me to have done it? I've been in Yorkshire all day.'

'You've had this over a week. You need to prioritise your activities if you're ever to make a sergeant.'

Cullen felt the red mist descend. 'I do prioritise, *sir*.'

'Okay, you need to prioritise *differently*.'

'Any time you feel like writing the book of *Police Procedure According to DI Brian Bain*, then I'll happily read it.'

Cullen killed the call and stared out of the window, trying to calm himself. He returned to the table and threw his phone down. He received an angry look from the old man for his trouble.

Angela looked across the table. 'You'll regret that.'

Cullen inspected his phone, finding a small chip on the back. 'Shite.'

'How was he?'

'Usual Bain. It's all my fault. That sort of bollocks.' Cullen rubbed the chip. 'I needed to get off the call to Bain before I said something I'll regret.'

'You didn't hang up on him, did you?'

'Might have done.' The display on his phone lit up — Bain. He switched the ringer to silent and put it down again.

'You're a brave man, Scott.'

Cullen turned to look out of the window as they pulled out of Newcastle station, through yet another industrial part of the city, glass and steel reflecting in the sunlight.

He glanced at the phone — a green text message showed a waiting voicemail.

'What did Bain actually want?'

Cullen glanced over at Angela. 'He was chasing me about Elspeth McLeish. Suppose I'd better chase the receptionist at the distillery.'

'I bet that's not all you want to do to her.'

Cullen glared at her. 'Stop it.' He grabbed his phone and dialled.

'Hi, this is Dunpender Distillery.' It was Amanda. 'How can I help?'

'You remember I asked you about the woman who had the job before you? Elspeth McLeish?'

'Of course.'

'Have you got an address for her yet?

'I do. She lives in Garleton.'

Cullen jotted it down in his notebook. 'Thanks for that. I'd have appreciated if you'd have phoned me.' He ended the call.

'Charming.' Angela chuckled. 'Why do you need to speak to her?'

'Can't remember.' Cullen flicked through his notebook looking for her name. 'Doug Strachan mentioned her. Paddy Kavanagh was seeing her.'

'So why is Bain chasing it now?'

Cullen shrugged. 'We deprioritised the search for her after it became clear it was Iain Crombie in the barrel.'

'So he's just covering his arse?'

'Aye. The continuing ambiguity around Paddy means it could be as good a lead as any. I'll have to head out there when we get back.'

Angela picked up her book. 'I'm keeping well clear of you.'

# 61

'I'm just saying, Cullen. You could have got me one.'

Cullen blinked at Bain as he sipped a large Americano from Caffe Nero, watching Angela at the far end of the empty Incident Room. 'I thought you preferred the coffee from upstairs?'

'Forget about the coffee.' Bain prodded him on the chest. 'If I've told you once, I've told you a million times. You *do not* hang up on me.'

'With all due respect, I was on a busy train with you swearing at me. I'm not sure the Chief Constable would appreciate a complaint from members of the public about the conduct of one of his officers down the phone to a subordinate.'

Bain scowled at him.

Cullen gestured round the room. 'This case seems to have kicked off at last. Thought you'd be out in the field.'

'Aye, well, had a summons from upstairs.' Bain stroked his moustache. 'Got a meeting with Turnbull and the Ice Queen in ten minutes. I was hoping you'd turn up some magic from Yorkshire but you arsed it up again. Two tickets you've wasted on nothing.'

'You can't pin losing this case on me.'

Bain glared at him. 'Who said anything about losing the case?'

'Nobody, I was just saying.'

'If you hear one word about me losing this case, then you tell me, all right?'

'Fine. How's it been here?'

'Getting there. I've got Lamb and Irvine, plus a few others like that Buxton boy. Up to a head count of twelve. Of course, Turnbull and Cargill are all over this like a bad rash.'

Cullen decided to throw him a bone. 'I got an address for Elspeth McLeish.'

'Sundance, this is going to take a long time if I have to remind you to do every single action.' Bain shook his head. 'I don't want you wasting hours on it. Just speak to her.'

'Hang on, you chased me on this.'

'Murray was nipping my head about it, that's all.'

'Fine, I'll get on to it.'

Bain scowled at him. 'Are you sure? You look banjaxed.'

'I feel fine.' Cullen felt the caffeine starting to kick in.

Bain folded his arms. 'Did you get anything out of Marion Parrott when you spoke to her?'

Cullen stared at the ceiling. 'Shite. I haven't spoken to her. With all that Paddy stuff and then going to Harrogate, I haven't had time yet.'

'Well, speak to her when you're out that way. I'd do it first if I was you.'

'Will do.' Cullen didn't mention the call from Iain Parrott.

'Right, well, I'd best go and face the music. Keep yourself out of mischief.'

Mischief was exactly what Cullen had in mind.

## 62

The Drem station car park was a hive of activity as the 18.12 from Waverley to North Berwick arrived. The other passengers getting off at Drem ploughed past him, heading for some early evening sunshine in their gardens beneath the blue sky.

Cullen only clocked Murray's Golf when the headlights flashed. He wandered over and got in. 'Thanks for picking me up.'

'I had to give up a round at Luffness for this.'

'If you're talking about golf, then I really don't care.'

'It's not a problem. I gave it to a mate.' Murray pulled into a queue of traffic trying to get out of the station onto the main road. 'Will get it another time. Didn't want to face the wrath of Bain if I pissed off early.'

'Just a matter of not getting caught.'

'I'll take your word for it, if it's all the same.'

Murray inched forward, blocking a Range Rover pushing in. 'You look like shite, by the way.'

'I feel it.'

'How was your jolly to Durham?'

'It was Harrogate and it wasn't a jolly.'

'Where the hell is Harrogate?'

'North Yorkshire.'

'Bloody hell.' Murray chuckled. 'Wouldn't catch me doing that trip in one day. I'd make sure I got a night in a swanky hotel out of it.'

'With Bain you'd end up in a shitty B&B two towns away and no taxi allowance.'

Murray turned right onto the road to Gullane. 'So how was it?'

'That's my fifth train of the day. I was stuck with hundreds of commuters in an end carriage.'

'Why didn't you drive out here?'

Cullen exhaled. 'I'm already shattered, despite all the coffee I've had. Getting a twenty-six back to Portobello from Waverley will be better than driving.'

'You wuss.'

Cullen laughed. 'I learnt a long time ago not to drive when I'm this tired. I drove my old man's car off the road when I was seventeen. I'd been working on a building site for him. Early starts, brutal days and late finishes. I misjudged a corner like that one back there and ploughed the car through a fence. Mum made me find the farmer. I lost a week's pay.'

'You idiot.' Murray turned left at the end, managing to sneak through a gap in the traffic from North Berwick to Gullane. 'Why didn't you get ADC Caldwell to head out here with you?'

'You and I work well together, don't we?'

Murray laughed. 'She's told you to piss off, hasn't she?'

'Maybe.'

'Don't you worry about the amount of aggro between you and Bain?'

Cullen looked out of the window, across the green fields. 'He's like that with everyone.'

'Not exactly.' Murray headed into the outskirts of Gullane. 'It looks unprofessional, Scott.'

Cullen inspected his nails. 'I hadn't thought of that.'

Murray glanced over. 'I'd suggest keeping a lid on it. He might be unprofessional, no need for you to follow him.'

'I'll bear it in mind.' Cullen rubbed his fingers together. 'I've noticed you and McLaren sucking up to him.'

'Have you?'

'McLaren got Bain a coffee yesterday. You've been all 'yes, sir' and 'three bags full, gaffer'.'

'Bill told us to watch it with him. He got a bit of a shoeing off DI Webster for that court case.'

'Right. It all makes sense now.' Cullen spotted the turning for Marion's street. 'It's down here.'

Murray frowned. 'Here?'

'Aye.'

'Right.'

'What have you been up to while Angela and I were on our jolly?'

Murray pulled up at traffic lights and signalled left. 'Irvine's been running around telling everyone what to do like he's SIO. Not that I've noticed him do much himself, mind.'

'He does that.'

'So basically trying to fob him and Bain off. Getting nowhere finding Paddy.'

Murray pulled in a few doors down from Marion's house. The street was busy with a group of teenagers playing football.

Cullen nodded over. 'A couple of them look pretty decent.'

Murray laughed. 'Pulling off the sort of Messi tricks you see in a computer game advert is enough to impress you, is it?'

Cullen laughed. 'I can't stand all that shite.'

'Me neither.' Murray smiled at a couple of kids on bikes. 'Don't see that so much these days.'

'Yeah, I used to be out on my bike most nights in summer when I was growing up.'

'Edinburgh?'

Cullen shook his head. 'Dalhousie in Angus.'

'Right.' Murray stared into the distance, his forehead twitching. 'Had a case on this street recently. That assault.'

Cullen got out and savoured the evening for a few seconds. The sun was hovering over the hill at the Crombie end of Gullane but it would still be light for a few hours. The earlier rain had been a freak storm — typical for Scotland — and the pavements were almost dry again. There was the familiar smell of charcoal in the air.

He opened the gate. 'Shall we?' He marched up to Marion's front door and pressed the buzzer.

There was a noise from inside. Through the living room window, two small boys huddled in front of the sofa, watching TV.

Marion Parrott and her husband sat behind them. She had a dour expression as she got up for the door.

Murray was still waiting by the front gate, fiddling with his phone.

The door opened. Marion looked irritated and harassed. 'What is it?'

'We need to speak to you about—'

She cut over him, staring straight at Murray. 'Have you found my son's attacker yet?'

## 63

Marion picked up a mug from the patio table. 'Give me a minute. I need to get the boys' tea out of the oven.' She turned and went back inside, shutting the door firmly behind her.

A small chunky tabby squeezed through the cat flap.

Cullen stabbed a finger at Murray. 'Why didn't you tell me you were investigating an assault on her son?'

Murray closed his eyes. 'I didn't know, I thought you were going next door or something but you powered on without me.'

'What about when we got to the street? All that Messi shite? It would have been useful to know then.'

Murray rubbed his eyes. 'Look, I'm sorry, all right? Be thankful you've never done anything wrong.'

'Bring me up to speed before she comes back.'

'What's there to tell? He got assaulted coming home from the pub a few weeks ago. Got done from behind. Someone chucked a brick at him.'

Cullen reached behind his head and patted the scar, still tender. 'Like with me and Fraser Crombie?'

'Aye, similar. He got taken to Edinburgh Infirmary. Eight stitches. Ewan and I were assigned to it and we've drawn a total blank so far.'

'You've got nothing?'

'That's why I'm avoiding her.'

'What about the boy Watson arrested at Archerfield?'

'You heard Bill yesterday. Solid alibi for that night. We had to let him go.'

'Shite...' Cullen buried his head in his hands. 'You need to be honest with people.'

Murray raised an eyebrow. 'And this is coming from you?'

'Don't.'

The door shuddered open. Marion appeared, carrying a packet of cigarettes and her lighter. The little tabby decided to head back in. Marion called it Tinkle.

She came over and sat, glaring at Murray. 'So have you found my son's attacker yet or not?'

'No, I'm sorry.'

Cullen got out his notebook. 'I'm afraid that's not what we're here about.'

'Right.'

'Unfortunately, we've confirmed the body in the whisky barrel is that of Iain Crombie.'

Marion closed her eyes. She was silent for a few seconds. 'I knew this day would come.'

Cullen leaned over. 'Do you need any help? I can get a Family Liaison Officer out.'

'I'll be fine.' Her eyes glossed over as she lit a cigarette, inhaling deeply. 'I never thought he'd be so close. I thought he'd run away to Spain or South America, maybe even South Yorkshire. I didn't think he'd be in the storage cellar in his dad's distillery.'

'I understand this is difficult for you, especially after all these years of not knowing. We'd like to ask you a few more questions, if that's okay?'

She wiped tears from her eyes, her make-up smudging at the edges. 'Go on.'

'Can you tell us about the day Iain and Fraser left to go on this trip?'

'Okay.' She sat and took a few drags. 'You know, I don't remember him leaving. He'd been for dinner with his family the previous night in Garleton and they'd usually stay out late on these things. I was working in Edinburgh at the time so I got up early.'

'Was Iain there when you left?'

'I think so.'

'How certain are you?'

She shrugged. 'How certain are *you* about who you woke up with eighteen years ago?'

Cullen refrained from pointing he would have been twelve. 'I'm sure I would be pretty certain if it was the last night I'd spent with them.'

'I *think* my husband was in the bed that morning, but I wouldn't swear on it, okay?'

'Fine.' Cullen made a note to validate the story. 'Iain suffered an injury to his arm about six weeks before he was reported missing. Do you know what happened?'

She nodded through the fug of smoke. 'I was in Spain with my parents and my sister. When I got back he had this big scar.' She drew a line across her forearm. 'He said he got it from an accident at work. I couldn't get any more out of him.'

'So you don't know how he got it?'

'No.'

'Did you check with his work?'

'I said no.'

Cullen scribbled some notes. 'Another question. Is your son due to inherit a share of the company?'

Her nostrils flared. 'I'm sorry?'

'I'll repeat the question. Is your son due to inherit a share of Dunpender Distillery?'

'I refuse to answer that.'

Cullen exchanged a look with Murray — the only way they were finding out anything was by taking her into the station for an interview. 'It would be very useful if you could give us an indication.'

'No.'

'We can find out by other means.'

Marion took a deep puff, exhaling slowly. 'Whether my son owns part of the distillery is irrelevant here.'

'I'm not sure about that.'

She exhaled a wall of smoke. 'Well, you'll just have to use your *other ways*, because I'm not telling you.'

Cullen grimaced. 'Is your son going to the board meeting tomorrow?'

She tipped the end of the cigarette into the overflowing ash tray. 'If this is your *other ways*, then I'm disappointed.'

Cullen flicked through his notebook. 'He phoned me earlier. Wanted to meet up but didn't say why. Did you give him my number?'

Marion lit a cigarette. 'Your card was sitting in the kitchen. That'll be how he got it.'

'I wanted to ask about Iain's relationship with Fraser.'

'He sees his uncle every couple of months.'

'No, I meant between your ex-husband and his brother.'

'Oh.'

'I understand there was some sort of argument?'

'There had been a bit of bad blood between them, aye.'

'We believe Iain and his brother were prone to violence.'

'No more than most brothers.' Marion flicked some ash off. 'My youngest pair are a nightmare for it. Iain's that bit older than them so he doesn't get involved.'

'So there wasn't any particularly excessive violence?'

'It was just toy fights. Nothing too serious, it was like they were wee kids, even though they were both in their twenties.'

'I understand Fraser wanted to sell the company and Iain and his dad were against the sale.'

'That's right.' Marion flicked some ash. 'Scottish Distillers were sniffing around at the time, looking for small distilleries to buy. I think they were bought out by Scottish & Newcastle themselves a few years later.'

'Why did Fraser want to sell?'

'He reckoned they'd make a good amount of cash out of it. He said they should push for senior roles in Scottish Distillers, take the cash *and* the jobs.'

'So why were Iain and Alec so against it?'

'Iain and his dad had this romantic notion of being the biggest independent distillery in Scotland. That's turned out amazing, by the way.'

'So, what was their plan?'

Marion took a deep drag. 'Iain got a good degree at uni. Business Studies and Accounting. Him and Alec believed they could make the distillery work.'

'How?'

'No idea. Business isn't my strong point. It was something to do with Iain's degree.'

'What made the argument so frosty?'

'All Fraser had done was make whisky. He didn't have an alternative career. I think he felt desperate. If they didn't sell and that place fell apart, he'd have nothing.'

'And that was what they were arguing about?'

'Alec got really annoyed with Fraser's attitude. He demoted him.'

Cullen's eyes shot up. 'He *demoted* him?'

'Aye. Made him the chief cooper. He said it would teach him some respect.'

'When was this?'

'It'll be a few months before Iain disappeared.'

'How did Fraser take it?'

Marion let out a breath of smoke. 'He wasn't pleased, put it that way. Fraser could be a bit of a spoilt child at times.'

'What position was he before he was demoted?'

'Managing director.' Marion laughed. 'Those titles were a joke, by the way. Alec expected his boys to grow into them. He could be very hard like that.'

'Did Fraser ever talk about leaving the company?'

'No.'

'Why not?'

'I've no idea. Loyalty to his father?'

'Did Fraser ever act angrily about it or anything?'

Marion shook her head. 'Not that I can think of.'

Cullen made a note to dig deeper.

## 64

They sat in Murray's Golf outside Marion's house, the engine running and the air conditioning starting to cool the car.

Murray yawned, his jaw giving a little click at the widest point. 'Reckon there's anything in this demotion?'

'Could be. We should speak to Fraser about it.'

'Now?'

Cullen checked his watch — it was just after six. 'We'd better see Elspeth McLeish first, otherwise Bain will be heating up his poker ready to stick up my arse.'

'Right, you are.' Murray pulled off, heading back the way they'd came. 'Sorry if I was a bit of an arse in there.'

Cullen rummaged around in his rucksack, finding his copy of the whisky ledger. He took it out and started skimming through. 'I still think you should have told me earlier.'

'The boy's got a different name from his old man. And besides, nobody wrote Parrott up on the board.'

Cullen looked over. 'Marion Parrott is all over Bain's whiteboard.'

'*Marion* is. Her surname isn't.'

'When I told Bain, he made a shite joke about her surname.'

'Well, I wasn't there. I was shitting myself when you led us there, hoping it was someone next door or something.'

'Fair enough, I suppose.'

'Do you think she could have done it?'

'Maybe.' Cullen was searching the ledger more carefully now, his stomach juddering as Murray turned onto the road to Garleton.

Murray leaned forward, drumming on the steering wheel. 'Doesn't matter if Iain Parrott owned a share in the company. She just needed to *believe* her son would inherit the company to make it worthwhile, right?'

Cullen looked over. 'I can buy that. The times still don't stack up though.'

'We need to check that, don't we?'

Cullen took a deep breath. 'Assuming Iain was put there after Glastonbury, she could have found out about his infidelity and killed him.'

'You think Fraser told her?'

'Maybe.'

'I'm liking this.' Murray tapped the steering wheel again. 'She would need help and not because she's a woman, despite what Angela says.'

'Agreed. I've seen some brutal crimes perpetrated by women in West Lothian. Hell hath no fury and all that.'

'Think Bain would buy it?'

'Whether he buys it or not, it's going on that whiteboard.'

Cullen turned to a sheet that showed the company structure. He held it up. 'Here we go. Marion wasn't lying.'

'What's that?'

'A structure chart.' Cullen checked it in more detail. 'Looks like it was part of the due diligence for the Scottish Distillers takeover. Iain was chief executive, Alec chairman and Fraser was managing director.'

'Still want to speak to Elspeth first?'

## 65

M urray pulled in on the high street, not far from the police station. Between the Starbucks and the McDonalds was a dark blue tenement door which matched the number for Elspeth McLeish. 'This is it.'

They got out and Cullen pressed the buzzer.

Murray thumbed at the door. 'Keep your hands off her. I know your reputation.'

'I've got a reputation?'

'Aye.' Murray smirked. 'Somebody was asking where Shagger was. Turned out it was you.'

Cullen pressed the buzzer again. 'I've got enough nicknames as it is.'

'What about you and Eva Law? Little knee trembler in the stationery cupboard back in January? Got a bit aggressive for her, did you?'

'Did Lamb tell you that?'

'I can't remember.' Murray shrugged. 'Is it true? She was tidy.'

Cullen ground his teeth. 'Of course it's not true. I've got a girl-friend and I told her that. She was flirting with me and I had no interest in her.'

'Just saying what I heard.'

'You got a thing for the receptionist at Dunpender then? Amanda?'

Murray grinned. 'We'll see. I asked her for her number and she gave me it. Still not called her.'

'Well, good luck.'

The door intercom sparked to life, the voice crystal clear. 'Hello?'

Cullen leaned forward. 'Is that Elspeth McLeish?'

'It's Elspeth Murison. I used to be Elspeth McLeish. Can I ask to whom I'm speaking?'

'Detective Constables Scott Cullen and Stuart Murray. We need to ask you a few questions.'

'Very well.' The intercom buzzed and the door clunked.

Cullen pushed it open and climbed the stairs. A curvy woman in her early fifties stood at the top. She had platinum hair and pronounced cheekbones — Cullen imagined she must have been quite something in her twenties.

Cullen showed her his warrant card.

Elspeth carefully inspected it, before handing it back. 'If you'd like to come through.'

The flat was palatial, like the sort of Manhattan apartment in a Woody Allen film, lots of intersecting corridors and wide halls.

She took them to a living room, gesturing for them to sit across from her armchair. 'Now, how can I help you?'

Cullen got out his notebook. 'We'd like to speak to you about one Paddy Kavanagh, who we believe worked with you at Dunpender Distillery.'

She leaned forward on the sofa, her tight blouse pushing her breasts together into a robust cleavage. 'My husband is in the other room. I would appreciate if you kept your voice down.'

'Is that because of your relationship with Mr Kavanagh?'

'Partially.' She scowled. 'Has something happened?'

'We're running an inquiry into a body found at the distillery.'

Her eyes widened. 'Do you think it's Paddy?'

Cullen shook his head. 'No. It's not Mr Kavanagh. We did, however, receive an anonymous tip-off that he's back in the area.'

She held a hand to her mouth. 'Oh my goodness.'

'Has he made contact with you?'

'Gracious, no. I would have gone straight to the police.'

'Why would you go to the police?'

She licked her lips. 'Because he's been missing so long.'

'And no other reason?'

She shook her head.

Cullen jotted it down. 'We'd like to obtain some background on him, if that's okay?'

She settled back, crossing her muscular legs. 'What do you want to know?'

'How would you describe your relationship with Mr Kavanagh?'

'We were lovers for a while.' Her eyes went misty, staring into the middle distance.

'And you both worked at Dunpender Distillery?'

'He worked on the whisky, while I practically ran the place. That family was hopeless at admin. It was a recipe for disaster. Their stock checks were all over the shop. Barrels missing, barrels found.'

'Why did you leave if you ran the company?'

Elspeth smoothed down her tights. 'In the end, I'd just had enough of it. It was a frustrating business to run, you know. Fortunately, I met my husband. He earns enough from his art business to take me on part-time.'

Murray cleared his throat. 'What can you tell us about Mr Kavanagh's disappearance?'

'It broke my heart.' She looked at the floor and blinked away a tear. 'I was thirty at the time and I thought maybe Paddy was the one. When he disappeared it just destroyed me.' She looked back at Murray, her eyes moist. 'I had such hopes.'

'I'm sorry to hear that.' Murray scribbled something in his notebook. 'Did you drink with Paddy at the Tanner's Arms?'

'I drank a lot more in those days.' She paused for a moment. 'Paddy was in there every night.'

'And were you?'

'Not as often, but fairly frequently.'

'We understand Mr Kavanagh had a tempestuous relationship with the other patrons of the bar.'

'There was a bad crowd in that place.' She tugged the collar on her blouse. 'Thank God it's closed.'

Murray looked up. 'Did Paddy ever get in trouble there? Fights, threats, that sort of thing?'

Elspeth pushed her bottom lip out for a few seconds, before

shaking her head. 'Not that I'm aware of, certainly.'

'Did Mr Kavanagh get on well with the Crombie family?'

'Why do you ask?'

'Paddy worked for them.'

'I didn't have much to do with that side of things but he worked hard by all accounts.'

Murray narrowed his eyes. 'He never fell out with either brother?'

'They were friends as far as I'm aware.' She twirled a strand of hair round a finger. 'From time-to-time Paddy took them to the Tanner's 'to experience real life' as he used to say.'

'Was that just Iain?'

She shook her head. 'Fraser usually went as well. Alec sometimes, too.'

Murray spent a few seconds writing a note.

Cullen decided to alter their approach. 'You were acquainted with both brothers, is that right?'

'Yes, I was. I dealt with both of them several times a day.' She looked away. 'Typical boys. My two nephews are the same, always at each other's throats but you can see they love each other really.' She stared at the floor. 'Of course, I never had children of my own.'

'Was there anything particularly violent?'

She shook her head. 'They were just arguing with each other all the time. Mostly about the distillery's future.' She laughed, cold and devoid of humour. 'Of course, anyone who knows that place will tell you the only person in charge of its destiny is Alec Crombie.'

'We understand Fraser was demoted as part of a restructure.'

She let out a breath. 'That's true. Alec made me write up the structure for the takeover.'

'Scottish Distillers?'

'That's correct.'

'And how did Fraser take it?'

She looked away. 'Not well.'

'In what way?'

'Just disappointed, I suppose. Fraser's a strong silent type, you know?'

'So he wasn't angry about it?'

'He was never particularly angry about anything. That was

Iain all over. Fraser knew how to wind him up. No, he just seemed to take it in his stride and get on with it after a while.'

'Were you well acquainted with any of the other workers there? Eric Knox? Doug Strachan?'

She shifted on her seat. 'Doug was a big friend of Paddy's. They both were but Eric's only friend was the drink. I occasionally see him staggering down the high street, a blue carrier bag full of whisky in his hand. I meet up with Doug for lunch on occasion. He still works there, you know, even after, well...'

'Even after what?'

'I really shouldn't say.'

Cullen gestured for to continue. 'Please do.'

She tugged a lock of hair. 'Do you know that Iain caught Doug stealing whisky?'

'We're aware of that, yes.

'There were no charges brought against him, but it was common knowledge.'

'How did it affect Mr Strachan?'

'It took him a while to rebuild his pride after that. He was a bit of a mess.' She sniffed. 'This was about the time Paddy disappeared and I wasn't in a good way myself. I wasn't able to give him any support. He just fell apart.'

'In what way?'

She fingered an earring. 'I remember seeing him through the window of the Tanner's, sitting at the bar drinking on his own. He was staring into space and his lips were moving, so I went inside.'

'What was he saying?'

'He was talking about killing.'

'Killing something?'

'He just snapped out of his trance when I sat down.'

'Not killing someone?'

She looked up at the ceiling. 'I just heard him say killing.'

Cullen underlined it four times. 'When was this?'

'I can't recall, I'm afraid. It was after Paddy went missing, as I say.'

Cullen looked at Murray, who just shrugged. 'Thanks for your time, Mrs Murison. We'll show ourselves out.'

Cullen waited for Murray to shut the door behind them. 'We really need to speak to Strachan.'

## 66

M urray tugged hard on the steering wheel, pushing his Golf over the railway bridge as they headed towards the distillery. 'What do you think he meant by 'killing'?'

'I've no idea.' Cullen gripped the grab handle above the door. 'Doesn't sound good, does it?'

'Could be making a killing.'

'Could be.'

'Or killing someone.'

Murray overtook a cyclist wearing a suit halfway down the hill. 'That must make Strachan suspect number one.'

'I'm sure Bain would be doing lots of underlining on his whiteboard just now.'

'If we'd told him.'

'Don't start.'

They turned off just after the bend for Dunpender, passing the metal sign for the farm swaying in the evening breeze. 'Bain was saying just how much of a game-player you are.'

'He can talk.'

Murray pulled into the busy car park, struggling to get a space. 'Must have a function on.'

'Even after Crombie's son's body has just been found?'

'Crombie's a businessman if nothing else.'

They got out and hurried across the gravel to the entrance.

Cullen opened the heavy oak door. 'Is your girlfriend on tonight?'

Murray ignored him.

In the reception, an elderly security guard sat behind the desk.

Cullen flashed his warrant card. 'We need to speak to Doug Strachan.'

The guard checked a sheet of paper. 'He's left for the evening.'

Cullen looked at Murray. 'What do you want to do?'

'Well, we've been to his flat and he's not here.'

'Probably in the pub.'

'Given we're here, let's speak to Alec Crombie.'

'Mr Crombie's upstairs, lads.' The guard pushed a clipboard over. 'If you'll just sign in.'

Cullen filled it in for both of them. 'We don't have to do this when Amanda's here.'

'Do I look like Amanda, son?'

They walked past the bar, a din emanating from the packed room. Cullen looked in — no sign of Doug Strachan.

Upstairs, Crombie's office door was open. He slumped in his chair, wistfully looking out of the window into the blue skies above the Scots pines.

Cullen knocked on the door frame.

Crombie turned around, sighing when he saw who it was. 'Haven't you had enough pleasure from taunting me?'

Cullen gritted his teeth. 'Believe me, it gives us no pleasure at all to discover it was your son in the barrel.'

Crombie looked at the desk. 'I find that hard to believe.'

'I mean it.' Cullen sat in front of Crombie. 'You have our deepest sympathies.'

'Well, I'm sure I'll see you at the funeral whenever you find it in your hearts to release Iain's body.'

'I'm sure you can understand there's a significant amount of analysis we require to undertake. It may be a while.'

Crombie picked up a document, stared at it for a moment, then casually tossed it aside. 'Very well.'

Cullen inspected the documents scattered over the desk, papers for the following day's board meeting. A bound document showed it was scheduled for noon.

'I still haven't got access to my barrels.'

Cullen got his notebook out. 'I understand your frustration. It's unlikely we'll lift the embargo until we've either secured a conviction or deemed the case unresolved.'

Crombie looked to the side. 'If it's not about my barrels, why are you here?'

'We're investigating a few leads into your son's murder. We'd like to speak to Doug Strachan.'

'He left at the back of five, I'm afraid.'

'Do you know where he's gone?'

'He'll be off to the pub, I expect.' Crombie adjusted his kilt. 'Why do you want to speak to him all of a sudden?'

Murray sat forward. 'Do you know anything about Mr Strachan talking about killing something?'

'Killing?' Crombie looked across his desk. 'I've no idea, I'm afraid. Maybe stopping drinking?'

'We have it on good authority that Mr Strachan had talked about murdering someone.'

Cullen glared at Murray — he was stretching it a bit.

Crombie's eyes widened. 'I've no idea what you mean.'

'You don't know who he might have been referring to?'

Crombie leaned forward and gripped the desk. 'Are you suggesting Doug killed Iain?'

'It's possible.'

Crombie shook his head. 'I don't think Doug is a murderer. He likes a drink and his punctuality is less than adequate but he's a good man. Any suggestion to the contrary is pure nonsense.'

'Were you aware Doug Strachan was stealing whisky?'

Crombie gave a slight nod. 'Iain told me.'

'And what was your reaction?'

Crombie leaned back in his chair. 'I was torn. First, I wanted to sack him, to make an example of him and stop anyone else thinking of doing it. But, of course, Doug was central to the process here. He would have been irreplaceable.'

'That's not what your son thinks.'

Crombie smiled. 'Fraser didn't really know the old Doug. He was a whirlwind and a perfectionist. He would put everything into making our whisky exceptional. He was the power behind the throne here.'

Cullen was surprised by his sudden humility. 'So Iain and Doug got on fairly well?'

Crombie stared at Cullen for a few seconds before speaking. 'Yes, other than the incident with the whisky. They used to go for drinks in Garleton every other week. There was a pub Doug and Paddy Kavanagh were regulars in.'

'Did anyone else join them?'

'Fraser and myself from time to time.'

'Did anything untoward ever occur?'

Crombie laughed. 'Just the occasional game of darts.'

'Why did you decide not to discipline Mr Strachan?'

'Who said anything about not disciplining him? We had a management restructure at the time and I moved Fraser into Doug's old role as master cooper and gave Doug a more generic role. He lost some of his salary as well.'

'How was Mr Strachan's relationship with Fraser after you gave him his job?'

'Doug had a perfectly amicable relationship with him. Still does.'

Cullen checked his notebook again. 'Why was Fraser demoted in the structure?'

'He wasn't demoted.'

'Managing director to master cooper looks very much like a demotion to me.'

'If you knew anything about the craft of whisky, you'd understand how key the role of cooper is.'

'Did his demotion have anything to do with the argument you had with Fraser about the direction of the company?'

Crombie stared at his desk. 'I don't see how that's pertinent to your investigation.'

Cullen leaned back on the chair. 'Let us be the judge of that.'

'We'd had a big disagreement about the future of the company. Fraser wanted to sell up, Iain and I wanted to stay independent.'

'Was there an offer on the table?'

'There was. Scottish Distillers.'

'Just them?'

'At the time.' Crombie ran his finger round the rim of the glass. 'As you know, Diageo are sniffing around just now. We've got a board meeting tomorrow to discuss our strategy.'

Cullen underscored it three times. 'How had this argument affected your sons?'

Crombie leaned on his elbow. 'Iain found it difficult being at war with Fraser. They were so close.'

'But they managed to resolve their disagreement?'

'I did. I was the peace broker in this. We had a family meal — the boys, my late wife and I.' Crombie looked away. 'Iain disappearing broke her heart. She passed away in 1998. Cancer.'

'I'm sorry to hear that.'

Crombie crossed his legs, showing their wiry grey hairs, the kilt mercifully staying in place. 'That was the last time I saw Iain. It was the day before they left for Glastonbury. It had been touch and go whether they actually went.' He got to his feet. 'Now if you don't mind, I've got to play Master of Ceremonies downstairs.'

'Is your son still here?'

'He'll be in the cooperage I expect.'

## 67

C ullen stopped at the bottom of the stairs, just by the door to the cooperage. 'Why did you mention Strachan talking about killing someone?'

Murray folded his arms. 'You were just going round in circles.'

Cullen's hand tightened on the door handle. 'Think you can keep that little nugget from Fraser Crombie?'

'Whatever. You lead this, given how you're a higher rank than me and everything.'

'Aye, very good.' Cullen paused. 'Look, if I adjust my tie, can you ask the question? Good cop style.'

'Fair enough, boss.'

Cullen opened the door and entered the cooperage.

Fraser Crombie sat on a wooden chair clawing the rim off a barrel. His eyes narrowed as they approached. 'Evening.'

Cullen nodded towards the barrel Fraser was stripping. 'We've just confirmed the body is your missing brother. You don't seem to be too upset.'

'I've got nothing else to do.' Fraser gave a slight shrug of the shoulders. 'This place is my life. I've got work to do and it helps clear my head. What are you two after?'

Cullen leaned back against a workbench. 'We have a few questions we wouldn't mind answers to.'

'Fire away.'

Cullen flipped through his notebook, more to intimidate than for retrieving information. 'What happened with your demotion?'

'Excuse me?'

Cullen handed him the organisation structure he'd found in the ledgers. 'This was in early '94.'

Fraser laughed and tossed it on the table. 'That company structure was just a show for the prospective purchasers.'

'Really?'

'Aye, it was. Just my old man and his vanity. Nothing more, nothing less.'

'You were demoted, though, weren't you?'

'Of course I wasn't.'

'Well, you were fairly senior here before, weren't you?' Cullen picked up the sheet. 'Says you were managing director?'

'How could I have been a managing director? I was twenty-one with some 'O' Levels and no experience of running a company. I used to make barrels with Doug Strachan, when he was sober enough to teach me. I was never a managing director.'

'This says you were.'

'Don't read too much into that structure chart. Dad did it when Scottish Distillers first approached us. He wanted us to look like a big company, trying to frighten them off. We were anything but.'

'You weren't angry at being demoted?'

Fraser held up his claw hammer. 'If I was angry at anything, it was at being stuck working here.'

'It's the family business, though.'

'It is, but there's no future here. We haven't invested in new technology and we haven't trained people up in the old ways. We've just kept my old man in a high standard of living.'

'Do you stand to take over the business when he dies?'

Fraser laughed, then attacked the barrel again, quickly tearing the rim off. 'Hardly. I'm certainly not inheriting the whole business. His will has strict terms. As far as I know, I get five per cent of the company. I've no idea what happens to the rest.'

'I would have thought your dad would have been keen on keeping everything in the family.'

'He's made it clear many times that I won't get any special favours or anything.' Fraser hacked at the rim. 'He's into his tough love.'

'This was why he demoted you?'

Fraser raised his hands. 'Fine, it's when I was demoted, if that's what you want to believe.'

'Why didn't you go and do something else?'

Fraser glared at him. 'Like what? I have no skills or qualifications.' He shrugged. 'I like the work. I like making barrels and I like making whisky. I'm proud of what I do. Not many people can drink high quality whisky they made themselves. I'm just angry it's such a bloody pigsty. We could be organised.'

'Wasn't Iain's argument that he should organise it?'

'Aye. Him and his degree. Disappearing like that left us in limbo. We hadn't sold out and Dad doesn't have a clue how to run this place. Elspeth tried, but she got fed up.'

Cullen tightened his tie.

Murray cleared his throat. 'Someone overheard Mr Strachan talk about killing or maybe a killing. Do you know what that might have been?'

Fraser stared at the barrel for a few seconds. 'No idea. Sorry. He does like a flutter, though. Could be gambling. He always talked about making a killing with Paddy.'

'That's interesting.'

Fraser put his hammer down. 'He was a man of many vices.'

Cullen picked up a hammer off the workbench and played with it. 'You mentioned earlier about Strachan being threatened with the sack by your brother. We spoke to him and he denied it.'

'That figures. My brother's body turns up, of course he's going to deny it.'

'He did admit to getting caught. He also admitted to being an alcoholic.'

'And?'

Cullen lay the hammer down. 'He said he had other offers of work if he left here.'

'And you believe him?'

'Do you want me to check with the other distilleries?'

Fraser laughed. 'There's nobody left alive who would even remember him let alone employ him.'

Cullen looked at the barrel he was fixing up, dated *13/06/1992*. He tapped it with his foot. 'Is this for the next batch?'

'Aye. No idea where we'll put it until you lot let us at this year's batch.'

'You and Iain were at Glastonbury when the barrel Iain was in was filled, weren't you?'

'Aye, we were.'

'How do you think Iain ended up in there?'

'I don't know.'

'Surely, he must have come here first rather than going to see his wife?'

Fraser shrugged. 'I'm not an expert in this. My brother was a dreamer. I've absolutely no idea what he was up to. He was besotted with that girl. Marion was probably the last person he wanted to see.'

'Why come here though?'

'Iain loved this place.' Fraser picked up a rag from the back of the chair and cleaned his hands. 'Unless you've got any other questions, I really wouldn't mind getting home. I've got a busy day tomorrow.'

## 68

They sat in Murray's Golf in the car park. The front door opened as the bar emptied, scores of punters heading to cars.

Cullen nodded over at them. 'Wonder how many of them are still within the limit?'

'They're all in pairs at least. Designated drivers, I suppose.' Murray pointed at Fraser as he got in his SUV. 'Shall we tail him?'

'What's the point? It's Strachan we need to speak to.'

'Is he the killer?'

'When we got here, I would have put money on it. If you offered me an each way bet, anyway.'

Murray laughed. 'What about now?'

'Now, I just don't know.' Cullen paused. 'We've got a reference to killing when Strachan was drunk from a woman who liked a drink as much as he did. He could have been talking about anything — killing the business, making a killing — not about killing Iain Crombie.'

Murray scratched his chin, the stubble making a rasping noise. 'If it's not Strachan, then who else is there?'

'Fraser?'

Murray tossed his car key in his hands a few times. 'Could work, I guess. Those brotherly fights. Then again, they seem to have made up before they went to Glastonbury.'

'There's still the problem of the timing. We're a month out on those barrels.'

'So they're a month out. Big deal.' Murray put his key in the ignition. 'You want a tenner each way on Paddy, then?'

Cullen chuckled. 'I think so. Two disappearances in a month is a hell of a coincidence.' He thought it through. 'He had to lay in wait for a month or so until Iain got back from Glastonbury. He disappeared and then waited. It doesn't stack up.'

'Maybe he was trying to throw us off the scent?'

'Someone's up to something like that here.'

'I still think Paddy's the most likely possibility we've got.'

'I just don't know what to make of this sighting of him yesterday.'

Murray reached over and prodded Cullen's wound. 'Attacking you, Fraser and Iain Parrott. Maybe he's decided the time's right to get some revenge?'

Cullen looked out of the window, watching the security guard shut the gates after the last car had left, cigarette in his mouth. 'Maybe you're right.'

Cullen's phone beeped — he took it out and checked.

He'd just missed the meeting with Iain Parrott.

## 69

Murray pulled into the car park outside the Old Clubhouse, a pub in Gullane on a green just off the main street.

Behind a low wall was an outside seating area — despite the sun, only two tables were occupied. One had two whippet-thin men in their thirties sitting beside road bikes, nursing pints of lager in elaborate glasses.

Iain Parrott sat at the other table, scowling at his mobile.

'Wait here.' Cullen opened his door. 'He's all cloak and dagger about this. I half expect him to hand over some microfilm or some shite like that.'

Murray laughed. 'Well, double oh seven, if you need any field help, I'll be... shite, I don't know. Who did Sean Bean play in that one he was in? Wasn't he a goodie?'

'He looks really pissed off so the Bond trivia will have to wait.' Cullen got out of the Golf and headed over. As he approached, Parrott evaded eye contact.

Cullen sat opposite him. 'Hello, Iain.'

'You're late.'

'I'm a police officer on an active investigation, Iain, it's the nature of the beast.' Cullen gestured at the pint glass on the table, full of cola. 'Can I get you another?'

'No, I'm good.'

Cullen looked through the window. It was busy inside and he figured he'd manage to get away without buying a drink. He looked Parrott in the eye, trying to get the measure of the boy. 'What do you want to talk about?'

'Is it Dad in the barrel?'

'It's Iain Crombie. I don't know if he's your dad or not.'

Parrott looked up into the night sky. 'Mum told me he was my dad when I turned seventeen. She said I deserved to know the truth. I like Craig, don't get me wrong, but he's not my real father.'

'He wasn't much older than you when he died. You weren't even born.'

'I've been convinced for months he was killed. Mum and my grandfather and my uncle have all been living in this fantasy he might appear next week out of the blue. Ta-da!' Parrott took a long drink. 'I *knew*.'

Cullen was wary of the boy already. He'd dealt with enough zealots to know he had to be careful. Everywhere zealotry went, bad stuff followed.

Parrott wrapped his hands around the glass and leaned over the table. 'It was a relief when Mum told me you'd found him.'

'Iain, you called me this morning. I didn't tell her till a couple of hours ago.'

'I know. I found your card and I wanted to speak to you anyway.'

'What about?'

'I want to find who killed my dad and I want justice.' Parrott wiped at a tear forming in his eye. 'I've lost a father. I'm seventeen and I should have had all that time with my dad and not Craig.'

'Craig's been your father. He'll continue to be your father, whether he's a blood relative or not. He's fed you, clothed you, given you everything you need. You need to make sure he's not excluded just because of what you've learnt. It doesn't change what you had or what you've still got.'

'I hear what you're saying.' Parrott looked at the table, drummed his fingers on top of a notepad. 'The reason I wanted to speak to you is I think I'm onto something with Dad's disappearance.'

Cullen didn't take his eyes off the pad. 'Go on.'

'It's probably nothing.'

'What is it?'

'I'll tell you when I know for sure.'

'Why don't you tell me now?'

Parrott shrugged. 'I just want you to know I'm onto something.'

A wave of fatigue hit Cullen — he'd had enough of the boy. 'So you phone me and meet me but you're not telling me what you've got?'

'I don't want to waste police time if it's nothing.'

'I can take you down the station if you want?'

'Listen, I'm sorry.' Parrott took a drink. 'It's just I'm, I don't know, a bit messed up by what's happened. A year ago I thought Craig was my dad, then I find out I've got a real dad. When I phoned you I thought I might be able to help find him. Now I find out he's dead I just don't know what to do.'

'It's okay to feel confused, Iain. Could your information help our investigation?'

'I don't think so.'

'Let me know if it becomes something.'

'I will do.'

Cullen got to his feet. 'Are we done here?'

'I'll call you if anything comes up.'

'Fine.' Cullen marched back to Murray's Golf, gleaming in the sunlight.

Murray looked up from his mobile as he got in. 'Turns out Sean Bean was double oh six.'

'He was a baddie, though.'

'He *was* a goodie.' Murray tapped his phone. 'I should have said I'll be Felix Leiter. He was the CIA agent in a couple of films.'

'Now who's sounding like Bain?'

Murray looked over. 'What did he want?'

'Nothing. He's just a confused kid.'

'So, what now?'

'Shall we try Strachan's flat again?'

## 70

Murray held the buzzer for longer than Cullen thought necessary. 'I don't think he's in.'

Cullen took a step back and looked up at Strachan's flat on Garleton High Street. Another wave of nausea hit him. 'Bollocks to it. I need to head back to Edinburgh.'

'I'll run you back to Drem so you can get the train.'

Murray got in first and started the engine, giving it a bit more throttle than he should. He tore off through the town. 'Seven a.m. briefing at Leith Walk tomorrow, right?'

'Aye. I'll enjoy the extra half an hour in bed.'

'Bastard.'

Murray turned right onto the main road, before shooting into Drem train station. 'Oh shite. The train's early.'

Murray pulled in at the front, the opposite side from the train.

Cullen shot out of the car and raced up the steps. At the top, the train hissed and pulled off. He closed his eyes.

'Bollocks.'

He caught his breath and trudged back to Murray's car.

Murray turned the engine off. 'Sorry about that, mate.'

'It's not your fault.' Cullen laughed. 'I thought of doing an Indiana Jones as it went off.'

'I wouldn't if I were you. Those things will clear a ton between here and Longniddry.'

Cullen checked his watch. Half eight. 'When's the next one?'

'Another hour.'

'Right.' Cullen looked across the car park. 'Fancy a pint?'

'Aye.'

'As long as you drive me back here.'

'I'll even make the train next time.'

## 71

Cullen walked up to the bar, the smell of steak and chips reminding him he hadn't eaten since a pair of Scotch eggs at Waverley.

The barman looked up. 'What can I get you?'

'Is the kitchen still open?'

'Sorry, pal. It's just shut.'

Cullen looked at the taps, finding the standard offering of a premium lager, a lager, a heavy and the ever-present Guinness. 'Two pints of Kronenburg and two bags of Kettle Chips.'

'Nine twenty, mate.'

Cullen paid.

The barman gave him his change. 'I'll bring them over.'

Cullen wandered to the table in the window Murray had acquired. He tossed the crisps down, then yawned as he undid his tie. 'I'm so tired.'

'You've been a busy boy.' Murray tore the crisps unevenly down the seam.

Cullen took a handful from his own bag. 'I hate people doing that.'

'Yet another pet hate of yours. I should write a book on them.'

The barman brought their tray over.

Murray chewed. 'Do you think we're any further forward?'

Cullen took a long drink of lager, relishing the hit of alcohol. 'Doesn't really feel like we are.'

'I think we've got four clear suspects.'

'Four vague possibilities, you mean.'

'Whatever. That's still people we need to eliminate. That's still work.'

Cullen took another drink and looked across the pub to the flat-screen TV, blasting out a football match. 'It's taken us nine days to get this far, Stuart. I can see this taking another nine to get nowhere.'

'Who's your favourite?'

'Paddy at the moment. But it's not exactly odds-on. What about you?'

When Murray didn't answer, Cullen looked up. He was staring out of the window. 'Look.'

Across the high street, Lamb walked hand in hand with Angela Caldwell, a good two inches taller than him.

'Jesus...' Cullen was tempted to hammer the window. 'Did you have any idea?'

Murray shook his head. 'Me and Ewan were bantering with him about it this morning. Didn't know it was actually *true*, though. Christ.'

'Thought Bill lived in Gifford?'

'He bought a flat just off the high street here. Think he's renting his house out.'

Cullen watched as they carried on down the street, oblivious to being watched. 'That's not something I expected to see.' He took another big drink of lager, now well under the halfway mark.

'Slow down, Scott. We've got ages.'

'There's no way I'm missing that train.' Cullen finished his crisps. 'Unless you want to give me a lift back to Edinburgh?'

'Aye, piss off.'

'Drink up, then.'

Murray laughed, then his face set into a frown. 'Sorry for all that shite about Iain Parrott. You were right. It should have gone on Bain's magic whiteboard earlier.'

'Don't worry about it.' Cullen checked his watch — twenty-five minutes to go. 'Was it the same as my attack?'

'Doctor said a blunt object. Could have been anything, though. Length of pipe, a hammer, a brick. She couldn't say.'

'Is Gullane that sort of town?'

Murray shrugged. 'It has been known, but once every five years or so. It's not like Tranent or Musselburgh.'

'That's three attacks in a short space of time, now.'

'Yeah.'

Cullen looked back out of the window. He saw a man stagger up the road, totally out of his skull. 'I've not been that pissed since I was a student.'

'Really?'

'Okay, maybe a couple of times.'

'Takes me back to being in uniform. Picking up some random pisshead on the street.'

'Tell me about it.' Cullen took another drink. 'I was based in Bathgate for a few years.'

'Rough.'

'I take the piss out of Bain about Bathgate but it's not that bad other than a Friday and Saturday night, when it's mostly neds from Blackburn or Ravencraig piling in.' Cullen stared at the man meandering down the street — something about him was familiar, but he couldn't place it. 'Is that Eric Knox?'

Murray squinted. 'Don't think so.' He put his face closer to the glass. 'Oh shite.'

'What?'

'It's Doug Strachan.'

Cullen closed his eyes in despair. 'Do you want to pick him up?'

Murray shook his head. 'Look at the state of him. It'll be *months* before he's sober. We'll nab him tomorrow. I'll get some uniform to keep an eye on his flat overnight.'

'I like your thinking.' Cullen put his jacket on and finished his pint. 'Come on, I'm not missing this train.'

## 72

Cullen parked the car and dug out his phone. 'Hi Sharon, you not in?'

Sharon yawned. 'Sorry. Wilko dragged me and Chantal out on an obbo again.'

'Right.'

'I'd offer to meet you in a car park but I think we'd get done for that.'

'I hoped there was more than the physical to our relationship.'

'There is, Scott. There's me listening to you moaning about still being a DC.'

Cullen laughed. 'How's it going?'

'Very dull. Got another suspect. Thought I was done with this. How was Harrogate?'

'Waste of time. It was lovely, though.'

'Well, let's head down there one weekend. Have you gone back to your flat, then?'

'Aye. I'm dreading it.'

'You know what to do.'

'I was out in Garleton and got the train, so I popped up to your flat from Waverley.'

'Oh, sorry. I should have texted you.'

'Don't worry about it. I went back to the station to get my car.'

'Anything but the bus with you, Scott.'

'I'm not that bad, am I? Besides, the timetable gets a bit weird after ten.'

'Look, I'd better go. I've got a call waiting. I'll see you tomorrow, maybe.'

'Aye.'

Cullen got out and trudged up the stairs to the flat, carry-out bag in hand. His stomach was rumbling, the acid tang of the crisps compounding things.

He pushed open the front door. Rich was sitting at the dining table, fiddling about on his iPad. He looked up and smiled. 'Oh, you must be our new flatmate. I'm Rich.'

'Aye, very funny.' Cullen shut the door behind him. He put his rucksack and the kebab on the table.

Rich's nostrils twitched at the blue bag. He scowled. 'Is that a kebab?'

Cullen put his suit jacket on the back of a chair. 'Yes, Richard, it's a kebab. I'm already salivating at the prospect of tucking into the marinated lamb, the pitta, the onions and the chilli sauce.'

'You're sickening me, Skinky.'

Cullen stabbed a finger at him. 'It's your fault that name's been resurrected.'

'If you eat that sort of shit you deserve worse names.'

'Not all of us can be gay, vegetarian fitness freaks. Sorry, gay, vegetarian, *alcoholic* fitness freaks.'

'That's me down to a T, Skinky. I'm just a walking stereotype.'

'That's the last thing you are.' Cullen opened the bag and got the tray out. 'Look, I got up at five, went to Harrogate for a complete waste of time and then I had to arse about in East Lothian for a few hours. I'm tired and hungry, so I'm having a kebab. And relax, it's not a doner.'

'Donor, you mean.'

'Very good.' Cullen went through to the kitchen, looking for a plate. They were all dirty and piled up in the sink. He went back out into the hall. 'Have you pair not done the dishes *again*?'

Rich looked over. 'Keep your wig on. When did you last do them?'

'Saturday *and* Sunday. Twice each day.'

'Well, you're hardly ever here.'

'You and Tom are made for each other.'

Cullen found a plastic chopping board in the cupboard and took it through to the hall along with a fork and knife.

Rich shook his head. 'Tell me you're not going to eat it off that?'

'There's nothing else.'

Rich shook his head. 'You're such a barbarian.'

'I'm not getting gastroenteritis from the state of the crockery in this place.'

'Stop moaning and eat your meat.'

'You say that all the time.'

Rich laughed. 'Never to you.'

Cullen sat and decanted his kebab onto the chopping board, leaving some of the sauce swilling around in the polystyrene container. 'Where's Tom?'

'Gone to bed. He's got an early start tomorrow.'

'Haven't we all.' Cullen chewed the congealed lamb. 'Who was playing tonight?'

Rich laughed. 'Czech Republic got tonked by Portugal. Of course, to Tom, it should have been Scotland getting into the second round. He started firing into his whisky in the second half and he went off to his bed moaning about Craig Levein.'

Cullen chuckled as he tore into the soggy pitta bread, the heat already building up in his mouth. 'Shite, I need some milk.'

He headed off to the kitchen and found three two-litre jugs of semi-skimmed in the fridge. He looked at the date on one in the door — best before tomorrow. He checked the others — they were the same.

He poured out a pint in a glass stolen from some pub and downed half. The fire abated slightly. He refilled the glass, feeling no guilt for taking so much given it was going out of date.

He went back through and sat. 'I take it Tom bought the milk.'

'However did you guess?'

'Because unless he's taken up baking, there's six litres of the stuff going off tomorrow.'

'He said it was on offer. Who am I to challenge the great man?'

'Great man, indeed.'

Rich flipped his iPad over. 'Have you talked to him yet?'

'About what?'

'Moving out.'

'No.'

'You really should.'

Cullen's nose was running from the chilli. 'I'll get round to it.'

'Really?'

'I've got another six months on the lease.'

'You should tell him before then.'

'I will.'

'I thought you'd like living with me.'

Cullen looked over. 'I do, Rich. It's just, I don't know, I'm trying to move on, I suppose.'

'You love Sharon.' Statement not question.

'I do, aye.'

Rich reached over and patted his arm. 'I'm glad.'

'You'll find someone one day.'

'Maybe.' Rich rubbed his piercing. 'Had another one at work.'

Cullen speared a lump of lamb with his fork and ate it. 'Another what?'

'Another colleague asking about you.'

'At the paper?'

Rich rolled his eyes. 'That viper's nest of journalists I spend my days with, yes. Aside from all that *Schoolbook Killer* stuff, you're now the destroyer of cults.'

Cullen jabbed the fork in the air. 'You know I'm not allowed to talk about that stuff, especially to you.'

'I told them that. Thought you'd find it funny, that's all.'

'I'd rather keep away from all that '*hero cop*' shite, if it's all the same. I quite like my anonymity.'

Rich laughed. 'Just as well. The number of times you've been out of your skull in public, there must be hundreds of opportunities for stories. *Hero cop pisses in phone box* or *Hero cop caught in sex act outside nightclub.*'

'Just as well you don't write about me.' Cullen took another drink of milk. 'Speaking of which, is The Outhouse a gay bar?'

Rich raised his eyebrows. 'Are you seriously asking me that?'

Cullen drank more milk — the fire wasn't in danger of letting up. 'Aye.'

'Just because I'm a *poof* doesn't mean I know every single gay bar in Edinburgh.'

Cullen pushed the empty chopping board away. He slowly pronounced each word. 'Do you know if it is a gay bar or not?'

'I've never even heard of it.'

'Fine, that's all I wanted to know.' Cullen finished the milk. 'I need a piss and then I'm off to bed.'

Rich grinned. 'Just because I'm gay doesn't mean I'm interested in what you do with your plonker.'

'Glad to hear it.' Cullen got to his feet and burped. '*Hero cop goes for slash then goes to bed.*'

# DAY 7

*Friday*
*22nd June*

# 73

C ullen looked out of the window at the back of the Incident Room across the Edinburgh skyline, waiting for the briefing to start.

'All right?'

He turned to see Murray. 'Morning.' He thumbed at the window. 'Seven am on a Scottish summer's day and it's pissing down.'

'And you're surprised?' Murray sipped a coffee through the lid.

Cullen had struggled to sleep, a combination of general fatigue, many strong coffees and the kebab congealing in his stomach. He glanced at his watch. 'Do you think I've got enough time to go up and get one myself?'

'Doubt it.' Murray nodded across the room at Angela and spoke softly. 'Did you speak to her?'

Cullen looked at her, sitting on her own, tapping her phone. 'Not yet. You spoken to Bill?'

'Not seen him today.'

Cullen noticed a couple of large photos on the wall, so wandered over. 'This is the first time I've seen what Paddy Kavanagh looked like.' He tapped the first one, which reminded him of a poster on Rich's wall. 'He looks like Morrissey.'

'Looks like he had a tough life, though. He was in his late twenties in this photo but he looks *old*.'

Bain stormed into the room, chucking a pile of papers on the table. He clapped his hands. 'Come on.' He moved over to the whiteboard, now virtually illegible with the number of cross-outs and arrows scribbled all over it.

Cullen got lost in the crush and had to sit in the middle of the front row, between Angela and Murray. Lamb and Irvine appeared and stood by Bain.

Bain took a sip of energy drink. 'We've got far too many suspects and I want us to narrow it down and progress the most likely. Rather than go through your updates one by one, I want to go through this whole thing collectively. All right?'

His left-handed writing had smudged a lot of the words. 'Let's start with the prime suspect, Paddy Kavanagh. What are our suspicions with him?'

Irvine raised a hand. 'He disappeared at roughly the same time Iain's body was put in the barrel. That's got to be suspicious in anyone's book.'

'Anything else?'

'The boy was a violent drunk.' Murray flicked a page over in his notebook. 'Used to go drinking with Iain in Garleton.'

Bain waited until Murray looked up. 'Do we know if he had any particular axe to grind with Iain?'

Lamb rubbed his stubble. 'You'll know as well as I do people like that don't need a valid reason to take against someone. I see it every other week in Prestonpans or Musselburgh.'

'I agree.' Murray thumbed to Cullen. 'Cullen has seen it in Bathgate a load of times.'

'Leave Bathgate out of this.' Bain scowled. 'Every time a copper mentions a crime in the town, I lose a grand off the value of my house.'

Angela smirked. 'Can't be worth anything now.'

'Shut it, Batgirl. You've been quiet so far. What's your take on this Paddy boy's motive?'

Angela crossed her legs. 'I agree with Stuart. As a violent drunk, Paddy's just as likely to turn on the people he's boozing with. He used to go out with Iain fairly often, so he knew him pretty well. The big thing, though, is he'd worked in the whisky industry for years so he knew the ropes and would certainly be capable of disposing of the body.'

'Assume they're pished in a pub in Garleton and he's just murdered Iain Crombie.' Bain focused on the whiteboard. 'Bit of a stretch to take him down to the distillery and chuck him in a barrel, isn't it?'

Angela shrugged. 'Assuming they're in Garleton. They could have been drinking at the distillery.'

'I'm prepared to accept he's a suspect.' Bain scribbled some more on the whiteboard.

Lamb walked over and made a T sign with his hands. 'Time out.'

'Don't you *time out* me, Sergeant.'

Lamb tapped the board. 'We've got eight officers working twelve-hour shifts around the clock looking for this man and you're 'prepared to accept he's a suspect'? If there's any doubt, I'm scaling the investigation back and returning these men to their normal duties.'

'Have you ever heard of playing devil's advocate?' Bain shook his head. 'Paddy Kavanagh is our primary suspect here.'

'You're treating him like a sideshow. We need to get focused. We need to find Paddy.'

'Are you expecting me to disagree with that? It sounds a hell of a lot like something I would say.' Bain made a pushing gesture with his hands. 'Now, clear off and let the Senior Investigating Officer lead his investigation.'

Lamb held his gaze for a few seconds, then sat down at the back.

'Right, I think we know we need to look into Paddy.' Bain tore the cap off the pen. 'Next, Doug Strachan. What could bring him to kill Iain Crombie?'

He counted on his fingers. 'One, Iain threatened him for nicking the whisky. Two, according to Sundance he was supposed to have muttered something about 'killing' around about this time. Three, he's got away with it — for the last eighteen years he's benefited by having a job and probably siphoning off more booze.'

Irvine raised his hand. 'Wasn't it him who found the body, though?'

'Aye, it was. Nice double bluff.'

Lamb scowled. 'Is it?'

'Isn't it?'

'He's a huge guy now. Could he really have done it?'

'Sundance?'

'We did some asking. He was quite athletic at the time, certainly nothing like as overweight as he is now. He could have done it on his own. Like Paddy, he's had years of experience making whisky and the whole process was automated by that point, except for some heavy lifting and rolling barrels.'

Bain scribbled on the board. 'We didn't find any splashes or wasted whisky so it would have to have been a professional filling the barrel, right?'

Irvine's hand went up again. 'Paddy was a pro.'

Bain nodded. 'So's Fraser.'

Cullen shook his head. 'Fraser had only been working there for a few years.'

Lamb frowned. 'So, he wasn't *as* experienced but he was still experienced. He could still have done it.'

'Right, Sundance, this is good stuff. You might make a DS one of these days.'

Irvine laughed.

Bain scribbled some more on the board. 'Next steps with Strachan?'

Lamb shrugged. 'We just need to get him in an interview room.'

'Agreed.' Bain took another drink. 'Anything else on him?'

Nobody had anything.

'Right, who's next?' Bain looked around at the blank faces.

Murray raised his hand. 'What about Marion Parrott?'

Bain looked around the room. 'Not to be outdone by Cullen, here's DC Stuart Murray to lower the bar.'

'Thanks for getting my name right for once.'

Bain chuckled. 'Entertain us and I don't mean in the way Cullen has.'

Murray sat forward in his chair. 'She could have been having an affair with Fraser.'

'Oh for Christ's sake.'

'I'm serious.' Murray's hands clasped his knees. 'Marion could have been seeing Fraser and they could both have killed Iain.'

Bain bellowed with laughter. 'Are you trying to wind me up

here? I haven't laughed so much since I saw Cullen's last annual appraisal form.'

'We've got a basic motive, sir. She might have believed the distillery would pass to Iain in the event of Crombie's death. That way, it would eventually go to her unborn child.'

'I think you pair need to quit while you're behind here.' Bain wrote *Implausible* next to *Marion*.

Angela smirked. 'She's more likely to have been angry at Iain having an affair.'

'Right.' Bain nodded. 'So, someone helped her with the technical whisky stuff, right?'

'She said she still meets up with Fraser every year. Even if she wasn't sleeping with him, she could have asked him to help.'

Bain scribbled on the board. 'Anything else on Marion?'

Murray sniffed. 'Fraser was assaulted.'

'Yeah, and?'

Cullen leaned back. 'She might have hoped the ownership passed to Iain junior. Maybe she's trying to kill shareholders to get it to pass now he's almost eighteen?'

Bain pinched the bridge of his nose. 'For Christ's sake.'

'We don't know when Fraser told her about Iain meeting this girl but she almost had an abortion because of it.'

'Right, you're finally getting somewhere with this. Next time, get in with the good stuff first.' Bain rubbed out *Implausible*. 'Right, Fraser next. What motive could he have?'

Angela put up her hand. 'The fights with his brother.'

'Right, the fighting.' Bain scribbled it up. 'What else?'

'Don't think there's anything else. They were at loggerheads over the future of the company. They had a history of violence, like many brothers do.'

Cullen leaned forward. 'Fraser was demoted. He played it low-key when we interviewed him last night.'

'So?'

'Being demoted to making barrels must have hurt.'

'Enough to kill his brother?'

'Maybe.'

'Fraser reported his brother missing.' Bain frowned. 'Is that a guilty man?'

Lamb got to his feet again. 'Is this another double bluff? I think we should rule it out.'

'Fine.' Bain added *Argument* alongside *Fighting*. 'So this fighting, could it be an accident?'

'Seems a bit strange.' Cullen tapped *Fighting*. 'I can buy Iain dying by accident after a drunken brawl with his brother, but I'm really struggling to see how.'

'What are you saying, Sundance?'

'They were supposed to be in Glastonbury. How did Iain end up in a barrel in Drem?'

'Fair point.' Bain scribbled *Implausible*. 'Next.'

'Hang on.' Lamb was doing the time out again. 'Why are we ruling him out?'

Bain put the pen on the whiteboard's shelf. 'Why did he do it?'

'Power?'

'Power?' Bain screwed up his face. 'What are you talking about?'

'Fraser had this argument with his brother and father about the company, right? He lost, they won. Fraser got demoted. Get his brother out of the picture and he's got more power.'

Bain snorted. 'But he's not, though, has he? He's still pissing about with barrels.'

'I'm just saying I don't think we should eliminate him just yet.'

'Right, that'll do on Fraser Crombie.' Bain didn't remove *Implausible*. 'Who else?'

Angela waved her finger in the air. 'What about Alec Crombie? He was in denial about whether it was Iain in the barrel.'

'So?'

'Well—' She came up short.

Cullen picked it up. 'I think it's a possibility, but I've been struggling with a motive. When we spoke to Marion, she made out like her and Iain were at war with his parents. Crombie and his wife didn't approve of her. In fact, they'd got married to spite him.'

'Is that enough to kill his own son, though?'

Cullen shrugged. 'I've seen people killed over a game of pool in Bathgate.'

Bain's eyes rolled as the room erupted into laughter. He stabbed a finger in the air. 'That's another grand.'

Cullen smiled. 'In all seriousness, what I think we have a real problem with is opportunity.'

Bain nodded. 'The elephant in the room.'

'Nobody has a clear opportunity. Iain's been at Glastonbury for a few weeks. The evidence points to him turning up at the distillery to meet up with his killer who shoves him in a barrel.'

'Or they did it remotely.' Lamb tapped the whiteboard. 'He could have been killed elsewhere, put in the barrel, taken there and the barrel filled.'

Angela sighed. 'We're nowhere near, are we?'

Bain wagged a finger at her. 'Hoy, hoy, stop that. We need to keep focused here. Is there anyone else we need to have a look at?'

No-one spoke.

'Right, actions.' Bain scribbled on the corner of the board. 'Batman and Robin, can you go and speak to Iain Crombie's doctor again?'

Cullen leaned back in his chair. 'Thought she was Batgirl now, not Robin?'

Bain glared at him. 'We need to find out who dropped him off at the hospital. We know it wasn't his bird.'

Bain looked at Lamb. 'Bill, you can progress with the hunt for Paddy Kavanagh. If there are any officers at all you can spare, then we should divvy them up among some other suspects.'

'I thought we agreed Paddy was the priority?'

'We did. I'm just saying.' Bain looked at McLaren. 'You—'

'McLaren, sir.'

'Aye, you, can you do some more digging into Paddy. Cast the net wide. Really wide.'

McLaren coughed. 'Isn't DS Lamb doing that?'

'I want you to do a much wider search. Bill's working in the here and now, looking for him as an active suspect. This boy disappeared in 1994 and we haven't seen him until two days ago. Where's he been, what's he been doing, why did he disappear?'

McLaren opened his notebook. 'Sir.'

Bain looked at Murray. 'Which leaves you.'

'Is that supposed to frighten me?'

Bain grinned. 'You and me are going to take Doug Strachan into an interview room in Haddington nick. I want to put him through the mill.'

'We might have bother getting anything out of him.'

'How?'

'He was absolutely paralytic in Garleton last night at about nine o'clock.'

Angela's eyes bulged.

'Sundance, what the hell were you doing not bringing him in?'

Murray shrugged. 'Got a couple of uniform to stake out his house. He's still there.'

'And you just happened to see him?'

'We'd spoken to about half the people on your whiteboard last night and Cullen had just missed the train back to Edinburgh, so we went for a pint.'

'Very romantic.'

Cullen grinned, looking at Angela. 'We weren't the ones romancing.'

Her eyes widened further as Lamb cleared his throat.

Cullen sat forward. 'One more thing, though. I spoke to Iain and Marion's son last night. Iain Parrott.'

'Why?'

'He called me. Said he's been looking into his father's disappearance for a few months and he's convinced he was murdered.'

'Sounds a bit weird.'

'Agreed. He's just found out the man he thought was his father isn't, so of course he's a bit confused.'

Bain stroked his moustache. 'Does he have anything?'

'Probably not, but I thought it was worth mentioning.'

Cullen stared at the page. Inspiration struck him. He clicked his fingers. 'It might be nothing, but Iain Parrott, Iain Crombie's son, was assaulted last week in Gullane.'

Murray avoided making eye contact with Bain. 'We were investigating an assault on Iain Parrott in Gullane.'

Bain glared at Lamb. 'Didn't think to mention it?'

'We obviously didn't make the connection. Sorry.'

'I'll connect my foot with your arse.' Bain clenched his fists.

'Calm down!' Cullen got between them, squaring up to each other like strutting cocks. 'If Paddy killed Iain then maybe he's back to get Iain's son.'

'Right, well find him.'

## 74

The wiper blades on Cullen's Golf were at full pelt, slicing through the streaks of rain dancing across the windscreen.

Cullen pulled into the car park of Edinburgh Royal Infirmary. He looked at Angela. 'Have you got through yet?'

She was lost to some train of thought she wasn't sharing. 'Got through to who?'

'Amardeep Singh. Who we're supposed to be meeting?'

'Right. Aye. No answer.'

'Bollocks.' Cullen grinned. 'We went to a nice boozer in Garleton last night.'

'Which one?'

'The Garleton Arms. Had a nice pint of lager in there.'

She looked away. 'Never been in.'

'You've been outside it, though.'

She folded her arms tight across her chest. 'What's that supposed to mean?'

'We saw you.'

'Saw who?'

Cullen grinned. 'You and a certain DS.'

'I don't know what you're talking about.'

'Angela, unless you've got a twin sister, you were walking down Garleton High Street hand in hand with Bill Lamb.'

She stared at the floor for a few seconds. 'So what if I was?'

'Well, you're married for a start.'

Tears started welling in her eyes. 'My marriage is dead in the water, Scott. It's over. I've been staying at my sister's in Mussel-burgh for the last two weeks.'

'I'm sorry. I didn't know.'

'I'm not likely to tell you, am I? It'll be half way round Lothian & Borders already, no doubt.'

'I can keep a secret.'

'Aye, right.'

'Seriously, I can. You've been hiding it well.'

She exhaled. 'It's tough. I've got so much going on. I just feel like I'm going to collapse.'

'You've been holding it together really well. You've got your DC role, your marriage is breaking apart and you're dealing with Bain.'

She closed her eyes. 'Thanks. I know if I can just get through the next few weeks then I can fall apart without Bain going ballistic about it.'

'How long has it been going on with Bill?'

'Since that case in January. We went for a drink the week after. Bill came into Edinburgh.'

'So it's serious?'

'I think so.'

'What about Rod?'

She looked out of the window at the rain. 'I've been with *him* since we were *fourteen*. I'm thirty-two now, Scott. I've changed so much and so has he. All he wants to do is piss about on his computer and watch the football. I need something different.'

'How's he taking it?'

'He's started filing for divorce.'

'Messy.'

'Aye, well, you can bloody talk about messy love lives. Sharon better watch she doesn't get kidnapped by any serial killers.'

Cullen laughed. 'Poor serial killer.'

She wiped the tears from her face. 'We're talking of moving in together. In Garleton. His flat's nice. It's not too much of a hassle to get into town, especially at stupid o'clock like we have to.'

'Well, good luck to you and I mean it.' He pointed up at the hospital. 'Are you okay to do this?'

'Aye, come on.'

## 75

Singh looked up from a document. 'What is it now?'

'We'd like to ask some follow-up questions. I don't suppose you're free now?'

Singh glanced at a clock on the wall. 'I can spare a few minutes.'

Cullen sat. 'We really need to know who brought Mr Crombie in.'

Singh took a deep breath. 'Listen, I don't know how many times I have to tell you this, but I do not know who brought him in.'

'Fine, *Mr* Singh, I will remind you this is a murder investigation and we really need to know this.'

'I can fully understand that, but I cannot tell you.' Singh threw the document on the table. 'I spoke to colleagues and I managed to acquire the admissions log.' He held up another file. 'Mr Crombie was self-admitted. Given the state he was in I would suggest someone *did* bring him in but I'm afraid the salient information just wasn't captured. This is a dead end for you.'

Cullen slumped back in his chair. 'Were you going to tell us?'

'I was planning on calling you later today.'

Cullen's mobile buzzed in his pocket. He'd set it to vibrate — he expected it to be more tedium from Bain, so he ignored it.

'Were there any extenuating circumstances pertaining to the admission?'

'Like what?' Singh leafed through the file. 'Mr Crombie was very drunk, despite the fact he'd had his arm sliced open. We had to wait over an hour to operate.'

'Is that unusual?'

Singh read again. 'I would usually expect an adrenaline spike which would cause sufficient sobriety. I noted he was rambling incoherently.'

'Does it say about what?'

Singh turned to a section at the back of the document, which looked like a questionnaire. 'I'm afraid not. I've tried to remember what he was ranting about, but I've come up blank.'

'Nothing?'

'You need to know I see hundreds of patients a year, sometimes thousands.' Singh looked at his pager. 'I would like to ask you to please contact me no further. I am a very busy man, I've given you a lot of my time and I can share no more with you.'

'Fine.' Cullen got to his feet. 'Please try and recall what he was rambling about.'

'Of course I will.'

Cullen left the room and stormed off down the corridor. 'We're getting bloody nowhere.'

He looked at his mobile, checking the missed call. 'That's all I bloody need.'

'What?'

'It wasn't Bain. It was Iain bloody Parrott.'

## 76

Cullen pulled in outside Marion's house. He tried Parrott's number again. 'Still nothing.'

Angela ran a hand through her hair. 'Think that means anything?'

'It's a pain in the arse is what it is.' He got out and knocked on the door.

Marion answered it quickly, scowling when she saw who it was. 'What is it now?'

Cullen held up his mobile. 'I got a missed call from your son. He's not answering or returning my calls. I'm getting a bit fed up with it.'

Marion closed her eyes.

Angela stepped forward. 'Have you seen him?'

Marion looked at her. 'I don't know where he is. He's not in his room.'

'When was the last time you saw him?'

'Last night at teatime, just after you visited. I told him about his father.' A tear slid down her cheek. 'I was just about to phone the police. I'm scared it's a follow-up to what happened a couple of weeks ago.'

Angela gave her a friendly smile. 'Can we have a look in his room?'

'Very well.' Marion led them upstairs. At the top, a white door had *Iain's Den — Keep Out* stencilled on.

The boy's room was very orderly, everything in neat piles. Cullen's room as a teenager was an absolute bomb site but this was structured and organised. He gestured at the meticulously tucked duvet. 'It doesn't look like the bed's been slept in.'

'Iain's like that. I've never had to moan at him about keeping his room tidy. Wish my other two bothered.'

There was a large computer desk beside the bed, with a sleeping laptop alongside stacks of papers and notebooks.

Cullen picked up the first one, which looked like a journal. 'Mind if I have a look through these?'

Marion leaned against the door frame. 'Fill your boots.'

It looked like notes relating to Iain's obsession with his father's disappearance. The handwriting was small and neat with each note dated, running from early February to April.

Cullen picked up another and flicked to the end, dated the previous day. He looked through the last few entries.

A photograph fell to the floor. He bent to retrieve it. It was of two men smiling and shaking hands. He flipped the photo over — on the back was a scribble. *With Paddy Kavanagh, June '95.*

Cullen's heart started racing. Paddy went missing a year before. Angela squeezed in beside him. 'What is it?'

'A photo.'

The Morrissey-alike Paddy was easy to place. He was holding up a copy of *The Sun*, Oasis on the cover.

The other man looked vaguely familiar. Cullen squinted and held it away, trying to add seventeen years on. He showed it to Marion. 'Do you know who this is?'

She spent a few moments examining it. 'It's Eric Knox.'

## 77

C ullen pressed the buzzer.
Angela flashed up the photograph. 'Paddy is holding a copy of *The Sun*. I found it in their archives. Saturday, the twenty-fourth of June 1995. Oasis headlined Glastonbury on the Friday night.'

'Did you check the previous year?'

'Aye. They played on the Sunday, pretty far down the bill.'

'So Paddy was alive a year after Iain Crombie was murdered.' He tried to kick his frazzled brain into gear. 'It can't be from before, right?'

'Yeah, I *know* that, Scott. What does it mean for the case?'

'Not only did Paddy Kavanagh disappear but he came back. You know what they say about a killer returning to the scene of the crime.'

'Yeah, but after a year?'

'Let's just see what Knox has to say about it.'

He buzzed again. The door opened and they climbed the stairs. When they reached the landing, Knox's flat door was open so they went inside.

Knox was in his armchair, his yellowy eyes bloodshot and struggling to focus. When he saw them, he reached over to a glass of whisky and knocked half of it back.

Angela sat near the window.

Cullen remained standing. He handed the photo over. 'Mr Knox. Is this your photograph?'

Knox squinted at it. 'I've no idea, pal.'

Cullen stood over him. 'Mr Knox, it's you in the photograph.'

Knox reached for the glass.

Cullen grabbed his hand. 'You'll get your whisky after confirming it's you.'

Knox sank back in the seat, his eyes locked on the glass of whisky. 'Aye, it's me.'

'And it was taken in 1995?'

'Aye.'

Cullen folded his arms. 'That's a year after Paddy Kavanagh disappeared.'

'I know that, son.'

'When we were here the other day you told us you don't know what happened to him.'

Knox evaded his look. 'Did you get it on tape, son?'

Cullen grabbed him by the shirt and pulled him to his feet. 'I've had it with you. You said you didn't know what happened to him and then I find a photo of you and him a year later.'

He let go and Knox fell back into the chair. 'I said I couldn't remember what happened. I didn't lie to you, son, it just slipped my memory.'

'I'm going to take you into the police station across the road and have you booked with about seven different charges.' Cullen started counting them off on his fingers. 'Withholding evidence—'

'Okay, fine.' Knox looked up. 'Will you drop it if I can remember the information now?'

'We'll see.'

Knox reached for the whisky. Cullen let him have it. His trembling hand put the glass to his lips, spilling some on his cardigan as he downed it. 'Paddy turned up just over a year later.'

'Where had he been?'

'Up north somewhere. Up past Inverness, I think, in a cabin in the middle of nowhere.'

'Why did he leave in the first place?'

'He wouldn't say. Kept it to himself.'

'If I find out you knew why, we can add accessory to murder to that charge list.'

'I swear, son, it's the God's honest truth.' Knox's eyes were already looking around for the next glass of whisky.

'What did he say?'

'He said his boat had come in. He was going to make a killing.'

'Did Doug Strachan know about this?'

'Who do you think took the photo?'

'Are you serious?'

'Aye. Paddy wanted the photo as evidence.'

'Did you ever hear from him again?'

'No. Neither did Doug.'

Cullen grabbed the photo back. 'You didn't think of going to the police with this?'

'We swore ourselves to secrecy.'

'So how the hell did Iain Parrott get this photo, then?'

'Aye, well.' Knox rubbed his hands together. 'He was a persuasive wee bugger, I'll give him that.'

'How did he get the photo?'

'He was here the other night. Wednesday, I think. I was a bit drunk, you know, and I passed out. The wee bugger started going through my stuff and he found that photograph. He was in my face, asking me all these questions about his dad and Paddy.'

'Was this the last time you saw him?'

Knox shook his head slowly. 'He was here last night as well. Pitched up at the back of nine.'

Cullen looked at Angela. 'This was after I met up with him.' Back at Knox. 'What was he after?'

'He was asking me about the photo. I couldn't answer half of his questions. My memory isn't as good as it used to be.'

'Do you know where he went afterwards?'

'Said he was off to see his uncle.'

## 78

A ngela ended the call and tossed her phone on the dashboard.

Cullen glanced over. 'Well?'

'Tommy Smith says the trace on Iain's phone will be ten minutes.'

'That's quick.'

'I name-dropped Bain.'

'Tommy'll love that.' Cullen turned right at Drem, heading to the distillery. His phone rang. He pulled in beside a row of post-war cottages and checked the display. Bain. 'Better not bounce him a sixth time.' He put the call on speakerphone.

'Better be some good news from you, Sundance, cos it's shite over here.'

'We found a photo of Paddy Kavanagh taken a year after he was supposed to have disappeared.'

'Are you kidding me?'

'I'm serious. Iain Parrott had it.' Cullen picked up the photo. 'It's of Paddy and Eric Knox. It was taken by Doug Strachan.'

'Are you sure?'

'Positive. It's got a newspaper in it. Angela checked and the paper is definitely from '95. Paddy swore them to secrecy.'

'So these pricks are lying to us?'

'It would appear that way. Have you got hold of Strachan yet?'

'Aye, he's still out of his skull. Managed to get in to work, mind. He's given us a statement and McLaren is chasing it up.'

'What did he say?'

'Strachan reckons he was on holiday at the time of Iain's arm injury. I've been thinking it's this Paddy boy for a while now and your photo just confirms it. Strachan has been hiding stuff from us and this gives me a big stick covered in shite to beat him with.'

'You think this confirms it's Paddy?'

'Too right. He's got these boys lying for him.'

'There's something else.' Cullen put the photo back down. 'Did you ask him what he meant about 'killing'?'

'Said he can't remember it.'

'Paddy told them his boat had come in and he was going to make a killing.'

'Right, Sundance. That closes that off, then. I'll chin Strachan about that as well.'

'We're going to speak to Fraser Crombie.'

'No way. Not without me, anyway. Those pricks are a ball-hair away from making a complaint against us, so I'd rather you had senior officers with you.'

'It's probably nothing. Iain Parrott went to speak to him last night and I want to know what it was about.'

'That boy tell you anything yet?'

'Can't find him. He might have gone missing.'

Bain's hand went over the mic at the other end and Cullen could make out him shouting at Murray. 'Better go, Sundance. Strachan's lawyer has just turned up.'

Cullen hung up. 'Great.'

Angela looked over. 'So what are we going to do now?'

Cullen turned the key in the engine. 'We're going to ask forgiveness rather than permission.'

'Not something I'd recommend in a sexual situation.'

Cullen laughed. 'That's more like the old you.'

He drove to the distillery, managing to find a space in the car park. He killed the engine. It coughed and spluttered and gradually switched off. 'Need to get a service.'

'Need to get a new car.' Angela let her buckle slide up. 'Why was Iain Parrott seeing Fraser Crombie?'

'That's why I want to speak to him. He disappeared just before he went to see his uncle.'

Angela checked her phone. 'We should get the trace back soon.'

'Here's hoping.'

He unbuckled his seat belt. 'Come on.'

Cullen jogged across the pebbles, the pouring rain soaking his suit jacket. They hurried inside to reception, a trail of wet footprints following them across the wooden floor.

Cullen made a beeline for the desk. 'Is Fraser Crombie in?'

Amanda looked up from her magazine. 'I'm afraid he can't be interrupted.'

'What's he doing?'

'He's preparing ahead of the board meeting.'

'I really need to speak to him. You'll know this is a police matter and you don't want to be accused of obstruction.'

Amanda's sass disappeared. 'He's in the cooperage.'

'Thank you.'

## 79

I n the cooperage, the machinery thundered, looking ready to deposit another batch of whisky.

Fraser Crombie sat on his own at the far end of the room, clawing at a barrel, muttering to himself. He glanced up at their approach then looked away again.

Cullen leaned back against one of the workbenches. 'Keeping yourself busy?'

Fraser didn't look up. 'Place doesn't run itself. Dad is running the company into the ground. Strachan's drunk all the time. We'll not get anything at this meeting this afternoon. Dad won't make the right decision. He'll sell out for nothing.'

'The receptionist upstairs said you were preparing for the board meeting.' Cullen pointed at the barrel. 'Is your strategy in there?'

'Fixing barrels helps me think. It's very therapeutic, taking something damaged and repairing it, ready for use again. You should try it.'

'I'm looking for Iain Parrott. Have you seen him?'

Fraser leaned against the rim of the barrel, resting his head on his forearms. 'I've not seen him for a week or so.'

'We've reason to believe he was coming to see you last night.'

'Coming to see me and actually seeing me aren't the same thing. As I say, I haven't seen the boy for a week or so.'

Cullen held his gaze.

Fraser looked away after a few seconds. 'Do you actually have anything specific to ask me or is it more fishing?'

'We need to ask you some other questions.'

Fraser got to his feet. 'Look, I'm going to get another barrel. It'll help me think.' He walked past them into the maze of casks and workbenches.

Cullen quickly lost sight of him in the mess, listening to the footsteps pace off up the room. He stood for a few seconds, running through everything in his head, trying to consolidate it.

He looked at Angela. 'I'm beginning to wonder if Iain did go to Glastonbury.'

'What?'

'It's only Fraser's word that Iain actually went. This stuff about a woman only came from Fraser.'

'What about the Harrogate stuff?'

'All they had on her were some sightings based on a photofit Fraser provided. What's to say he didn't forge it based on someone from Harrogate so there would be actual sightings? Nobody has placed Iain at Glastonbury other than Fraser.'

'You could be onto something, Scott. What about the phone calls Marion got from Iain?'

Cullen thought about it. 'She could be colluding with Fraser. She could have lied.'

'You seriously think that? Why would Fraser kill his brother, though?'

'The argument? Being demoted by his father? As well as killing his brother, he's managed to totally screw up his parents. His old man has waited eighteen years for his son to turn up. Fraser worked here, clocking in every day, watching Alec worry about where Iain was.'

'And the mother died of cancer, right? Could be brought on by stress.'

'Has Tommy Smith called back yet?'

She checked her phone. 'No missed calls and I've got reception.'

'Call him.'

She held the phone up to her ear and waited.

Cullen looked around the room — the machinery still

whirring. Despite liking whisky, he knew next to nothing about the process of making it. Something to do with distillation but, other than the tidbits he'd picked up on this case, they could be passing the stuff through a toad for all he knew.

Angela tugged on his jacket sleeve, her eyes wide.

'Well?'

'Iain Crombie's in this building.'

'What?'

'The cell trace placed him in this building. There's a tower on the train line.'

'Is he upstairs?'

'With Crombie? I don't know.'

Cullen stood and turned around. 'I'm going to find him.'

The lights turned off.

'What the—?'

In the gloom, Cullen saw something flash.

Angela screamed and slumped to the floor.

Cullen ducked and reached for her. Her head was bleeding and her eyes were rolling in her head. She was still breathing.

Through a shaft of daylight, he saw Fraser approaching, a large claw hammer in his left hand.

He swung it at Cullen, claw first.

Cullen tried to swerve, but stumbled. Fraser caught his left shoulder, sending him sprawling.

Cullen screamed. He glanced down. The hammer had torn through his suit, the wool and cotton were frayed and already turning red.

Cullen's shoulder burned. He screamed again.

Fraser knelt over him before pushing Cullen onto his front and digging his knee into the small of his back. 'Think you're smart, do you? I'll show you.'

Fraser flipped Cullen back over, the movement sending a jolt of pain through his shoulder. He raised the claw and hit the same spot. The hammer dug in and Fraser yanked it.

Cullen almost passed out with pain. He reached around with his right arm, trying to grab hold of anything.

He caught Fraser's wrist.

His hand slipped.

Fraser stood up and turned the hammer around.

Cullen rolled over, facing away from him. He tried kicking out but missed.

Fraser smashed the hammer at Cullen's head.

Cullen reached his hand out, managing to deflect the blow onto his shoulder.

Fraser stumbled forward and braced himself against the edge of a bench.

Cullen scrabbled around, crawling from where Angela lay.

He scrambled to his feet and started running, clutching the gash on his shoulder, blood pouring down his arm. He looked around and saw Fraser following.

He wove in and out of the workbenches, heading for the door. He looked for a weapon but the worktops were empty. He made it to the door, trying the handle.

Locked.

He kicked it. It was a solid oak door — it wasn't going to budge.

He turned, pressing his back against the wood. His shoulder was burning and blood dripped from his fingertips. He felt cold. His hands were shaking.

Fraser approached him, his face now an evil rictus.

Cullen swallowed hard, his pulse racing. 'What happened to your brother?'

Fraser laughed. 'You'll find out soon enough.' He held up the hammer, running a finger down the length of it. 'It's amazing what trained hands can do with one of these.' He moved forwards and started swinging the hammer, inching closer to Cullen.

'Stop. I'll let you go.'

Fraser was inches away. 'No, you won't.'

Cullen leaned back against the door, realising he had to act quickly. He waited for Fraser's hammer to hit the top of the swing and pushed off on the backswing, ploughing into Fraser with his good shoulder, knocking them both over and sending the hammer flying.

Cullen wriggled on top of him. He raised his good hand up to punch him.

Fraser prodded his thumb into the gash in Cullen's shoulder. A jolt of pain seared through his body.

Fraser kicked him, pushing him backwards.

He got on top of Cullen. His hand reached for the hammer.

Cullen tried to grab his arm but his fingers couldn't grip.

Fraser smashed his head on the concrete floor.

Cullen blacked out.

He came to.

Fraser Crombie stood over him, hammer raised, ready to strike.

A wooden chair smashed over Fraser, the seat connecting with his skull. He collapsed in a heap.

Angela stood there, rubbing her head. 'Can't let you get a reputation for getting Acting DCs killed.'

## 80

Cullen got to his knees. 'Now I see why Bain calls you Robin.' He laughed through the pain. 'Batman tells Robin to stay behind, but he always ignores him and saves the day.'

Angela clutched the gash in the back of her head, her hair matted with blood. 'Does he get battered on the head with a hammer?'

Cullen tried to laugh again, but the searing pain from his shoulder made him draw breath.

She frowned at him. 'Are you all right?'

'Not really.' He unbuttoned his shirt to get a better look.

Her eyes darted away. 'I hope I don't have to look at your peely-wally chest.'

'I might not be as rugged as Bill Lamb, but I'm not exactly peely-wally.'

'Any more of that and I'll use his hammer on you.'

Cullen coughed, pain shuddering through his body. 'What about you?'

'I was out cold.' Her eyes locked on his fingers. 'I don't think he caught me cleanly.'

Cullen had pulled his shirt open, recoiling at the dark ridges of flesh, the subcutaneous fat layer sliced open and blood already starting to coagulate.

'You need to go to hospital, Scott.'

'The door's locked and, unless we can find the keys, we're stuck. I hope they're in his bloody pocket.'

'Great.'

Fraser started moving again.

Cullen couldn't get his fingers to reach his pockets. 'Have you got your cuffs?'

Angela reached into her jacket, producing a pair with a click. 'Never leave home without them.'

'Did you smash that chair?'

She inspected it. 'Looks like it's still intact.'

'Help me put him on it.'

She looked at his chest. 'Scott, you're in no state to do anything. Call back-up while I get him up.'

'Give him a blast of pepper spray.'

'Are you serious?'

Cullen grimaced. 'No.'

The adrenaline spike was starting to fade. He was feeling woozy with the pain.

He supported himself against a workbench and got his phone out. He called Bain.

'What is it, Sundance?'

As Cullen spoke, he felt a distance from the scene in front of him. 'We went to see Fraser Crombie. He attacked us.'

'What are you saying?'

'He killed his brother.'

'Get him over here.'

'That's a bit difficult. He's torn my shoulder open and knocked Caldwell out.'

'Is she okay?'

'Just a few cuts and bruises.'

Angela hauled Fraser onto the chair, tying his hands together under the seat and securing him in place. She reached into his pocket and retrieved a set of keys. She held them up.

Cullen winced. 'Can you get an ambulance over here?'

'Sundance, for Christ's sake.'

Fraser started to blink.

'Look, sir, I need to go.' Cullen ended the call and pocketed his phone before staggering over. 'Bain's on his way. Along with an ambulance.'

Angela prodded Fraser with her finger. 'He's awake.'

Fraser had a large bump running along the side of his head, growing by the second.

'You're lucky you didn't take his head clean off.'

She rubbed her wound. 'He'd deserve it.'

The machinery was still whirring in the background.

Cullen leaned against a bench. 'Can't hear myself think. Could you go and turn that off?'

'I'll try.' She headed off to the far end of the room.

Cullen grabbed hold of Fraser's shirt collar. 'Fraser.'

He laughed.

Cullen had to stop himself from headbutting him. 'You're in a lot of trouble, you know that?'

'You've got nothing on me.'

'You've just assaulted two police officers. That's something.'

'Fair enough.'

'Fraser, what happened in '94 between you and your brother?'

'Nothing. I don't know what you mean.'

'We know Paddy Kavanagh appeared a year later.'

'So?'

'We know Iain Parrott went to see you last night. We've had a trace done. We know he's here.'

Fraser slumped back on the chair. 'That's nothing. You attacked me first. I was just defending myself. We'll see where that gets us.'

The machinery stopped.

Cullen took in the silence for a few seconds. 'What was your nephew wanting to speak to you about?'

'You'll have to ask him.'

'Was it about Paddy Kavanagh?'

Fraser shrugged. 'No idea.'

Angela reappeared. 'You need to come and see something.'

She helped him to the other end of the room. In the corner, a pair of large barrels sat with their lids off. She pointed at the one nearest the corner. 'Have a look inside.'

Cullen peered over the edge. There was a man inside.

'I think it's Iain Parrott.' Angela snapped on a pair of blue nitrile gloves. 'I didn't want to move him.'

Cullen reached into the barrel, putting his fingers under Parrott's neck and felt for a pulse. 'He's still alive.'

Cullen helped Angela ease the barrel over, making his shoulder burn anew. He breathed hard.

Angela got the boy out. 'It's definitely Iain.' She clicked her fingers by his ears. 'He's totally out of it.'

'What about the other barrel?'

'Empty.'

Cullen slumped on a chair opposite.

'You don't look very well, Scott.'

'I'm not very well.' His shoulder throbbed and a wave of nausea hit him. 'What's going on here?'

'I've no idea.'

Cullen staggered to his feet and set off back to Fraser.

'Scott, you need to sit down.'

Cullen had to lean against a workbench halfway down. 'I need to get to the bottom of this.'

'Sit down!'

Cullen soldiered on. He grabbed Fraser by the lapels and got in his face. 'What are you planning on doing with Iain?'

'I was going to make him disappear just like his father.'

'What happened?'

Fraser stared up at the ceiling. 'After the meal, me and Iain drove here to get some whisky for the trip to Glastonbury. We were both drunk and started arguing about the takeover again. We got into a fight. We were pushing each other. Iain tripped and clattered his head off the corner of a workbench.'

'Did you plan this?'

Fraser shook his head. 'I panicked. I sat for about an hour, thinking what to do. Iain didn't wake up. They were going to pour the whisky the next day, so I put him in a barrel.'

'Was he still alive?'

'Yes.'

'And you smashed his head in with a hammer?'

Fire burnt in Fraser's eyes. 'I wanted to make him pay. He'd made my life a misery. It was all his fault, all him and Dad. I just wanted to sell to Scottish Distillers. Dad and Iain didn't. Dad sidelined me. He said I'd never amount to anything. He took me off the board, made me the bloody cooper. I was left with nothing. Dad would much rather have a legacy than a son.'

Cullen's shoulder gave another spasm of pain. 'Why didn't you come clean?'

'I needed to get away with it.'

Angela shook her head. 'But it was an accident.'

Fraser looked at her. 'Yeah, well, it was, but I thought sod it, here's some luck at last.' He scowled. 'I'd finally got that bastard brother of mine out of the way. I could watch Dad suffer for siding with Iain and screwing me over.'

He grinned. 'He's been through eighteen years of agony. I could see his face every day, wondering where Iain was. Every time the door opened he'd look up to see if it was him. When he finally found his precious son rotting in a barrel of his bloody whisky, he finally knew Iain wasn't coming back.'

'It's quite an extreme thing to do.'

'I don't regret it.'

'What happened after you put him in the barrel?'

'I took Iain's keys. I waited till Marion left for work then packed a bag and made it look like he'd left.'

'Did you go to Glastonbury?'

Fraser shook his head. 'I stayed around and watched to see if I needed to go on the run.'

'So you made the whole thing up?'

'I led Stanhope on a merry dance.' Fraser smirked. 'I called everyone from a phone box in Dirleton, pretending to be Iain. I saw Dad giving you his usual shite about the family trait. Got it to work in my favour for once.'

Cullen rubbed his eyes. 'Were you really assaulted down by the beach?'

'Chucked a brick at myself.' Fraser's eyes looped up then back down again. 'I caught you clean though.'

Cullen gripped his lapels again. 'Did you assault Iain Parrott?'

'The boy was getting too close. I thought I'd killed him, but I just knocked him out.'

'How does Paddy Kavanagh fit into this?'

'He was working that night. I didn't know. He must have heard the machinery going, but he caught me at it.'

'What happened?'

'He blackmailed me. I paid him ten grand to leave.'

'And he just left?'

Fraser nodded.

'Where did you get the money from?'

'Iain and I had trust funds till we were eighteen. I still had mine but Iain spent his on his bird.'

'Did Paddy come and see you a year later?'

'He did. He wanted more money. I thought I'd seen the last of him, but no, he turned up at my flat.'

'What happened?'

Fraser thumbed at the door. 'He's in one of the '95 barrels.'

## 81

C ullen lay on a gurney in the back of the ambulance, buckled in. The rain thundered on the roof, sounding like it was leaving a trail of dents.

He tried calling Sharon. Her phone was still off. He left another voicemail and sent another text, painfully typed with one hand.

The paramedic jumped in the back. 'Let's see if that's settled down any.'

'I'm fine.'

'You're not fine, pal. You've lost a lot of blood and you've been charging around in there. You've left a nice trail in that barrel room.'

'It's called a cooperage.'

'Quite the expert, are you?'

'I am now.'

'Until someone who earns a lot more than you or I works out if you've seriously damaged yourself, you're staying still. That hole in your shoulder is going to take some fixing.'

A voice called outside the ambulance. 'Where the hell is he?'

The paramedic turned. 'He's not in a fit state to speak to anyone.'

Bain climbed in. 'I'll be the judge of that.'

'I really must insist.'

'Just give me two minutes.'

The paramedic shook his head. 'Two minutes, not a second more. The ambulance leaves then and I don't want you in it.'

'Magic.' Bain pushed past and sat next to Cullen.

Angela appeared, her fingers tracing the outline of the bandage on her head.

Bain leaned over Cullen's gurney. 'You are an idiot, Sundance.'

'Thanks for that, sir.'

'I'm serious. That's the last time you go in two-footed. I'm on a sticky enough wicket as it is. I don't need to lose two officers in a year.'

Cullen nodded at Angela. 'She's okay. Minor injury.'

'It's not her I'm talking about, you tube!' Bain stroked his moustache. 'You've got to stop all this cowboy shite.'

'I had a few questions to ask him. *He* attacked us, not the other way round.'

'Aye, well, I still would have appreciated being on the inside track on this one.'

Cullen looked away. 'I told you. You weren't interested.'

'I was going by due process, eliminating Doug Strachan from the investigation.' Bain shook his head. 'As ever, you knew best though didn't you, Sundance? You just had to ignore me and go and speak to him.'

'Where's Fraser?'

'He's in a meat wagon en route to Leith Walk.'

'Have you spoken to him?'

'I've got that pleasure to come.' Bain stood up again. 'We found Paddy in another barrel. Would have found him a week ago if I'd got my way.'

'I'm sure you'll remind DCI Turnbull.'

Bain grinned. 'We finally got a trace back on the Paddy sighting. Fraser again. Still, good result there.'

'Is that you thanking me?'

'It's as close as I get, Sundance.'

## 82

SCOTT CULLEN WILL RETURN IN

# NEXT BOOK

The next Police Scotland book is out now!

## "STAB IN THE DARK"

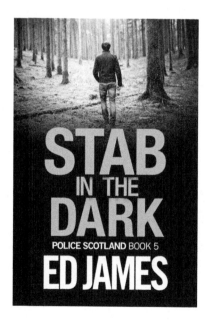

Get it now!

If you would like to be kept up to date with new releases from Ed James and access free novellas, please join the Ed James Readers' Club.

# AFTERWORD

Thanks for reading this — I hope you enjoyed it.

This one had a very interesting gestation.

It started with a competition — Bloody Scotland, the Scottish crime writing festival, had a short story competition with a theme of 'Worth the wait' which was sponsored by a distillery. Within a minute I had the germ of an idea — the body in the barrel and the motive. I did a lot of research into whisky — unlike Cullen, I cannot stand the stuff, I'm much more of a red wine, real ale and continental lager drinker (okay, not so dissimilar to Cullen) — and started to understand the process of making whisky, from malting through distillation and barrel-making through to bottling. I wrote the short story called WHISKY IN THE JAR — 3,000 words — and I submitted it in June. I didn't win.

Given the amount of research that I had done and I had the full Crombie dynasty plotted out (even if I hadn't used it), I thought it'd work as a novella to bridge the gap between DEVIL IN THE DETAIL and DYED IN THE WOOL. So I extended it, mostly in gaps in the editing of DEVIL, and bumped it up to 27,000 words. I gave it to my alpha readers (C and Pat) and the feedback wasn't as positive as I'd have liked — the idea and the story were good, but it missed that certain Cullen-ness of the first two — mostly Bain nonsense — and focused a lot on the deep history rather than the present. Ultimately, the story wasn't that enthralling.

So, back to the drawing board — I jotted down some ideas and quickly realised that I had enough (and enough good stuff) for a full length novel. I'd started to hate the title, so renamed it to FIRE IN THE BLOOD. I wrote it pretty quickly and got it up to 84,000 words and published it.

Fast forward to February 2014. I'd published the fourth and fifth Cullens and had just gone through editing GHOST IN THE MACHINE and DEVIL IN THE DETAIL to bring them in line stylistically. What I saw in FIRE was a fairly solid first draft but it needed serious work. This version is almost a rewrite of the book — the story is largely the same from the short story — and I've added a few little bits and pieces that pave the way for the stuff that happens in BOTTLENECK, but everything I've learnt since has gone into this book. I think it's as good as I can make it.

As ever, there are a few things I made up in this book. Dunpender Distillery doesn't exist and is entirely fictional. Garleton still doesn't exist, and I drove up that way at the weekend. The site of Leith Walk station is still a derelict plot. There's a brief mention of Ravencraig — it doesn't exist except in STAB IN THE DARK...

Thanks again go to C for the alpha and beta editing. Also, thanks go to Pat for the editing help from the novella to the final novel. For the final version of the novel, thanks to Rhona for the editing and Allan for distracting me with hatred of pleonasms and summary narrative.

I promise I won't set in any more books in East Lothian for a while...

Thanks again for buying and reading this — do let me know what you think of my books.

— Ed James
East Lothian, May 2014

# ABOUT THE AUTHOR

Ed James is the author of the bestselling DI Simon Fenchurch novels, Seattle-based FBI thrillers starring Max Carter, and the self-published Detective Scott Cullen series and its Craig Hunter spin-off books.

During his time in IT project management, Ed spent every moment he could writing and has now traded in his weekly commute to London in order to write full-time. He lives in the Scottish Borders with far too many rescued animals.

If you would like to be kept up to date with new releases from Ed James, please join the Ed James Readers Club.

Connect with Ed online:
Amazon Author page
Website

# OTHER BOOKS BY ED JAMES

## DI ROB MARSHALL

Ed's first new police procedural series in six years, focusing on DI Rob Marshall, a criminal profiler turned detective. London-based, an old case brings him back home to the Scottish Borders and the dark past he fled as a teenager.

1. THE TURNING OF OUR BONES
2. WHERE THE BODIES LIE (May 2023)

Also available is FALSE START, a prequel novella starring DS Rakesh Siyal, is available for **free** to subscribers of Ed's newsletter or on Amazon. Sign up at https://geni.us/EJLCFS

## POLICE SCOTLAND

Precinct novels featuring detectives covering Edinburgh and its surrounding counties, and further across Scotland: Scott Cullen, eager to climb the career ladder; Craig Hunter, an ex-squaddie struggling with PTSD; Brian Bain, the centre of his own universe and everyone else's. Previously published as SCOTT CULLEN MYSTERIES, CRAIG HUNTER POLICE THRILLERS and CULLEN & BAIN SERIES.

1. DEAD IN THE WATER
2. GHOST IN THE MACHINE
3. DEVIL IN THE DETAIL
4. FIRE IN THE BLOOD
5. STAB IN THE DARK
6. COPS & ROBBERS
7. LIARS & THIEVES
8. COWBOYS & INDIANS
9. THE MISSING
10. THE HUNTED
11. HEROES & VILLAINS
12. THE BLACK ISLE
13. THE COLD TRUTH

## 14. THE DEAD END

### DS VICKY DODDS

Gritty crime novels set in Dundee and Tayside, featuring a DS juggling being a cop and a single mother.

1. BLOOD & GUTS
2. TOOTH & CLAW
3. FLESH & BLOOD
4. SKIN & BONE
5. GUILT TRIP

### DI SIMON FENCHURCH

Set in East London, will Fenchurch ever find what happened to his daughter, missing for the last ten years?

1. THE HOPE THAT KILLS
2. WORTH KILLING FOR
3. WHAT DOESN'T KILL YOU
4. IN FOR THE KILL
5. KILL WITH KINDNESS
6. KILL THE MESSENGER
7. DEAD MAN'S SHOES
8. A HILL TO DIE ON
9. THE LAST THING TO DIE

### Other Books

Other crime novels, with Lost Cause set in Scotland and Senseless set in southern England, and the other three set in Seattle, Washington.

- LOST CAUSE
- SENSELESS
- TELL ME LIES
- GONE IN SECONDS
- BEFORE SHE WAKES

# STAB IN THE DARK

## PROLOGUE

The sleeping man's head rocks forward and hits the steering wheel. The orange Range Rover, the bright orange glowing in the darkness, trundles towards the slip road down the hill. Behind it, the West Lothian skyline stretches out, small islands of yellow light in an ocean of black.

He starts walking, his footsteps crunching the red soil as he matches the pace of the Range Rover. It starts accelerating as it nears the edge of the plateau. The wind whips at his clothes. 'The breeze is a lot stronger up here.'

'Of course it is.'

And the screaming starts.

He has to jog now. 'He's supposed to be unconscious.'

'I know. Don't know what happened there. Not my department.'

'I don't like this.'

'It's a crime whether he's dead or alive, awake or asleep.'

He stops, resisting the urge to shake his head, and watches the SUV race down the hill, an orange blur against the dark-red shale bing. Halfway down, the Range Rover loses grip, and lists to one side. Then it all happens too fast, tumbling over and over. It rolls to the bottom and bounces across the scrub land beyond, then shudders to a final halt, crumpled and ruined, sitting on its roof.

'That's the ticket.' The other man squeezes his shoulder. 'Our friend will be as battered as the motor.'

'Come on.' Ignoring the burning guilt in his gut, he starts back to his own Land Rover, ready for their own controlled descent. 'Time to call the police.'

～

THE FIFTH POLICE SCOTLAND BOOK, STAB IN THE DARK, is out now. You can get a copy at Amazon. I hope you enjoy it!

If you would like to be kept up to date with my new releases, please join the Ed James Readers Club.

Printed in Great Britain
by Amazon

38837692R00199